A KILLING
for
CHRISTMAS

C.K.
Harewood

ISBN (Paperback): 978-1-912968-76-3
ISBN (eBOOK): 978-1-912968-75-6

A Killing for Christmas

C. K. Harewood

Chapter One

FRIDAY, 9TH MAY 1930

The night out had been a bad idea. Benjamin Scott felt sure of that as the train screeched into the station and came to a stop beside him.

He'd thought an evening out in town would be just the thing to cheer everyone up. But their dinner had been mediocre, the musical dreadful, no one's mood had lifted, and he wished he'd accepted the invitation to his golf club's anniversary dinner instead.

The carriage doors opened with a squeal, and Benjamin waved his wife and daughter inside before stepping in behind them. He settled the two women into their seats, then took one opposite and set his top hat on the seat alongside, snatching it away a moment later as the fourth member of the party fell down beside him. Benjamin shot Maxwell an exasperated look, which his son-in-law entirely failed to notice, for his attention was solely on his cigarette case. Maxwell took out a cigarette and lit it. Blowing out a plume of smoke, he appropriated the armrest between them, stretched out his legs, leant his head back and closed his eyes.

Benjamin folded his arms over his chest with a huff, his eyes settling on the women. Victoria, fat and vulgar in a revealing dress she thought made her look at least a decade younger than her fifty-nine years, was flicking through the theatre programme while Imogen, still lovely at thirty-two, stared out of the window, clutching a beaded handbag in her lap, her satin gloves straining at the seams. Familiarity and experience warned him a row was brewing.

The doors closed, and the train lurched as it pulled away from the station, jolting them all. Imogen let out a small cry, put a hand to her mouth and squeezed her eyes shut.

Victoria closed her programme with a loud tut. 'What is the matter with you?' she demanded.

And they're off! Benjamin rolled his pouchy eyes at the inevitability.

'It's the motion.' Imogen said, keeping her eyes closed. 'I have a headache, and it's making me queasy.'

'You and your headaches. Take something if it's that bad.'

'I don't like taking pills, you know that.'

Victoria opened her programme again with an exasperated shake of her head. 'I don't think you've got a headache at all. You just want attention.'

'My head's been hurting all day, Mother.'

'Then you should have said so earlier and saved your father the cost of your ticket. If I'd known you'd be complaining all evening, I'd have told Max to leave you behind.'

'I haven't complained.'

'You were moaning all through the interval.'

'Because my head hurts. You know I suffer from headaches.'

'Then get the doctor to have a look at you.'

'Imogen won't go to the doctor,' Maxwell piped up,

tapping the ash from his cigarette to drop onto the wooden slatted floor. 'She positively refuses. Don't you, darling?'

'What's this?' Victoria said sharply. 'I thought Imogen saw the doctor every three months.'

'Not anymore,' Maxwell said. 'She cancelled all those appointments.'

'And you let her? Oh, Max, how do you expect her to get pregnant if you let her do things like that?'

'Shush, Mother, please.' Imogen looked around the train carriage uneasily. 'People will hear you.'

'I don't care if they do. They shouldn't be listening.' Victoria glared at the heads that turned towards her. 'Now, about the doctor. I'll make an appointment for you.'

'Please don't,' Imogen begged. 'I'm tired of being pulled about and prodded by doctors. I just want to be left alone.'

'And what about Max? Doesn't it matter what he wants?'

'Of course it matters, but—'

'But nothing.' Victoria sliced the air with her hand. 'You tell her, Ben.'

'Your mother's right, Imogen,' Benjamin said. 'Max wants a son, and it's your duty to do everything you can to give him one.'

'After all,' Victoria went on, 'he's waited long enough. Most men would have got rid of you long ago. Isn't that right, Max?'

Maxwell smiled at his mother-in-law and took a drag of his cigarette.

'So you will see the doctor. I don't want to hear any more of your nonsense.'

Victoria resumed her reading, and Benjamin watched his daughter, glad Imogen had decided not to argue. She was staring down at her silver satin shoes, the only sign of her anger a biting of her bottom lip, a familiar curb on her temper. He glanced at Maxwell beside him, who had gone back to dozing. *Not a bad idea*, Benjamin thought, and closed his eyes.

As the train's motion rocked him with its predictable, soothing rhythm, Benjamin decided he would organise no more nights out for his family. He should have learnt by now they never turned out well.

———

Nigel Frye took a sip of his cocktail, set the glass down, and smoothed his trim moustache with a long, tapered finger. With a sigh of resignation, he reached into his jacket pocket and took out the letter he had received that morning and which had been playing on his mind ever since. Popping a green olive from the bowl on the bar into his mouth, he read the few typed lines.

We write to respectfully remind you that the bill issued to you on 16th November 1929 is still outstanding. Unless the amount of £47 5/ 2d is paid within the next fourteen days, we shall be forced to take legal proceedings against you.

We remain, yours faithfully,
Messrs Holman and Hunt, Solicitors

His lips curling with disgust, Frye shoved the letter back into his pocket and drained his glass. Of course, the bill was still outstanding; he didn't have the money to pay it. And even if he had the money, he didn't see why the hell he should pay the damn bill; his ex-wife had racked up those solicitor fees. Not that she cared. She wouldn't be satisfied until he was out on the street, begging for his bread.

Frye rapped on the counter to get the barman's attention and order another drink. While he waited for it to come, he took out his cigarettes, turning his back to the room so no one would see they were in a crumpled packet rather than a case and that he used the bar's matches to light one. His silver case and lighter had been sold more than a month earlier, and the few banknotes in his wallet were all that remained of what he had got for them. Frye knew he shouldn't be wasting his money on over-priced drinks in West End clubs, but damn it, a man had to maintain standards at certain times. Times when it mattered. Times when a chap was on display.

Desirous of a little uncomplicated female company to take his mind off his financial affairs, Frye scanned the room for a suitable companion. His practised eye caught an attractive blonde looking his way, but his attention was diverted from her to the man who left her side and walked up to the bar. Frye recognised him at once and held out his hand to force a reacquaintance.

'Saunders, old man. How good to see you.'

'Frye,' Saunders said, taking the hand without pleasure. 'It's been a long time.'

'Yes, hasn't it? What are you up to these days? Still being run into the ground by old Allinson?'

'No, no. I left Allinson's practice a few years ago. I'm with Marriott now.' Saunders added smugly, 'On Harley Street. He's tipped me the wink that he's soon to retire, so this time next year, I'll be running the whole show. What about you? I heard a rumour you were slumming it at a free hospital.'

Frye was quick with his refutation. 'You heard wrong. I have a practice in Craynebrook.'

'Really? Old Rathbone swore he saw you at Sawyers Cross.'

It was no good; Frye saw that. If it had got around the old crowd that he was doing shifts at a hospital, he would have to own up. But at least he could make out it was his choice. He was good at that sort of thing. As his wife had once said, there were few things he couldn't turn to his own advantage.

'He probably did see me,' he said. 'I do regular shifts at Sawyers Cross. It's one of the best hospitals in this area. Though you're wrong in saying it's a free hospital; only a few wards are given over to free patients. But I like those the best. The working class has such interesting medical problems. And I like to keep my hand in. I do find a GP's work to be dreadfully dull. There's no challenge in it, is there? I don't know how you put up with all those middle-aged women moaning about their imaginary complaints. You must get so bored.' And Frye scored a victory. Saunders' self-satisfied smile faltered, and he moved in for the killing blow. 'You should give a free hospital a try, Saunders. Then you could be a proper doctor instead of just pocketing guineas like some quack.'

Saunders glowered at Frye, grabbed the drinks he'd ordered and returned to his table and the blonde without another word.

'Nicely done,' a voice said.

Frye turned to the woman on the bar stool beside him. She was forty-something with hair too dark to be natural and a cleavage he could get lost in. He gave her his charming smile. 'Thank you,' he said, and held out his hand. 'Nigel Frye.'

The woman gave him the tips of her blood-tinted fingers. 'Olivia Thurloe.' She glanced over at Saunders. 'Rather a pompous ass, isn't he?'

'I couldn't agree more.'

'So, you're a doctor?' she said, raising a plucked eyebrow. 'Are you a good one?'

'I've never had any complaints.'

Her mouth widened, showing nicotine-stained teeth. 'I'm sure you haven't.'

There was no mistaking the look she gave him or the promise in the sultry tone of her voice. Frye glanced at her left hand and was pleased to see the gold band on her third finger. He smiled and pointed at her empty glass. 'Let me get you another.'

———

Sarah Kempe's body tensed as the crabby, gnarled hand inched its way around her hip and pinched her backside. Her jaw tightening in anger, she grabbed the bony wrist and thrust it back at its owner.

'You can pack that in or I'll tell Matron you're well enough to go home,' she snapped.

The old man in the hospital bed smirked. 'You love it.'

'I do not. I do not love being groped by a dirty old man like you one little bit.'

His face screwed up in disgust. 'You know what's wrong with you, don't you?'

'No, Mr Stevens. What?'

'You need a good seeing-to. That's what.'

'Oh, that's what I need, is it?' she said, straightening. 'And I suppose you're the man to give it to me?'

'I'll sort you out, good and proper, Nurse Kempe.' Mr Stevens threw back the blanket. His arthritic fingers fumbled with the cord on his pyjama bottoms.

'I wouldn't bother,' she said, tossing the blanket back up to cover him. 'You've got nothing to write home about.'

His face screwed up. 'You what?'

'I expect that's why your wife left you,' Sarah went on. 'Mrs Stevens grew bored with you trying to make something out of your pathetic little thing, so she went off and found herself a real man who knew what he was doing.'

'What do you know about it?' he snarled. 'What man's ever laid a finger on you?'

'You'd be surprised, Mr Stevens. I know what a real man is, and trust me, you're nothing like one.' Sarah smiled at him coolly. 'Good night, Mr Stevens.'

'Dried-up, ugly old cow,' he muttered as she walked towards the nurses' station.

Sarah reached the desk and snatched up a pencil, bending low over the ward logbook to write an entry.

'Was Mr Stevens at it again?' Nurse Crewe, seated at the desk, asked.

'He's always at it, Nurse Crewe,' Sarah sighed.

The young nurse's face screwed up in distaste. 'You wouldn't think an old man would be so crude.'

'Old men are the worst. You'll find that out for yourself if you stay on the geriatric ward.'

'I don't want to stay here. Not if I have to tend to men like Mr Stevens. I think we should tell Matron about him.'

'And what do you think she'll do? Throw him out?'

'Well,' Nurse Crewe said, a little indignant, 'he's not paying for his treatment, is he? I don't think we're obligated to treat people who are rude.'

Sarah gave her a pitying smile. 'You have a funny idea about this place. If we tell Matron about Mr Stevens, and all the other men like him, and trust me, there are plenty, do you know what she'd say? "It's part of the job, ladies. Stop complaining and get back to work".'

'Well, I don't think it's right,' Nurse Crewe said sullenly. 'I didn't become a nurse to be groped and insulted by dirty old men.'

'Did you think it would be romantic? That there would be handsome young men in here, all wanting to marry you when they got back on their feet?' Sarah tutted and shook her head. 'If you're going to do this job, Nurse Crewe, you need to realise that nursing is hard. It's dirty. It's long hours and being ordered about all day and told off by the matrons, and yes, having to put up with men like Mr Stevens who think they have a right to stick their hands up your skirts and grab at you. That's what nursing is. We're not angels. We're just ordinary women doing a very unpleasant job. The sooner you accept that, the easier you'll find it.'

'Why do you do it if you hate it so much?' Nurse Crewe asked, chastened.

'Because,' Sarah opened the desk drawer and rooted around inside, looking for the packet of cigarettes she had stashed in there, 'I have to earn my living and this is the only thing I'm good at.'

'I'd like to work on the children's ward,' Nurse Crewe said after a moment of awkward silence between them. 'It would be lovely to be around all those kiddies, don't you think?'

Sarah slammed the drawer shut, making the desk shudder. 'Mind the ward.'

'But your break's not due for another five minutes,' Nurse Crewe called after her as Sarah walked away.

Sarah paid her no attention. She continued on her way, out of the ward and along the corridor that smelt of antiseptic and carbolic, and which she never seemed to be free of, wanting to get as far away as she could from Nurse Crewe and her pathetic ideas and Mr Stevens and all the other men like him on the ward.

If only, Sarah thought, *I could walk right out of this hospital and never come back.*

Chapter Two

Frye groaned and pulled his crusted eyelids apart, mentally cursing whoever was ringing his doorbell.

Throwing back the bedcovers, he sat up and dropped his feet to the floor. A moan of protest came from behind him, as Olivia Thurloe turned over onto her side and tugged the covers up to her ear. Pulling on his silk dressing gown, he slipped his feet into his monogrammed slippers before making his way down the stairs.

'All right, all right,' he called irritably as the doorbell rang again. 'I'm coming.' He turned the latch and yanked the door open. 'Victoria!' he gasped, tightening his dressing gown by a sharp tug of its belt. 'I'm so sorry. I didn't realise it was you.'

Victoria smiled, her bright blue eyes twinkling with amusement as she looked him up and down. 'I didn't get you out of bed, did I? At this hour? Tut tut, Nigel.'

'I had a late shift at the hospital last night,' he lied.

'I suppose that's a reasonable excuse. Well?' She raised her eyebrows at him. 'Aren't you going to invite me in?'

Frye hesitated. He didn't want her in his house, not with Olivia upstairs and him naked beneath his dressing gown. But

Victoria had already put her foot over the threshold, and he reluctantly opened the door wider. 'Please go into the sitting room. I'll just put some clothes on.'

'Before you do that,' Victoria halted him, giving his bare legs a swift but appreciative stare, 'let me tell you why I've come. I want you to have a look at Imogen. She's complaining about headaches again, and it's getting us all down.'

'I'm very sorry to hear that,' Frye said, 'but I'm not your daughter's doctor, Victoria. Dr Woodrow—'

'Oh yes, I know.' She cut him off with a wave of her hand. 'But Dr Woodrow's no good. He listens to Imogen going on about how difficult everything is for her when really he should be giving her a good talking-to. Paying her attention only encourages Imogen. So, you will come and see her, won't you?'

Oh God, she means now, Frye realised. He heard a creak from upstairs and stared nervously at the ceiling. He really didn't want her to find out about Olivia. For all her flirting, Victoria was a prude, and a jealous one at that. Frye sensed her good favour towards him would evaporate if she knew he had a woman in his bed.

'Let me get dressed,' he said, 'and I'll see you there.'

'Oh, there's no need for that,' Victoria said, making herself comfortable on his sofa. 'I'll wait and we can go together. Off you go and get dressed. Don't be too long.'

Seeing he wasn't getting rid of her, Frye left the sitting room and climbed the stairs. Returning to his bedroom, he quietly closed the door and leant onto the bed to shake Olivia's shoulder.

'What?' she grumbled loudly, turning towards him a mascara-streaked face that had none of the allure he'd encountered in the club the night before.

He shushed her. 'I have to go out. But there's someone

downstairs, so don't move until I've gone in case they hear you.'

'And how am I supposed to get home?'

'Get a taxi.'

'I don't have enough money on me for a cab.'

'Then get a bus,' he snapped. 'Just make sure no one sees you leave.'

'Pig!' Olivia spat as he headed for the bathroom.

———

Benjamin nudged the blind aside a few inches and peered out.

A Rolls-Royce pulled up on the forecourt, parking between the company's delivery van and his Bentley. He drew back out of sight as the driver climbed out of the car and let the blind fall back into place. Benjamin tugged his tie straight, adjusted the handkerchief in his top pocket and fixed a smile on his face as he waited for his visitor to be shown into the office.

'Mr Prince,' his secretary announced.

'Harold,' Benjamin cried. 'Do come in.' He dismissed the secretary with a wave of his hand even as he stretched out the other to his visitor. 'Thank you for coming.'

'I was intrigued by the invitation.' Harold Prince turned to the view outside the office partition window, where men and women laboured at the printing machines.

Get a good look, Benjamin thought, following his gaze. Then he said, 'Come and sit down. A drink? Or is it too early for you?'

'It is a little early,' Prince said, taking a seat by Benjamin's desk. He pointed at the desk opposite. 'That belongs to Maxwell, I suppose. You share an office?'

'You sound surprised.'

'I am. I would have thought you'd have an office all to yourself. You are the senior partner, after all.'

'I'm the owner, Harold. The business is all mine.'

Prince's bushy eyebrows rose. 'I didn't know that. The way Maxwell talks—'

'You don't want to pay too much attention to what my son-in-law says,' Benjamin said curtly, this talk of Maxwell irritating him. 'Let's get straight down to business. You want to know why I've asked you here.'

'I do,' Prince said. 'And also why I wasn't to breathe a word to anyone that we were meeting. You made it all sound very cloak and dagger.'

'I just want to keep this meeting between you and me. There's a good reason for it, I promise you.'

'Well, I'm here and I'm all ears.'

Benjamin took a deep breath, his eyes twinkling. 'I'm thinking of selling the business, Harold.'

'Selling?' Prince's eyes widened in surprise. 'But you've always said you would go on until you dropped.'

'Things change. I want to retire while I'm still young enough to enjoy it.'

'Of course.' Prince nodded understandingly. 'But what about Maxwell? Surely the business goes to him? I'm certain that's what he expects.'

'What Maxwell expects is of no account.'

Prince made a face. 'I'm sorry, Ben, but I disagree. I've heard Maxwell talk often enough at the club to know he plans to be in charge here one day. And I wouldn't want to be piggy in the middle if it came to a row between you two.'

'I can handle Max,' Benjamin assured him. 'This is my business. I started it. I've made it what it is. And I've every right to dispose of it as I please.'

'But if you want to sell, why not sell to him?'

'I have my reasons,' he snapped. 'All I need to know, Harold, is whether you're interested in buying?'

'You know I am. But it'll depend on what you want for the business. What figure do you have in mind?'

Benjamin named a sum. 'That's a good price,' he insisted when Prince raised his eyebrows.

'It's a hefty one,' Prince said. 'I'll be honest, Ben, that's a lot more than I was expecting. I'll have to think about it.'

'That's fine. I don't need an answer straight away.'

'And this really has to be on the QT?'

'Absolutely. No one can know. Not even our wives. This stays between us. Agreed?'

Prince studied him for a long moment. 'Agreed,' he said eventually, and rose, buttoning his jacket. 'It's been an interesting meeting, Ben. I'll be in touch.'

———

Maxwell finished the newspaper article about the Blackbird Farm murder and turned the page.

An exclamation of irritation came from his lips as his eyes raked over the adverts. It seemed that every time he opened a newspaper or magazine these days, he was confronted by printers' ads. Here was an ad for posters, mail order catalogues, even billboards, for heaven's sake! The very printing services he had been telling Benjamin they should have been doing for years!

He tossed the newspaper aside and pushed himself out of the armchair. Snatching the lid off the marquetry box on the mantelpiece, he took out one of the few remaining cigarettes inside and slammed the lid back down.

'Imogen!' Maxwell yelled. 'Why the hell haven't you bought more cigarettes? We're almost out.' There was no response and he yelled her name even louder. But still no answer came. Cursing, he snatched up the onyx lighter from the table. As the flame flickered at the end of his cigarette, his eyes caught movement outside the sitting-room window.

'Oh, bloody hell,' Maxwell muttered as he saw Victoria marching purposefully up the garden path with Dr Frye a few steps behind.

The doorbell rang, and he heard the maid exit the kitchen and run down the hall to open the front door. Then Victoria barked, 'Where's my daughter?' and Jane answered in a quivering voice, 'She's in the bedroom, madam. But the master's around somewhere.'

The next moment, the sitting-room door was flung open, and Victoria cried, 'There you are!'

'Yes, here I am,' Maxwell sighed.

Victoria gestured at Frye. 'I've brought Nigel to see Imogen. Your girl says she's in the bedroom.'

'She is. Sulking.'

'Oh, what is she sulking about now?'

'Apparently, we all ganged up on her last night,' Maxwell said carelessly, dropping back into the armchair and putting his feet up on the footstool.

'Oh, for heaven's sake.' Victoria turned to Frye. 'I'm so sorry about this, Nigel.'

'It's fine, Victoria,' Frye assured her. 'I can see her some other time.'

'Certainly not. You'll see her now. She can stop her sulking.'

'No, really. If Mrs Carr doesn't want to see me, ethically—'

'Don't talk to me about ethics. Imogen will be seen by you whether she likes it or not. You wait there.'

Victoria bustled out, her bulky body thumping up the stairs, and Maxwell heard her jiggling the bedroom door handle. It was locked, as he knew it would be, and Victoria banged on the door angrily.

'Imogen, open this door at once,' she bellowed.

'Victoria can shout all she likes,' Maxwell told Frye, who was hovering half-in, half-out of the sitting-room doorway. 'She won't come out. Imogen can be a stubborn mare when she wants to be.'

'Perhaps Victoria could bring your wife to the surgery?' Frye suggested. 'It would be more proper.'

'Since when have you cared about what's proper?' Maxwell sneered and was delighted with the scornful look he received in return. 'If you're that bothered, why did you come?'

'I didn't have a choice. Your mother-in-law turned up on my doorstep and demanded I come here.'

'You could have said no.'

'Have you tried saying no to Victoria?'

Maxwell shrugged. 'It's a waste of time Victoria bringing you here. A simple look at Imogen won't tell you anything. She's had plenty of doctors examine her over the years and not one of them could say what's wrong with her. They just put the miscarriages down to nature's way. As if that makes everything all right.'

'Have you considered having any tests done?'

'Why should I have tests?' Maxwell demanded indignantly. 'There's nothing wrong with me, Frye. My equipment's working perfectly, I assure you.'

Victoria thundered back down the stairs, and Frye backed away as she entered the sitting room.

'Imogen's impossible,' she declared. 'She absolutely refuses to open the door.'

'Best leave her be, Victoria,' Maxwell said. 'She'll come out when she wants something.'

'It's so rude of her. And poor Nigel here—'

'Please think nothing of it,' Frye said. 'I should go.'

'Oh no, don't hurry away.' Victoria grabbed his arm. 'You'll come back home with me and we'll have tea and cake.'

'I thought Dr Woodrow told you to lay off the cake?' Maxwell said. 'Something about all those cakes and pastries not doing your heart any good? Don't look at me like that, Victoria. I'm looking out for you, old girl. Isn't that right, Frye? My mother-in-law needs to lose some weight?'

'Well,' Frye said, smiling uneasily at Victoria. 'I understand Dr Woodrow did advise you might find things easier if you were a little lighter. Personally, I think there's nothing wrong with your weight,' he hastened to add as Victoria's lips tightened.

'There, you see?' Victoria said to Maxwell, mollified. 'Come along, Nigel.' She hooked her arm through his and turned back to Maxwell. 'You're not invited,' she said as they left.

'Thank God for that,' Maxwell muttered as the front door banged shut behind them.

———

The guard opened the door, and the visitors trooped in.

Sarah took a seat at a table, her heart beating too fast for comfort, not only because she hated coming here, but because she would set her eyes on Nick once more.

Glancing around, Sarah saw the other women visitors patting their hair into place, adjusting their blouses, and some applying fresh lipstick as if they expected to be kissed. There was no hope of that, she knew, but Nick would like her to make an effort.

Sarah took out her compact and self-consciously dabbed a little powder on her nose, to take off the shine, as the advertisements said. Except her nose wasn't shiny; it was red and flaky, and the powder accentuated the crow's feet around her lips and at the corners of her eyes. She snapped the compact shut and stuffed it back in her handbag as the doors at the far end of the room opened and the prisoners filed in.

Nicholas Baddowes walked through the door, and as always, Sarah's breath caught in her throat at the sight of him. Even in prison clothes, he was handsome. A roguish handsome, admittedly, with his lock of unruly black hair falling over his forehead, and the five o'clock shadow that always decorated his jaw no matter how recently he'd shaved, but handsome, nonetheless. He looked around, saw her, and made his way over.

'Hello, love,' she said, beaming up at him as he pulled out the chair and sat down.

'I thought you weren't coming back,' Nick said. 'You haven't been in for a month.'

'Three weeks,' she corrected. 'I couldn't get away before this. But I've been dying to see you, Nick.'

He grunted, unconvinced. 'What have you brought me?'

Sarah reached into the shopping bag at her feet and drew out three packets of cigarettes and a box of matches she'd bought on her way to the prison with the last of her money. She put them on the table before him.

'Bloody Capstan?' Nick grumbled, snatching up a packet.

'They're all I could afford. I thought they were better than nothing.'

'Not much better.' Nick took out a stick, lit it and glanced around the room. 'Blimey. Brandon's got a looker visiting him.'

Sarah turned to see who Nick was looking at. Opposite the said Brandon was a very smart young woman in an expensive-looking green suit that set off her alabaster complexion and auburn hair, set in the latest style, superbly.

She must have sensed she was being stared at, for she suddenly looked over and met Sarah's eye, then shifted her gaze to Nick. Her perfectly moulded lips spread in a wide smile, and Sarah turned back to see Nick grinning at her. Her stomach lurched.

'Is she his wife?' Sarah asked, trying to keep the pain out of her voice.

'Nah, his wife's nothing to look at.' She was sure he would have added, 'Like you,' if a guard hadn't chosen that moment to pass their table and Nick took a drag of his cigarette instead, keeping his eyes on the auburn-haired woman.

Sarah reached across the table and grabbed his hand, but the guard saw the movement and said sternly, 'No touching, miss.' Reluctantly, she withdrew her hand. 'It feels so long since we were alone together. You can't imagine how much I miss you, Nick.' Sarah wanted him to say he missed her too but all he did was make a face. 'It won't be for much longer. Just a few more months. The twenty-first of October isn't so very long away, really.'

'Not for you, maybe,' he said. 'For me, it's a lifetime.'

'I know, Nick, but if nothing else, it'll give you time to work out what you're going to do when you're released.'

Nick frowned. 'What do you mean, what I'm going to do?'

'For work. Have you given any thought to what you'll do?'

'Yeah,' he grinned. 'I'm going to walk out of here and into every pub I can find.'

'I meant for a job, Nick.'

The grin disappeared. 'What do I want a bleeding job for?' He leaned forward and stabbed the table with his fore-finger. 'You want to know what I'm going to do when I'm out of here? I'll tell ya. I'm going to break into every house worth breaking into and steal everything I can. That's what.'

'Oh, Nick,' Sarah cried, a little too loudly, for heads turned in their direction. She leaned in closer, lowering her voice. 'I hoped you wouldn't be doing that again. I don't want you back in here.'

'Who says I'll be back?' Nick slid the cigarettes and matches into his pocket. 'Who says I'll even stay in London?'

His words hit her like a punch to the stomach. 'Where are you thinking of going?'

'Dunno. I might go home.' He smiled slyly. 'Norah came to see me last week.'

The mention of his wife made a chill run down her spine. 'And what did Norah have to say for herself?'

'She wants me back.'

'She threw you out,' Sarah reminded him angrily.

'Well, what can I say? The poor cow misses me. The kids do, too.'

Sarah swallowed. Her mouth had gone dry. Tears pricked her eyes. 'I love you, Nick,' she burst out. 'You know that, don't you? I'll die if you leave me.'

'Pack it in, will you?' he said, looking around uneasily. 'You're showing me up. Oh, Christ!' he growled as her tears fell. 'As if it's not bad enough being in here, I've got to put up with you blubbing.'

She pulled her handkerchief from her sleeve and brushed the tears from her cheeks. 'Please don't leave me, Nick. I'll do anything you want. Just tell me.'

'I want you to stop nagging me to go straight,' he muttered sourly.

'I won't say another word,' Sarah promised.

Chapter Three

Jane Prior yawned as she set the boiled eggs and toast down on the tray.

She hadn't slept well; yesterday had been such a horrible day. What with Mrs Scott turning up, bringing that doctor with her, and then Mr and Mrs Carr having that blazing row after dinner… Jane had hurried up to her attic bedroom as soon as she could just to get out of their way. Why did they always have to be arguing?

She picked up the breakfast tray, kicked open the kitchen door, and took the tray up to the first floor. Balancing the tray on her forearm, Jane knocked on the bedroom door and entered.

The room was in darkness. Inching her way to the ottoman at the foot of the bed, she set down the tray and moved to the window to pull back the curtains. Jane had already begun her 'Morning, madam,' before she'd even turned back to the bed. The 'madam' died in her throat. The bed was empty and didn't appear to have been slept in.

Frowning, Jane returned to the landing and crossed to the spare bedroom, putting her ear to the door. She heard snoring and poked her head inside. Daylight flooded the room, for the curtains hadn't been drawn, and she saw Maxwell lying on the bed on his stomach, wearing only his underwear, head turned to one side. She retreated, closing the door as quietly as she had opened it.

Scurrying down the stairs, Jane checked each of the ground-floor rooms in search of her mistress. Imogen wasn't in any of them.

She returned to the kitchen, drawn there by the sound of scratching, and found Imogen's elderly white Scottish terrier, Tinker, clawing at the back door to be let out. Jane unlocked the door, and the little dog darted out into the garden, heading for the patch of ground where he always did his business. She watched him, wondering where her mistress could have gone without taking Tinker.

Noises from inside the house caught her ears, and Jane hurried up the stairs to see Maxwell just as he put his hand on the bathroom doorknob. He was still wearing only his underwear.

'Sorry, sir,' she said, a little flustered with embarrassment, 'but I can't find the mistress. She's not in the house. And I've got her breakfast all ready, and—'

'For God's sake, girl,' Maxwell snapped, rubbing his forehead. 'Stop wittering. My head's pounding. My wife's probably gone to church.'

'Yes, sir,' Jane agreed obediently, but thought it was a bit early for Imogen to have left for church. As far as she knew, the service didn't start until ten o'clock, and it was only half-past eight. Although, she mused, Imogen being at church would explain why Tinker was still in the house. She tutted in irritation as she realised that wouldn't explain why she hadn't let him out to do his business before she left.

Maxwell opened the bathroom door and stepped inside before turning back to her. 'I'll have her breakfast if it's still hot,' he said.

'Yes, sir. It's in the bedroom. Will you be going to ch—?' she began, but Maxwell had already shut the door.

Jane went back down to the kitchen. Tinker came in, wagging his tail, and she forked a tin of his food into a bowl for him.

It's all a bit odd, she thought as she watched the little dog eat.

Chapter Four

THURSDAY, 15TH AUGUST

Deirdre Johnson swore under her breath as the pram banged into the shop counter.

Why had she allowed Albert to talk her into buying this monstrosity? The smaller pram would have been so much easier to manoeuvre, but Albert said the bigger one was sturdier. What he really meant was that it looked more expensive, and looking expensive was all that mattered to Albert. But it was all very well for him to show off to the neighbours; he didn't have to push the blooming thing around all day.

Her bladder painfully reminding her it was full, Deirdre steered the pram towards the Ladies. After struggling to get the pram inside the lavatory door, she parked it by the row of basins, knocking over a mop and bucket propped against them. Grateful the bucket was empty and she hadn't caused a flood, Deidre entered the nearest vacant cubicle, hearing a toilet flush as she locked the door and pulled up her skirt. She sank onto the seat with a groan of relief.

There was a squeal from outside the cubicle. Recognising this as the noise the pram wheels made, she called out, 'Just move it over if it's in the way.' No one answered her, but she heard another squeak of the hinges and the clank of metal and supposed whoever it was had done as she instructed.

She finished, astonished she had held her water as long as she had, and unlocked the cubicle door, barely glancing at the pram as she crossed to the basins. Examining herself in the mirror as she washed her hands, she groaned. *God, I look old*, she thought, pushing a stray strand of greying hair back beneath its pin. *No more babies*, she decided, even if it meant exiling Albert to the spare bedroom.

Deirdre turned to the pram. 'Come on, then,' she said with a sigh. 'Let's go home.' She grabbed the handle and tugged the pram towards the door.

Frowning, she halted. The pram felt lighter than usual. She ducked down to examine the shelf between the wheels, thinking perhaps one of her shopping bags had fallen off, but they were all there. Straightening, she peered into the pram and stared confusedly at the space where her baby had been, where now there was only the white blanket her sister had knitted.

When asked later, Deidre was unable to give an account of what she did next. All she could remember was that she had been screaming.

———

Maxwell drained his glass and banged it on the counter. 'Another,' he ordered, clicking his fingers at the pub landlord.

He wanted to get drunk. He wanted to get so drunk he wasn't thinking about Benjamin, wasn't thinking about the business, wasn't thinking about anything, at least for a few blessed hours. Damn Ben and his dyed-in-the-wool attitude, his complete lack of understanding that they needed to move on or be left behind.

The entrance door opened to his left, and out of the corner of his eye, he saw a gaggle of women enter. They were talking ten to the dozen and laughing, and he wondered bitterly what they had to be so happy about.

The fresh drink appeared before him, and he flicked the payment towards the landlord carelessly.

'Mr Carr?' a voice enquired at his elbow.

He turned and stared at the woman standing there. His vision was already a little faulty, and he struggled to place her.

'It's me,' she said, sensing this.

'Mrs Pearson, of course,' he said, finally recognising the voice. She looked so different from how she looked in the office. Her lipstick was brighter, redder, and her hair was curled more exuberantly. She was really a great deal prettier than he had realised.

'You're here alone?'

'Yes, all alone. You?'

'I'm with some friends,' she said, gesturing at the women seated at a corner table. She looked him up and down. 'I don't like to see you here all by yourself. Why don't you come over?'

'I wouldn't dream of intruding,' he said, unable to think of anything more trying at that moment than being surrounded by giggling women.

'You mean you don't fancy it,' she smiled, showing her teeth. 'I can't say I blame you. I'm not really in the mood for them, either.'

'Then why come with them?'

'I was bored at home. My husband's away, you see.' She climbed up onto the stool beside him. 'Your wife's still away, isn't she?'

Maxwell nodded reluctantly, annoyed by her mentioning Imogen. She was another thing he didn't want to think about.

Mrs Pearson went on. 'I expect you're lonely at home with no one to look after you.'

'I do have a maid, you know?' he said indignantly. 'Jane cleans for me. Cooks for me. And now, she toddles off home of an evening and comes back in the morning. Can you believe her mother didn't think it was decent for her to be alone in the house with me? As if I'm going to lay a finger on her.'

'I'm sure any woman is safe with you,' Mrs Pearson cooed. When Maxwell made no reply, she went on. 'I heard you had a row with Mr Scott today.'

He rounded on her. 'How do you know about that?'

She shrugged. 'Everyone knows.'

Maxwell's jaw tightened. 'I can't get him to understand we need to invest in the business if we don't want to go under.'

'I don't understand about business,' she said with a very feminine laugh. 'But it is rotten for you. I feel for you, I really do.'

Maxwell was touched. He smiled at her. 'Would you like a drink, Mrs Pearson?'

'Ooh,' she said, her shoulders jiggling with pleasure. 'I'll have a gin and orange, if you're offering. And it's Linda. Not Mrs Pearson.'

Maxwell got her the drink, and she cupped the glass with both hands, staring at it, suddenly awkward. He saw her cast a surreptitious look over her shoulder at her friends, saw them wave for her to come over, and, by their faces, guessed she'd mouthed a refusal at them so she could stay chatting to him.

'So, Linda,' he said, smiling. 'Your husband's away, you say?'

———

DI Barnaby Walsh signed his name at the bottom of the report he'd written and set it on top of all the other pages in the case file with a heavy sigh.

'Still here?' a voice asked.

Walsh looked up to see Police Inspector Colin Fowler standing in his doorway, the lamplight glinting off the silver buttons on his uniform. 'I had to finish my report,' he said, closing the file and heaving it into his In tray. 'You heard?'

'About Elaine Johnson?' Fowler nodded. 'Yes, I heard.'

'That makes four. Four babies snatched over the last four years.'

'And you're no nearer catching the person who took them than Morris was when he retired.'

'Thanks,' Walsh said flatly.

Fowler frowned. 'For what?'

'For reminding me I haven't got anywhere with it.'

Fowler leant over the desk and picked up the case file. 'Feeling sorry for ourself, are we?'

'Well, if no one else will.' Walsh yanked open his desk drawer, took a boiled sweet from a paper bag and popped it in his mouth.

Fowler flicked through the case file papers. 'I remember Morris pulling his hair out over these cases. He said if there was one good thing about them, it was that all the kids were found.'

Walsh nodded. 'I suppose, at the end of the day, there was no harm done.'

'I wouldn't say that. There was plenty of harm done.' Fowler pointed at the page he'd been reading. 'Billy Spinner. Found with severe nappy rash and sores. Susan Banks. Found with a cut and a lump on her head the size of an egg where she'd either fallen or been hit. Sean Walls. Found suffering from whooping cough. That poor kid spent six weeks in hospital. And that's not to mention the distress the parents went through, not knowing what had happened to their children.' He threw the file onto the desk contemptuously. 'Don't tell me there was no harm done.'

Walsh held up his hands. 'All I meant is the parents got their kids back. They're safe.'

'You mean alive. Who's to say Elaine Johnson will be so lucky? This woman who's snatched her doesn't take care of the babies properly. What if this time she doesn't give Elaine back before it's too late? You need to find this snatcher, Barnaby.'

'You don't need to lecture me, Colin,' Walsh snapped. 'I know. The Chief Constable has already made it perfectly clear I need to get a result.'

'You've spoken with the Chief Constable about this case?' Fowler was surprised.

'He cornered me the other night. The mayor has been on at him as to why the snatcher hasn't been caught yet, and the Chief Constable is getting calls from the press. There's a danger of a public outcry, he says, and that's the last thing he wants. So, he's told me if there's no arrest and soon, there's no promotion for me and he's going to hang me out to dry.' Walsh slammed the desk drawer shut. 'And on top of all that, my wife thinks the promotion's in the bag. She's telling all our friends, the neighbours, her family, that I'll be DCI this time next month. She'll kill me if I don't get it.' He groaned and ran his hands through his thin brown hair. 'I've had enough. I'm going home.' He rose and took his hat and coat down from the hook on the door.

'Maybe you should warn your wife you might not get the promotion?' Fowler suggested, following Walsh out of his office. 'Let her down gently.'

Walsh turned on him angrily. 'Forget Julia. *I* want the damn promotion, Colin. I'm fed up with all this.' He waved at the CID office. 'I've had enough of the late nights and early mornings. With getting called out just as I've got into bed because some tramp's died and I've got to work out if it's a suspicious death or not. I want to be sitting behind my desk all day, having long lunches and going home at six o'clock, no matter what. So, I don't have a choice. Whatever it takes, I have to solve this case.'

Chapter Five

SATURDAY, 27TH SEPTEMBER

Frye closed the staff room door, glad to shut out the hospital, if only for a few minutes. He was tired, and tiredness had made him grumpy, and having to carry out five ward rounds all by himself hadn't improved his mood one bit. He needed a smoke, but a pat of his pockets told him he had no cigarettes. Frye looked around the staff room, hoping someone had left a packet on a table, but he was out of luck. His eyes strayed to the row of hooks where the staff hung their hats and coats and, checking he had closed the door, he hurried across the room and searched a shabby blue coat. All he found was a screwed-up handkerchief, but beneath the coat was a hand-bag, the brown leather scratched and scuffed. He opened it and delved inside.

He found an envelope and read the address to see whose bag he was searching. 'Miss Sarah Kempe' was written on the front, and it was stamped with HMP Pentonville in the top left corner. Curious about who was writing to Sarah from prison, he peered inside and saw the words 'Visiting Order' at the top of the page. Frye shook his head in surprise. Well, well, well. Sarah consorted with criminals. Who would have thought it?

He returned the envelope to the handbag and rooted around inside, giving a satisfied noise when he found a packet of cigarettes. A cheap brand, but better than nothing. There were three left, and Frye helped himself to one before replacing the packet in the handbag. Just as he snapped the clasp shut, the staff room door opened and Sarah walked in.

'What are you up to?' she asked, her eyes narrowing with suspicion.

'Nothing,' he said, putting the hand with the cigarette behind his back. 'Just taking a break.'

Sarah went over to her coat. She lifted it off the hook and laid it over her arm, reaching up to take her handbag down.

'You look tired, Sarah,' Frye said as she unclasped her bag and took out her packet of cigarettes. 'That holiday you had doesn't seem to have done you much good.'

'I wasn't on holiday,' she said.

Frye watched as Sarah took out a cigarette; she hadn't seemed to notice one was missing. 'But Nurse Crewe told me you'd gone away for a few days to Clacton or Southend or some other Godawful place. I'm sure that's what she said.'

'It wasn't a holiday.' She lit her cigarette, closing her eyes in pleasure as she took the smoke down.

'If not a holiday, then what?'

She glared at him. 'What business is it of yours?'

'Just making conversation, old girl,' he said, moving away and falling down into a battered armchair. 'Touchy today, aren't we?'

'I'm tired,' she admitted, half in explanation, half in apology. 'I haven't been sleeping well.' She sat down and rubbed her eyes.

'Noisy neighbours or something else?'

'Something else. Worrying about money, if you must know. I'm running very short. The truth is, I don't know what I'm going to do.'

'You're that hard up?'

'I will be soon. My landlady is raising the rent.'

'Then take a room here. They're cheap enough. That's what hospital accommodation is for, after all.'

'And be under Matron's nose all the time, telling me what I can do and what I can't?' Sarah scoffed. 'No, thank you. This place has enough of my life as it is. They're not getting my hours off as well.'

'Find new digs?'

'They're the cheapest I could find. Ordinarily, I can just about manage, but I've had a few unexpected expenses lately.'

'I know the feeling.'

Sarah tutted and shook her head. 'I'm talking about not having enough money to buy food for myself. Your idea of being hard up is not having enough to take a lady to the Ritz.'

Frye glared at her. How dare she presume that was all he had to put up with? 'There are all kinds of hardships, Sarah.'

'I suppose it is hard for you. Being forced to work here. What?' she said, smiling at the alarm on his face. 'You thought no one knew that working here was a condition of Dr Woodrow taking you on?'

'Does everyone know?' he asked, dismayed.

'I expect so. You've made it clear you're not here by choice.'

Was he really that transparent? 'Hopefully, it won't be for much longer,' he said before he could stop himself.

'Oh? And why's that?'

He hesitated, unsure he wanted to confess his hopes to

Sarah. For months now, he had been cultivating Victoria Scott, making himself available and attentive to her needs. Victoria, like so many of his former elderly female patients, had grown enamoured, and he'd had indications she was willing and able to be of service to him. She hadn't yet said how that service would manifest, but he had his own ideas, chief of which was getting his private practice back. It was an ambitious hope, he knew; still, one had to dream big.

And Sarah, he thought, could be of use to him. She wasn't a gossip, either. What he told her would stay between them, he was sure. To hell with it. He would tell her.

'There's a private patient of mine who may be interested in becoming my patron,' he said.

'One of your fancy ladies?'

'A mature lady of considerable means who thinks highly of me and has hinted she'd like to help.'

'Well, aren't you the lucky one?'

'You could be lucky, too,' he said meaningfully.

Sarah frowned. 'How?'

Frye leaned forward, suddenly animated. 'This lady's got a few health issues. Nothing serious, but she likes to be fussed over, and she hasn't had anyone doing that since her daughter ran off months ago. If I were to suggest she needs a private nurse keeping an eye on her, she'd be grateful. It would be financially rewarding for you, and you could put in a good word for me now and then. We could fit your hours with her around your shifts here easily enough.'

'I could do with the money,' she said thoughtfully, but then narrowed her eyes at him. 'You're sure that's all you're after? Me helping to put you in her good books?'

'That's all, I swear it. You're off shift, aren't you? So am I. Let's go and see her now.'

'She won't mind us just turning up?'

Frye grinned and shook his head. 'She's always pleased to see me. So, you'll come?'

Sarah studied him for a long moment, then nodded. 'I'll come.'

———

Frye smiled at Sarah encouragingly and took a drag of his cigarette.

She was doing rather well, saying all the right things, letting Victoria lead the conversation. Sarah knew how to play the game, he could tell, even though the occasional barb of Victoria's made her spine stiffen and her lips purse. Frye understood. He'd had to bite his tongue more often than not with Victoria.

There was a lull in the conversation, and he hurried to keep it going. 'Miss Kempe is our finest nurse, Victoria,' Frye assured her as her censorious eye raked over Sarah. 'Everyone says so. Even Matron, and that's saying something, believe me.'

'Oh, I believe you, Nigel,' Victoria said with either a wink or a twitch, Frye couldn't tell. She turned to Sarah. 'Do you enjoy your work, Miss Kempe?'

'It's very satisfying, Mrs Scott,' Sarah said, and Frye could tell it angered her to tell the lie. He suspected she hated the hospital even more than he did.

'Of course, it's a vocation for women like you,' Victoria said. 'After all, you have nothing else to occupy you, do you?'

Frye saw Sarah's face harden. *Bite your tongue, Sarah,* he mentally begged.

Sarah smiled. 'I don't have a husband or children, so yes. I put everything into my work.'

Frye let out a quiet breath of relief. 'You couldn't ask for anyone better, Victoria. It would ease my mind if I knew you were in Miss Kempe's capable hands.'

'And I don't want to make you worry about me, do I?' Victoria said, reaching over to pat his hand. 'Very well. I will take Miss Kempe on.'

'Excellent.' Frye turned to smile at Sarah and saw her gaze shift over his shoulder towards the sitting-room door. He turned to see Benjamin come in.

'Hullo!' Benjamin said, frowning. 'What's all this?'

'This is Nurse Kempe, Ben,' Victoria said. 'She'll be looking after me for a few hours each day.'

'Oh yes?' Benjamin nodded at Sarah. 'How do you do.'

'Pleased to meet you, Mr Scott,' Sarah said.

Frye felt Benjamin's suspicious gaze settle on him, and he decided it was time to leave. 'Well, I should be going.'

'I'd like a word before you go, Frye,' Benjamin said.

'Yes, of course,' Frye said uneasily, bending to take Victoria's outstretched hand. 'I'll leave you and Miss Kempe to iron out the details.' He hurried into the hall, taking his hat down from the stand as Benjamin closed the sitting-room door.

'This is your doing, I take it,' Benjamin said, jerking his head at the door.

'Miss Kempe is an acquaintance of mine from the hospital,' Frye acknowledged.

'I didn't think she looked the sort to be one of your lady friends.' Benjamin smirked. 'So, Victoria's got a nurse to fuss over her. What's in it for you?'

'I don't know what you mean,' Frye said indignantly.

'Yes, you do. What are you getting out of putting this woman in my house?'

'Nothing at all, other than the reassurance Victoria will be well looked after.'

'Professional concern, is that it?'

Frye wasn't prepared to let Benjamin goad him. 'I really must be going, Ben.' He put his hat on his head and reached for the front door latch.

'It's Mr Scott,' Benjamin said as Frye stepped down onto the doorstep. 'And I'm on to you, Frye. Don't think I'm not.'

Frye stared back at him in surprise, and Benjamin, with an unpleasant smile, slammed the door in his face.

Chapter Six

MONDAY, 20TH OCTOBER

Jane strolled along the road, deliberately catching the rim of her sole on every other paving stone. She'd had a lovely weekend; her parents had taken her to see her nan and grandad in Kent and she'd spent the two days playing with their dog's puppies. She'd begged her father to let her bring one home, but her father had reminded her it would need a lot of attention, and she'd be too busy with work to do that. So, the puppy with the floppy ear had stayed with its siblings and Jane had come home feeling she'd been denied a little piece of happiness.

She was particularly annoyed by her father's decision because she really didn't want to go to work anymore, least-ways, not at the Carrs. It hadn't been the same there since her mistress had been gone. Jane never got a kind word from Maxwell, only orders to hurry up, to get his breakfast or clean the house. She'd complained to her mother about him, hoping she would say she could leave, but all her mother had done had changed her working hours, so she was now a 'daily', arriving early in the morning and leaving after she'd served dinner. It meant a lot of to-ing and fro-ing, and she was fed up with it.

Jane raised her eyes with a heavy sigh and saw Maxwell emerge from his garden path onto the pavement and yank open the door of his car. What was he doing up this early? she wondered, checking her wristwatch in case she was running late. No, there were still five minutes to go before she had to be at the house, but she quickened her pace as Maxwell left the car door open and returned to the house. A few moments later, he came out once again, this time with Tinker in his arms.

'Mr Carr,' she cried, hurrying towards him. 'What is it?'

Maxwell glared at her. 'There you are. I've had my breakfast,' he snapped, as though him being up earlier than usual was her fault. 'I'm going out.'

'With Tinker?' she asked, staring at the dog through the car window.

'Yes,' Maxwell said, moving around the car to the driver's seat. 'I want the house cleaned today, Jane. All over, and no sweeping the dirt under the rugs. You hear me?'

'Yes, sir,' she replied sulkily, watching him start up the engine and drive off. 'I always clean properly,' she muttered and turned into the house, slamming the front door behind her.

She took off her coat and hung it up on the hall stand, putting her hat on the same hook and dropping her handbag on the shelf at the bottom. She went into the kitchen and saw the tray with the remains of a breakfast Maxwell had left for her to clear up. If she was being fair to him – and Jane was in no mood to be fair to him – it looked like he'd only had a cup of tea and a slice of toast, and so there was very little for her to do. She'd cleaned the kitchen only the evening before, so she grabbed her cleaning cloths and her tin of Vim and headed up the stairs to the bathroom.

Jane cleaned the bath, wiping away the tidemark left by Maxwell's bath salts. Getting to her feet, she bent and rubbed some feeling back into her knees, then turned to the basin to clean away the shaving soap suds and short bristles he'd shaved off that morning. Satisfied with her work, she bent to pick up the waste bin so she could empty it into the dustbin outside. As she lifted it, she heard something clink on the tiles and peered into the semi-darkness behind the basin's pedestal. Something cylindrical was lying there, and she was surprised, for she had cleaned the floor on Friday and whatever this thing was, it hadn't been there then. She snatched the object up.

Her eyebrows rose as she saw it was a lipstick. Taking the top off, she studied the colour, and her brow creased. Strange, she thought, staring at the bright red lipstick she'd revealed. Mrs Carr never wore bright red lipstick; she'd always said it didn't suit her skin colouring, preferring a raspberry shade. Jane turned the lipstick upside down to see the brand on the base. It wasn't one she'd ever seen on her mistress's dressing table.

Jane went into the bedroom and put the lipstick on the pink glass tray on the dressing table where Imogen had kept her makeup and turned to the bed.

She stared at it in surprise. Normally, only Mr Carr's side of the bed would be rumpled, but this morning, both pillows had indents in them where a head had lain, and the sheets were tumbled over the sides.

Maybe, Jane thought excitedly, Mrs Carr had returned. That would explain the bed. But that wouldn't explain the different shade of lipstick. No, it wouldn't explain that.

Jane hurried over to the dressing table and snatched up the lipstick and, without really knowing why, slipped the metal tube into her pocket. She'd tell her mother about it, she decided, and see what explanation she came up with for it being in the house.

———

In one sense, and in one sense only, it had been a good morning for Walsh.

Elaine Johnson had been found on the steps of St Luke's church at 6 a.m. alive and, if not exactly well, at least not as bad as everyone had feared. Elaine had been taken to the local hospital and reunited with her parents, who had thanked Walsh profusely for finding her.

Except he hadn't found her. She'd been returned, and once again, Walsh had no clues to follow and nothing to go on. He'd said as much to the Chief Constable the night before at a police function, a stupid, drunken mistake for which his wife berated him roundly. He'd said a lot more too that he didn't tell her, how it wasn't fair his promotion hinged on him solving the case when he had so much to do, how overworked he was. Walsh had thought the Chief Constable had been sympathetic, understanding, but now that he'd been summoned to Chief Superintendent Goodridge's office, he wasn't so sure.

He winced as the secretary adjusted the angle of the Venetian blind behind her desk and sunlight pierced his eyes. The intercom on her desk buzzed and a deep voice growled, 'Send in Walsh.'

Walsh was already on his feet, straightening his tie, when the secretary waved him to the door.

'You wanted to see me, sir?' Walsh said as he entered the office.

Goodridge waved him to a chair. 'I heard the baby turned up?'

'Yes, sir. It was found this morning by the church cleaner

when she arrived to begin work. It was wrapped in a filthy blanket and was very dirty but otherwise unharmed.'

'Any notion of who put it there?'

'I'm afraid not. Neither the cleaner nor the vicar saw anything.'

'Unfortunate.' Goodridge's nostrils tightened as he studied Walsh. 'The Chief Constable had a word with me last night.'

Here it comes, Walsh thought unhappily. 'Ah, yes. I can explain about that. You see—'

'You complained of being overworked.'

'I didn't complain, sir. I made an off-hand remark that I have rather a lot on my plate.'

Goodridge tapped the newspaper lying folded on his desk. 'I've had reporters calling me this morning. This return of the baby will be in the late editions, and I don't need to tell you, the 'papers will not be kind to us. The press believes we're incompetent. That we're incapable of catching this woman.'

'I'm not responsible for what the press prints, sir,' Walsh protested. 'The problem is that despite the number of snatches, there simply aren't any leads to follow. DI Morris had the same problem. And with Turner not being replaced and Batten on light duties, we're short-staffed in CID. I can't devote the time the cases demand.'

'Yes, yes, I understand the problem,' Goodridge said thoughtfully. 'The answer, as I see it, is to second an officer from Russell Street to come here for a month or so and ease your burden.'

'Thank you, sir.' Walsh breathed a sigh of relief. It was going to be all right. Goodridge would hand the case over to someone else. It would be off his hands by the time he walked out of the office. 'I'll brief him fully on the case and give him all the assistance I can.'

Goodridge frowned. 'You misunderstand me, Walsh. I'm

not taking you off the snatch case. I'm making it the only case you're working on.'

Walsh stared at him. 'But … but…'

'The officer I'll second will take over your other cases and deal with anything else that comes in. There's nothing to be gained by handing the case over to another officer at this late stage. You know it inside out; it makes sense to keep you on it. And with you working on the case full time, I'm expecting you to have it solved very soon. As is the Chief Constable. But I'm sure you already know that.'

'Yes, sir,' Walsh nodded miserably. 'I know that.'

Goodridge dismissed him, and Walsh returned to his office in CID and fell down into his chair. A photograph of Elaine Johnson smiled at him from his desk. Walsh closed the case file cover on her with a curling of his top lip. Reaching for his coffee, he took a mouthful and made a face.

'Crossley!' Walsh yelled, and the young detective constable hurried into his office.

'Yes, sir?'

'Coffee's cold,' he said, banging the cup down onto the saucer.

'I'll get you another. And there's someone to see you.'

'Tell them I'm busy,' Walsh growled.

'I don't think I can do that, sir,' Crossley said, looking uneasily over his shoulder into the main CID office. 'You see—'

'I apologise for bothering you, Inspector Walsh.'

The tone was sardonic, and Walsh looked up to see a man in his late thirties with salt-and-pepper hair and dressed in a smart three-piece suit standing in his office doorway.

'This is DCI Vickery, sir,' Crossley explained awkwardly.

Walsh scrambled to his feet. 'I'm sorry, sir. I didn't realise…' His words trailed off as he struggled to find an excuse for his rudeness. 'Please come in,' he said instead and gestured Vickery to a chair.

'Thank you.' Vickery sat down, putting his briefcase on the floor beside the chair.

Walsh jerked his head at Crossley to leave. 'How can I help you, sir?' he said, resuming his seat.

'Actually, I'm here to help you. I understand you're working on a baby-snatching case?'

'That's right,' Walsh said, his brow creasing as he wondered what it had to do with Vickery. 'In fact, the last baby to be snatched turned up this morning.'

'I heard. That's why I'm here.' He took a file out of his briefcase. 'I'm over at Minerva Road now, but I was stationed in Witham a few years ago. We had a similar case there.' He passed the file across the desk.

'In Witham?' Walsh flipped open the file and scanned the first page it contained. It was an incident report detailing how a baby had been snatched from a mother while she was shopping and found weeks later on the steps of a church.

'November 1927,' Vickery said. 'I never found the woman who took the baby. So, I'm wondering if she could be at it again here?'

'There have been four cases in Colchester,' Walsh said, astonished by this information. He pulled out his case file and turned to the handwritten summary he had made at the front. 'One in 1926, one in 1928, another in '29 and this most recent one. But there was nothing here in '27.' He groaned and shook his head. 'Because—'

'Because the snatcher wasn't in Colchester in 1927,' Vickery said with a nod. 'She was in Witham. I'm afraid, Walsh, you'll have to widen your search for this woman.'

Chapter Seven

Sarah nestled a little closer, angling her head so the hairs on Nick's chest tickled her cheek.

He had turned up at the hospital as her shift was ending, reeking of booze and cigarette smoke, evidence he had done what he'd said he would as soon as he came out of prison and gone in every pub he passed on the way to her. She hadn't cared that he'd taken his time; he was with her now. Sarah closed her eyes and smiled to herself.

'What are you smiling about?' Nick asked lazily.

'I'm happy,' she said, giving him a squeeze. 'To finally have you home.'

'Home?' He snorted and waved his hand at the dingy room. 'This?'

Sarah propped herself up on her elbow, making sure the sheet still covered her. 'I know it's not much, Nick, but it's better than a prison cell.'

He gave her a disparaging look, then raised his arm over her head and snatched up the half bottle of whisky from the bedside cabinet. He drank from the bottle, then offered it to Sarah.

She shook her head. 'I can't. I have to go to work.'

'You've been to work. Your next shift doesn't start until the morning.'

'Not at the hospital. It's a private patient. A lady.'

'You didn't tell me you were doing private work.'

'I didn't think you'd be interested.'

Nick lit a cigarette. 'Does it pay much?'

'Five shillings a week.'

'She's rich, then?'

'I would say so. It's a nice house, and they have a cook and a maid. The husband owns a printing works.' Sarah checked the clock and groaned. 'I've got to go.' She reached for her slip from the end of the bed, pulling it on over her head before sliding out from between the sheets.

'How long have you been working for them?'

'Since September.'

Nick did a quick mental calculation. 'Then you've made close on to five quid. Where's it all gone? Or are you hiding it from me?'

'I'm not hiding it. It's been spent.'

'On what?'

She turned her back to pull on her stockings. 'On the usual things. Food, heating, rent. It all mounts up.'

Nick shook his head. 'Not five quid's worth. What have you spent it on, Sarah? Because it bloody well isn't on me.' He held up the near-empty whisky. 'I shouldn't have to drink this gut rot if you've got money.'

'I had to go away a few times,' Sarah explained unhappily, knowing Nick wouldn't let the matter lie. 'There were train fares and other expenses. And I haven't spent it all. I'm just being careful. After all, we need the money.'

'For what?'

'For a flat, Nick. We talked about getting a nice place together once you were out. Remember?'

His face hardened. 'I want to see this money. Show it to me.'

With a sigh, Sarah opened the top drawer in the chest of drawers and pulled out a small battered purse. She threw it onto the bed. It clinked as it landed in Nick's lap, and he tipped the contents onto the blanket.

'See, I haven't spent all of it.' She slipped her feet into her brogues and bent to tie up the laces.

'Is this woman the only one you're doing this private work for?' he asked, putting the few coins back into the purse.

'She's the only one.'

'How did you find her?'

'She's a patient of Dr Frye's. He asked me if I was interested in some private nursing work.'

'And who's this Dr Frye?'

'He works at the hospital.'

'Why is he arranging private work for you?' Nick asked suspiciously. 'Is he taking a cut of your wages? Because I'm not having that.'

'He isn't taking a cut.'

'Then what's in it for him?'

'He wants to get in with this lady, that's all. He wants me to put in a good word for him now and then.'

'That's all?'

'That's all, Nick. Look, I've got to go. I'll bring supper back.' She headed for the door. 'It'll be about nine.'

'Don't bother,' Nick said. 'I won't be here.'

Sarah whirled around and stared at him in alarm. 'Where are you going?' she cried.

'Out. You don't need to know where.'

He was waiting for her to protest; Sarah could see it in his eyes. But she didn't want a row. So she nodded and smiled and said, 'I'll see you when I see you, then.'

She yanked the door open and stepped out into the hall. Closing the door behind her, she raised her eyes to the ceiling and mouthed a silent prayer. *Please, God, don't let him leave me.*

Chapter Eight

SATURDAY, 1ST NOVEMBER

Matthew Stannard threw back his head and yawned, wishing that just once he could wake refreshed and not feeling more tired than when he went to bed.

The kettle whistled, and he poured the boiling water into the mug with its heaped teaspoon of coffee powder. He'd decided against tea that morning; he needed caffeine.

A loud meow made him look down. A black and white face with round yellow eyes stared back up at him. 'Woken up at last, have you?' he said, smiling down at Bella. She stretched upwards, placing her paws on his leg and extending her claws. 'I'm feeding you,' he protested, wincing.

Matthew emptied a tin of tuna onto a saucer and set it on the floor. He whistled, and a moment later, three kittens came gambolling into the kitchen. He put down a saucer of milk and watched as they lapped it up.

Matthew made his breakfast – a bowl of cornflakes and a slice of toast to go with the coffee – and took it to his sitting-room table, where a week's worth of post waited to be opened. Most were bills, and he set these aside, not in the mood to deal with them, but one had handwriting on the front, and he recognised it as his sister's. Wondering why Pat was writing to him instead of telephoning, he ripped open the envelope. There was a note and a newspaper clipping inside. He unfolded the clipping with a sigh, anticipating it would be an article about him and the Foxhall Green cinema shooting, but his breath caught in his throat as he read the first sentence. It wasn't about him. It was about the man who had tried to kill him.

Wilfrid Gadd was executed at 8 o'clock this morning. Mr Gadd was sentenced to death for the murder of Mr Leonard Gibbs and convicted of other charges of assault and the attempted murder of a police officer.

His hand was shaking as Matthew lit a cigarette. He closed his eyes, taking the smoke deep into his lungs before daring to pick up the clipping again. He read it once more, then set it aside and read Pat's note.

I don't expect you've had the time with all that horror at the cinema to have a look at a newspaper recently, so I thought I'd better post you this. He's dead now, Mattie, so you don't have to worry any more.

A memory exploded in Matthew's brain. He was seven years old, and Pat was sitting on his bed, squeezing his hand and talking in a whisper, saying, 'You don't have to worry any more.'

Matthew had been playing cricket in the street with his friends when the ball had gone over the wall of No. 36. Mr Burland lived in that house, and everyone knew he was mad;

all the mothers along the street warned their children to stay away from him. But the boys needed the cricket ball, and deciding Matthew had to get it back, he'd got a leg-up from his friend and dropped down into the rubbish tip that passed for Mr Burland's backyard. There were so many places the cricket ball could have landed, and it took Matthew a while to find it behind a rotting wooden box by the back door.

He'd bent to pick it up when a hand grabbed his hair. Long, sharp fingernails dug into his scalp and wrenched him backwards. Mr Burland had caught him! Grunting like an animal, the old man dragged Matthew into his house, through the kitchen and into the passage, where he yanked open the door to the under-stairs cupboard.

Matthew had grabbed hold of the doorframe, his nails splitting as they dug into the wood. Just as he thought he couldn't hold on any longer, Mr Burland's grip loosened. Taking his chance, Matthew kicked at the old man's legs, and he stumbled backwards with a curse. Matthew ran, and didn't stop until he had buried himself beneath his blankets in the bedroom he shared with Pat.

That was where his sister had found him several hours later, and she dragged the tale of what had happened out of him. Knowing he shouldn't have been in Mr Burland's garden in the first place, and not wanting to get into trouble, Matthew begged her not to tell their parents, and Pat promised she wouldn't. So when the nightmares came, night after night, it was his sister and not their mother who comforted him, climbing into his bed, wrapping her arms around him and whispering soothing words into his ear.

And when the police had broken down the front door of No. 36 because the neighbour had complained about the smell, and Mr Burland had been carried out in a wooden box, it had been Pat who told him the old man was dead and that he didn't have to worry any more.

But when Gadd attacked Matthew and hunted him down, and the nightmares had come again, Pat wasn't there to reassure him everything was all right. All he had was Bella, but she didn't always appreciate being grabbed in the middle of the night and held tight. And Bella never cuddled back.

But now Gadd was dead; he wasn't ever coming back. And Matthew didn't have to worry any more.

Chapter Nine

'Ah, inspector.' Sergeant Turkel waved at Matthew from the front desk as he entered the station's lobby.

One day, Matthew thought wryly, *I'll walk in here and Turkel won't have something for me.* 'Yes, sergeant?' he said. 'What can I do for you?'

Turkel nodded towards the door of the private waiting room. 'There's a mother and daughter in there who want to report a missing person. I was going to give it to one of the lads, but Denham and Rudd are busy, and Barnes has been called out to a burglary. So, would you mind taking it, sir?'

Matthew said he would take it and crossed the lobby to the waiting room. Two faces looked up at him as he entered. One was young, a little plain and looked very nervous. The other was middle-aged, heavily made up, and full of barely suppressed eagerness.

'Good morning,' Matthew said, taking a seat at the table. 'I'm DI Stannard.'

'I recognise you from the 'paper,' the elder woman said with a smile. 'As soon as you came in, I thought, that's him. That's the detective who caught that horrible man over in Foxhall Green. It was you, wasn't it?'

'Yes, that was me. And you are?'

'I'm Mrs Abigail Prior, and this is my daughter, Jane.'

Matthew smiled at the young girl. She smiled back but said nothing. 'And I understand you want to report a missing person? Is it a relative?'

'No,' Mrs Prior said. 'It's the woman my daughter works for. A Mrs Imogen Carr.'

This was new. Matthew had never had an employee care enough about their employer to report them missing. 'What's your job, Miss Prior?' he asked Jane.

Jane opened her mouth to reply, but her mother answered for her. 'Jane's her maid. Well, I say maid, but she does everything for them. Maid, cook, cleaner. They really ought to pay her more, you know?'

'I'm sure,' Matthew said. 'And how long has Mrs Carr been missing?'

'It's been about six months,' Mrs Prior said.

'When did you last see her?' Matthew asked Jane.

Again, it was her mother who answered. 'It was the tenth of May. A Saturday, and—'

'Forgive me, Mrs Prior,' Matthew interrupted her with his most charming smile. 'But it would be better if your daughter told me herself.'

Mrs Prior's mouth pursed in indignation, but it stayed shut.

Matthew turned back to Jane. Jane was looking at him in astonishment, and he guessed no one had silenced her mother before. 'So, she's been gone around six months. Why have you waited this long to report Mrs Carr missing?'

'Because I didn't think she was missing until now,' Jane said. 'Just that she'd gone away. You see, there had been a big to-do on the Saturday. Mrs Carr had shut herself up in her bedroom for most of the day. She only came down at dinner-time and then she and the master had a big row. That was the last I saw of her.'

'Mr Carr hasn't reported his wife missing,' Matthew said.

'Well, he wouldn't, would he?' Mrs Prior put in.

'Why wouldn't he, Mrs Prior?'

'Because he's done her in, that's why,' she said as if the answer was obvious.

His eyes widened. 'You think Mr Carr's killed his wife?'

'He has a row with her, and then she's gone? Disappeared?' She shook her head in disbelief. 'He goes around telling the neighbours she's off in Scotland, visiting relatives, but—'

'But they don't have any relatives in Scotland,' Jane cut in. 'Mrs Carr once told me the only relatives she has are her parents, and they live just around the corner.'

'And,' Mrs Prior stabbed the tabletop with her finger, 'he's carrying on with another woman. In the house, if you please. Jane found her lipstick in the bathroom. And the bed,' she raised her eyebrows meaningfully at Matthew and lowered her voice, 'had been used by two people.'

'I see,' Matthew said, thinking it sounded more like a marriage breaking down than a murder. 'Her parents are local, you say? Yet they haven't reported her missing, either.'

'Probably because they believe Mr Carr when he says she's away,' Mrs Prior said. 'But Jane says there has been nothing from Mrs Carr. Not a letter, not a telephone call. Not a thing. Don't tell me that's not suspicious.'

'It is unusual,' Matthew agreed, a little reluctantly. 'But they could have separated. If, as you say, they were quarrelling—'

'It's not just the rows,' Jane burst out. 'Mrs Carr left her dog behind. She loved Tinker, and I don't think she would have gone anywhere without him. And Mr Carr, he—' she broke off, her voice catching. 'He had Tinker destroyed. He killed the poor little thing.'

'Oh, Jane, don't cry,' her mother chided, handing Jane her handkerchief and gesturing for her to wipe her eyes. 'There,' she said defiantly to Matthew. 'Mrs Carr goes off without the dog she loves, and Mr Carr has it put down because he knows she isn't coming back. And how does he know that? Because he's done her in, that's how. I don't know what you call it, but I call it very suspicious.'

If he was honest, Matthew thought it sounded suspicious too, but he wasn't ready to believe Mr Carr had murdered his wife just yet. 'I will certainly look into this, Mrs Prior,' he said.

'Are you going to talk to Mr Carr?' Jane asked.

'To him, and to Mrs Carr's parents.'

'But you won't tell them I told you about Mrs Carr being missing, will you? He'll be ever so angry.'

'I'm afraid I can't promise your name won't be mentioned.'

'Jane's worried about losing her position,' Mrs Prior explained. 'But I told her not to worry about that. I don't want her working for that swine. God knows what he might do to her.'

'There may be nothing in this,' Matthew said. 'Mr Carr may have a perfectly reasonable explanation for his wife's absence.'

'If you say so, inspector,' Mrs Prior said. 'But if I were you, I wouldn't believe a word that man says.'

———

Maxwell was washing his hands when Benjamin burst into the lavatory. He checked the cubicles were empty, then shoved a newspaper in Maxwell's face and demanded, 'What's this?'

Maxwell's heart sank. The newspaper was turned to the page where he'd placed an advertisement for commercial printing. 'I was going to talk to you about that.'

'How much did it cost?' Benjamin asked stonily.

'A few pounds. What does it matter if it brings in orders?'

'And how are we supposed to fulfil them? We don't have the machines for this sort of printing.'

'I can get them. I've already had estimates from manu-facturers.'

'Something else you've done without my say-so.'

'I don't need to ask you about every damn thing, Ben,' Maxwell cried. 'I've told you. We've got to move with the times. If we don't get into commercial printing, we'll be left behind.'

'Utter rot,' Benjamin scoffed. 'There'll always be a need for printed stationery.'

'At a few quid here, a few quid there? With these kinds of jobs,' Maxwell pointed at the advertisment, 'we can earn in one month what it would take us a year to do with letterheads and business cards.'

'It's a good business as it is,' Benjamin growled.

'It's a stagnant business. Our profits haven't risen in years.'

'At least we have profits. I can just imagine how much these machines of yours would set us back.'

'Listen, Ben, please,' Maxwell pleaded. 'We've got the space. We've got the manpower. All we need is a little ambition.'

'And money. Where's that supposed to come from, eh?'

'We go to a bank. We take out a loan.'

'Oh no.' Benjamin wagged a finger at Maxwell. 'I've not

been in debt for more than fifteen years, and I won't go back to owing a bank money for anything. Not at my time of life.'

'Well, that's just it, isn't it?' Maxwell shot back. 'You've got your eyes set on retirement and to hell with what you leave behind for me. I'm telling you, the machines would pay for themselves in just a few months. We'd pay the loan back in no time.'

'No, we won't, because we're not doing it.' Benjamin screwed up the newspaper and tossed it into the waste bin. 'I've cancelled the ad.'

'You've no right to do that.'

'I've every right. It's my company.'

'For now, maybe,' Maxwell nodded. 'But as soon as you're gone, I'll do exactly what I want, and then you'll see what could have been.'

Benjamin's top lip curled in a sneer. 'You'd run this business into the ground within six months with your harebrained schemes.' He was about to say more when there was a knock on the door. Benjamin yanked it open to see their secretary standing outside. 'What is it?' he demanded.

'I'm sorry to disturb you,' Linda said, looking past him to Maxwell. 'But there's a policeman here to see Mr Carr.'

Chapter Ten

'What do you mean my wife's been reported missing?'
Maxwell cried.

Matthew sized Maxwell up. He was younger than he'd
imagined, roughly the same age as he, and handsome in a
boyish kind of way, he supposed, with dark blond hair that
flopped over his forehead, blue eyes and a square jaw. Carr
was full of bluster and outrage, one of those men who
shouted a lot, he guessed, but a wife killer?

'Exactly that, Mr Carr,' Matthew said, making himself
comfortable in the chair by Maxwell's desk. 'I'm told your
wife hasn't been seen for almost six months.'

'Who reported her missing, inspector?' Benjamin asked
from his desk across the room.

'It was Jane, wasn't it?' Maxwell said. 'She's been
looking sideways at me for weeks.'

'Miss Prior is very concerned about Mrs Carr.'

'My daughter isn't missing, inspector,' Benjamin said.
'She's just gone away.'

'Where?'

'She's in Scotland,' Maxwell said. 'Visiting relatives.'

'I've been told that your wife doesn't have any relatives

except for her parents.' Matthew turned to Benjamin. 'And I understand you live just around the corner. Of course, if you can give me the address where she's staying in Scotland, I can speak to her and clear this up.'

Matthew noticed the uneasy glance Benjamin and Maxwell exchanged. So there was something in Mrs Prior's claim, after all, he thought.

'Imogen's not in Scotland, inspector,' Maxwell admitted with a sigh. 'I said that was where she'd gone because I grew tired of the neighbours asking about her.'

'So, where is she?'

'I don't know.' Maxwell flipped open the lid of the box on his desk and took out a cigarette.

'You don't know?' Matthew queried as Maxwell lit it.

'No, I don't. But wherever she is, I'm sure she's fine.'

'So, she's left you?'

'Not exactly. Not in the way you mean.'

How many ways are there? Matthew wondered. 'She left her dog behind,' he said.

'That's right.'

'And you had it put down.'

Maxwell made a noise of impatience. 'Yes, I did. Tinker was old, and he was suffering. I took him to the vet, and he said the kindest thing would be to put him down. So that's what I did.'

'I understand your wife was very attached to her dog. Why would she leave him behind?'

'You tell me!' Maxwell cried, throwing up his hands. 'I don't know why Imogen didn't take the bloody thing with her.'

'I need the name of the vet,' Matthew said.

'Charles Marsland on Southbury Avenue. You don't mean to say you're going to check up on me?'

Matthew said nothing as he noted the name and address

down in his notebook. 'You had an argument with your wife just before she disappeared?' he said when he'd finished.

Maxwell closed his eyes in irritation. 'I've told you, she hasn't disappeared. All this fuss. It's ridiculous.'

'You don't seem very concerned about your wife, Mr Carr,' Matthew said. 'Nor you about your daughter, Mr Scott.'

Benjamin shook his head. 'There are things you don't understand about my daughter, inspector. I can assure you she's not missing. Imogen chose to leave. This isn't the first time she's gone off. It's the... what is it, Max? The third time?'

'Fourth,' Maxwell said.

'You see,' Benjamin went on, 'Imogen has always been rather highly strung. She gets upset at the slightest thing. She has tantrums. When things get too much for her, Imogen runs away. The first time she did it, she worried us dreadfully. But then we had a letter from her, telling us she was all right and would be back when she felt better. She returned to us nearly seven months later.'

'Then she went off again a few years later,' Maxwell said. 'She was gone for four months that time. And we didn't hear from her at all. Nor the time after that.'

'And you didn't know where she was?' Matthew asked.

'Imogen never told us where she went,' Benjamin said.

'But surely you asked her?'

'Of course we did, but she absolutely refused to speak about where she had gone or who she had been with. And we didn't want to insist she tell us in case it set her off again.'

Matthew turned back to Maxwell. 'So, what upset her this time? What was the row about?'

'The usual things, I suppose. What do you argue with your wife about?'

'I'm not married, Mr Carr.'

'Huh. Fortunate man.' Maxwell sighed and rubbed his forehead. 'If you must know, it was all Victoria's fault. She upset her.'

'Victoria is…?'

'My wife, inspector,' Benjamin said.

'And what did Mrs Scott do to upset your wife, Mr Carr?'

'She brought the bloody doctor to the house,' Maxwell said. 'Imogen had complained about headaches, and Victoria knew Imogen wouldn't go to the doctor if left to her own devices, so she brought the doctor to her. But Imogen had locked herself in the bedroom and refused to come out, so it was all a waste of time.'

'Mrs Carr was ill?'

'No, not as such.'

'What does that mean?'

'It means it's none of your business.'

'Max!' Benjamin chided. 'The inspector's just doing his job.'

'He's poking his nose in where it doesn't belong. He has no right to know about my private life.'

'He has to know.' Benjamin turned to Matthew. 'My daughter has been unable to have a child, inspector. This is why Imogen has these bouts of…' He searched for the right word.

'Insanity?' Maxwell suggested sourly.

'Nerves,' Benjamin said, glaring at him. 'She had two miscarriages early in her marriage, and nothing since. She's been examined by many doctors, but none of them has ever been able to tell us why she can't have a baby. The examinations distress Imogen a great deal.'

'So, a doctor coming to examine her without her knowledge or consent would have upset her?' Matthew said.

'Imogen didn't want to be poked about,' Maxwell said. 'She'd said so the night before.'

'Then it seems rather cruel to force her to be examined,' Matthew said accusingly.

'I've just told you, it was nothing to do with me. It was her mother.'

'Surely, you could have prevented Mrs Scott from bringing the doctor to your house?'

'You try to stop Victoria from doing anything,' Maxwell said sulkily. 'I suppose you want to talk to the doctor as well?'

'Yes,' Matthew said. 'I do.'

'His name's Nigel Frye. He works at the surgery on Sherwood Close.'

'That's Dr Woodrow's practice,' Matthew said in surprise.

'That's right. So you know Frye?'

'No, I know of Dr Woodrow. He's taken over as the police doctor.' Matthew made another note in his notebook and then looked back at Maxwell. 'My next question is very personal, Mr Carr.'

'And all your other ones haven't been?' Maxwell scoffed.

'Is it possible your wife left because she found out you were having an affair?'

Maxwell stared at Matthew, taken aback by the question.

'What's this?' Benjamin demanded.

'No,' Maxwell said to Matthew through gritted teeth. 'That isn't possible.'

'Because she didn't know you were having an affair?'

'Because I wasn't.'

'You weren't? But you are now?'

'That's it.' Maxwell jumped out of his chair and jabbed a finger at Matthew. 'I've had enough. I refuse to answer any more of these damned impertinent questions. You get out. Go.' He waved Matthew towards the door.

'I do think you ought to leave, inspector,' Benjamin said, rising as well. 'We've answered your questions. Imogen will be back when she feels like it. I'm sure the police have far more important matters to investigate. This isn't worth your time, I assure you.'

'I'll decide what's worth my time, Mr Scott,' Matthew said testily. 'I would like a photograph of Mrs Carr, please.'

Maxwell snatched up a picture frame from his desk and held it out to Matthew. 'Here. Take it.'

Matthew took it. 'Thank you. I'll sure we'll be speaking again.'

He left the printing works and climbed into the waiting police car. Telling the driver to take him back to the station, Matthew looked at the black-and-white photograph in the frame Maxwell had given him. A very lovely woman with dark wavy hair, high cheekbones, a Cupid's bow mouth and sad eyes looked out at him.

Matthew shook his head in disbelief at Maxwell. If Imogen Carr was his wife, he thought, he wouldn't rest until he found her.

Chapter Eleven

Two men turned to look at Matthew when he was shown into the office at the Sherwood Close Surgery. One was in his late sixties, dressed in a rather tired-looking three-piece suit with a gold watch-chain hanging from his waistcoat pocket. This, Matthew supposed, was Dr Woodrow, the new police doctor. The other man was younger, in his early forties, slim and elegantly turned out in a dark tan suit, with light brown hair and a wispy moustache. His mother would have described Frye as debonair.

'You want to see me?' Frye asked, a look of alarm crossing his face.

'I'm the police doctor, inspector,' Woodrow said, 'so actually, I think it's me you want to see. But I don't think I've had the pleasure?'

Matthew held out his hand. 'I'm Matthew Stannard.'

'Of course you are,' Woodrow said, shaking his hand. 'I've seen your picture in the 'paper.'

Who hasn't? Matthew thought ruefully. 'I'm not here for me,' he explained. 'I'm making enquiries about a patient of yours. A Mrs Imogen Carr. She hasn't been seen for several months.'

'I believe she's in Scotland, inspector,' Woodrow said.

'She isn't,' Matthew said. 'In fact, her family doesn't know where she is. I understand, Dr Frye, that you went to see her the day she disappeared.'

'You went to see Mrs Carr, Frye?' Woodrow asked. 'But she's my patient.'

'Yes, I know.' Frye gave a nervous laugh and shrugged. 'It was Victoria, Edward. She insisted.' He turned to Matthew. 'I can assure you I had nothing to do with Mrs Carr leaving home. After all, I never even saw her that day.'

'You had no right to go there at all,' Woodrow chided. Frye looked contrite but said nothing. 'Why are you asking about Mrs Carr, inspector?'

'Mrs Carr has been reported as missing by her maid,' Matthew said. 'She's concerned something's happened to her. A concern not shared by her husband and father, which I find very odd.'

Woodrow invited Matthew to take a seat. 'It isn't all that odd. I'm sure Mr Carr has already told you that his wife has a very fragile temperament. She gets upset very easily. Running away is how she copes when things become too much for her.'

'So, Dr Frye arriving at her house unannounced to examine her against her will would be enough for her to take off?' Matthew asked.

Woodrow gave Frye a hard stare. 'Yes, I believe it would.'

'I may be persuaded that Mrs Carr left of her own voli-tion,' Matthew said, 'but after what I've heard, I am concerned about her safety. Would she be in a fit state to take care of herself? Would she do herself harm?'

'Oh no.' Woodrow shook his head. 'I'm sure Mrs Carr wouldn't be that silly.'

'She's fine, inspector,' Frye said, reaching into his pocket to take out his packet of cigarettes. He put one in the corner of his mouth and lit it, composure regained. 'If her family isn't worried about her, then I don't see any reason why the police should be. Now, if you don't mind, I'm due at the hospital. Excuse me.'

'I apologise for Dr Frye, inspector,' Woodrow said when Frye had gone. 'He can be rather touchy.'

'Is he a partner here?' Matthew asked.

'No, he works for me.'

'And for the hospital?'

'No, still me. It's part of his contract with me that he carries out shifts at Sawyers Cross. I don't want to only treat patients who can afford my care. We must look after those less fortunate too.'

'Dr Frye doesn't strike me as the kind of man who would choose to tend to the needy.'

Woodrow smiled. 'I wouldn't like to comment on his character. Frye does his shifts. That's all I need to know.'

'Even if he acts unethically?' Matthew challenged.

Woodrow drew in a deep breath. 'I shall be talking to him about this incident with Mrs Carr, inspector. I'll make sure that sort of thing doesn't happen again.'

Matthew rose. 'I'm glad to hear it.'

———

Matthew's next visit was to the vet, Charles Marsland. Marsland confirmed that the elderly dog had been suffering and he advised it be put down. Everything tallied. It seemed no one but the Priors believed Imogen Carr had done anything but left Craynebrook of her own free will, and Matthew was inclined to agree. Mindful of the other cases waiting for him back at the station, he decided to postpone any further enquiries until Monday and headed back to CID.

The next few hours were spent reading through the junior detectives' crime reports, and he only looked up from his paperwork when DS Denham rapped on the office window and stuck his head around the doorway.

'It's six o'clock, sir,' he said.

Matthew glanced up at the clock on the wall. 'I didn't realise it was that late.' He glanced through the office window to see the other detectives pulling on their coats.

'All right to call it a night?'

'Yes, if everything's done.' Matthew rose from his chair and stretched, arching his back that had grown stiff from sitting still for too long. 'You're eager to leave tonight.'

Denham made an apologetic face. 'Me and the wife are taking the baby over to her parents. It's my wife's birthday, and they're putting on a bit of a do.'

'Ah,' Matthew nodded. 'Wish your wife a happy birthday from me.'

'Will do,' Denham nodded. 'I'll see you Monday, sir.'

He exited the office, joining DS Bissett as he grabbed his coat from the hat stand and handed Barnes his. They were about to leave when Matthew remembered he had wanted to talk to them and hurried out of his office.

'Just a minute,' he called, and saw them turn back to him, dismay evident in their expressions. 'I won't keep you. I just want to say something about DI Lund.'

The three detectives glanced at each other. Denham's expression had grown hard, and Matthew knew the sergeant hadn't forgiven Lund for his mishandling of the Foxhall Green cinema shooting.

'Now,' Matthew went on, 'I know he didn't leave in the best of circumstances, and feelings,' he caught Denham's eye, 'ran a little high over what happened. But that's all over now. I don't want there to be any trouble when DI Lund walks in here on Monday. I don't want any recriminations. I don't even want mutterings or dirty looks.' He was about to add that none of the detectives knew what Lund had been going through at the time, but stopped himself. He'd promised Lund he wouldn't say a word. So he settled for, 'Is that understood?'

'Yes, sir,' Barnes and Bissett replied immediately.

'Denham?' Matthew queried.

Denham took a deep breath, nodded, and said, albeit reluctantly, 'Yes, sir.'

Satisfied, Matthew nodded. 'Good. Off you go, then.'

They tramped out. A few minutes later, DC Tapper came into CID to cover the night shift, and Matthew left him to it, heading for the King George on the high street, hoping no one would bother him there.

Chapter Twelve

'And this policeman was there because that silly maid of yours reported Imogen missing?' Victoria tutted and shook her head, making her sapphire earrings jiggle. 'I never liked that girl. I hope you've sacked her, Max.'

Maxwell swirled his brandy around the glass, staring moodily into it. 'I haven't seen her to sack her. I expect her mother's told her she's not allowed anywhere near me in case I murder her as well.'

'What nonsense! I've a good mind to go round to their house and tell them both what I think of them.'

'A lot of good that will do,' Benjamin said sourly. He was standing by the mantelpiece, fiddling with the spills used to light the fire. 'You sticking your oar in will make everything ten times worse than it already is.'

'What's the matter with you? Why are you so grumpy?' Victoria demanded. 'Anyone would think the police suspect you of murdering Imogen. It's Max who's under suspicion.'

Benjamin turned to her. 'Keep your voice down. That Kempe woman's here, remember? I'll tell you what's the matter with me. You don't seem to realise the damage this could do to the business if it gets out Maxwell is under any kind of suspicion.'

'How can it hurt the business?' Victoria said derisively. 'This has nothing to do with the printing works.'

'That detective came to the office, Victoria.'

'But he didn't arrest Max, did he? He didn't walk him out in irons or anything like that.'

'It doesn't take much for people to gossip and then for them to speculate,' Benjamin said. 'It starts off with a detective asking a few questions about Imogen, but then people begin to doubt our integrity. We've got the police asking questions, so we must be up to something, they think. Is there something wrong with the business? Are we doing anything illegal? That's what they'll start wondering, you can bet on it.'

'Oh, you're exaggerating,' she said dismissively, but then glanced up at Maxwell. 'He is, isn't he?'

'To hell with the business,' Maxwell cried. 'What about me? I'm suspected of murdering my wife.'

'But you explained to this detective what Imogen's like,' Victoria said. 'You told him she goes off whenever she feels like it.'

'You don't imagine that will satisfy him, do you? Especially if there's gossip going around that Max is—' Benjamin broke off and shook his head.

'Max is what?' Victoria asked. 'Max, what is he talking about?'

'Nothing,' Maxwell said, turning away.

'It's not nothing,' Benjamin muttered.

'Will one of you tell me what you're talking about?' Victoria demanded. 'I insist on knowing.'

'He's got another woman,' Benjamin burst out. 'That's what.'

'It's a lie,' Maxwell said.

'That's not what you said to that policeman. You didn't deny it. You just refused to answer his questions.'

'Because my private life is none of his business. I didn't see why I should have to deny I'm having an affair.' He rounded on Benjamin. 'To him or to anyone else.'

'Oh, enough, you two,' Victoria said, putting her hands over her ears and shaking her head. 'We're not talking about Max, but Imogen. If this detective is going to be asking around town about her, I say, let him. He'll soon find out what she's like, and that'll be an end to it. He'll realise there's nothing for him to investigate. And I tell you, when Imogen does waltz back here again, I'll put an end to her going off and causing trouble like this.'

'And how are you going to do that?' Benjamin asked.

'I'm stopping her allowance. It's only because she's had the money that she can go off the way she has.'

Maxwell stared at her. 'You're not serious?'

'I most certainly am.'

'But that's rather drastic, isn't it?'

'It'll serve her right. Don't trouble yourself worrying about her being upset.'

'He's not,' Benjamin said sourly. 'Max is worried about the money. Your money, Victoria, goes into Imogen's bank account, but Max here had the signatories on the account altered so he can take money out without Imogen needing to sign for it. You don't imagine Max has just let all that money sit there, do you?'

'Have you been helping yourself to my money, Max?' Victoria asked.

'If you've given it to Imogen, it's not your money any longer, is it?' Maxwell shot back. 'And once it's Imogen's, it's mine too. What's hers is mine, remember?'

'Well, yes, I suppose so,' Victoria conceded.

'What's he been spending it on, though?' Benjamin wondered. 'Expensive, is she? This mistress of yours?'

Maxwell's fists clenched. 'You want to watch what you say, Ben, or so help me God—'

'You'll what?'

'I'll…' Maxwell drew his right hand back as Benjamin raised both of his.

Victoria clambered out of her chair and stood between them. 'For heaven's sake, will you two stop? You're like children, both of you.'

When they didn't move, she put her hands on both men's chests and shoved them away. Reluctantly, they lowered their fists.

'I still don't think it's fair of you to stop Imogen's allowance,' Maxwell said.

'Nonsense,' Victoria said. 'I've been more than fair all these years. After all, I wasn't under any obligation to continue her allowance once you married her. I chose to do it out of the goodness of my heart.' She put her hand to her chest dramatically. 'And besides, I may have a better use for my money.'

Benjamin frowned at her. 'What are you talking about, woman? What better use?'

'Never you mind,' Victoria said, her eyes twinkling mischievously as she took a sip of her sherry.

Chapter Thirteen

SUNDAY, 2ND NOVEMBER

Frye knew people were talking about him and Sarah. Even now, here in the hospital canteen, heads were turning in their direction, people looking over their shoulders and whispering as Sarah stirred her mug of tea and he dropped sugar into his.

'They all think you're trying to get me into bed,' Sarah said, smirking at him. Then her face hardened, and she dropped her gaze to the tabletop and played with her mug. 'Probably wondering why you're bothering.'

'Do you have to do that?' he snapped.

'Do what?' she asked, surprised by his tone.

'Put yourself down all the time? It makes me feel as if you're angling for a compliment. Like you're expecting me to protest that you're beautiful.'

'Don't be ridiculous. I know what I am.'

He studied her for a moment, her sadness and resignation making him regret speaking to her so harshly. 'My wife was always doing that,' he said, both an explanation and an apology. 'It got on my nerves. I'm sorry for snapping.'

Sarah shook her head to imply it didn't matter. 'What did you want to talk about?'

'I just wanted to know how things are going with Mrs Scott. Has she said anything to you about her daughter and the police?'

'You know about that?'

'The detective came to the surgery yesterday to question me.'

'Did he? Well, she hasn't talked to me about it, but it caused quite a ruction between Mr Carr and Mr Scott. Mrs Scott had to stop them from coming to blows. Apparently, Mr Carr has a mistress. He denied it, but Mr Scott doesn't believe him.'

'How do you know?'

'I listened at the door. Don't look so shocked. That's what you wanted me to do, isn't it? Listen in, hear what's being said, especially if it's about you, and report back.'

Frye couldn't deny it; that was what he wanted her to do. It just seemed a bit underhanded when Sarah said it so bluntly. 'Was I mentioned?'

'I'm not sure.'

'What do you mean, you're not sure? Was my name mentioned or not?'

'Not. But Mrs Scott was talking about money. She plans to cut off the allowance she gives Mrs Carr when she finally comes back. Mr Carr wasn't at all happy about that, but Mrs Scott said she might have another use for her money, and I think she meant you.'

'You think she's going to do something for me?' he asked eagerly.

'I wouldn't be surprised. She's always asking me about you. You've charmed her.'

'Well, that was the idea,' Frye grinned. 'But she hasn't said what she's got in mind?'

Sarah shook her head. 'I could try to get it out of her, I suppose, but to be honest, you could ask her yourself. If she is going to give you money, I reckon she'll be pleased as punch to tell you. But if I were you, I'd do it when Mr Scott isn't there. You haven't charmed him.'

'You don't have to tell me that. Ben hates my guts.' Frye considered. 'I might pop round when you're there tomorrow.'

'Not tomorrow. I'm going away for a couple of days. I'm leaving after my shift at the hospital.'

'Again?' Frye cried in exasperation. 'You went away only a few weeks ago. You can't leave just when we might be getting somewhere. There's money in this for you as well, you know?'

'I know, but this can't be helped. I have to go.'

Frye heaved a deep sigh. 'Well, don't be away too long, or Victoria might start wanting a different nurse, one who doesn't go off gallivanting. And then we'll both be stuffed.'

Chapter Fourteen

Victor Sands' eyes snapped open.

He stared at his bedroom ceiling, ears pricked, certain he had heard something. But now he couldn't hear anything except the light snoring of Beryl beside him. Tutting, he closed his eyes, annoyed to have awoken for nothing.

There was another noise. This time, Sands sat up, staring at the closed bedroom door. What had he heard? He thought it sounded like the tinkling of glass. He threw back the blankets, taking care not to disturb Beryl, and prised his feet into his slippers, reaching for his dressing gown lying at the end of the bed.

Sands pulled it on, ears still pricked as he tied the belt tight. His heart was beating fast as he tiptoed to the door and put his ear to the wood. There it was again, the clink of glass. Someone was out there! He glanced around the room, looking for something he could use as a weapon, but there was nothing.

Beryl stirred in the bed. 'Vic?' she mumbled. 'What are you doing?'

He shushed her as he heard footsteps on the stairs. 'There's someone in the house,' he whispered.

'What?' Beryl gasped and clutched the blankets to her chest. 'Call the police.'

'The telephone's downstairs,' he hissed at her.

'Don't go out there,' she pleaded as he put his hand on the doorknob.

'I can't just hide in here.'

Part of him wanted to do that very much. But another part was angry that someone had broken into his house and was ransacking it. He took another look at Beryl, at her frightened face, and that decided him. No one came into his house and scared his wife.

He turned the knob, yanked the door open and stole out into the darkened hall, fumbling for the light switch. Before he found it, something… no, someone, large and dark bore down on him.

Sands didn't stop to think. He lunged at the intruder, arms outstretched, ready to do… he didn't know what.

He didn't see the blow coming. Pain exploded across his face, and he fell, hitting the ground hard. Then he felt a blow to his stomach, and another and another. He heard Beryl cry out, 'Vic?' and thought, *For God's sake, don't come out here.*

The figure moved away. Sands heard hurried footsteps on the carpeted stairs, the opening of the back door.

Then the lightbulb above him flickered into life, and he heard Beryl scream, 'Oh my God! Vic!' And she was bending over him, crying, her hands shaking as they caressed his head.

'Call the police,' he croaked.

———

Sarah peered at the clock on the bedside cabinet and groaned as she saw the hands were pointing to twenty past two. Where on earth was Nick?

She flopped onto her back and stared at the ceiling. Nick

had been out every night since he'd got out of prison, and he never told her when he'd be back, or if he would be back at all. That was what worried her most. What if he decided to stay away? Or go back to his wife? What would she do then?

Sarah shook the unwelcome thoughts away. She wouldn't think about Nick not coming back to her. There were too many other things to worry about. While he was happy and getting good hauls at the houses he burgled, he'd stay. She was sure of it.

She sat up as she heard a noise outside the door and looked at it expectantly. It opened quietly and Nick tiptoed in.

'Where have you been?' she said in a loud whisper.

Nick jumped. 'Bloody hell, Sarah. Don't do that.' He closed the door and dropped his tool roll onto the bed.

Sarah threw the blankets back. 'Come to bed.'

'In a minute.' Nick dropped onto the mattress, making the springs squeal. He grinned. 'Want to see what I've got?'

'Show me,' she said, humouring him.

Nick delved into his jacket pocket. 'Ta-dah,' he said, pulling his hand back out and dropping banknotes onto her lap.

Sarah gathered them up. 'Oh, Nick,' she breathed. 'All this money!'

'God bless Craynebrook,' he said, grinning, 'and people with more money than sense. Easy pickings, Sarah. Easy pickings.'

'And you didn't have any problems?'

'Had a run-in with a fella in the second house. The bleeder rushed me as I got to the landing.' Nick rose and began undressing.

'What did you do to him?' Sarah asked.

'Gave him what for, didn't I? Went down like a sack of spuds, he did.'

'But he's all right?'

'Who cares?' Nick climbed into bed and put his head on the pillow, pulling the blankets up to his chin. Sarah lay down beside him and rested her arm on his chest. 'Leave it out,' he said, pushing her arm away. He turned over onto his side, his back to her. 'There's no point you waiting up for me every night,' he said, his voice growing sleepy. 'I've sorted out some digs.'

A lump formed in Sarah's throat. 'That was quick,' she said. 'I thought we were going to wait until we got somewhere together.'

'That could be a while. We need more money for that. And I'm fed up with sneaking in here.' He turned his head to look over his shoulder at her. 'It's better for you this way. You won't have to worry about that old cow downstairs seeing me.'

'Where are these digs?' she asked.

'A few streets away.'

She breathed a sigh of relief. Nick wasn't going far. 'That's all right, then,' she said, and settled down to sleep.

Chapter Fifteen

MONDAY, 3RD NOVEMBER

Lund was already at his desk when Matthew walked into CID a little before eight o'clock. He was astonished; Matthew had never known his fellow detective to be in before him. In fact, despite what he'd said to the others on Saturday, he'd been half-expecting Lund not to turn up at all.

He was relieved to see Lund was looking a lot better when last they'd met. The heavy purple bags under his eyes had shrunk and faded a little, his skin had lost its greyness and was back to its unhealthy pasty colour, and he looked tidy, at least as tidy as it was possible for Lund to be. His shirt, though still bulging at the buttons, looked clean and ironed, and his suit jacket had been brushed down.

Matthew entered their office a little awkwardly, unsure how best to greet Lund. Would Lund even remember just how much of his marriage troubles he'd confided to him? He wasn't going to mention it if Lund didn't.

'Morning,' he said brightly, hanging up his hat and coat.

'Morning,' Lund returned, and carried on with what he was doing.

'All right?'

'Yep. You all right?'

'Me? Yeah. I'm fine.'

'That's all right, then, isn't it?'

Matthew nodded and breathed a silent sigh of relief. Sitting down at his desk, he reached for the topmost case file in his In tray, glancing through the partition window as Denham and Barnes entered the main office. They saw Lund and nodded a greeting.

'So,' Lund said, throwing down his pen and leaning back in his chair, 'what have I missed? How many murders have you solved since last week?'

Matthew smiled at the mockery. 'Hundreds. In fact, I don't know why you bothered coming back.'

'Well, someone needs to stop your head getting too big, don't they?' Lund smirked, but then his expression turned serious. Keeping his voice low, he said, 'By the way, I didn't say thanks the other week for coming round.'

'You don't have to thank me,' Matthew said.

'I think I do. You could have put the boot in with Old Mouldy about me, told him the state I was in, and I know he wouldn't take much persuading to throw me off the Force. So, I'm saying it now. Thank you.'

'You're welcome.' Sensing Lund wanted to talk, Matthew asked, 'How are things at home?'

'Better,' Lund said. 'Me and the wife are talking, not shouting at each other, which is something. And I've seen my girls. So, yeah. Things are looking up.'

'Good. I'm glad for you.'

Lund gave him a rueful smile. 'You mean you're glad you don't have to worry about me ballsing things up again.'

'No,' Matthew protested, despite thinking Lund had got him dead right. 'I am glad. I know what your family means to you.'

Lund nodded in agreement. 'I didn't realise it until they were gone. But that's always the way, isn't it? You never appreciate what you've got until you've lost it.'

'I suppose,' Matthew said, then called to Barnes to bring in the report book.

'So,' Lund went on, 'I imagine you've been busy while I've been away?'

Matthew tapped his overflowing In tray. 'Just a bit.'

'Well, you can pass some of it over to me now I'm back.'

Matthew stared at him in astonishment. Lund never offered to take on more work. 'Really?'

Lund shrugged. 'I've got to get back into it. I might as well make a start right away. So come on. Give me something.'

'Well…,' Matthew stared at his case files, wondering which he wouldn't mind handing over, when Barnes came into the office.

'Good to have you back, sir,' Barnes said to Lund.

'Ta,' Lund said.

Barnes handed Matthew a hardbound logbook. 'We had another spate of burglaries, sir. This time over on Mallory Drive and Somerset Road.'

'I'm reading those now,' Matthew said. 'The homeowner in the second burglary was assaulted.'

'Yes, sir. Mr Victor Sands. He disturbed the burglar and got a pasting for it. He's in the hospital. And I was thinking. Now these burglaries have turned nasty, you might want to come in on them? You see,' he went on hurriedly, 'this burglar doesn't leave much in the way of clues, and well, I don't seem to be getting anywhere. And I'm sure Mr Mullinger would prefer it if you were working on them too, now there's been an assault.'

'He's right,' Lund said. 'Old Mouldy will want Craynebrook's finest on the case.'

Matthew gave Lund a disparaging look. 'All right, Barnes.' He handed the DC the report book. 'I'll come in on the burglary cases with you.'

'Very good, sir,' Barnes said with evident relief. 'I'll get you both a cuppa, and I'll call the hospital. See if Mr Sands is fit to be questioned.' He hurried out.

'There you go,' Lund said triumphantly. 'You'll have to pass something over to me now, won't you? So, what have you been working on?'

'A missing person case,' Matthew said. 'But it looks like the lady left of her own free will. It will probably turn out to be nothing.'

'That's all right. I'm good at nothing cases.' Lund held out his hand. 'Let me have the file and I'll go through it. If it's nothing,' he added as Matthew hesitated, 'you won't miss it, will you?'

Reluctantly, Matthew carried the Imogen Carr file over to Lund. 'It's all in there. I've made some enquiries, but I was going to check on a few more things today before I wound it down.'

Lund opened the file cover. The picture frame with Imogen's photograph in it stared back at him. He whistled. 'Nice looking lady. So, what's still to be done?'

'Talking with public transport drivers to see if anyone remembers seeing her.'

'On the tramp, eh? I can do that.'

Barnes brought in their tea. 'The hospital says we can interview Mr Sands. Shall I tell the driver to bring the car round in about ten minutes?'

Matthew made a face. 'It takes him that long to turn the engine over. Tell him I want it straightaway. That way he might actually be ready in ten minutes.' Matthew gulped down the tea as Barnes hurried away. He reached up to take his hat and coat down from the stand and cast a worried look back at Lund. 'You're sure you don't mind taking that case over? I can carry on with it when I get back from the hospital. I don't mind.'

Lund smiled ruefully up at him. 'I'm not going to mess it up, Stannard, I promise. Quite frankly, you shouldn't even be working on a case like this. This is a DC's job.'

'They were busy,' Matthew shrugged.

'How are they going to learn if you keep everything to yourself? You know what you're not good at, Stannard? Delegating. Good at everything else. Lousy at that.'

'But you are going to follow that up, aren't you?' Matthew asked worriedly, pointing at the file. 'You won't give it to one of the others?'

'It'll be me on it. Scout's honour,' Lund said, giving Matthew the three-finger salute. 'So, off you go to the hospital and interview your burglary victim. Go on.'

'I'm going,' Matthew declared.

Chapter Sixteen

Sarah stood beside the doctor as he bent over Victor Sands, watching as he examined him, feeling sick. She knew Sands was the man Nick had told her about the night before, the man whose house he had burgled and whom he had attacked, relating the story with a grin on his face. She should have known that, with her luck, Nick's victim would be brought to Sawyers Cross and end up on her ward.

The doctor straightened and replaced his stethoscope around his neck. 'You're very lucky, Mr Sands. It could have been a lot worse.'

Sands nodded, but seemed unconvinced. His eyes closed, and he turned his bandaged head away.

The doctor turned to Sarah. 'Let me know if there's any change in his condition,' he said, leaving her to gently tuck in the blankets around Mr Sands.

'How about tucking me in, Nurse Kempe?' Stevens, lying in the next bed, said.

'You can tuck yourself in, Mr Stevens. There's nothing much wrong with you. I can't think why you're back in here.'

'Oh, go on. Admit it. You missed me.'

Sarah didn't even bother to answer.

'I heard he got done over when he was burgled,' Stevens went on, jerking his head at Sands. 'The silly sod. Fancy going for the burglar. I mean, you don't know what they're carrying, do you? He could have had a cosh or a knife, even. You wouldn't catch me doing what he did. I'd say let 'em have whatever they can find. It ain't worth dying for.'

'I think it was very brave of him.' Sarah's face hardened as she turned to Mr Stevens. 'But I wouldn't worry. I don't expect a burglar would bother with your house. You can't have anything worth stealing.'

'That's what you think,' he said, his top lip curling.

'You've got valuables at home, have you?' Sarah said, her eyebrows raised in disbelief. 'What would that be? The family silver?'

'I've got money. That's what I've got. What? You don't believe me?'

'No, Mr Stevens, I don't. You've never paid for the treatment you've had here, which means you don't have the means.'

Stevens grinned at her. 'I'm not daft. I'm not going to tell this lot I've got money.'

'Well, go on, then. Tell me. How much do you have?'

'Ten quid saved up,' he declared proudly.

'So, a burglar going into your house would have a good night, then, wouldn't he?'

'A burglar would never find it. It's too well hidden.'

'So you say.'

'It is, I tell you. No one would ever think to look where I've put it.'

Sarah studied him with an appraising eye, then shook her head. 'I don't believe you. You don't have any money, and even if you did, you wouldn't have the sense to hide it.'

'I tell you, I have. I've got ten quid hidden in the false

bottom of my wardrobe. So, you can shut your mouth and stop calling me a liar.'

Sarah glared at him and stooped to pick up the magazine he'd let fall earlier. As she did so, she felt her skirt lift and his cold, crabby hand stroke the back of her thigh, his finger creeping beneath the hem of her knickers.

With a sudden burst of rage, Sarah grabbed his hand and crushed his fingers with her own. He cried out in pain and tried to snatch his hand away, but she held on tight and dug her nails into his paper-thin skin.

Matron came hurrying over. 'What is going on here?' she demanded.

'Nothing, Matron,' Sarah said, letting go.

'That bitch hurt me,' Stevens cried, cradling his hand.

'Now, now. Enough of that, Mr Stevens,' Matron said imperiously. 'We'll have no bad language from you.'

'But she—'

'Nurse Kempe,' Matron cut him off. 'A word, if you please.' She led Sarah to the nurses' station. 'Care to explain yourself?'

'Mr Stevens has wandering hands, Matron,' Sarah said, 'and I don't like it.'

'I'm sure you don't, but I'm afraid that's something we have to put up with on a men's ward, as well you know. This isn't the first time I've had to remind you of your duty. Now, you're off for a few days, aren't you, when your shift ends? Well, when you return from your leave, I expect you to carry out your work without your personal feelings intruding and for there not to be any more incidents like today. Is that understood?'

'Yes, Matron. Understood.'

'Good.' The matron walked away, her expression suggesting she was a little surprised Sarah hadn't argued with her.

But Sarah hadn't really been listening to a word she'd said. Her mind was on her conversation with Mr Stevens; it had given her an idea, and she needed to tell Nick.

Her eyes, meanwhile, were on the two men walking towards Mr Sands' bed. Policemen, she decided, come to question him and get a statement.

Sarah made her way back down the ward towards Mr Sands' bed. She wanted to hear what he told the police and, most importantly, whether he could identify Nick.

Chapter Seventeen

The Imogen Carr case file was open on Lund's blotter when Matthew walked into the office the next morning. He paused, checked over his shoulder, then leaned over the desk, attempting to read Lund's scrawled notes.

'Checking up on me?'

Startled, Matthew turned. Lund was standing in the doorway, an eyebrow raised at him. 'I was just looking,' he protested and quickly moved to his own desk.

Lund smirked and sat down in his chair, depositing his tea and his Bath bun on the blotter. He closed the file with a glance over at Matthew, who was doing his best to interest himself in the messages that had been left for him. 'How did you get on yesterday with the burglary enquiries?' he asked.

'I spoke with the latest victim. Mr Sands,' Matthew said, glad Lund wasn't going to go on about his snooping. 'He couldn't give a description of the burglar, but the MO is the same as the others. A pane of glass was broken in the back door, key still in the lock. Easy to get in. Only money and alcohol were taken. But what's worrying is that this burglar carried on kicking the victim even when he was no longer a threat.'

'So, he's a vicious bugger,' Lund said, taking a bite of his bun. 'You better find him before he kills someone.'

'Yes, thank you, Lund. That was my intention.'

Lund grinned and he tapped the Imogen Carr case file. 'Do you want to know how I've been getting on?'

Matthew shrugged. 'If you like.'

The grin stayed on Lund's face, and Matthew knew he hadn't fooled him for a second with his pretended indifference.

'I've spoken to the staff at the train station and bus depot,' Lund said. 'There's a bus driver who recognised Mrs Carr from her picture and remembered her getting on his bus late on the Saturday night.'

'What made him remember her?'

'Said he liked the look of her, which is fair enough. But I also had a word with the conductor, and he remembered her because he said she was crying and he asked her if she was all right. She told him she'd had an argument with her family. So, that all tallies with what her husband and father said, doesn't it? She left town of her own volition.'

'I suppose it does. Where was the bus going?'

'Romford. And before you ask, yes, I checked. The family doesn't know anyone in Romford.'

'Is it worth asking the Romford Police to look into it?' Matthew wondered.

'Stannard,' Lund sighed. 'Everything points to Mrs Carr leaving because she wanted to. She's not missing. Just run away. I'm closing the case. Unless you don't trust me and want to take it back—'

'Of course I trust you.'

'There's no 'of course' about it,' Lund muttered.

Matthew held up his hands. 'I just thought there might be more to it, that's all.'

'What? You thought the Priors were right and the husband

had done his wife in?' He shook his head. 'You can't have a murder every time, sunshine.'

'I don't want people to be murdered, Lund,' Matthew said testily. 'I just thought Maxwell Carr acted very shifty when I questioned him. As if he had something to hide.'

'I expect he did, and I reckon I can tell you what. In my opinion, Mrs Prior is right about him having another woman on the go. He's got all the telltale signs. And I wouldn't be surprised if his bit on the side is that secretary of his.'

'How have you come to that conclusion?'

Lund shrugged. 'I saw the way she was with Carr when I went to the printing works to see him.'

'You went to see him?'

'I had to find out about Romford, didn't I? And I had to give him his picture back. Bissett's done a copy for the file. I'm writing up a final report. So, that's that. Case closed. All right?'

'Yes,' Matthew said reluctantly. 'All right.'

Chapter Eighteen

WEDNESDAY, 5TH NOVEMBER

I don't bloody believe this, Walsh thought as he yanked open the hospital's entrance door and charged into the reception.

He had only just climbed into bed when his telephone rang. Listening to his wife grumbling, he had hurried downstairs and snatched up the receiver. Bellowing 'Walsh' into the mouthpiece, he heard the news he had been dreading. Another child had been snatched!

The woman at the hospital reception desk was anxiously awaiting him. He had barely introduced himself when she pointed him towards a staircase, where a sign pointed to the maternity ward. As he hurried up the stairs, she called after him, 'You are going to find it, aren't you?'

Walsh left her question unanswered, wishing he had one for her. He hadn't found the others before they were returned, so why should he find this one?

He reached the maternity ward corridor and saw Colin Fowler already heading towards him, his hand outstretched.

'Slow it down, Barnaby,' Fowler said.

'Don't tell me to slow down. I mean, for God's sake,

Colin, a newborn? And from a hospital? Please tell me someone saw something.' But Fowler made a face, and Walsh groaned. 'The Chief Super's going to have my head when he hears another one's been taken.'

Fowler's expression hardened. 'The mother's frantic, Barnaby. She's had to be sedated. Worry about her, not yourself.'

Walsh glared at him. 'Just tell me what happened.'

Fowler gestured for Walsh to follow him back down the corridor and pointed at a door. Walsh looked through the window and saw several cots, each with a baby asleep inside. One of the cots was empty.

'The baby was in there,' Fowler said. 'The nurse on duty had gone outside to look at the fireworks. When she came back, the baby was gone.'

'How long was she gone?'

'Ten, fifteen minutes. Not long.'

'Long enough.' Walsh rested his forehead on the glass and found the coolness soothing. 'What about the baby that was taken?'

'It was premature, just under a month early. Underweight. It will need a lot of looking after. And bearing in mind this woman's history of looking after babies...'

'Don't,' Walsh groaned and slumped against the wall. He sighed. 'She's never taken a newborn before.'

'She's never taken one from a hospital before,' Fowler pointed out. 'That sounds deliberate to me.'

'You think she came in with the intention of taking one?'

Fowler shrugged. 'The alternative is that she was visiting someone and saw an opportunity.'

'Visiting hour was over a while ago, though, wasn't it?'

'She could have hidden somewhere in the hospital. Waited until no one was around.' Fowler crossed his arms and leant against the opposite wall. 'What about the other case you were looking into? The one DCI Vickery told you about?'

Walsh grimaced. 'It's opened up a can of worms. I've found other snatches with the same MO in Chelmsford and Brentwood. And I'm still looking.'

'Any clues to go on?'

'Nothing.' Walsh swore and thrust himself away from the wall to look through the window once more. 'Why has she taken a newborn? And one so delicate? She's always gone for kids that are several months old before.'

'Perhaps she wanted a baby that was brand new? One she could pass off as her own?'

Walsh ran his hand through his hair and shook his head. 'I've got a horrible feeling this one isn't going to turn out well.'

Chapter Nineteen

TUESDAY, 25TH NOVEMBER

Barnes rapped on the window and put his head around the doorway. 'There's been another one, sir.'

Matthew looked up from his desk. 'Another one what?'

'Another burglary. Old fella just called it in. He's come home from the hospital and found his house broken into.'

Matthew threw down his pen in annoyance. 'What progress have you made looking into recent prison releases?'

Barnes made a face. 'Not much, if I'm honest. There were fourteen convicted housebreakers released in London in the two weeks before the first burglary. I've located four of them and I'm in the process of confirming their alibis.'

'And the others?'

'I'm still trying to find them, sir.'

'Still?' Matthew said, glaring at Barnes. 'What's taking you so long?'

'I'm sorry, sir,' Barnes muttered. 'I'll do better.'

'And when you find them, they'll probably have alibis as well,' Lund piped up as Barnes turned to go. 'All nicely worked out. And it's not as if you'll find anything you can trace back to the victims. This burglar's only taking money and booze, isn't he? He's probably keeping those for himself and not passing them on to anyone, so there's no trail to follow.'

'Are you saying we shouldn't even try?' Matthew asked scornfully.

'Of course not. But you know as well as I do, you have to work out what's worth spending our time on and what isn't. Is it worth Barnes spending all his time checking up on all those recent releases, for example?'

'It's his job, Lund,' Matthew said.

'Do you want to attend this one, sir?' Barnes interjected, watching the two inspectors warily. 'Or leave it to me?'

Matthew glanced down at the report he had been working on. It was a petty affair – criminal damage by one neighbour against the other – and he was bored by it. Barnes was quite capable of attending the crime scene and interviewing the victim, but…

He closed the file. 'Get the car,' he ordered Barnes. 'I'll be down in five minutes.'

Barnes scurried away, almost barging into Rudd, who took his place in the doorway.

'Blimey. It's like Piccadilly Circus in here,' Lund said. 'What do you want, Rudd?'

'I've just had a call from Essex County Police, sir,' Rudd said. 'A DI Walsh.'

Lund frowned. 'Essex County? What are they bothering us for?'

'DI Walsh is asking if we've had any incidents involving babies or children being snatched. Is it all right if I look into it?'

'This is the Met, Rudd. Let Essex County do their own dirty work.'

'It did sound rather important, sir.'

'We haven't had any snatched babies. I'd remember if we'd had.'

'Not necessarily recent cases, sir. DI Walsh is asking about any incidents going back ten years or more.'

'Does he think we've got the time to go through all those years of records?' Lund cried.

'I'm sure it won't take me long.'

Lund raised an eyebrow at Rudd. 'Did this DI Walsh ask nicely?'

'Sir?' Rudd said.

'Oh, for God's sake, Lund,' Matthew said, rising to take down his hat and coat, and seeing his fellow inspector smirking. 'It's all right, Rudd. You can look into the records. But don't spend too much time on it. Understand?'

'Yes, sir,' Rudd said gratefully. 'Thank you, sir.'

'I was enjoying that,' Lund protested as Rudd hurried away.

Matthew shook his head at him. 'He's just a boy, Lund. He hasn't got used to your peculiar sense of humour.'

'At least I've got one, sunshine,' Lund said as Matthew strolled out of their office.

———

'It's a flaming liability, that's what it is.'

Matthew looked around the room, thinking something seemed off. It looked like the normal workings of a burglar – drawers pulled out, sofa cushions tossed aside – but to his experienced eyes, it had been staged to look that way, to give the appearance of a ransacked room.

'Could you tell me what's been taken, Mr Stevens?' he asked.

'My money's gone,' Stevens said sourly. 'Ten quid, the

bleeder took. All my savings. What are you going to do about it? I want my money back.'

'We will do our best to recover your money,' Matthew said, knowing full well the old man would never see his ten pounds again.

Stevens fell into his armchair. 'That's what you say,' he muttered, taking a battered tin from his pocket and opening it on the arm. He pinched out some tobacco and rolled a cigarette.

Barnes came into the room. 'He got in through the back door, sir. Same as the others. There's a pane of glass broken. The key was in the lock. All he had to do was put his hand through and turn it.'

Matthew nodded and turned back to Stevens. 'I understand you've been in hospital, Mr Stevens?'

'That's right. I'm on my last legs and I come home to this. Lovely, ain't it?'

'How long were you in hospital?'

'From the Thursday before last until this morning.'

'And you live alone?'

Stevens nodded, licked the cigarette paper and sealed it.

'So, the burglary could have been any day or night during that time?'

'Cor blimey, it's easy to see why you're a detective.'

Matthew ignored the sarcasm. 'Do you keep any alcohol in the house?'

'I did!' He pointed to the sideboard opposite. 'The bleeder's taken my rum as well!'

Alcohol and money taken. It was definitely the same man as in the Sands' burglary, Matthew thought. 'Where did you keep your money?'

'Up in my bedroom. Hidden in the bottom of my wardrobe.'

'Hidden in what way?'

'It was in a box. I'd made a false bottom in the wardrobe.
I could have sworn no one would find it.'

'No one knew your money was hidden there?'

'You think I go around telling people where I keep my
money?'

'It sounds like someone knew,' Matthew insisted. 'And
perhaps someone also knew you were in hospital and that
your house would be empty.'

Stevens's eyes narrowed at him. 'My neighbours knew I
was in the hospital,' he said thoughtfully. 'The milkman. The
newsagent.'

'Anyone else?'

'I wrote and told my brother.'

'What about your wife?'

'I ain't spoken to her in years. I don't even know where
she is.'

'But none of the people you mentioned knew where you
kept your money?'

'Course they don't.'

'Then who did?' Matthew asked impatiently. 'There has
to be someone who knew. You say your money was well
hidden and yet this burglar found it. He knew where to look.'

'All right, all right. Shut up and let me think.' Stevens
stared at the carpet for a while, then he looked up at Matthew
and groaned, 'It was her.'

'Who?' Matthew asked.

'The nurse at the hospital. I told her about my money.'

'I need her name, Mr Stevens.'

Stevens made a face. 'You want to talk to an old bag
called Nurse Kempe.'

Chapter Twenty

'Sarah Kempe?'

The woman turned, and Matthew saw that Stevens had described Sarah Kempe accurately if not at all politely. He held up his warrant card. 'I'm DI Stannard. This is DC Barnes. We're from Craynebrook CID.'

'I remember you,' she said, gesturing for Matthew to move aside so she could continue making the bed. 'You were here to talk to Mr Sands the other day.' She pointed down the ward. 'He's still over there if you want him.'

'No, we're not here to talk to Mr Sands. We'd like to talk to you about another patient of yours. Mr Stevens.'

Sarah didn't stop what she was doing. Instead, she said, 'Well, I'm on duty at the moment, as you can see. So, it will have to wait.'

'I've spoken to the matron,' Matthew persisted. 'You can give me five minutes.'

He saw her body heave as she took a deep breath before turning to face him. 'What about Mr Stevens?' Sarah asked.

'He was a patient here. Discharged this morning. When he got home, he discovered he'd been burgled.'

Her expression didn't change. 'That's rotten for him.'

Her words sounded sympathetic, Matthew thought, but she didn't mean them. 'The burglar took all his savings. A matter of ten pounds.'

'Mr Stevens says he had ten pounds?' Sarah smiled and shook her head. 'Then he shouldn't have been getting free treatment here. I should tell Matron.'

'Mr Stevens had it very well hidden, but the burglar seemed to know exactly where to find the money.'

Sarah smoothed her apron down, then looked up coolly into Matthew's eyes. 'This is all very interesting, inspector, but why are you telling me?'

He held her gaze. 'Mr Stevens said the only person he'd told where he hid his money was you.'

'Are you accusing me of burglarising his home?'

'Is it true you knew where he hid his money?'

'What do I care about his money?'

'That's not what I asked, Nurse Kempe.'

She drew a deep breath. 'No, inspector. Mr Stevens did not tell me where he kept his money.'

'He says he did.'

'Then he's mistaken.'

'He seemed very sure he told you.'

'And I'm very sure he didn't.'

Matthew glanced at Barnes, who gave him a look in return he understood only too well. Barnes knew as well as Matthew did that it was Mr Stevens' word against Nurse Kempe's. If she remained adamant she didn't know about the money, without witnesses to the contrary, there was nothing they could do.

'When was he burgled?' Sarah asked.

'While he was in here.'

'Obviously. I meant what day or night?'

'We don't know.'

She gave him a mocking smile. 'You don't know?'

'I know you were here last Monday,' Matthew went on, bristling. 'But can you tell me your whereabouts since then?'

The smile left Sarah's face. 'I went away after my shift on Monday. I didn't come back until late last night.'

'Where did you go?'

'That's none of your business.'

Matthew raised an eyebrow. 'You object to telling me where you were?'

She folded her arms and narrowed her eyes at him. 'Are you arresting me?'

Matthew sensed where she was heading. 'No,' he said tightly.

'Then I don't have to answer any of your questions, do I?'

'No, you don't.'

'Then I'll be getting on with my work, if it's all the same to you. Matron may have been polite to a couple of policemen, but she won't be to me when you're gone and I've not done what I'm supposed to. Excuse me, inspector.'

Matthew stepped aside as Sarah brushed past him and he watched her walk away to the far end of the ward.

'What do you think, sir?' Barnes asked.

'I think she knows something,' Matthew said. 'Otherwise, she wouldn't have been so cagey with us. Stick around here, Barnes. Chat to some of the other staff. See what you can find out about her. But discreetly. Let them just think we're following up on the assault on Mr Sands. I'll go back to the station and see if she's in our records. Got that?'

'Yes, sir,' Barnes said. 'Got it.'

———

Sarah hurried home after her shift, ran up the stairs to her room and locked her door, leaning against it and willing her heart to stop banging in her chest.

The rest of her day at the hospital had been an agony. She'd been sure the police would return and march her off to a police cell just like that other time. That inspector hadn't believed her; she could see it in his eyes. He'd be back for her. She knew it.

They can't prove anything, she reminded herself as she moved away from the door and unbuttoned her coat. The inspector could have his suspicions all he liked as long as he couldn't prove anything. That's what Nick had always said. Oh, Nick! She shook her head sorrowfully. She had to make sure they didn't find out about Nick.

There came a loud rap on the door, making her jump.

'Who is it?' she called, certain it would be the police. She was relieved to hear Nick reply, 'Let me in, you silly cow.'

She opened the door and Nick entered, falling down onto the bed and lifting his booted, muddy feet onto the coverlet.

'What's the matter with you?' he asked, seeing her anxious expression.

'The police came to the hospital to see me,' Sarah said. 'You didn't tell me they would question me, Nick.'

'It was obvious they would. That old fella was bound to tell them he had told you about his money. So, what did you say to them?'

'Nothing. I said they couldn't prove anything against me, so they had to leave me alone.'

'And they left?'

She nodded.

He shrugged. 'Why are you getting your knickers in a twist, then?'

'Because they'll be back. And if they work out I know you—'

'You didn't tell them about me, did you?'

'Of course I didn't. But what if they find out?'

Nick shook his head. 'We've only been together in public in that cafe, and no one there has paid us any attention.'

'The police might find out I visited you in prison.'

Nick groaned in impatience. 'So, you visited me. So what? That doesn't prove anything. And even if they do get on to me, they won't find anything. I only took money, didn't I? Money and booze. Well, the booze is all gone,' he grinned, 'and money doesn't have a person's name on it. So they can't prove where I got it. And if I need an alibi… well, that's what I've got you for, ain't it?'

Sarah heaved a sigh. 'I suppose you're right. But you shouldn't have come here again, Nick. We agreed it would be best not to.'

'Yeah, well, I need some money.'

'More?' she cried. 'But you got ten pounds from Mr Stevens!'

'It got spent.'

'On what?'

Nick's eyes hardened at her. 'I lost it at a game, all right? Now, you gonna give me some or not?' He held out his hand and crooked his fingers a few times at her.

Reluctantly, Sarah opened her handbag and took out her purse. 'This is all I have,' she said, giving him a handful of coins.

'It'll have to do, then, won't it?' Nick pocketed the coins. 'You got another address for me yet?'

'Not yet. And maybe it isn't such a good idea. Not if the police can trace your burglaries back to me so quickly.'

'They've got nothing otherwise they would have collared you.' His expression hardened. 'Get me an address, Sarah, or I might start wondering why I bother with you.'

Chapter Twenty-One

MONDAY, 1ST DECEMBER

'You're late this morning, Mr Stannard,' Turkel observed as Matthew entered the police station lobby. 'It's not like you.'

'I overslept,' Matthew said, keeping to himself that it was the fault of his three kittens. They had spent most of the night clambering over him in bed, not settling until dawn, when he had finally drifted off to sleep.

'You picked the wrong morning to do that. Mr Mullinger wanted to see you first thing.' Turkel checked the clock on the wall. 'He's been waiting half an hour.'

Matthew cursed. 'I'll go straight up,' he told Turkel and headed for the stairs.

'There you are!' Miss Halliwell declared as he reached the landing. 'Mr Mullinger—'

'I know. I'm late.' Matthew tugged his gloves off, stuffed them in his coat pockets and threw his hat and coat over the back of a chair. He rapped on the superintendent's door and opened it.

'Ah, Stannard,' Mullinger said, adding pointedly, 'at last.' He gestured at the man who had been sitting in the visitor's chair and was now on his feet, looking at Matthew with a smile on his face. 'This is DI Barnaby Walsh from Essex County Police.'

Walsh held out his hand. 'How do you do?'

Matthew took it. 'How do you do?' he said, wondering why he recognised the name. He turned to Mullinger. 'I'm sorry I'm late, sir.'

Mullinger grunted and gestured for them both to sit. 'I was just telling DI Walsh about the Foxhall Green shooting case.'

'Extraordinary,' Walsh said. 'I've never heard of anything like that happening before.'

'It was unusual,' Matthew agreed.

'The crime made the national press,' Mullinger added.

'I must have missed it. But you must be used to that kind of attention, Stannard,' Walsh said. 'You've been in the 'papers quite a bit, I understand. My chief constable told me about you.'

Mullinger leaned forward with interest. 'That would be George Dancey?'

'That's the fellow,' Walsh confirmed. 'You know him, sir?'

'We've met on several occasions at functions uptown. Do you know him well?'

'Very. My wife and his wife are quite close.' Walsh wagged a finger. 'And now I think of it, he has mentioned you too, Mr Mullinger.'

Mullinger swelled with pride. 'Favourably, I hope?'

Walsh smiled and nodded. 'He says you run a very tight ship.'

You smarmy sod, Matthew thought, watching Walsh out of the corner of his eye. He doubted whether Walsh's chief constable even knew who Mullinger was, let alone talked about him, favourably or otherwise.

'What did you want to see me about, sir?' he asked irritably, keen to put an end to the small talk.

Mullinger's eyes narrowed at Matthew, annoyed at the interruption. 'DI Walsh is here to follow up a lead in connection with a case of his in Colchester.'

Now Matthew understood why he knew the name. 'You were the officer asking about baby snatches,' he said to Walsh.

'That's right,' Walsh said. 'Your DC Rudd dug up a case you had in 1920. A baby was snatched and then found dead on the church steps. It bears a striking similarity to my cases.'

'Cases?' Matthew raised an eyebrow. 'How many snatches have you had?'

'In Colchester, five, since 1926. But I've found three more. One in Witham, one in Chelmsford and one in Brentwood.'

'Going back to when?'

'The Brentwood one was in '22. Chelmsford, '24. Witham, '27.'

'But your cases have been going on for four years?' Matthew asked, incredulous.

'I've only been working on them this year, when I took over from my predecessor,' Walsh said, bristling. 'Clues are a bit thin on the ground, Stannard. I'm sure you've had cases you don't seem to be getting anywhere with.'

'Actually, no,' Matthew said.

'Stannard has an excellent track record of solving cases,' Mullinger said proudly. 'As I'm sure you're aware if, as you say, you've read about him in the newspapers.'

'I haven't,' Walsh said sharply. 'If you remember, sir, I said my chief constable had. I'm afraid I'm too busy to pay much attention to the newspapers. Or,' he added with a sideways glance at Matthew, 'get my name in them.'

'Yes, well,' Mullinger cleared his throat and fiddled with

the pens on his desk. 'I understand you want to look at the case file we have from 1920?'

'I do, sir,' Walsh nodded. 'And maybe talk to a few of the people involved in the investigation. If I could have one of your men to assist me?'

'That sounds perfectly fine. Yes, Stannard?'

'We're really quite busy, sir,' Matthew said. 'I don't know if anyone can be spared.'

'Oh, nonsense. I'm sure you can let him have someone. DC Rudd, as he's already dug up the case and knows about it.'

'I'm very grateful, sir,' Walsh said. 'I'm sure Chief Constable Dancey will be, too.'

Mullinger beamed. 'Anything we can do to help our Essex brethren. Now, if that's all, Walsh, I would like a word with Stannard.'

'Of course. I'll go to CID and find DC Rudd.'

Walsh left the office, and Matthew waited for the telling-off he knew was coming. Mullinger didn't hesitate.

'What the devil's come over you, Stannard?' he demanded. 'Berating Walsh like that for not solving the case? Showing off, was that it? And refusing to cooperate.'

'I didn't refuse, sir,' Matthew said. 'I just said we were busy.'

'We're always busy. There would be something wrong if we weren't. I won't have it said that we in the Met are deliberately obstructive to provincial constabularies. We should make an effort to cooperate whenever we can.'

'Especially if it will look good to Chief Constable Dancey,' Matthew muttered.

He knew he'd gone too far the moment the words were out of his mouth. Mullinger's eyes bulged from their sockets and his lips pursed beneath his moustache.

'You're to give DI Walsh all the assistance he requires, Stannard,' Mullinger growled. 'That's an order.'

—————

Walsh had settled himself at Rudd's desk when Matthew walked into CID. Rudd was standing beside him, handing him a mug of tea.

'Good morning, sir,' Rudd said brightly as Matthew passed him by.

Matthew grunted a greeting, ignoring Walsh as he walked into his office and shut the door.

'Morning, Stannard.' Lund jerked his head towards the partition window. 'I hear we've got a guest for a day or two?'

'Mullinger's orders,' Matthew said, hanging up his hat and coat. 'We're to render all assistance necessary. He wants to make a good impression.'

'On this Walsh fella?'

'On his chief constable.'

'Ah,' Lund nodding, understanding. 'Not content with crawling to the Met's top brass, Old Mouldy wants to get in with the Essex lot as well. Is that it?'

'I'd say so.' Matthew slammed a case file down on his desk, making Lund jump.

'Is it Old Mouldy who's got your back up or this Walsh? I have to say,' Lund said, watching Walsh as Rudd offered him the biscuit tin, 'he doesn't mind making himself at home, does he?'

Barnes appeared in the window and rapped on it. Lund gestured for him to come inside.

'The front desk just put a call through,' he said to Matthew. 'A Mrs Deeley has returned home and found her house burgled. Same method of entry as the others. Do you want to attend?'

'Yes, I do,' Matthew said, rising and grabbing his hat and coat.

'And what am I supposed to do with him?' Lund asked, pointing at Walsh as Matthew moved towards the door.

Matthew shrugged. 'Cooperate.'

———

Mrs Rosemary Deeley was crying. Matthew stood before her, his hat in his hand, waiting for her to stop.

She wiped her reddened nose with a soggy handkerchief. 'I'm so sorry,' she said.

'Not at all,' Matthew assured her. 'You've every right to be upset. Do you live here alone, Mrs Deeley?'

'Yes. Ever since my husband died last year.'

'And I understand you haven't been here for a while?'

'No, I've been in the hospital for the last three weeks. I had an operation on my hip.'

The hospital again. Matthew's interest was piqued. 'While you were in hospital, did you come into contact with a Nurse Kempe?' He described Sarah.

'I don't remember her. Why? Has she got something to do with this?'

'Just a routine enquiry,' Matthew said, disappointed the answer had been a negative. 'Who knew you were in the hospital?'

'My neighbour. A few of my friends. That's all.'

Matthew glanced around the room. The place had been ransacked and a pane of glass in the back door had been broken, just the same as the Stevens' burglary. But unlike before, the ransacking here looked genuine. 'Can you tell me what's been taken?'

'That's just it. I don't think anything has,' she said, a note of incredulity in her voice. 'I know it's all a mess, but my silver candlesticks and my jewellery are still here. I would have thought the burglar would take those.'

'What about alcohol?'

'I don't drink, inspector. There's just a bottle of sherry in the cupboard I keep for visitors.' She pointed to a cupboard whose doors were open.

Matthew saw a sherry bottle sitting on the shelf. Maybe the burglar didn't have a taste for sherry, only strong spirits?

'What about money? Do you have any money in the house?'

'Why, yes, I—' She broke off, staring at him in alarm. 'Oh my God,' she gasped and tried to get out of the chair. Her face screwed up in pain, and Matthew put his hand on her shoulder.

'Stay there. I'll look. Where?'

'The kitchen dresser,' she said, rubbing her hip. 'In the tea caddy on the top shelf.'

Matthew went into the kitchen. He didn't need to touch the pine dresser, for the tea caddy was on the counter with its lid off, and there was nothing inside. He returned to the sitting room.

'Well?' she asked.

'I'm sorry. The money's gone.' She started crying again. 'How much was in there?' he asked.

'A few pounds,' she said, wiping her nose. 'It was my housekeeping.'

There were footsteps in the hall, and a moment later, Barnes appeared in the doorway. He jerked his head for Matthew to join him in the passage.

'I've spoken to the neighbours, sir,' Barnes said in a low voice. 'No one heard or saw a thing. And their houses haven't been touched. It looks like chummy only did here.'

'Because he knew it was empty,' Matthew nodded, and told Barnes about Mrs Deeley being in the hospital.

'We should question Nurse Kempe again, then, sir,' Barnes said.

'And ask her what? We don't know when the burglary took place. It could have been any time in the past three weeks. And Mrs Deeley says she didn't come across Sarah Kempe in the hospital. We don't have any witnesses to place her here. And Kempe's too careful. She won't tell us a thing, and all we will have done is warned her and her accomplice we're on to them.'

'Her accomplice?'

Matthew nodded. 'I don't think Sarah Kempe carried out the burglaries herself, Barnes, but I reckon she knows who did.'

Chapter Twenty-Two

Matthew had had CID to himself for more than an hour the next morning before Rudd came in and put an end to his solitude. The young detective stood at his desk as he took off his coat. Matthew saw a frown crease his forehead and then Rudd searching frantically in his desk drawers.

He rose and stepped out into the main office. 'Looking for this?' he asked, and held up a file.

Rudd was startled to see him. 'Sorry, sir. I didn't realise you were here.' He nodded at the file in Matthew's hand. 'Is that the dead baby file?' His tone implied he was wondering what Matthew was doing with it.

'It is,' Matthew nodded. 'I thought I'd have a look through it. You don't mind, do you?'

'Of course not, sir. Are you working on it with DI Walsh?'

Matthew shook his head. 'I was just curious.' He held the file out to Rudd.

Rudd took it. 'What do you make of it, sir?'

'Sad,' Matthew said, moving to the tea urn to make himself another cup of tea. 'And peculiar.'

'Peculiar?'

'Dr Wallace not being able to explain how the baby died. There were no wounds on the body. The coroner called it a murder, but I think it should have been an open verdict.'

'What else could it have been but murder, though, sir?' Rudd wondered. 'Babies don't just die. Something has to be done to them. After all, the baby was healthy when it was taken.'

'I know,' Matthew agreed. 'It's just peculiar, as I said.' He took a mouthful of tea. 'By the way, did DI Walsh take some of the papers from that file with him?'

'I don't think so, sir. Why?'

'It seemed to me there were some statements missing.'

Rudd opened the file and rifled through it. 'It looks like everything's here. What statements, sir?'

'In Mrs Burns' second statement, she says the police aren't doing enough and asks why they haven't talked to certain people who might know something about her baby.' Matthew held his hand out for the file, and Rudd passed it back to him. 'Yes, here it is. She says they ought to talk to her friend, the cleaner and the milkman. But there aren't any statements from them.'

'I know about that, sir,' Rudd said, relief evident on his face that he had an answer. 'DI Vaughn made some notes.' He took the file from Matthew and turned to the back, taking out a creased and faded sheet of paper. 'If you read this, DI Vaughn said Mrs Burns named a dozen people over the course of the investigation who they should talk to, and some of them weren't even anywhere near her house when the baby was taken.'

'So, DI Vaughn never followed those people up?'

'No, sir. At least, if he did, it's not in the file.'

'And Walsh?'

'Um,' Rudd shifted his feet awkwardly. 'Well, DI Walsh never said anything about them. The only person he was interested in was a nurse Mrs Burns mentioned. He thought a nurse might be significant considering the last baby was taken from a hospital.'

'And where is he this morning?'

'He's gone back, to Colchester, I think. He's going to try to track down Mrs Burns. She left Craynebrook soon after her baby was found dead and no one seems to know where she went.'

'Does he still think his cases and ours are connected?'

'He's certain of it. Says the similarities are too strong for them not to be. Do you think he's right, sir?'

'I expect he knows what he's doing,' Matthew said, perhaps a little insincerely. 'Got on all right with him, did you?'

'Yes, sir, I think so. We had a drink before he went, and he told me about some of the cases he's worked on. Do you know he's solved every one of his cases before these snatches? And he's got a commendation for bravery from his chief constable. Mr Walsh wrestled a man waving a gun around in a park to the ground. Got it off him before he could hurt anyone.' Rudd shook his head in admiration. 'That takes some courage, don't you think, sir?'

'No more so than trying to apprehend a dangerous criminal single-handed,' Matthew said, raising his eyebrows at Rudd.

Rudd coloured, knowing what Matthew was getting at: his attempt, while off duty, to arrest Wilfred Gadd when he stumbled upon him at a cemetery. That foolish but brave action had landed Rudd in hospital for weeks. 'Well, Gadd wasn't armed, sir,' he said, looking down at his feet in embarrassment.

'For all you knew. Did you tell Walsh about that, or was it him doing all the boasting?'

'I didn't tell him anything, sir,' Rudd said.

Probably because you couldn't get a word in, Matthew thought as he checked his wristwatch. 'I have to go.' He headed back into his office to get his hat and coat.

'Where are you off to, sir?'

'I've got my annual medical examination,' Matthew said, pulling on his coat and heading for the door. 'I'll be back later, but if you want me, I'll be at the Sherwood Close Surgery.'

———

Matthew took a deep breath.

'Again,' Woodrow said, moving the stethoscope to another spot on Matthew's chest. 'And again.' He straightened and pulled the instrument from his ears. 'That all sounds fine.' He moved to his desk and studied the notes lying on his blotter. 'I see you told my predecessor you've suffered headaches since the attack. Frequently?'

'Now and then.' Matthew picked up his shirt from the end of the examination table.

'The truth, inspector, if you please.'

'Fairly often,' he admitted. 'When I've had a long day, mostly.'

'And how often do you have a long day?'

'It depends. Some days are longer than others. If I have a big investigation—'

'Such as this recent shooting? I imagine that involved many long days, yes? So, I assume the headaches have been quite bad of late?'

'The investigation's over, Dr Woodrow. The headaches will pass.'

'There's no need to be so defensive, inspector. I'm not for one moment suggesting you're unfit for duty. Just that you may need to take things a little easier.'

'I'd love to,' Matthew said. 'Just tell the criminal fraternity to stop committing crimes and I'll take as long a rest as you want.'

His sarcasm didn't amuse Woodrow. The doctor raised an eyebrow, then put his signature to Matthew's medical report. 'There. I've declared you fit for duty.'

Matthew knotted his tie, his eyes catching sight of a framed photograph on the wall of Woodrow surrounded by other serious-looking men. The caption beneath the photograph said the men formed the medical staff at St Bartholomew's Hospital. 'You were at St Barts?' he asked.

Woodrow looked up in surprise at the question until he saw what Matthew was looking at. 'Oh, you're looking at that old thing, are you? Yes, I was there for almost twenty years. Mostly in medical research rather than actual doctoring.'

'Researching what?'

'Oh, many things, inspector. Respiratory conditions. Digestive ailments.'

Matthew pulled on his jacket. 'Women's problems?'

'Yes, for a time.'

'Can you tell me what kind of woman snatches another woman's baby?'

'Well,' Woodrow frowned, screwing the cap back on his fountain pen and placing it in his pen tray, 'there hasn't been a great deal of study into that kind of criminal act, as far as I'm aware, and I didn't come across any cases personally. I do remember reading some literature on the subject, however, and if you want a medical opinion, then I would say the woman who snatches another woman's baby is either incapable of having a child of her own or has had a child and lost it.'

'Not a woman who already has children?'

Woodrow shook his head. 'I wouldn't say so, no.'

'What about age? How old would this woman be?'

'That's difficult to say. It could be a young woman with reproductive problems or it could be an older woman who has gone through the change. One of the papers I read was of a woman who was married to a man who had children from a previous marriage. He was disappointed his current wife hadn't provided him with a child and was threatening to leave her. She kidnapped a child to present him with a son and so give him no reason to leave.'

Matthew frowned. 'But the man would know the child wasn't his, so why would he accept it?'

'I know, I agree. But the woman couldn't have seen it that way. Possibly she was hysterical.'

'Dangerous?'

'In that case, yes. The husband left the wife. She blamed the child and attacked it. The baby barely survived.'

'So, a woman who steals a baby is likely to harm it?'

'I wouldn't say likely. I doubt whether causing harm would be the motive for taking a child. But I can imagine scenarios where mistreatment might occur. If the woman has no idea how to care for a baby, for example, never having had one of her own and perhaps no one to tell her what to do. She may get frustrated and angry if the baby cries too much and lash out at it. Oh yes, I'm afraid harm could occur.'

'So, the woman who snatches babies could be of any age, who's either had children and lost them or can't have them at all. That doesn't exactly narrow it down.'

'I wasn't aware that was what I was supposed to be doing for you, inspector.' Woodrow's tone suggested he'd taken Matthew's words as an accusation. 'You're looking for such a woman?'

Matthew shook his head, annoyed at himself for being rude. What was the matter with him lately? He seemed to find fault with everyone. 'Not me. Another officer. He has an ongoing case of babies being snatched and returned. The most recent one was a premature newborn. It's still missing.'

'But the others were returned, you say?'

'Is that significant?'

'It may be,' Woodrow nodded. 'Possibly, the woman realised she couldn't look after the children properly, but cared enough to make sure someone else would. If I were your colleague, inspector, I would begin by consulting local maternity hospitals and midwives. Enquire whether they've had any patients whose behaviour could be considered suspicious. Women who've had miscarriages and who reacted very badly, for example, or who had stillborn children.'

Matthew suddenly thought of Imogen Carr and her photograph in the case file.

'Inspector?' Dr Woodrow said.

'Yes, sorry,' Matthew said, pulling himself together. 'Thank you. That's very helpful.'

'I'm glad. Do tell your colleague he's welcome to contact me if he requires more information.'

Matthew shook his head. 'I doubt it would occur to him to ask.'

Chapter Twenty-Three

FRIDAY, 12TH DECEMBER

'So, when my solicitor has finished going through the contract,' Prince said, twisting his cigar in the ashtray to put it out, 'we can go ahead and sign. At least, as far as I'm concerned.'

Benjamin nodded from the other side of his desk. 'And how long will that take?'

'A couple of weeks, I should think. He's rather busy at the moment.'

'I would have thought you would tell him to give this priority, Harold.'

'I know you're eager, Ben,' Prince said with a smile, 'but these things shouldn't be rushed.'

'How is this rushing?' Benjamin burst out in exasperation. 'We've been negotiating for months. I thought we'd get it all agreed and finalised before Christmas.'

'And we still might. Let my solicitor do his job. Anyway, what's the hurry?'

'I just want it done. I'd like to start the new year fresh.'

Benjamin smacked the desktop. 'But I suppose you're right. We shouldn't rush things.'

Prince rose and buttoned up his jacket. 'I'll be off then.'

'Before you go,' Benjamin said, holding up a hand to stop him. 'There's something I wanted to ask you.'

'And what's that?'

'You're friendly with Nigel Frye, aren't you? What can you tell me about him?'

Prince shrugged. 'I wouldn't say we're friends as such, but we have a drink together at the club now and then. He's a decent chap.'

'Decent?'

'Well, good for a chat and a game of billiards, that sort of thing.'

'What about women?'

'Well, there are rumours. Gossip.'

'What's the gossip?'

'Really, Ben! I don't think you ought to ask things like that. It's not done to spread these things, you know.'

'If someone's talked about Frye with you, you can talk about him with me,' Benjamin snapped. Then he sighed and held up his hand in apology. 'I have a good reason for asking, Harold.'

Prince considered him for a moment, then nodded. 'All right. I'll tell you what I've heard. Frye makes out he was blameless in his divorce, that his wife was the one who had the affairs. He tells the story she wanted to marry again and so he did the decent thing and gave her evidence for a divorce so there would be no taint attached to her.'

'And that's not true?'

Prince's mouth pursed. 'I met a chap who knew both Frye and his wife. He said it was all balderdash. Frye was a notorious womaniser, and his wife finally decided she'd had enough and demanded a divorce. I would have thought Frye would want to be free of his wife so he could carry on without hindrance, but apparently, he didn't want a divorce. This chap reckoned Frye used his being married as a defence. You know, he couldn't marry his mistresses because he was already married. But his wife was adamant, and…' He trailed off.

'What, Harold?' Benjamin prompted.

'This is all speculation, Ben, you have to appreciate that. But there is a rumour his wife threatened him to make him agree to a divorce.'

'Threatened him with what?'

Prince licked his lips and shuffled his feet uneasily. 'Look, I'm not happy about this, Ben. Talking about a chap behind his back.'

'I need to know, Harold. For God's sake, this bounder has got Victoria in his claws. I'm trying to protect her.'

'Oh, I didn't realise,' Prince said. 'In that case, I'll tell you. His wife apparently claimed Frye had coerced several of his female patients into giving him money and naming him as a beneficiary in their wills. There may be nothing in it, but you know what they say. There's no smoke without fire.'

'If there wasn't anything in it, why did he agree to the divorce?'

'You have to wonder, don't you? Now, that is all I've heard, Ben, and I really must be going.' Prince hurried out before Benjamin could stop him again.

But Benjamin had heard all he needed. He stared out of the office window for a long while, then reached for the newspaper on his desk and flicked through the pages until he came to the one he had been looking for. He studied the advertisement that bore the headline 'PRIVATE ENQUIRY AGENT' and lifted the telephone receiver out of its cradle.

Chapter Twenty-Four

Barnes and Denham were poring over a sheet of paper when Matthew walked into CID on Saturday morning.

'What's going on?' he asked, curious what was absorbing their interest so greatly.

'It's the Christmas roster, sir,' Barnes said. 'Denham's got Boxing Day. I've got Christmas Day. Rudd's got it off. How did that happen? He's the new boy. He should have to work Christmas Day.'

'You're not down here, sir,' Denham said to Matthew, pointing at the roster.

'Mr Mullinger wants me to take my days that are owing,' he explained, referring to his leave that had been interrupted because of the Foxhall Green shooting. 'So I'm off for Christmas and Boxing Day.'

'Got any plans?'

Matthew shook his head. 'Nothing special.'

He knew exactly what his Christmas Day would be like. He would be at the pub, arriving as late as he could get away with, but in time for the extravagant Christmas dinner Pat would put on. Everyone would eat too much, and he and Fred would drink too much. After dinner, there would be a row between Pat and his mother about something – who should do the washing-up, what they should listen to on the wireless – and it would be left to Georgie to calm them down. The pub would be open later, and Fred would go down to serve behind the bar. Matthew would be forced to remain upstairs with his mother and sister until he could get away for a drink downstairs with Georgie. Then he would be asked to stay overnight; he would refuse, not wanting to put Georgie out of his bed, and make his weary way home. And he'd be back there for Boxing Day to do it all over again.

'I was hoping I'd get Christmas Day off,' Barnes moaned. 'Judy said if I wasn't working, I could spend the day with her and her family. I suppose it'll just have to be the evening now.'

Denham rolled his eyes. 'Listen to him. Anyone would think he's in love.'

'What if I am?' Barnes shot back, his cheeks reddening. 'You can shut up.'

But Denham was having fun, and he continued to mock his friend until Lund's voice cut him off.

'Leave him alone, Denham,' Lund said. 'If Barnes is happy with his girl, good luck to him. What's it to you?'

'I was only having a joke, sir,' Denham protested. 'I didn't mean anything by it.' He glanced at Barnes, who was looking equally surprised by Lund's outburst.

Lund turned on his heel and returned to his desk.

'It was just a bit of fun, sir,' Denham muttered to Matthew.

'I know,' Matthew said, and joined Lund in the office, closing the door. 'What's the matter?' he asked.

'I thought I'd have Christmas Day as well as Boxing Day off, that's all,' Lund said. 'But I'm down for it. The fact is, the wife's come back with the girls. She wants us to have a proper Christmas, all of us together. I don't know why I did it, but I told her I wouldn't be working for the two days. We were going to have Christmas Day just us four, then we'd go over to the in-laws for Boxing Day. But now I'm going to miss Christmas and just have Boxing Day, no chance for me to be on my own with the wife and my girls. Just my luck.'

Matthew sat down at his desk and lit a cigarette, feeling awkward. He knew what he should say, knew what Lund wanted him to say, but for some reason, he didn't feel like making the offer.

Lund put his elbows on his desk and leaned forward. 'I don't suppose—' he broke off, shaking his head, then tutted and started again. 'You can tell me to get lost, Stannard, but I'm going to ask. Would you swap Christmas Day with me? I know Old Mouldy wants you to take your days, and I know it's a bleeding cheek me asking, but would you? After all, it's not as if you've got a wife who's going to complain, is it? And you said yourself you're not doing anything special.'

Matthew took a drag of his cigarette, knowing everything Lund said was true, but hearing it stated so bluntly didn't make it sting any the less. 'I'll talk to Mr Mullinger,' he said. 'I'll sure he'll agree.'

Lund groaned in relief. 'I'm grateful, Stannard. And I'll make it up to you. I promise.'

———

Matthew dropped by The Fiddler's Retreat after work to tell his family he wouldn't be there for Christmas. He readied himself for their complaints.

Entering the pub, he nodded to his brother-in-law Fred, who had his hands full behind the bar. Catching Ruby's eye, he smiled at the barmaid and let himself through the bar counter flap and mounted the stairs leading to the family's private area.

'Hello?' Matthew called out as he reached the top landing.

'Mattie?' his mother's voice rang out. 'Is that you?'

'Yes, it's me, Mum.'

He entered the sitting room and found his mother in her armchair, closing a copy of the *Radio Times*. He leant over and kissed her cheek.

'Pat,' Amanda said, raising her voice, 'Mattie's here for tea.'

'No,' he said hastily as Pat emerged from the kitchen, wiping her hands on a tea towel. 'I can't stay tonight. I thought I'd just pop in.'

His mother's face fell. 'Why can't you stay, Mattie?' she whined.

'As if you need to ask, Mum,' Pat said, rolling her eyes. 'He's working. He's always working. What are you doing here, Mattie?'

'It's nice to see you too,' he said, a little put out by her bluntness. 'I just came to tell you,' he said, readying himself for the outburst, 'about Christmas Day.'

'I suppose you're not coming,' Pat said. 'Oh, don't look so surprised. We've been expecting it. Haven't we, Mum?'

Amanda nodded unhappily. 'Fred bet your sister five bob you'd be working.'

'More fool me to bet against him,' Pat muttered. 'What about Boxing Day? Can you manage that?'

Manage it? Matthew thought irritably. *Anyone would think I was always letting them down and trying to get out of being here.* 'I should think so,' he said. 'If nothing comes up.'

'We won't hold our breath, then. So, you're not staying for tea?'

'I can't,' he said, thinking he definitely wouldn't now, not with Pat in such a Bolshie mood. 'Things to do.'

She nodded with a roll of her eyes and returned to the kitchen.

'What's up with her?' he asked his mother sulkily.

'Oh, she's just in one of her moods,' Amanda said dismissively. 'Probably annoyed that Fred was right about you. Don't pay any attention, Mattie.'

'I'll be off, then,' he said. 'I am sorry about Christmas, Mum.'

'It's all right, Mattie,' she said, giving his hand a squeeze. 'I know you're busy. Now, off you go if you're going. There's a play on the wireless I want to listen to.'

A little hurt by this dismissal and by the lack of protestations about him not making Christmas, Matthew left the sitting room, leaving his mother tuning the radio. *It's nice to be wanted*, he thought as he descended the stairs.

Chapter Twenty-Five

'You've been a difficult lady to find, Mrs Burns,' Walsh said as he pushed the Pekinese off the settee, brushed the upholstery free of its hairs and sat down.

Margaret Burns wasn't what he had been expecting. He thought he'd encounter a woman worn out with sorrow over the loss of her child, aged beyond her years, perhaps grubbing out a living and watching every penny. But when he finally tracked her down, he found Margaret Burns living in a large, detached house in Surrey, dressed in clothes that were made to measure and wearing jewellery that probably cost more than six months of his wages. Her hair was perfectly set, her eyebrows plucked to perfection, her fingernails painted an alarming shade of red. And when she spoke, it was with an accent that took care to pronounce every tee.

A plume of smoke obscured her face from him for a few seconds, then was wafted away with a wave of her elegant hand. 'It's Mrs Hollins, inspector,' she corrected him coolly. 'I haven't been Mrs Burns for some years.'

'My apologies,' Walsh held up a hand. 'Mrs Hollins.'

'And as for being hard to find, well…' She tapped her cigarette, being smoked through a long ivory holder, against a crystal ashtray. 'I had no idea anyone would be looking for me. Why are you here?'

'I'm here to talk to you about what happened to your baby in 1920.'

Her lips tightened. 'That's not a subject I want to talk about,' she said, smoothing her skirt over her knees. 'I've done my best to forget that time in my life.'

'I'm sorry, but I do need to ask you about it.' Walsh was damned if he would let her reluctance stop him. 'The detective in charge made a note about something you said regarding a nurse the police ought to talk to. It was never followed up, but I'd like to know why you said that.'

'Did I say that? I don't remember.' Margaret shook her head at her poor memory and then narrowed her eyes. 'But yes, there was a nurse at the hospital who was very kind to me at first. Fussed over me a great deal until Alice was born and then I was just in the way. She was only interested in the baby.'

'But you suspected her of taking your child?'

'I don't know if I thought that. You have to appreciate, inspector, I was in rather a state at the time. You can't imagine what it's like to have a child taken from you. I was so very angry, and I remember thinking the police weren't doing enough to find her. But as for suspecting that nurse…' She shrugged and shook her head. 'I wouldn't go that far.'

Walsh was disappointed. 'What was her name?' he asked sulkily.

'It was a long time ago, inspector.'

'It's important, Mrs Burns. Think.'

'Hollins, inspector,' she corrected sharply, glaring at him. She heaved a sigh and studied the carpet for a long moment. Then she looked up at him and said, 'Madden. Her name was Susan Madden.'

Chapter Twenty-Six

SATURDAY, 20TH DECEMBER

Frye watched the second hand ticking round on the mantelpiece clock as he listened to the beating of Victoria's heart. There was the the odd flutter, but nothing to worry about. He smiled down at her and unplugged his ears.

'That all sounds fine,' he said, tucking the stethoscope into his bag. He glanced at Sarah, sitting on the sofa, and flicked his eyes towards Victoria.

She took the hint and rose, helping Victoria to button her blouse back up. 'That's good news, isn't it, Mrs Scott?' she said, forcing a smile.

Victoria slapped her hands away. 'You can clear your things away upstairs, Miss Kempe.'

Sarah stiffened, and Frye hoped she wasn't going to ruin everything by losing her temper. But she left the sitting room without another word, and Frye breathed a sigh of relief. He sat down and turned back to Victoria.

Victoria was grinning at him, her wide, fat mouth showing her yellow, uneven teeth. He raised his eyebrows at her in query.

'I wanted her out of the way so we could talk in private,' she explained.

'About what?' he asked, taking a cigarette from the box on the table beside him, having been instructed he was to help himself.

'I'm going to set you up in a private practice,' she said.

Frye's heart beat faster. This was it, the moment he had been hoping for. *Don't blow it*, he told himself. 'Victoria, I'm—'

She laughed with delight. 'Pleased?'

'Pleased? I'm staggered. You can't mean it?'

'Of course I mean it. I'm going to lease a set of rooms for you here in Craynebrook in the new year. I'll have a plaque made up with your name on it, and you will have your very own private practice once more. You won't have to work under anyone ever again or do your duty at that wretched hospital.'

Frye shook his head as if bewildered. 'I don't know what to say.'

'How about thank you?'

'Thank you,' he laughed, grabbing her hands and kissing them, making her giggle. 'How will it work? Between us, I mean?'

'Well, I'll be putting all the money in. You'll be doing all the work. So I thought a fifty/fifty split would be the best thing.'

Frye kept his expression the same, but his mind was busy. He didn't think Victoria getting half of his fees was fair, but it wasn't the time to say so.

'Absolutely,' he said. Then an unpleasant thought occurred to him. 'And what does Benjamin say about this?'

'Ben? Oh, he doesn't know.'

'You haven't told him? But surely, in a matter of business—'

'You think I need a man to tell me how to do business?' she said indignantly. 'That I'm not clever enough to work everything out for myself?'

'I don't think that,' he said hastily. 'You're one of the most intelligent women I've ever known. But your husband is bound to find out.'

'Oh yes, Ben will find out.' Victoria waved her hand dismissively. 'But by then, it will be too late to do anything about it. So, you're not to tell anyone, Nigel. If Ben found out before our arrangements were made, he would do all he could to stop us.'

'I'm sure he would,' Frye agreed. 'But the new year is nearly upon us, Victoria. There's such a lot to do. Premises to find, leases to be agreed. A contract to be written up.'

'Aha.' Victoria reached over the side of the armchair to pick up her handbag. She unclasped it and took out a brown envelope. 'Look inside,' she said, handing it to Frye.

He opened the envelope and took out the contents. 'A contract already done?' Frye cried in surprise.

'I didn't want to waste any time,' she nodded, pleased with his reaction. 'We just need to sign that, have it witnessed and we're in business. Or at least, we will be, once I've given it to my solicitor. That won't be until after Christmas now, but that's not too long to wait.'

Frye quickly scanned the document. It all seemed in order; there was even an option to renegotiate terms after two years. Victoria really had done it all properly. He was impressed.

'Then I shall sign,' he said, taking a pen out of his jacket pocket and turning to the last page of the contract. He scribbled his signature and handed the document and the pen to Victoria. She signed her name.

'Now, we just need a witness,' she said, blowing on the ink to dry it.

Sarah came into the sitting room, pulling on her coat. 'I'm all done, Mrs Scott.'

'Miss Kempe can witness it,' Frye cried, grabbing Sarah by the elbow and pulling her over to Victoria.

Victoria looked at Sarah doubtfully, but then nodded. 'I suppose so.' She held out the document and pen to Sarah.

Sarah looked quizzically at Frye, who nodded urgently. 'Sign it,' he mouthed at her, and she took the pen and paper and signed her name beneath theirs.

'Thank you,' Frye said, taking them from her. He handed the document back to Victoria and replaced his pen in his pocket. 'And as for you, Victoria, I really can't thank you enough.'

Her face crumpled with pleasure. 'We must celebrate.'

'Indeed, we must,' he agreed, then checked his wrist-watch. 'But alas, not right now. I'm due at the hospital.'

'Oh,' she cried, disappointed. 'Can't you give it a miss just this once?'

'I could not be so cruel to my patients, dear lady,' he said, and took her hand once more to kiss it. 'Perhaps I may call on you tomorrow?'

'You may,' Victoria said, letting her hand linger in his. 'Come for tea.'

'What was all that about?' Sarah asked as they walked down the garden path to the pavement.

'Mission accomplished,' Frye said with glee. 'That document you just witnessed was Victoria setting me up in a private practice.'

'So that's what she's been up to, is it? I wondered what she was so excited about. Well, aren't you a lucky boy? Does that mean I can stop singing your praises to her?'

'It won't hurt to continue. I want the whole thing in the bag before you stop.'

'In case Mr Scott gets a whiff of it?' Sarah said shrewdly. 'He won't be pleased when he finds out, you know?'

'He's not going to find out,' Frye said. 'Not until it's too late, anyway. So, don't you go saying anything to him.'

'Oh, don't worry,' she said with feeling. 'That old bugger won't hear it from me.'

Chapter Twenty-Seven

MONDAY, 22ND DECEMBER

Benjamin slammed the bureau drawer back in with a curse. Why could he never find anything in this blasted house? He opened another drawer, rooted around inside for the stamps he was after, didn't find any and slammed it shut. Benjamin swore loudly and kicked the bureau.

Take a deep breath, he told himself. *Don't let him get to you.*

The 'him' was Maxwell. They'd had another quarrel that morning, and the tension between them had become so bad that Benjamin hadn't trusted himself to stay in the same room as his son-in-law, so he had left the office to work at home. But everything he needed to work he couldn't find at home. He couldn't find a ruler, a pencil sharpener or a bottle of ink. Then he couldn't find a notepad until finally he couldn't even find a single stamp!

There was one more drawer to try, the one where Victoria kept her correspondence. She was bound to have stamps in there, he felt sure. She was always writing to someone.

Benjamin opened the drawer. Inside was a long brown envelope. Recognising it as the type of envelope that held legal documents, and curious as to what it contained, he took it out and pinched out the document inside. His eyes widened as he read the first few lines. It couldn't be...? Surely Victoria wouldn't be so stupid?

Benjamin hurried out of the sitting room and mounted the stairs to their bedroom. He threw open the door, yelled, 'What the hell is this?' and threw the document onto Victoria's lap as she lay on the bed in her dressing gown. It was only then he saw Sarah standing by the dressing table, rolling a crepe bandage. 'Out,' he said, and jerked his thumb at the door. Sarah looked enquiringly at Victoria, who nodded, and she scurried past Benjamin onto the landing. He slammed the door on her. 'What have you been up to, Victoria?'

'You've been going through my things,' she said carelessly, picking up the contract. 'Sneaking around.'

'If you didn't want me to see it, you should have hidden it better.'

'It wasn't hidden. I don't have to hide anything from you. This is my business. It's nothing to do with you.'

'Setting Frye up in a private practice?' he cried incredulously. 'Are you really such a fool?'

'It's a business venture, Ben. Surely you can understand that?'

'I understand that weasel has got you wrapped around his little finger, you stupid cow.'

'Don't talk to me like that!'

'Have you given him money? Cash, Victoria. Have you given him cash?'

'Of course I haven't. But I am setting him up in a practice.'

'You think so?'

'I know so.'

'You won't say that once you hear what I've found out.'

Victoria's piggy eyes narrowed at him. 'What have you found out?'

'I hired a private enquiry agent to look into Frye,' Benjamin said. 'He's done this before, Victoria. Got in with silly old women who believe all his talk of being hard done by.'

'I am not a silly old woman.'

'He's got money out of them,' he went on. 'Plenty of it. And then spent it all on other women, wining and dining them in fancy hotels and restaurants to get them into bed.'

'That's not true,' Victoria said, though his words had shaken her, he could see that. 'Nigel's not like that. He's a gentleman.'

'A gentleman?' Benjamin scoffed. 'Why do you think his wife divorced him?'

'Because she wanted to marry the man she was carrying on with.'

'It was because she'd had enough of his womanising. And because she knew him for what he was. A gold digger. I knew he was up to something with you. Why else would he keep coming round here all the time?'

'Because he likes me,' Victoria protested feebly.

'Likes you,' he repeated scornfully. 'I'll show you every-thing this private enquiry agent dug up about him and then you'll see what he likes about you.' Benjamin leaned across the bed to retrieve the contract 'Who drew this up for you? Deakins?'

She nodded.

'I'll see Deakins and tell him it's all off. And next time you decide to do something stupid like this, Victoria, tell me first, eh?' He yanked open the door to see Sarah jump away. Barking a humourless laugh, he looked back at his wife and jerked his head at Sarah. 'Now, do you believe me? He put her in here to make sure you did exactly what he wanted.'

Victoria stared at Sarah. Then her face screwed up, and she tugged her pillow out from behind her and hurled it through the door. 'You get out!' she screamed. 'I won't have any creature of his in this house ever again.'

Chapter Twenty-Eight

'And you've been to the hospital and checked with them?' Miss Richardson asked as she handed Walsh a cup of tea.

'I have,' he said, resting the saucer on his knee, resisting the urge to yawn. All this running around from Colchester to London was wearing him out. 'But they threw out all their personnel records up to 1920 and couldn't tell me anything about Susan Madden. Your name was in a police report concerning her from 1919. That's how I found you. You were a senior nurse at St Catherine's Maternity Hospital then.'

Miss Richardson smiled. Her thin, pale face lit up. 'For twenty-five years, yes.'

'Susan Madden worked under you?'

Her expression changed to sorrow. 'For a while. A most trying woman. I suppose the police report you mean was the complaint Mrs Freeman made against her?'

'Yes. You remember it?'

'Of course I remember. It was the only time I've ever been questioned by the police. Until now,' she added with a rueful smile at him.

'Tell me about the complaint.'

Miss Richardson took a deep breath. 'Mrs Freeman had

been at the hospital to have her baby. She contacted us a few weeks after her discharge to say Nurse Madden had been making a nuisance of herself. Turning up at her house, insisting on seeing the baby. Claiming the hospital had sent her. It was all nonsense; we had done no such thing. Mrs Freeman wanted us to have a word with Nurse Madden to make her stop. So I had a word, and I thought I'd got through to her, but another couple of weeks went by and the police turned up at the hospital to question Nurse Madden. Apparently, she'd gone into Mrs Freeman's house uninvited and Mrs Freeman had found her in her sitting room holding the baby. It quite unnerved her.'

'According to the police report,' Walsh said, 'Susan Madden claimed she had heard the baby crying for some time and was concerned for its safety.'

'That's what she said, yes,' Miss Richardson nodded. 'She made out Mrs Freeman wasn't a good mother, that she wasn't looking after the child properly. Again, complete nonsense. Mrs Freeman was perfectly capable, and I told the police so.'

'You also told the police you'd had cause to speak to Susan Madden before Mrs Freeman complained, but the police report didn't elaborate. What was that all about?'

'There had been complaints from other patients about how clingy Nurse Madden was with the babies and some of the other nurses said she was too attentive, that she spent too much time fussing over them when she should have been working. These complaints never got back to the board. We dealt with those ourselves.'

'I see,' Walsh nodded. 'The police cautioned Susan Madden about the Freeman incident. Was any action taken by the hospital?'

'Not really. I was told to keep an eye on her, but that was about it.' Miss Richardson shook her frizzy-haired head in disapproval. 'The board thought the police involvement would have given Nurse Madden enough of a fright and that she would have learnt her lesson. They didn't want a fuss made. Personally, I thought she ought to have been dismissed, but the board were reluctant to let such a capable nurse go. We were extremely busy at the time. It was the end of the war, inspector.' Her nostrils pinched prudishly. 'A lot of babies were being born.'

'Yes, I can imagine,' Walsh said. 'Were you still working at St Catherine's in 1920?'

'Oh yes. I didn't retire until 1927.'

'Do you remember Margaret Burns?'

'The woman who had her baby stolen from her garden? I'm not likely to forget her.'

'Susan Madden was still working at the hospital then.'

Miss Richardson's eyes screwed up as she searched her memory. 'I think she was. Just.'

'Just?'

'It was a day or two either before or after the poor little thing was found. It was very close, I do remember, and we all thought that it had set her off. Everyone at the hospital knew the trouble she had got herself into with the police and people started talking about her behind her back. And when we heard about Mrs Burns' baby, one of the nurses joked that there was another woman as batty as Nurse Madden in Craynebrook, and Nurse Madden heard her and... well, let's just say she failed to see the funny side. She got into a frightful state, shouting and screaming, right there on the ward. Oh, the things she said. It was really quite dreadful, inspector. Such language. Her behaviour was so bad, some of the staff even left in disgust.'

'And that prompted the board to dismiss her?'

Miss Richardson's mouth pursed and she shook her head. 'The board never heard about it. Nurse Madden left. Had her tantrum, stormed out of the hospital and never came back. I can't say I was sorry to see her go.'

'Do you have any idea where she lived or where her family was?'

'Actually, I do. When there was all that trouble with the police, I looked at her personnel file to give them some details, and I remember she had named her parents as her next of kin.'

'And?' Walsh cried a little desperately. 'Where did they live?'

'They lived in your neck of the woods, inspector. In Colchester.'

———

'I think I've got it, sir,' Barnes declared, striding into the inspectors' office.

Matthew looked up to see the young detective constable brandishing a piece of paper. 'Got what?' he asked.

'Who the burglar might be.' Barnes put the paper down on the desk in front of Matthew. 'Sarah Kempe visited Nicholas Baddowes in HMP Pentonville almost every two weeks when he was inside. And Baddowes is on my list of recent releases with a history of housebreaking.'

Matthew read the prison inmate report Barnes had put in front of him. 'Where is Baddowes now?'

'Well, he's not at his home. His wife lives in Gravesend. I asked the local plod to go round there to see if Baddowes is there, and they've reported back that his wife claims not to have seen him since she visited him in the prison back in early October.'

'So, we don't know where he is?'

'No, sir,' Barnes said regretfully, then raised his eyebrow suggestively. 'But maybe Sarah Kempe does?'

Chapter Twenty-Nine

Sarah emptied the contents of the bedpan down the plughole and rinsed it out, placing it on top of all the other bedpans she had cleaned in the last half hour, and picked up the next.

Why had she thought her life would get any better? she wondered. For a few days, she'd had a wonderful idea. More than an idea; a dream. When Frye got his practice, he would need someone to run it for him. And she would make sure that someone would be her. He wouldn't refuse; it would be good for him, too. He would have a trained nurse on hand to assist him, while she acted as receptionist and secretary the rest of the time. No more drudgery doing shift work at a hospital, but a nice, clean job in a posh private establishment with sensible hours and good pay. Enough to get a decent flat for her and Nick. But now, that dream had been dashed because Frye had been found out. She should have known it would never happen. After all, when had life ever been good to her?

Sarah was surprised she wasn't angrier with Frye for messing everything up. If she was angry with anyone, it was with the Scotts. For months, she had put up with Victoria, listening to her complaints, soothing her, taking her put-downs and rudeness, pandering to a stupid old woman who had nothing wrong with her except boredom. And as for Mr Scott! He'd never even bothered to be civil to her, always looking down his nose whenever he saw her, shouting abuse at her, even calling her a filthy sneak that time Victoria had sent her to fetch him from his study. Just because she'd walked in on him opening his safe. The way he'd reacted, anyone would think he had the Crown Jewels in there. It would serve him right if—

'Oh! There you are!'

Sarah turned towards the doorway to see Nurse Crewe looking in at her. 'What's that supposed to mean?' she snapped.

'Nothing,' Nurse Crewe said. 'That is, I mean, I didn't realise you were in here.'

'Someone's got to clean the bedpans. And you were conveniently not around, as usual.'

'I was at reception. The police came in and asked for you.'

Sarah dropped the bedpan she had been cleaning. It banged noisily in the sink. 'The police?' she gasped.

'Two detectives. They want to talk to you.'

'Did they say why?'

Nurse Crewe shook her head. 'No. They just asked where you were. I thought you'd disappeared again, so I couldn't tell them. '

'What do you mean, disappeared again?' Sarah asked sharply.

'No one can ever find you lately,' Nurse Crewe said indignantly. 'You're always off somewhere. If I'd known you were here, I would have told them so. Shall I find them and tell them you're here?'

'No,' Sarah said hastily. 'I'll find them. You finish cleaning the pans.'

'But I'm needed on—' Nurse Crewe began.

But Sarah wasn't listening. She hurried out of the sluice room, grabbed her hat, coat and handbag from the staffroom and made her way down to the back of the hospital where no one else ever went. She slipped out of the door that opened on to a small, gloomy courtyard with a solitary, derelict shed. Stepping inside, she peered inside the hatbox she had secreted there weeks before, then replaced the lid with its punched-out holes and made her way to the hospital exit.

Sarah froze when she saw the police car parked outside, the driver with a newspaper open across the steering wheel. But he was too absorbed in his reading to notice her walk past and head for the gates. When she was out of sight, she quickened her pace towards the bus stop, expecting someone to shout out, 'Stop that woman!' at any moment.

A bus pulled up at the stop and she climbed on board. Settling the box on her lap, Sarah lifted the lid an inch and looked inside.

'It's all right,' she said under her breath. 'No one's going to take you away from me.'

———

Mullinger peered at Matthew over the top of his spectacles. 'And you have no idea where this Kempe woman is?'

'I'm afraid not, sir,' Matthew said. 'She left the hospital before we could talk to her and cleared out of her digs, owing three weeks' rent. We've contacted all the local stations to be on the lookout for her and Baddowes. With any luck, they'll be picked up soon.'

'I think you may have to rely on more than luck, Stannard,' Mullinger said. 'What I can't understand is why, if you suspected this woman had something to do with the burglaries, if she's associated with this Baddowes, you didn't pick her up sooner?'

'We had no proof she was involved, sir,' he said. 'To be honest, we still don't. All we have is a series of coincidences and likelihoods.'

'Those would have been enough for Lund to bring her in. Maybe he should be working on these burglaries.'

'He's welcome to take them over, if that's what you want,' Matthew said testily, seeing the superintendent's eyes widen at his impertinence. He knew he shouldn't have said that, should have kept his mouth shut, but if Lund had suddenly become flavour of the month with Old Mouldy, then he could sit here and take the criticism instead of him. Matthew agreed with Mullinger that Lund probably would have brought Sarah Kempe in for questioning, but he would also have ended up releasing her for lack of evidence and she would have done a runner, just the same.

'I want you to find this pair, Stannard,' Mullinger said sternly. 'From the reports I've read, this Baddowes is a violent character and an irredeemable criminal. Put the two together and we may find him committing more than an assault. Do a better job of keeping on top of this, Stannard. You may go.'

Chapter Thirty

TUESDAY, 23RD DECEMBER

It was late in the afternoon when Walsh knocked on the Maddens' front door in the poorest part of Colchester. The door was opened by an elderly woman with more lines than Walsh could count running down her cheeks and eyes that looked as if they wouldn't mind being permanently closed. He showed her his warrant card, and she invited him to step inside.

'I'm afraid we can't give you tea,' Mrs Madden said. 'The gas has been turned off.'

It was freezing in the house, and Walsh turned down her offer to take his coat, preferring to keep it on. He followed Mrs Madden into a poky front room, where an elderly man, huddled in blankets, sat in a straight-backed armchair in the corner next to a pitiful excuse for a Christmas tree. He looked at death's door.

'That's my husband, Stan,' Mrs Madden said, taking a seat. 'What's this all about?'

'It's about your daughter,' Walsh said, and waited for the alarmed response that usually followed such a statement. But it didn't come, and he continued. 'Do you know where she is?'

Mrs Madden shook her head. 'In London somewhere. She doesn't give us her address.'

'How do you get in touch with her, then?'

'We have to send anything to one of those Post Office boxes. What's she done?'

Walsh was surprised by the question. He'd not been able to find a single police record about Susan Madden in any of the Colchester stations, which suggested she had never done anything criminal, at least not in her hometown. And yet, here was her mother asking quite casually what she had done to warrant a policeman turning up on her doorstep.

'I'm not sure she's done anything. I'm investigating the babies that have been stolen recently and I—' Walsh broke off as Mrs Madden slid her husband a worried glance, and with that glance, he knew he was on the right track. 'Mrs Madden?' he probed.

She turned back to him. 'You think Susan has something to do with those?'

'Do you?'

'When we read about it in the newspapers, we both thought,' she gestured between herself and her husband, 'that it was the sort of thing Susan might do.'

'Why would she steal babies, Mrs Madden?' Walsh asked, trying to keep his excitement under control.

Mrs Madden shrugged. 'She's done it before. Well, sort of. Not quite what was in the 'paper. Look, Mr Walsh, I'm not sure I should be saying any of this. After all, you said yourself Susan's not done nothing.'

'Nothing I'm aware of. But I wouldn't be here if I didn't have my suspicions.'

Mrs Madden nodded unhappily. 'Go on, then. Ask your questions.'

'You said she's stolen babies before?'

'I didn't say that. I said she did something similar. A long time ago.'

'Tell me about it.'

'It was before the war. Susan got in the family way when she was twenty-five. God knows who the father was because she never told us, and Susan had never had any man look at her that way, so it was a shock, you can imagine. But anyway, she gave it away and then she got a job at a nursery. One day, I came home and found her with a kiddie in the kitchen. I asked her where she'd got it, and she said she'd brought it home from work as if it was the most natural thing in the world to do. I said she had to take it back, and we had a row, but then the police turned up and took the kiddie and Susan away. She was lucky not to get locked up for it, but the nursery didn't want any bother, and they persuaded the parents not to press charges or whatever you call it.

'Things got worse after that. She wasn't working, wouldn't get another job, and we had lots of rows. She said we'd made her give her baby away, but we hadn't, Mr Walsh. She agreed she couldn't keep it. We were hard up enough as it was without another mouth to feed. I know it wasn't easy for her, but she wasn't the only one that had happened to. I've known plenty of girls in my time who've found themselves in trouble and done the same thing, and it's been for the best. But after that, we never had a moment's peace with her. We were always arguing, and when she upped and left one day… well, we were glad. We didn't hear from her from that day until a few years later when she sent us a letter saying she was all right and working in a hospital as a nurse.'

Mrs Madden got up suddenly and went over to the mantelpiece, picking up a faded and creased photograph from behind a framed picture of her husband taken in his youth.

Holding the photograph out to Walsh, she said, 'That's Susan. It was taken when she was working at the nursery.'

Walsh looked at the picture. A plain woman, aged in her mid-twenties but looking older and dressed in drab, ill-fitting clothes, looked sullenly out at him. 'Can I keep this?' he asked.

'If you like,' she shrugged.

He tucked the photograph into the back of his notebook. 'Have you been in contact with her recently?'

Mrs Madden settled back in her chair. 'We've seen more of her this year than we've seen in the last ten because of Stan.'

Walsh glanced at the man in the corner, who began coughing violently. He hoped whatever was wrong with him wasn't catching.

'I wrote and told her Stan wasn't well,' Mrs Madden went on. 'Said she ought to come and see her dad before they carry him out in a wooden box. So, she came to see us.'

'When was that?'

'The first time was back in August.'

August! That was when Elaine Johnson was snatched from Jarrold's Department Store, Walsh thought excitedly.

'And she came again in the middle of October.'

When Elaine was put on the church steps!

'But then the doc said Stan's getting better, not that we've noticed, mind, and so she didn't bother coming again until last month.'

Walsh's pulse quickened. 'Susan was here in Colchester in November? Do you remember when? Exactly when?'

Mrs Madden's weary eyes blinked at him. 'She came down for two days. She left on the fifth.'

'Bonfire Night?' he asked breathlessly.

Mrs Madden nodded.

Chapter Thirty-One

Frye opened his front door and bent to pick up the post from the mat, covering his mouth with his hand as he yawned.

God, he was tired.

It had been a long day: the morning at the hospital, the afternoon and early evening at the surgery. All he wanted was a drink, a good dinner and a hot bath before bed to ease his aching bones.

Just a few more weeks, he reminded himself, and his duty at Woodrow's surgery and his shifts at the hospital would be nothing but an unhappy memory.

He shrugged off his overcoat, hung it up with his hat on the hook, and flicked through the post. Bills were tossed aside, but he frowned at a heavy cream envelope, recognising the handwriting on the front as belonging to Victoria.

He ripped open the envelope and took out the letter. The salutation said, *Dr Frye,* and he frowned. Why not, *Dear Nigel?*

He read on.

I cannot bring myself to see you, so this letter

is to tell you that you are no longer welcome at my house. Ben has had you investigated and exposed your lies and disgraceful behaviour to your wife and all those old women you charmed into giving you their money. Well, that's not going to happen this time. You won't get a penny more from me! I have torn up the contract between us. There will be NO private practice for you.

I daresay you will feel outraged by this letter and want to explain yourself. I don't want to hear any of your excuses. If you try to call on me, or contact me in any way, I shall have the police on you and I will be informing Dr Woodrow what a scoundrel he has employed.

I have nothing more to say to you.

Victoria Scott

Frye stared at the letter in disbelief. Benjamin had had him investigated? Some grubby private eye had been digging around in his personal life? What had he found out?

He reread the letter, and his stomach turned over at the last few lines. Victoria said she was going to tell Woodrow whatever the gutter rat had uncovered. Woodrow was such a Puritan, he'd fire him for sure. And then he'd lose everything. His job at the surgery, his shifts at the hospital. Word would get around, and he'd not be able to get another position. No money coming in. No savings to fall back on. He'd be ruined.

Oh, God! What was he going to do?

———

'Max, what is this?' Victoria demanded when Maxwell opened his front door. She gestured at Benjamin beside her. 'We get a telephone call from you telling us to come round at once. No word of explanation. Do you know how inconvenient this is? We were on our way out. I insist you tell us what this is all about.'

Maxwell shook his head helplessly and gestured them to step inside. Closing the front door, he pointed his in-laws towards the sitting room and followed them in.

Victoria and Benjamin both gasped in surprise. Imogen was sitting on the sofa.

'Hello,' she said.

'Hello?' Victoria cried. 'Is that all you can say?'

'Mother, please,' Imogen said, and put her hand out to the woven basket sitting beside her on the sofa. 'You'll wake the baby.'

'The baby?' Benjamin asked in astonishment. He turned to Maxwell. 'You didn't say anything about a baby on the telephone.'

Maxwell shrugged helplessly. 'I didn't know what to say. I'm still reeling.'

'You've had a baby?' Victoria said in astonishment.

Imogen smiled proudly. 'Yes, Mother, I did. Come and see him.'

Victoria obeyed and peered into the basket. 'I can't believe it.' She made a move to pick up the sleeping child, but Imogen threw out her arm to stop her.

'Don't,' she said. 'Not while he's sleeping. You can hold him later. Besides, Max hasn't even held him yet, and he should be first.'

'I need a drink,' Maxwell declared and moved to the drinks cabinet. He poured himself a large brandy and swallowed the lot in one gulp.

'Where have you been, Imogen?' Benjamin asked as Victoria sank into an armchair.

'It doesn't matter where I've been,' Imogen said with a toss of her head. 'I'm back and there's no need to go on about it.'

'Oh, that's typical,' Victoria declared. 'Never a thought for anyone else. All the trouble you've caused. Do you know what that stupid maid of yours did? She went to the police. Told them you were missing and that Maxwell had murdered you.'

Imogen stared wide-eyed at Maxwell. 'That's not true, is it?'

He nodded. 'They questioned me at the office. I was lucky not to be arrested.'

'I never meant for that to happen, Max, you must know that. I just had to get away.'

'For God's sake, why?' he cried. 'You must have known you were pregnant when you left.'

'You were all getting at me,' Imogen cried angrily. 'I couldn't bear it.'

'So it's our fault. I might have known.' Victoria's mouth pursed in irritation. 'Well, at least you've finally done your duty and given Max a son. Congratulations, Max. You must be very pleased.'

'I don't know what I am,' Maxwell confessed, staring down into his empty glass. He really didn't. A few hours earlier, he had been considering leaving Craynebrook, telling Benjamin to stuff the printing works and running off with Linda. Now, his wife was back with the son he'd always hoped for, and he didn't know what he wanted anymore. And then a thought burst into his mind. 'But this changes everything, Ben,' he said, turning to his father-in-law. 'You've got to let me run the business the way I want. Not just for me, but for your grandson. He'll inherit it one day.'

Benjamin laughed hollowly and shook his head. 'I wondered how long it would take you to get back to what's best for you. You're so predictable, Max.'

'I'm serious, Ben.'

'I know you are, and that's the problem.' He sighed. 'Let's get Christmas over and done with, and then we'll talk about the future. Let's just have a nice, quiet Christmas. God knows we could all do with that after these last few months.'

'I agree,' Victoria said. 'We'll all go to Midnight Mass tomorrow and then you come round for Christmas Day and—'

'I was thinking,' Imogen cut in, 'that we, Max and me and the baby, would have Christmas alone this year. Just us.'

'What nonsense! Of course you're coming to us. I have all the food being delivered, and you won't have a thing in the house. And besides, you don't have a maid anymore, so who would cook? You?' Victoria laughed derisively.

Imogen sighed resignedly. 'Well, we're not going to Midnight Mass. Not with the baby.'

'No,' Benjamin said, waving a hand at Victoria as she opened her mouth to protest. 'Imogen's right. A church at midnight is no place for a baby. It'll be crying all through the service, spoiling it for everyone else. You don't want that, Victoria. People tutting at us.'

'I suppose not,' Victoria said, narrowing her eyes at the basket. 'Very well. You don't have to come. Come round for Christmas Day around half-twelve, one o'clock. Yes, Max?'

Maxwell shrugged and said, 'If you like.'

'And when Christmas is over,' Victoria went on, 'I'll find a nanny and get you another maid.'

'I don't want a nanny for the baby, Mother,' Imogen protested.

'Of course you'll have a nanny for him. We can't leave you to look after a baby.' She sat up and peered into the basket. 'Has he woken up yet? No? Well, we're not waiting.' She clambered out of the armchair. 'Bring him round to us tomorrow, Imogen, so we can have a proper look at him. Come along, Ben. We're going home.'

They left, and Maxwell watched Imogen tuck the blanket around the baby. 'Where the hell have you been?' he asked quietly.

'You don't need to know, and I'm not telling you,' Imogen said, raising her chin defiantly.

'You're a cow, you know that? Do you have any idea what you've put me through? Do you care about me at all?'

She closed her eyes and sighed. 'I'm back, Max, and you've finally got your son. Be grateful for that.' She rose and grabbed the handles of the basket, heaving it off the sofa. 'I'm going to bed. It's been a long day, and I'm very tired.'

Imogen left the sitting room, and Maxwell heard her climbing the stairs. After a moment's consideration, he poured himself another double brandy.

Chapter Thirty-Two

CHRISTMAS EVE

The kittens were curled up in a ball on the sofa. Matthew picked out the one with the white smudge on its nose and handed the furry little body to Lund with care.

'She's just been fed, so she's sleepy.'

'She's a pretty little thing, isn't she?' Lund said, holding the kitten up to his face and smiling. 'My girls are going to love her.'

'Have you told them you're giving them a kitten for Christmas?'

'No, it'll be a surprise. I'm going to put her in a box with a big ribbon on it, and they'll open it tomorrow.'

'You're not going to leave her in a box all night, are you?' Matthew asked, aghast.

Lund chuckled. 'Of course I'm not. We're going to keep her in our bedroom, and put her in the box just before we give her to the girls. She's going to be fine, Stannard. Honestly, the look on your face! Are you sure you want to get rid of them?'

Matthew wasn't sure at all. He loved having the kittens, but he knew he couldn't keep all three; his flat wasn't big enough for four cats. 'I'm sure,' he said with as much conviction as he could muster.

The doorbell rang, and Matthew silently cursed. He had hoped Lund would be gone by the time Dickie arrived. It had been Dickie who had caused the uproar that led to Lund being taken off the Foxhall Green shooting case, and though it had all turned out for the best, Matthew wasn't sure Lund would be entirely forgiving.

He answered the door, and Dickie grinned at him. 'I'm here to collect,' he announced.

'Lund's here,' Matthew said in a low voice.

'Ah.' Dickie's face fell. 'Should I come back later?'

Matthew shook his head. 'You're going to meet sometime. You might as well get it over with.' He beckoned Dickie inside.

'Evening, Lund,' Dickie said uneasily as he entered the sitting room.

Lund, who had been playing with the kitten, looked up, the smile on his face instantly fading.

Obviously not forgiven, Matthew mused.

'Waite,' Lund greeted him stonily, and got to his feet. 'You said you had a box to put her in, Stannard?'

'Yes, I'll get it.' Matthew retreated to the kitchen and took down a cardboard box from the top of the cabinet. When he returned, Dickie was studying the books on his shelves with a determined interest.

Bella had followed Matthew from the kitchen, and jumped up on the sofa as he put the box by Lund's feet. She cried as Lund put the kitten inside and closed the flaps, and Matthew's stomach lurched.

'I won't drag it out,' Lund said. 'I don't want to upset the mother. Here.' He fished in his pocket, pulled out some coins and held his hand out to Matthew.

Matthew pushed Lund's hand away. 'I don't want money for her,' he said reproachfully.

'You sure?' Lund said. 'All right. If that's what you want.' He put the coins back in his pocket and bent to pick up the box. A pitiful cry came from inside. 'I appreciate this, Stannard. My girls are going to love her.'

'I hope so,' Matthew said earnestly, resisting the urge to snatch the box from Lund and return the kitten to her siblings.

'Well, I'll be off,' Lund said. 'Thanks again for swapping your day with me.'

'Don't mention it.' Matthew walked him to the front door and pointed at the box. 'The bus ride might upset her, so make sure you put your hand in and stroke her on the way home.'

'Will do,' Lund promised. 'Well, I'll see you after Christmas. Have a good one.'

'He's still got the hump with me,' Dickie said as Matthew returned to the sitting room.

'Lund will get over it.' Matthew went over to the cupboard where he kept his alcohol. 'You want a drink?'

'If you're offering,' Dickie said, taking the seat Lund had occupied. He glanced around the sitting room. 'No Christmas tree?'

'What's the point?' Matthew said, handing him a tumbler of whisky. 'It's only me here and I've got nothing to put under it.'

'Where's your Christmas spirit?' Dickie said scornfully. 'I shall start calling you Scrooge.'

Matthew shrugged to show he didn't care. As far as he was concerned, Christmas was for kids and as he didn't have any... He picked up the two remaining kittens and sat down, depositing them on his lap. Bella was poised on the arm beside him.

'I should have brought a box to put the kitten in,' Dickie said ruefully.

'It's all right. I've got another.'

'Good. And I won't insult you by offering you money.'

'I should hope not,' Matthew said, and ducked his head down so Bella could rub her cheek against his. 'As if I could sell them.'

Dickie chuckled. 'You know, you're a soppy sod when it comes to these cats. Where's the hard-bitten detective everyone thinks you are?'

'Who thinks I'm hard-bitten?'

Dickie shrugged. 'What was that Lund said as he was leaving? Something about you swapping days with him?'

'Tomorrow,' Matthew nodded. 'I was down to have Christmas Day off and Lund was supposed to be working. But he asked if I would swap with him.'

'And you said yes?' Dickie was incredulous.

'Why not? He wanted to be with his family.'

'And what about your family?'

Matthew sighed. 'They didn't care. They were expecting me to work Christmas Day anyway.' He looked up. Dickie was looking at him strangely. 'What?'

'What's the matter, Matthew?' Dickie asked seriously.

'Nothing's the matter.'

'Don't give me that. What's wrong?'

'There's nothing wrong, Dickie,' he insisted. 'It doesn't matter if I'm working Christmas Day. Like Lund said when he asked me, it's not like I've got a wife at home, is it?'

Dickie smiled uncertainly. 'You've got the cats,' he joked.

Matthew nodded. 'Yeah. I've got the cats. Two of them, anyway.' He lifted the kitten with three white socks and held it out to Dickie. 'This one's yours.'

'This is the other girl, yes? So, that makes that little fella,' Dickie nodded at the kitten being forced to make room on

Matthew's lap for Bella, 'the boy. That's the one you're keeping?'

'His name's Hobbs,' Matthew said, tickling the kitten under the chin.

'After the cricketer. It would have to be, wouldn't it?'

Matthew grinned. 'Lund would have liked to have two, one for each of his girls, but I can't take all Bella's kittens away from her. Hopefully, she won't miss the other two too much.'

'Cats aren't like women, Matthew. She'll forget all about them before long, you'll see. But you'll have to get him fixed, you know? He'll be after his mother if you're not careful.'

'I know, and I will. In the new year.'

Dickie took a mouthful of his whisky. 'So, do you still have Boxing Day off?'

'That's the plan,' Matthew sighed. 'I'll be at the pub.'

'If it all gets too much for you, why not come to us for the evening?' Dickie suggested. 'It won't be much. Just leftovers. But you'll be very welcome.'

The offer was appealing. 'You're sure Emma won't mind?' Matthew asked. 'I don't want to be a nuisance.'

'Don't be a chump. Emma thinks the sun shines out of your whatsit. She'd love to have you round. And besides, if you come round, you can make sure we're taking care of this little thing properly. I know that's what you're worrying about.'

He grinned at Matthew, and Matthew, knowing he was being made fun of, grinned back.

'All right,' he said. 'I will.'

Chapter Thirty-Three

Maxwell gulped his whisky, his eyes fixed on the door. He checked his wristwatch and hoped the man he was waiting for would be in soon.

He lit a cigarette while he waited, his thoughts turning to earlier in the day. Benjamin had been more insufferable than ever. Maxwell had hoped that with Imogen's return and the arrival of his grandson, Benjamin would relent and stop being such an obstinate old man. But that hope had gone up in a puff of smoke that afternoon when Benjamin had absolutely refused to consider any of Maxwell's new marketing ideas for the new year. Driven to desperation, Maxwell had begged his father-in-law to give him a free hand, just for a few months. But Benjamin had laughed and waved him away as if he were a child begging for more sweets. When he thought how he had abased himself before Benjamin, Maxwell wanted to curl up in shame.

His only solace was that the printing works had closed for the holiday and he wouldn't have to sit opposite him every day. Except for Christmas and Boxing Day, Maxwell would be free of him until January. Time to think about what he was going to do. The fantasy he had had about chucking the business and running away with Linda had been destroyed by Imogen's return. He couldn't think about leaving, not now he had a son to consider. Everything had changed and he would need to change too.

Maxwell had made a start that afternoon after the office closed down for the holiday and everyone but he and Linda had gone home. He'd told her then about Imogen and the baby and that he couldn't see her anymore. Linda had taken it well, saying she understood, though adding a little bitterly that she wished Imogen had stayed away. He had been about to say the same, but she hurried on, saying she didn't think she could stay at the printing works, that it would be best if she left in the new year.

'You don't have to leave,' Maxwell said.

'It would be too awkward between us,' Linda insisted. And then she shrugged and said, 'But maybe I won't have a choice anyway, not if Mr Prince takes over. There's no saying he'll want to keep any of us on.'

Maxwell frowned at her. 'What are you talking about?' he said.

'It's just a rumour,' she shrugged again, shaking her head and reaching for her coat.

'What's a rumour? What's all this about Prince?'

Linda pulled her coat on and buttoned it up. 'Mr Prince and Mr Scott have been having meetings,' she said. 'What else would they be talking about if not the business?'

'What meetings?' Maxwell cried. 'I don't know about any meetings.'

'Don't you?' Linda said carelessly. She hooked her handbag on her arm and moved to step around him.

But Maxwell grabbed her and held her fast. 'Ben's been having meetings with Harold Prince and you never told me?'

Linda jerked herself out of his grip. 'You never wanted to hear about Mr Scott, did you? I would have told you, if you'd bothered to ask me anything. Now, I've got to get home to my husband. Merry Christmas, Mr Carr.'

And she had left, leaving Maxwell standing in the darkened office, feeling as if he'd been kicked in the stomach.

When he'd pulled himself together, he knew what he was going to do. Benjamin wouldn't tell him anything, so he would have to ask Prince. And he knew where he would most likely be.

Maxwell had jumped in his car and driven like a madman to the club Prince frequented. He was all ready to have it out with him, but Prince wasn't there when he arrived. And so Maxwell had settled down to wait for him.

He didn't have to wait long. After about twenty minutes, Harold Prince sauntered into the bar with a pack of his cronies, all jolly and full of Christmas cheer. He ordered champagne, and one of his friends cried, 'Champagne? Are we celebrating?'

'We certainly are,' Prince replied, and Maxwell, keeping out of sight, saw him raise his glass in the air. 'Here's to an even more profitable 1931.'

His friends clinked their glasses and drank.

'How can it be more profitable?' one of them asked. 'What scheme have you got up your sleeve this time, Harold?'

Prince tapped his nose. 'Wait and see,' he said with a smile.

'Oh, come on, don't tease,' the man said, jogging Prince's elbow as he drank. 'Tell all.'

'I know what it is,' another said, wagging a finger. 'It's something to do with all those secret meetings he's been having.'

'David,' Prince chided, wiping champagne from his shirt front, 'I told you about those in confidence.'

'I know, but there can't be any need for secrecy now. You said whatever it was would all be settled by the new year, and here we are, Christmas Eve, and the new year just a few days away. So, tell us.'

The others urged the same, and Prince gave in. 'Very well. I'll tell you. It is almost done, after all. I'm expanding.'

'Don't we know it!' one laughed, patting Prince's bulging stomach.

Prince knocked the hand away. 'My business is expanding,' he explained irritably. 'I'm buying Scott's Printing Works.'

A lump of lead landed in Maxwell's stomach. Linda had been right.

'Old Ben's selling up?' David said. 'But I thought he'd go on forever.'

'He's keen to retire,' Prince said, holding his glass out for a refill. 'Wants to enjoy it before he's too old.'

'Well, well. What a turn-up! But what about young Maxwell? Doesn't he have something to say about all this?'

Prince shrugged. 'I'm not concerning myself with Carr. The deal will be done before he even knows about it.'

'You mean he doesn't know?' David said incredulously. 'I say, that's a bit thick. Old Ben selling the business out from under his son-in-law. So, are you taking Max on?'

'I certainly am not,' Prince declared.

Maxwell couldn't bear it any longer. He had to know if this was true or some cruel practical joke. He stumbled towards Prince, knocking over a table.

Prince turned at the noise and the smile dropped off his face. 'Max! Good Lord. I didn't see you there.'

'Is it true?' Maxwell croaked.

'Now, now, Max, I don't want any—'

'IS IT TRUE?' he yelled.

Prince swallowed. 'Yes, it is. But keeping you out of it wasn't my idea. If there is a problem, Max, you need to take it up with your father-in-law.'

'Oh, don't you worry,' Maxwell said, his jaw hardening, his fists clenching. 'I will.'

Chapter Thirty-Four

'And you're to be here by no later than one,' Victoria said, adjusting a decoration on the Christmas tree. 'Not a minute later, you hear?'

'Yes, Mother, you said,' Imogen said with a sigh, shifting the baby from her shoulder to her lap.

'And you're certain you won't come to Midnight Mass tonight? It's such a shame. You could show the baby off to everyone.'

'I don't want to show him off. And it wouldn't be good for him. It will be so cold in the church. And he'll be tired.'

'Oh, all these excuses. Have it your own way.' Victoria turned to her daughter with a wide smile. 'I've got a new dress for Midnight Mass, Imogen. It'll be here any moment. Holly green with berry red cuffs. Christmas colours. It's so pretty.'

'It sounds perfectly horrid,' Imogen muttered.

'Oh, what would you know?' There came a bang on the front door and Victoria clapped her hands together and cried, 'Oh, there it is,' as the maid answered it.

But the next moment, Maxwell's voice could be heard demanding, 'Where is he?'

'Max!' Victoria cried as Maxwell burst into the room. 'What is it? What's wrong?'

Maxwell stormed over to Benjamin sitting in the armchair by the fire. 'What the hell do you think you're doing?'

Benjamin set down the novel he'd been reading and looked up at him impassively. 'I suppose this means you've heard? Prince was meant to keep it to himself.'

'Ben, what is all this?' Victoria demanded.

'He's selling the business,' Maxwell cried. 'That's what this is.'

She stared at her husband in astonishment. 'You're selling?'

Benjamin took a puff of his pipe before answering. 'Yes, it's true. I've decided to sell up to Harold Prince. The contract will be signed in the new year.'

'How much are you selling it for?'

'Enough.'

'How much? I want to know.'

'I'll show you the bank statement when the deal's done, Victoria. Don't be so impatient.'

'But I—'

'Will you both shut up?' Maxwell yelled, and the baby woke and bawled.

'Oh, Max, please don't shout,' Imogen cried, holding her baby to her breast, staring at her husband and father in horror.

Maxwell ignored her. 'You have no right to sell the business without consulting me.'

Benjamin laughed. 'I have every right. I don't have to consult you. You're an employee, Max. You do as you're told.'

'The business was to be mine. You promised. You told me when I married Imogen that the business would come to me when you retired. You said that.'

'What if I did?' Benjamin shrugged, frowning at the baby

whose bawling had grown louder. 'It was years ago, and I've changed my mind. You think I'm going to retire and watch you run it into the ground? I'd rather sell it to a man who knows how to run a business properly than watch you ruin everything I built.'

'But it's not fair,' Maxwell cried despairingly. 'I've done everything you ever asked of me.'

'Stop your whining. You've done well out of me all these years. I've given you a good job. I gave you my daughter. And all I've ever had from you is complaints. If you were any kind of man you would have set up on your own years ago. But no, you wanted to take the easy path and just have it all come to you when I'm gone.'

'It's what you agreed,' Maxwell insisted stubbornly. 'You can't do this.'

'It's done.'

'Don't you even care about your daughter? How am I going to support her if I'm out of a job?'

'Don't you try that on with me, Max,' Benjamin warned him. 'Don't pretend to be concerned about Imogen while gadding about with that mistress of yours.'

'Mistress?' Imogen looked up at her husband with wide eyes. 'Max, what does he mean?'

'Nothing,' Maxwell spat. 'Ben's just stirring because he knows he's in the wrong.'

'You're having an affair?'

'Of course I'm not.'

'And if you believe that, you'll believe anything,' Benjamin muttered.

'Max!' Imogen cried.

'Oh, for heaven's sake, don't you start as well,' Victoria cried. 'You can't blame Max if he has got another woman. You can't keep running off and expect him to stay faithful.'

'We swore vows,' Imogen whimpered.

'If you're going to start snivelling, you can go. All this noise is giving me a headache. Max, take your wife and child home.'

'Not until Ben says he won't sell,' Maxwell said.

Benjamin got out of his chair and squared up to his son-in-law. 'I am selling, Max, and there's nothing you can do about it.'

'I won't let you do this.'

'Oh no? How are you going to stop me?'

Maxwell held Benjamin's gaze for a long moment, then turned on his heel and stormed out of the house.

'Go after him, Imogen,' Victoria ordered. 'My dress will be here soon, and I need to get ready. And for heaven's sake, don't make a fuss about Max.'

Frye looked down at his glass and saw with surprise that it was empty once again. He raised his hand and signalled to the bartender. 'Another,' he called.

Frank Greader came over. 'I think you should call it a night, Dr Frye, don't you?'

'Certainly not. I'm just getting into my stride. Another, if you please, Greader.'

Reluctantly, Greader poured out a measure of brandy and put the glass on the counter, holding his hand out for payment. Frye carefully counted out the correct coins and handed them over. He lifted the glass to his lips and swallowed the lot in one gulp.

A sudden burst of laughter made him look around. The laughter had come from a group of men and women in their mid-twenties. They were well dressed, their voices plummy. A few years earlier, they would have been called Bright Young Things, he supposed, but judging by the disapproving looks they were getting from the regulars, to them they were just yahoos.

One of the women in the group turned, her Pre-Raphaelite red curls bouncing delightfully, and caught Frye's eye. She held his gaze for a long moment, then her wide mouth broadened into a smile, showing a row of perfect teeth.

Frye smiled back, and a warm feeling crept over him. Had he been sober, he might have sauntered over and asked if she wanted a drink. But he was drunk and almost out of money, and besides, she was fifteen years younger if she was a day, and he wasn't so much of a fool as all that. He turned back to lean on the bar and stared down into his empty glass.

'Hello.'

He turned. The woman with red hair was at his elbow. 'Hello,' he said, unable to keep the surprise out of his voice.

'All alone?' she asked.

'Afraid so.'

'Why don't you come over and join us?' She jerked her head at her friends.

The suggestion held little appeal. Frye had never been one for socialising in groups; he much preferred tête-à-têtes. 'Oh, you don't want an old chap like me barging in.'

'But I like old chaps like you,' she said, leaning a little closer so he could smell her musky perfume. 'Come over. It'll be fun.'

'What will be fun?'

She smiled coquettishly. 'Are you coming over or not?'

The young woman was really quite delightful. So what if she was almost young enough to be his daughter? He'd had enough of older women. This pretty thing would make a very pleasant change.

Frye gave her his charming smile. 'How can I refuse?'

Chapter Thirty-Five

CHRISTMAS DAY

Mrs Peggy Keeling unlocked the side door of No. 9 Brampton Drive and pushed open the door, her body very keen to get out of the cold and her mind busy with all the things she had to do that morning.

There was the goose to put in the oven. That had to be done first; it would take the longest. Then she would have to put the plum pudding on to steam. That would take a while too. Then she should get on with preparing the vegetables: there were potatoes to be peeled and parboiled, Brussel sprouts to be trimmed, carrots and parsnips cut. Batter made for the Yorkshire puddings. When all that was done, it would be time to put the rib beef in the oven, as the Scotts didn't like it too well done. Take the goose out to rest. Make the gravy. And once all that was done, she would leave the family to get on with the rest and toddle off home to do it all over again for her and Larry.

Peggy dumped her bag on the kitchen table, smiling at the box of chocolate liqueurs Mrs Scott must have left for her. She was good like that, always leaving her a present on

Christmas Day, and Larry would like those liqueurs. She turned the oven on to heat up, filled the kettle and put it on the gas ring for a cup of tea. Opening the door to the hall, she cocked her head for any sounds of movement in the house but heard nothing. The Scotts were having a lie-in. *All right for some*, she thought as she closed the kitchen door and got on with her work.

It was half-past ten before everything that could be done had been done, and she sat down on a kitchen chair with a grateful groan and sipped at her second cup of tea. It was only then Peggy realised Mrs Scott hadn't been down to check on her.

Setting her cup back on its saucer, she opened the kitchen door and took a few steps into the hall. There was still no sound of movement, and that was odd because she'd never known the Scotts to stay in bed this late.

'Hello?' she called in a quiet voice, not wishing to disturb them and risk a telling-off. But she got no reply and, feeling bolder, went along the passage to stand between the two reception room doors.

The sitting-room door was ajar, and she could see the sofas and the fireplace through the gap. The room was empty. There was no fire burning in the grate, despite the cold, and the ashtray on the side table beside it was full of ash and had Mr Scott's pipe in it. That was odd, too. Mrs Scott was always very particular about the ashtrays being emptied every night; she didn't like the room smelling of stale smoke in the morning. If the maid didn't see to the ashtrays, then Mr Scott would take them to the kitchen and empty them into the bin.

She turned to the dining-room door, which was also ajar, and poked her head inside. The maid had laid the table the evening before, and it looked lovely. Peggy forgot her curiosity about the Scotts for a moment as she wandered in to admire the place settings, the candles in their seasonal holders and the holly that decorated the tablecloth. She wished she could set a table like this at home, but she didn't have the fine cutlery or the crystal wine glasses. She didn't even have napkin rings.

Peggy reached the head of the table near the bay window and turned to go down the other side when she froze. Her eyes widened. Her mouth formed a perfect O.

'Mrs Scott?' she cried when her brain finally understood the sight before her.

Victoria was lying on her back on the floor between the fireplace and the table. Peggy's first thought was that she had had a heart attack, but then she understood what the dark red stain on the front of Victoria's dress was and she recoiled in disgust and alarm. Her horrified gaze stared at the grey face and staring eyes, and she knew the old woman was dead.

Peggy stumbled backwards, nearly tripping over the legs of a dining chair, and hurried towards the door. She froze again. Sticking out from behind the door was a pair of slippered feet. Her legs shaking beneath her, she edged slowly towards the door, one arm outstretched to pull it towards her.

'Oh my God,' she whimpered as she looked down on Benjamin, slumped against the wall. His pullover was stained with blood.

———

Mrs Parker deposited a mince pie on the table. 'There you go, love. You eat that up.'

Matthew smiled up at the dinner lady. 'Thank you,' he said, not wishing to hurt her feelings by admitting he didn't really like mince pies. 'That's very kind of you.'

'Not kind at all. I think it's such a shame you have to be in here, working today of all days.'

'You're working,' he pointed out.

She shrugged carelessly. 'I'm too old for it to matter, love. In fact,' she elbowed Matthew playfully, 'I'm blooming glad to get out of the house. Don't tell my hubby.'

He grinned. 'I won't say a word,' he promised. Realising Mrs Parker was waiting for him to take a bite of the mince pie, he gingerly picked it up. The treat was halfway to his mouth when the canteen door burst open and Barnes hurried over to his table.

'Sir,' Barnes panted. 'Front desk has just taken an emergency call. A woman has called to say she's found her employers dead in their dining room. Blood all over them.'

Oh God, Matthew thought. *Not again.* But he immediately got to his feet and asked, 'Where?' as they headed for the canteen door, taking his hat and coat from Barnes that the DC had brought with him from CID.

'Brampton Drive,' Barnes said. 'The lady who called in is a Mrs Keeling. She'd gone in to cook the Christmas dinner and found the man and woman dead. Uniform are already on their way. And the car's waiting outside.'

'What's the dead couple's name?' Matthew asked.

'Scott,' Barnes said. 'A Mr and Mrs Benjamin Scott.'

Chapter Thirty-Six

A crowd had gathered outside the house, and Matthew reflected ruefully that not even Christmas Day celebrations could keep gawpers inside when there was a murder in the vicinity.

Or two murders, as this case seemed to be, he thought as he climbed out of the police car and stared up at the front of the house. All but the upstairs right-hand window had their curtains drawn.

Matthew approached the constable standing guard at the gate. He jerked his head at the neighbours who were edging forward, drawn by the arrival of plain-clothes detectives. 'Can you handle them?' he asked.

'I can manage, sir,' the constable assured him.

'Has the pathologist been called?'

'Dr Wallace said he'd come right over.'

Matthew nodded and bent to study the front door. There was no sign of forced entry – no glass broken, no lock forced – and he stepped inside the hall, Barnes at his heels.

Another constable was guarding the dining-room door. 'The bodies are in here, sir,' he told Matthew. 'And Sergeant

Turkel's in the kitchen with Mrs Keeling. She was very shaken up.'

'I expect she was. Has anyone else been in the house since she called? Any of the neighbours come in for a look?'

'I don't think so, sir. She waited outside for us to arrive. Didn't want to be in here on her own.' He stepped aside and Matthew used a gloved forefinger to push open the dining-room door.

The dining table was laid for the Christmas dinner. Matthew counted four place settings. One each for the Scotts, perhaps one for Maxwell Carr. Who was the other one for? he wondered.

He walked around the table towards the bay window. Everything seemed normal; nothing was disturbed until Matthew turned at the end of the table and saw the body, stretched out full length between the table and the fireplace. Victoria was on her back, eyes open, arms by her sides. Blood stained the entire front of her dress. There was a tear in the fabric right over her heart.

'Sir?' Barnes said quietly.

Matthew looked up to see Barnes staring at something behind the door. He stepped around Victoria and moved to the end of the table to see the body of Benjamin Scott. His head was forward, chin against his chest, his grey hair flopped over his forehead. He was wearing a shirt and cardigan, and both were stained with blood. Beside him on the floor lay a bloodied carving knife.

'We've got the murder weapon, then,' Barnes said ruefully.

Matthew looked back at the table. There was a carving board with a carving fork lying upon it, but no knife. The handle of the fork matched the handle of the knife beside Benjamin.

'The murderer used what came to hand,' Matthew said.

'He didn't come with his own knife, which suggests the murders weren't premeditated.'

'If he snatched the knife up without thinking,' Barnes said, 'we might get some prints off it, if we're lucky.'

Matthew nodded. 'I want pictures of everything in here before we start dusting. Everything photographed exactly as it is.' He took another look around the room, then said, 'Let's talk to the cook.'

Peggy was seated opposite Turkel at the kitchen table, a cup of tea before her. She glanced up as Matthew and Barnes entered. Turkel rose and gave Matthew his chair.

'I'm DI Stannard, Mrs Keeling,' Matthew said. 'You've had quite a shock. How are you?'

'I don't blooming well know how I am, if you want the truth,' Peggy said. 'I can't believe what I saw in that room. Them lying there like that.' A shaking hand lifted her teacup to her lips, and she took a sip, setting it back down with a clatter. 'Look at me. I'm shaking.'

'I put three sugars in it, sir,' Turkel said in an undertone. 'It's good for shock.'

'Like tea's going to help me,' she muttered.

'I do need to ask you some questions, Mrs Keeling,' Matthew said. 'Are you up to answering them?'

She nodded. 'What do you want to know?'

'I'd like you to talk me through what happened this morning.'

'Everything?'

'Everything.'

Peggy took a deep breath. 'I got here just before nine. I came in, put my bag down on the table there, and got straight to work.'

Matthew glanced at the table, saw the vegetables, the gravy and sauce boats, the box of chocolate liqueurs. 'Which door did you use to come in?'

'The side door.' She pointed at the door behind her. 'I always use the side door. That way, no one has to let me in. I have a key.'

'It was locked?'

'Yes.'

'Go on, please.'

'I hadn't heard a thing from upstairs,' Peggy went on, 'but I just thought the Scotts were having a lie-in. I got on with everything, then as I still hadn't heard anything, I thought I would go and have a look around. I saw there wasn't a fire going in the sitting room and that the ashtray was dirty, and I thought that was peculiar. Then I looked into the dining room and that was when I found them. I'd been working down here all that time while they were dead up there.' She shook her head and took a mouthful of tea.

'When did you last see the Scotts?' Matthew asked when she'd returned the cup to the saucer.

'Last night at eight when I left.'

'Is there a maid?'

'Phyllis. She left after she'd cleaned away the Scotts' dinner, a little after seven.'

'And where is Phyllis today?'

'She's gone away for Christmas down to her parents. She was leaving as soon as she got home last night. Getting the last train.'

'Was there anyone else in the house last night when you left?'

'Not that I know of. And I don't think they would have had any visitors. They were going out for Midnight Mass. Mrs Scott bought a new dress to wear to it. It came just before I left. She showed it to me. It was the one she was wearing in there.'

She suddenly burst into tears and buried her face in her hands.

'The doctor's here, sir,' Barnes said in Matthew's ear.

Matthew nodded and told Turkel to see Mrs Keeling home. He and Barnes returned to the dining room. A large man with grey, grizzled hair was kneeling by Victoria's body.

'Good morning,' Matthew said.

The pathologist turned his head. 'Morning, inspector. Couldn't you have picked a better day for this?'

'Would that I could.' He said no more, waiting for Dr Wallace to make his preliminary examination. 'Well?' Matthew asked when the doctor clambered back to his feet.

'Death from a wound to the heart. No defensive wounds that I can see, so she didn't fight off her attacker.'

'Or didn't see the attack coming?' Matthew suggested.

'Possibly.'

'Time of death?'

Wallace pointed at the fireplace where burnt logs and embers lay. 'The fire would have been on last night, which would have made the room warm. Rigor has passed, but only just, so I would say they've been dead approximately twelve hours, which would,' he glanced at the carriage clock on the mantelpiece, 'place them as being dead by roughly midnight.' He moved around the table to Benjamin. 'This poor chap was stabbed twice. Once in the side here,' he pointed to a spot just above Benjamin's left hip, 'and in the stomach. It would have taken him quite a while to die.'

'We're still waiting for the photographer, so please don't touch it, but is that knife the weapon used?'

'Inspector, you know better than to ask,' Wallace admonished but studied the knife all the same. 'It has blood on it. It's by the body. The likelihood is that it is the murder weapon, of course, but please allow me to conduct my postmortems before saying so. And before you ask, I will do the postmortems first thing tomorrow morning.' He grimaced. 'I shall have to call my assistant in. He won't be happy about it.'

Matthew didn't care about the assistant's feelings. 'I'll see you tomorrow morning, then.'

'Eight o'clock.' Wallace snapped his medical bag shut and left.

Matthew turned to Barnes. 'Get back to the station and call everyone in,' he instructed. 'All leave is cancelled.'

When Barnes had gone, Matthew crossed the hall to the sitting room. He saw the dirty ashtray Peggy had mentioned, the hardback novel hanging over the arm of the armchair and the Christmas tree in the bay window with presents around the base. There was no sign of a disturbance.

He returned to the kitchen. The smell of goose was stronger than it had been when he interviewed Peggy and Matthew realised the oven was still on. He turned it off, thinking what a shame that all the food would not now be eaten.

He examined the side door Peggy had used to enter the house and saw nothing amiss. Then he looked down the passage at the back of the kitchen and saw two more doors. The one to the right revealed a scullery; the other was a back door leading to the garden. A pane of glass just above the lock was missing and there were shards of glass on the doormat beneath. Nicholas Baddowes' MO. But then, Matthew thought ruefully, the MO of a hundred other burglars too.

Returning to the hall, Matthew mounted the stairs to the first floor. Along the landing to what he supposed was a guest bedroom. The curtains were open, the bed made, but there were no personal items to speak of.

The master bedroom was next. Here, there was disarray. Victoria's discarded clothes – a dress, cardigan, stockings – lay over the bottom of the bed next to a rectangular box spilling white tissue paper, undoubtedly the box Victoria's new dress had arrived in. Make-up littered the dressing table, leaving only a corner for Benjamin's use, where his two hairbrushes lay next to a leather cufflink box.

The bathroom and box room revealed nothing of interest, and Matthew made his way back down the stairs to the hall. Across the passage from the kitchen was another door, this slightly ajar, and he pushed it open.

Matthew's eyes immediately fell upon the safe in the corner of the room. Its thick lead door was open and he could see it was stuffed with documents. At first glance, it appeared nothing had been taken, but then he saw that one stack of papers had been disarranged and were partially covering an empty space on the top shelf. It seemed that something was missing after all.

He returned to the hall and studied the framed photographs on a console table behind the front door. A wedding photograph caught his attention and he recognised Maxwell Carr, dressed in his army uniform, and Imogen from the picture in her case file. The difference between her on her wedding day and whenever the later photograph had been taken was striking. In the former, she was smiling and happy; in the latter, she had been smiling too, but the smile had been wistful, sad, as if conscious of having disappointed.

Maxwell Carr needed to be told of his in-laws' deaths, not least because he would be the best person to formally identify the Scotts. Matthew took out his notebook and flicked back to the notes he had made when he'd been investigating Imogen's supposed disappearance and found the Carr address. He left the Scotts' house as Barnes came hurrying along the pavement, and Matthew told him they were off to inform the son-in-law.

Chapter Thirty-Seven

Maxwell answered their knock, still in his pyjamas.

'Oh, for God's sake,' he cried at the sight of Matthew and Barnes. 'What do you want?'

'I'm sorry to disturb you, Mr Carr,' Matthew said, prepared to be patient in view of the reason for his call, 'but can we come in?'

'No, you can't. I have nothing more to say to you.' Maxwell started to close the door.

Matthew put his hand to the wood and held it open. 'I'm going to have to insist, Mr Carr. It's important, and I'd rather not do this on the doorstep.'

'Do what? You know, I would have thought even you would have better things to do on Christmas Day.' Maxwell tutted, then opened the door and waved them in impatiently. 'Come in, then. Get it over with. If it's about my wife, I can tell you—'

'I'm afraid there's been an incident at your in-laws' house,' Matthew cut him off. 'Their bodies were discovered a short while ago by their cook.'

Maxwell stared at him, uncomprehending. After a long

moment, he ran a hand through his hair and said, 'Is this some kind of joke? Because if it is, it isn't very funny.'

'No joke, Mr Carr,' Matthew assured him. 'Mr and Mrs Scott are dead.'

'Jesus,' Maxwell breathed, and sank down onto the stairs. He looked up at Matthew. 'How?'

'They were stabbed by an intruder.'

'Do you know who?'

'Not yet.'

'My God! But we were going round there in an hour.'

Matthew pounced on the word. 'We?'

'What?' Maxwell frowned up at him. 'Yes. Imogen and me. If you'd let me finish just now, I would have told you. Imogen came back.'

Matthew was astonished. 'When?'

'Two nights ago.'

'Two nights—? You should have informed us.'

'Why should I?' Maxwell said petulantly and got to his feet. 'That other detective said the case was closed. And this is hardly the time to rebuke me for not informing you my wife decided to come home. I've got to tell her about her parents. How the hell do I do that and not set her off?'

Matthew understood Maxwell's concern. If Imogen was so fragile, how would hearing her parents had been murdered affect her?

'Perhaps you should call her down?' he said.

'I suppose I should. You can tell her the news. At least that way it'll be your fault.' Maxwell thumped up the stairs. Matthew heard a door opening and then Maxwell say, 'You've got to come downstairs. There's a policeman who wants to see you.' And then, a few seconds later, 'Of course you're not in trouble. It's something else... No, you don't need to dress. Stop fussing and come on.'

Matthew turned to the mirror on the hall wall and examined his appearance. He smoothed down his hair, adjusted his tie, then caught sight of Barnes looking at him in surprise. Reddening, Matthew turned back to the stairs to see Maxwell coming back down, followed by a woman in a peach satin dressing gown and feathered mules. Her unbrushed, jaw-length brown hair was held back by silver clips and she wore no makeup. Her skin was pale with a dusting of freckles across her nose. Matthew thought he'd never seen a lovelier woman.

Imogen stared at him with wide, wary eyes, one hand grasping the banister rail, the other tugging at her dressing-gown collar.

'This is my wife,' Maxwell said with a showman-like gesture. 'Very much alive, as you can see.'

'My husband said you wanted to see me,' Imogen said. 'Why?'

'Perhaps it would be better if you sat down.' Matthew caught her husband's eye, and Maxwell grabbed her hand, tugging her into the sitting room. Matthew and Barnes followed.

'Max, don't,' she said, trying to pull her hand out of his.

'Just sit there,' he ordered, pushing her down onto the sofa.

Matthew glared at him, but Maxwell didn't notice; he was too busy lighting a cigarette. Matthew remained standing, as he wasn't invited to take a seat. He felt Imogen's eyes upon him and wondered how to begin.

'Well, get on with it,' Maxwell said impatiently.

'I'm very sorry to have to tell you, Mrs Carr,' Matthew said, 'but I have some bad news about your parents.'

Imogen's throat tightened. 'What is it?' she asked in a tremulous voice.

'They were attacked in their home last night. I'm very sorry, but they were killed.'

A cry escaped Imogen. Her hands went to her mouth, and her eyes brimmed with tears. 'Dead?' she whimpered.

Matthew nodded and stared down at his feet as Imogen sobbed. He expected Maxwell to go to her, to join her on the sofa and comfort her, but he stayed by the fireplace, smoking his cigarette.

'When did you last see Mr and Mrs Scott, Mr Carr?' Matthew asked, trying to keep his loathing for Maxwell out of both his expression and voice.

'Around half seven last night, I think it was. I called round to fetch Imogen home.'

'And they were going to Midnight Mass, I believe?'

'Yes, that's right.'

Imogen's sobs were subsiding now, Matthew noted with relief. She felt inside her dressing-gown pocket, probably searching for a handkerchief, but came up empty-handed.

Matthew gave her his. She took it with a look of surprise, as if no one had ever offered her a kindness before, and wiped her eyes.

'Mother wanted me to go with them to Midnight Mass,' she said, sniffing. 'Maybe I should have. This might not have happened if I hadn't been so stubborn.'

'I'm sure it wouldn't have made any difference,' Matthew hurried to assure her. 'You didn't want to go to Midnight Mass?'

Imogen shook her head. 'I couldn't. Not with the baby.'

'The baby?' Matthew asked.

'My wife had a child while she was away, inspector,' Maxwell said, and Matthew could hear the pride in his voice. 'It was quite unthinkable to take the baby to Midnight Mass and, of course, we couldn't leave it here alone. You may remember I no longer have a maid. She's gone to work for somebody else.' He said this pointedly, as if it was Matthew's fault Jane Prior had left his employ.

'Do you know who killed them, inspector?' Imogen asked.

'Not at present, Mrs Carr,' Matthew said. 'Was there anyone who had a grievance against Mr and Mrs Scott?'

'A grievance?' Maxwell said. 'You mean, did anyone loathe them enough to kill them?'

'Yes, that's what I mean,' Matthew replied.

'I wouldn't have thought so. Ben and Victoria were pretty harmless, you know.'

Matthew looked at Imogen. 'Mrs Carr?'

Imogen shook her head. 'I can't imagine anyone hating my parents.'

A cry came from upstairs, and Maxwell tutted in irritation. 'He's awake,' he told Imogen. 'You better go up and see to him.'

Without a word, Imogen did so.

Matthew watched her go, thinking she had taken the news better than he had hoped. 'So, your wife left because she was pregnant?' he said to Maxwell.

'Yes,' Maxwell said. 'Bloody stupid thing to do. Going away just when she needed her family most. But then, that's Imogen all over.'

'Where did she go?'

'God knows. She won't say. And quite frankly, I'm beyond caring where she went or what she got up to. The baby's well enough, that's the main thing.' He turned to the doorway at the sound of footsteps and gave an exclamation of exasperation. 'I didn't mean for you to bring him down, for heaven's sake.'

Imogen came back into the sitting room with the baby in her arms. She resettled herself on the sofa, putting the child on her lap. She looked up at Matthew. 'Will you find out who killed them?'

'I will catch them, Mrs Carr,' he said. 'I promise you.'

'I wouldn't hold your breath, Imogen,' Maxwell muttered, leaning forward to look into the bundle of blankets at the baby. He studied the tiny face with curiosity.

'I haven't failed yet, Mr Carr,' Matthew said, his jaw tightening in irritation.

'Always get your man, do you?' Maxwell said with a smirk.

'Always,' Matthew said, holding his gaze sternly. 'Tell me, Mr Carr. Do you know what valuables were kept in the safe in the room across from the kitchen?'

'Ben's study, you mean? I don't think there were any valuables in it. Just papers. Why? Is something missing?'

'That's what I need to find out. There were plenty of papers still in there, but there seemed to be an empty space, perhaps so big.' He made the size of something smaller than a shoebox with his hands to show Maxwell. 'Any idea what that might have been?'

'No, I can't thi— No, wait.' Maxwell put a hand to his forehead. 'I'd forgotten. There would have been a money box in there. Ben brought it back from the office.'

'How much was inside?' Matthew asked.

'I don't know exactly,' Maxwell said. 'But around fifteen pounds, I think. The bank had misread the figure we gave them to cover the staff's wages and sent more than we needed. By the time we realised, the bank was shut, so Ben said he'd take the extra home and put it in the safe until after Christmas.'

'Who knew the money was in the safe?'

'Ben and I, obviously. Our bookkeeper. No one else that I know of. And it couldn't have been in there for more than a day. But it's gone, you say? I suppose that means a burglar got in, doesn't it? And he killed Ben and Victoria.'

'That's a theory,' Matthew admitted.

'What else could it be?' Maxwell said impatiently, falling

down into the armchair. 'It's obvious. Victoria and Ben caught this fellow at it, so he killed them. And I know for a fact a burglar's been operating here in Craynebrook for weeks now and that he only takes money. It's been in the newspapers. Haven't caught him, have you, for all your boasting? So, it's clear you'd be wasting your time looking for someone else or trying to fathom out another motive. Keep things simple and concentrate on finding this burglar.'

'I think I know how to run a murder investigation, Mr Carr,' Matthew said stiffly.

'You should let the inspector do his job, Max,' Imogen agreed.

'If I want your opinion, I'll ask for it,' Maxwell snapped. 'What the hell do you know about anything?'

'That's no way to talk to your wife,' Matthew burst out.

Both Imogen and Maxwell stared at him; Imogen in surprise, Maxwell in anger. Matthew heard Barnes shuffle his feet and cough pointedly.

'What the devil has it got to do with you how I talk to my wife?' Maxwell yelled, and the baby on Imogen's lap stirred. Fists emerged from beneath the blankets followed by a loud cry. 'Now, look what you've done. You want to mind your own business, inspector, and stop sticking your nose into mine. You've done far too much of that already.'

'Max, please,' Imogen begged, lifting the baby up and putting it over her shoulder, wincing as it screamed in her ear.

'Oh, for God's sake,' he returned. 'Can't you shut him up? Ben and Victoria dead, a flatfoot who doesn't know his place, and now I've got to listen to that noise!' He jumped up and stormed out of the sitting room, thundering up the stairs. A moment later, a door slammed.

'I'm sorry he was so rude to you,' Imogen said.

'It's all right, Mrs Carr, I've had far worse,' Matthew

assured her. 'And I know it's not my place to say, but he really shouldn't talk to you like that.'

She shrugged. 'I'm used to it.'

He wanted to say she shouldn't have had to grown used to such treatment, but Matthew knew he'd already overstepped the mark. And besides, Barnes was there. He could feel the young detective's eyes upon him.

'We should be going,' he said. 'Don't get up,' he told Imogen. 'We'll see ourselves out.'

'You don't like the husband, do you, sir?' Barnes said as he held the car door open for Matthew.

'What's to like?' Matthew climbed into the back and told the driver to take them back to the station as Barnes got in beside him.

'He does seem right about it being a burglary gone wrong, though, sir,' Barnes said. 'You said the back door had Baddowes' MO all over it, and we know Baddowes is violent when confronted.'

Matthew nodded. 'Yes, but with his fists. There's nothing in his record to suggest he uses weapons. And if he was going through the safe and the Scotts came upon him, why weren't the bodies in the study? There's nothing to suggest a burglar was in the dining room at all.'

'Maybe he was walking through the house and had just got to the dining room when the Scotts discovered him? He killed them, then found the safe and took the money, and left. We know he only takes money.'

'And alcohol. Yet there were bottles of wine on the dining table,' Matthew pointed out. 'Brandy and whisky in the sitting room. Why didn't he take those? And what about the presents under the tree? You ever heard of a burglar passing on those? Ready-made gifts for his family?'

'Well,' Barnes said, frowning, 'if he'd just killed them,

Baddowes would have been in a bit of a panic and probably wouldn't have stopped to think about those.'

'You just said he went down to the study and through the safe after killing the Scotts,' Matthew pointed out. 'That doesn't sound panicked to me.'

'Oh yeah.' Barnes held up a finger. 'Unless he did the safe first, then went through the house, and that's when they caught him.'

'Too much speculation for my liking, Barnes. We don't know enough yet to say what did and what didn't happen.' Matthew sighed and rubbed the side of his head where it was starting to ache. 'Oh God,' he groaned as the car turned the corner and he saw a huddle of reporters outside the police station.

'The vultures are here,' Barnes muttered as the car came to a stop. 'Are you going to talk to them, sir?'

'I'll suppose I'll have to.'

Matthew clambered out of the car and the reporters immediately began shouting at him. Spotting Dickie amongst them, he pushed his way through to the front steps, turned back to them and held up a hand.

'If I could have quiet, please,' he asked. The reporters quietened. A flashbulb popped, and Matthew blinked as dark spots danced before his eyes. 'I have only a short statement to make. Mr and Mrs Scott of Brampton Drive were found dead in their home this morning. The deaths are being treated as suspicious.'

'How did they die?' someone shouted.

'The investigation is ongoing, and I'm not at liberty to divulge any details of our enquiries.'

'What was the motive?'

'We can't say yet. That's all for now.'

Chapter Thirty-Eight

Matthew and Barnes hurried up the stairs to CID. As he reached the landing, Matthew heard voices from inside.

'This is so flaming unfair,' DS Bissett said. 'I'm supposed to be on leave.'

'We're all supposed to be on leave,' Denham replied. 'We don't like being here any more than you do, so stop your whinging.'

'I've a right to whinge. I was going to a party tonight. I've a good mind to complain to Old Mouldy. The inspector shouldn't have called us in. I notice Lund isn't here. It just goes to show, doesn't it? You can get away with anything if you're an inspector, even if you are a flaming liability like him. A right bleeding Christmas this is turning out to be.'

Matthew strode into the main office, Barnes at his heels. The other detectives turned to him expectantly and he moved to stand in front of the corkboard.

'I realise none of you were expecting to be called in today,' he said, eyeing Bissett sternly. 'But this is the job we do. Crimes happen, and we have to investigate, even when it's not convenient. So, I'm sorry your Christmas has been spoilt, but I promise you, Mr and Mrs Scott have had a far worse Christmas than any of you. Just go down to the mortuary and see for yourselves. So, I don't want to hear any more complaints. Is that clear?'

The detectives glanced at one another shamefacedly, then nodded and muttered, 'Yes, sir.'

Satisfied, Matthew continued. 'An emergency call came in just after ten-thirty this morning made by a Mrs Peggy Keeling saying she'd found her employers, Mr and Mrs Scott, dead in their dining room. Mrs Keeling is the Scotts' cook. Both of the victims had been stabbed; Mrs Scott once in the heart, Mr Scott twice in the stomach. Dr Wallace estimated they had been dead at least twelve hours. We know they were still alive at 8 p.m. when Mrs Keeling left the house so, assuming the doctor doesn't change his estimate, that means we're looking at a time of death between 8 p.m. and around midnight.'

'Could it be a domestic, sir?' Rudd suggested. 'A quarrel turned violent? Each attacked the other?'

'I'm not ruling anything out until we have more information,' Matthew said, 'but it seems unlikely. There was no sign of a struggle, nothing to suggest there had been a fight. Besides which, it looks like there was only one murder weapon. If it had been a domestic, I would expect two. And there is the fact of the broken glass in the back door, suggesting an unlawful entry.'

'A burglary gone wrong, sir?' Denham wondered.

'Possibly,' Matthew nodded. 'I've spoken with their son-in-law, Mr Maxwell Carr. He told me there was at least fifteen pounds in a money box in the Scotts' safe, and that money box is missing. So, Bissett,' he nodded at the sergeant, 'I want you at the house dusting for prints. We have a suspect in mind. Nicholas Baddowes, a convicted housebreaker who may have been operating in this area over the past month or so. Check any prints you get with Baddowes' prints. Barnes will give you his case file.'

Barnes flipped through the paperwork on his desk, found Baddowes' file and handed it to Bissett.

'Dr Wallace,' Matthew went on, 'will be doing the post-mortems tomorrow morning. We have plenty to be getting on with in the meantime. The Scotts were planning to attend Midnight Mass, so I'll be contacting the church to see if they went. Denham, go with Bissett to the house. You're in charge of the evidence. That includes bringing back all the papers from the safe. I want to go through them. Barnes, Rudd. You're on the house-to-house enquiries with Uniform. That's all for now. Be back here by…' Matthew checked his wrist-watch, 'seven o'clock to see what we've got. Dismissed.'

The men filed out and Matthew retired to his office. He had just sat down at his desk when he heard footsteps and looked up to see Dickie walking towards him.

'How do?' Dickie said.

'How did you get in here?' Matthew said, lighting a cigarette.

'The front desk sergeant said I could come up.' Dickie took a seat. 'Well, this is a turn-up, isn't it? A double murder on Christmas Day? So, what's the story?'

'You were out there, Dickie,' Matthew said, jerking his head at the window. 'You heard my statement.'

'Wasn't much of a statement, though, was it? I got more from the neighbours.'

'Then you don't need me.'

'Come on. You must be able to give me something.'

'I can't discuss an investigation, Dickie. You should know better than to ask.'

Dickie sighed. 'Then tell me who's identifying the bodies.'

'The next of kin.'

'Who is?'

'Maxwell Carr. Son-in-law.'

'Why not the daughter?'

'Because I don't want to put her through that. Her husband can do it.'

'Postmortems?'

'Tomorrow morning. Dr Wallace.'

'And you can't tell me how they were killed?'

'There'll be a full statement when we're ready, Dickie,' Matthew said, rubbing his temples.

'Will Mullinger be making it or you?'

'I don't know. I haven't informed Mr Mullinger yet.'

'I can't see him giving up his Christmas Day,' Dickie muttered. 'He'll leave it to you. So, you might as well tell me what you know now.'

'For Christ's sake, Dickie,' Matthew burst out, 'give it a rest. I've told you all I'm going to.'

'All right, all right. I'll leave it.' Dickie, a little taken aback, watched as Matthew fished inside his drawer and pulled out a bottle of aspirin, tipping two tablets into his palm. 'Headache?' he asked.

Matthew nodded, throwing the tablets into his mouth and swallowing them dry. 'I've got to get on,' he said.

Dickie took the hint and rose. 'I don't expect you'll be coming round tomorrow night now you've got this case?'

'I don't think I'll be able to make it,' Matthew said apologetically, embarrassed by the way he'd snapped at his friend. 'Unless I catch the killer today, and I don't think I'll have that kind of luck. Apologise to Emma for me, would you?'

'Will do. And don't worry. You'll catch this killer. You always do.' Dickie took a step towards the door, then turned back. 'Oh, by the way, Emma loves the kitten.'

Matthew smiled. 'What's she called it?'

'Bitsy.' Dickie made a face. 'Don't ask me where she's

got that from, but she's as pleased as punch. I daresay you're going to get a little something from her to say thank you.'

'She doesn't have to do that.'

'She'll do it all the same. You know what women are like. Well, I'll see you when I see you.'

Matthew smiled ruefully. 'I expect that will be in a few hours' time, Dickie. When I make the statement.'

After Dickie left, Matthew telephoned Mullinger at home. The superintendent was not at all pleased to be disturbed and asked testily if Matthew could handle the press. After assuring him he could, Mullinger told Matthew to keep him informed and hung up.

Then Matthew called the Fiddler's Retreat. Georgie picked up the telephone and Matthew told him what had happened and that he wouldn't be able to make Boxing Day after all. Georgie was disappointed but seemed eager to get back to his Christmas dinner, hanging up almost before Matthew said goodbye.

He spent the next hour calling all the local stations to make sure they were still looking out for Baddowes and Kempe. After that, he telephoned the rectory and asked the vicar if the Scotts had been at Midnight Mass. The vicar had said they hadn't turned up, which had surprised him. When Matthew told him the Scotts were dead, there was silence for a few seconds at the end of the line before the vicar asked what had happened. Matthew told him as little as possible and rang off.

The next few hours were spent going through recent burglary reports as well as the file Barnes had got on Baddowes from Scotland Yard. It was a little after 7 p.m. when the junior detectives came back into CID for the debriefing. They gathered around him as Matthew took up his accustomed position before the corkboard.

'The vicar,' he began, 'has confirmed the Scotts didn't

show up at Midnight Mass, which backs up Dr Wallace's estimate of them being dead by midnight. That gives us a four-hour time frame. From 8 p.m. when the cook left to midnight when they were supposed to be at the church. So, what have you found out?'

Bissett spoke first. 'Plenty of prints at the house to sort through, sir. The carving knife had smudged prints on it, so I don't know if we're going to be getting anything useful off it. I'll need to get elimination prints from the family and servants. And the bodies, of course.'

'I'll bring back the victims' prints from the postmortems,' Matthew said. 'You arrange getting the others. Denham?'

'All the photographs have been taken and are being developed and evidence has been bagged up. I've sent the knife to the mortuary for Dr Wallace,' Denham said. He pointed to the box he had carried in and put down by the blackboard. 'In there's the contents of the safe you said you wanted.'

Matthew nodded in approval. 'What about the house-to-house enquiries?'

'We got something interesting,' Barnes said. 'Several of the neighbours said there was a rowdy crowd on Brampton Drive and the surrounding streets around 11 p.m. last night. They knocked on a few doors claiming to be carol singers, but they weren't the Sally Army or any other charity, and in fact, the neighbours said they were very drunk and making a nuisance of themselves. They left when one neighbour threatened to call us. But according to the Bearmans, who live a few doors down from the Scotts on the other side of the road, a man and a woman from the party lingered on the street for a while after the others had gone.'

'Near the Scotts' house?'

'Not exactly. More on the street corner.'

'Descriptions?'

'The man was tall, slim, may have had a moustache. They

thought the woman had red hair, but couldn't be sure because of the street lamps throwing the colour off. It might have been brown.'

'If this crowd were that drunk,' Matthew said, 'chances are they were drinking locally and would have been noticed. So, I want you going round the local pubs. See if they were in any of them.' The detectives grinned at each other, and Matthew held up a warning finger. 'I'm not sending you on a pub crawl. It might be Christmas, but remember you're working. Once you've done that, you can call it a night. But make sure you're all here for when I get back from the postmortems tomorrow.'

The detectives left. Matthew returned to his office, grabbed his hat and coat, picked up the box Denham had brought back from the Scotts, and left the station to go home.

Chapter Thirty-Nine

BOXING DAY

Matthew had spent much of the previous night reading through the papers from Benjamin Scott's safe. Most had been tedious business papers, and he had been about to give up and go to bed when he came across a large brown envelope. He took out the contents, his eyebrows rising as he read the letterhead at the top of the first page: George McNamara, Private Enquiry Agent.

All tiredness vanished as Matthew read the report the private investigator had sent to Benjamin about Frye. There were tales of affairs with married women, rumours of sexual encounters with female patients, allegations of coercion in financial matters. And the report was of recent date; so recent, in fact, Matthew wondered if he held in his hands a motive for murder.

He put the report back in the envelope and put the envelope on the hall table so he wouldn't forget it in the morning. Then he scooped up Bella and Hobbs and carried them into the bedroom, where they settled on the end of his bed as he climbed beneath the blankets. His dreams were of geese and dead bodies. And of Imogen Carr.

———

He was yawning as he entered the mortuary a few hours later, and Dr Wallace greeted him by instructing his assistant to provide Matthew with a cup of strong black coffee. Matthew kept back in the examination room, as he usually did during postmortems, keeping his eyes off the bodies and Wallace's dissections as much as possible. When they were over, Wallace invited him to his office.

Matthew took a seat by the desk and reached into his pocket for his cigarettes. 'You don't mind?' he asked the pathologist, showing him the packet.

'I know you need one,' Wallace said, taking his seat. 'So,' he said, glancing over the notes his assistant had made while he performed the postmortems, 'both died from their wounds. Mrs Scott suffered one wound to the heart. She would have died almost instantly. Mr Scott had one wound in his stomach, another on his left side. The poor man. It would have taken him a while to die. No defensive wounds on either of them. The murder weapon was indeed the carving knife in both instances. The depth and width of the blade fit.' He leaned back in his chair and looked over at Matthew. 'All as expected.'

Matthew nodded. 'Do you find it odd that neither of the Scotts defended themselves? Considering that the position of the wounds suggests both were facing their attacker?'

'It is a little odd,' Wallace agreed. 'But perhaps the attacks happened so fast, they had no time to react?'

'Can you tell who was attacked first?'

'I'm afraid not. Though if I were to speculate...?' He raised an eyebrow at Matthew, asking for permission.

'Please do,' Matthew said.

'Then I would speculate Mrs Scott was attacked first. The stabbing was swift and sure. Possibly she never saw it coming. Mr Scott's double wounds suggest to me the killer panicked and stabbed wildly.'

'But that would imply Mr Scott did see the attack coming? So, why no defensive wounds?'

'I couldn't say, inspector. Fortunately, it's not my job to find out. It's yours.'

Matthew sighed, acknowledging the truth of this. 'You'll let me have your full report as soon as possible?'

'By the end of the day,' Wallace nodded. 'Is that all?'

'Actually, no. There are a couple of other things I'd like to ask you. Have you come across a Dr Nigel Frye?'

'Yes, I've seen him at Sawyers Cross quite often. Why are you asking?'

'He was acquainted with the Scotts. What can you tell me about him?'

Wallace pursed his lips. 'He's very competent.'

Matthew frowned. 'Is that all you can say about him?'

'Indeed, no. I could tell you a lot more, but how much of it might be true, I couldn't say. A hospital is a perfect breeding ground for gossip, inspector. Doctors and nurses love nothing more than to talk about one another. And Frye has more than his fair share of gossip spoken about him.'

'Why is that?'

'I suppose because he's very charming, very handsome. Very attractive to certain people.'

'You mean to women?'

'He certainly is a ladies' man. Of course, he is no longer married, so there's no bar to him enjoying himself, but…'

'But what?' Matthew asked.

'If rumour is to be believed, Frye prefers married women, some of them the wives of his fellow doctors. And there are other rumours that he is over-familiar with some of his female patients.'

'What about nurses? For example, do you know if there are any rumours about Dr Frye and Nurse Sarah Kempe?'

'Strange you should ask, inspector,' Wallace said. 'They have been in each other's company quite a bit of late. Everyone thought it very odd because Nurse Kempe is not Dr Frye's usual type. She's not young, rather plain and unmarried. Oh yes, people have been talking about them.'

———

Frye woke up.

At least, he thought he did, but he couldn't be sure, for everything was still dark. He did know he felt sick, and tried swallowing to push the nausea away. That didn't work, and he licked his dry lips with the tip of his tongue, brushing away the crust upon them.

He did his best to concentrate and forced his eyelids apart, feeling them tug and split. Slowly, things came into focus. A pendant light shade above him, a painting of something garish on the wall opposite.

Frye lifted his head. A bare foot was lying on his chest, and he frowned at it, trying to work out how his foot had got there. But, he thought as he stared at it, surely his foot wasn't that small or so delicate? He wiggled his toes. The toes before him remained still.

He pushed himself up onto his elbows, and his eyes followed the length of the leg all the way up the body and along to the mass of red hair that covered the shoulders and face of a woman. Who was she? Frye wondered, feeling he should know.

His nostrils twitched. There was something acrid, unpleasant under his nose. He glanced down at his left shoulder and saw that his shirt was speckled and stained with vomit. He presumed it was his own. Groaning, he sat up, pushing the woman's leg away. She didn't stir as he twisted his body and set his stockinged feet on the floor.

Frye stared at the table beside the sofa. There were over-flowing ashtrays, empty gin and champagne bottles, and a syringe! What was that doing there? Why had he got a syringe out of his bag?

But no ... wait a minute. Frye shook his head. That syringe couldn't be his. He hadn't had his doctor's bag with him when he went down the pub.

Yes, the pub. That was it. He'd gone to the pub. Last night, was it? Or the night before?

Frye looked over at the woman still asleep. He'd met her there, hadn't he? He'd had a few drinks with her, her and her friends. They'd had the drinks and… then what?

'Where am I?' he asked himself in a whisper as he looked around the room. Wherever it was, it wasn't up to his usual standard. Mismatched furniture with fraying upholstery, dirty clothes hanging off the back of chairs, dust layering surfaces, rubbish strewn on the floor.

Frye looked down at himself. He wasn't in a much better state. His soiled shirt was pulled out of the waistband of his trousers, and these were also spotted and stained with the contents of his stomach. His braces were hanging down. His flies were undone. His clumsy fingers buttoned them back up, and he got unsteadily to his feet. The movement caused his brain to rock inside his skull, and he closed his eyes, blowing his cheeks out as a wave of nausea hit him. He waited for it to fade before moving around the table and making his way to the door, grabbing his jacket on the way out.

The sunlight blinded him as he emerged onto the pave-ment. Blinking, a hand shielding his eyes, Frye looked first left, then right down the street, trying to determine which way to go. The Royal Albert Hall loomed over him. *Dear God,* he thought. *How did I get to Kensington? And what day is it?*

The cold was waking him, sobering him. He turned his collar up, pulled his jacket tighter across his chest, and turned his feet to the left.

Chapter Forty

Barnes had a mug of tea ready when Matthew arrived in CID. 'Thought you might need that, sir,' he said with an understanding smile. None of the detectives liked attending postmortems. 'Denham's called in. He apologises for not being here, but says he's looking into a lead he got last night, and he'll be in as soon as he's finished.'

'We won't wait for him, then.' Matthew gestured for everyone to gather round. 'The postmortems,' he began, 'confirm the murder weapon was the carving knife. Neither victim had defensive wounds, so they didn't attempt to fend off their attacker. We don't know who was attacked first, although Dr Wallace has speculated Victoria Scott was the first victim. I don't want us treating that as fact but it's reasonable to assume that whoever was attacked second would have had time to react, so the fact that they didn't is something we need an answer to.'

'Shock, sir?' Barnes suggested.

'It's possible,' Matthew conceded as Denham entered the CID office.

'Sorry I'm late, sir,' he said to Matthew, unwinding his scarf from his neck. 'Barnes told you—'

'Yes,' Matthew said. 'What was the lead?'

Denham hitched himself onto the edge of a desk. 'The crowd that was on Brampton Drive seemed to visit every pub in Craynebrook from Christmas Even afternoon onwards. But they finished up at the King George. They were there from around nine o'clock until just before chucking out time.'

'Names?'

'No one knows who they were. They weren't locals. Mr Greader, landlord at the King George, reckoned they were from uptown, slumming it here.'

'Slumming in Craynebrook?' Matthew raised an eyebrow.

'Yeah, I know,' Denham laughed. 'We're not exactly Whitechapel. But they seemed like toffs to him. Anyway, while no one seems to know who they were, Greader says one of his regulars hooked up with them, so he might be able to tell us something. That's where I was this morning, sir.'

'Who was this regular?'

'A man called Nigel Frye.'

Matthew started. 'Dr Frye?'

'Yes, sir. Do you know him?'

'I met him when I was investigating Imogen Carr as a missing person. He's friendly with Sarah Kempe, who is associated with Baddowes and Benjamin Scott had Frye investigated by a private enquiry agent. Turned up quite a lot of unsavoury things on him. What did Dr Frye have to say about this crowd?'

Denham shook his head. 'I haven't been able to talk to him yet. He wasn't at home when I called.'

'Try his surgery,' Matthew said. 'And if he's not there, try Sawyers Cross.' He nodded at Denham's telephone. 'Do it now.'

Denham rose to get the telephone directory and make the calls.

'Sir!' Bissett, who had been peering at prints through a

magnifying glass while Denham talked, called out suddenly. 'I've got a match!'

'With Baddowes?'

'Yes, sir.' Bissett grabbed the prints from the case file and the prints he had taken at the Scotts' house to show him. 'It's only a partial print. This one,' he said, showing Matthew a photograph, 'I got from the handle of the safe. But I reckon that is a match with Baddowes's right thumb.'

Matthew took the two sets of prints and the magnifying glass Bissett handed him, and studied the prints, going back and forth between them to examine the swirls. He wasn't an expert when it came to fingerprints, but he could see the similarity.

'Looks like a match,' he agreed, handing the prints back to Bissett.

Denham hung up his receiver and turned to Matthew. 'Dr Frye isn't at the surgery, sir, and he hasn't turned up for his shift at the hospital. They haven't heard from him. I've told them to call us if he turns up. But it sounds a bit dodgy, don't you think?'

'More than a bit,' Matthew agreed. 'Get a constable posted outside Frye's house. If he comes home, I want to know. I'm going back to see the Carrs to ask if the Scotts had any association with Sarah Kempe.'

———

Matthew heard the baby crying as he approached the Carrs' front door and rang the bell.

'The door, Max,' he heard Imogen call.

'You get it,' Maxwell shouted back.

'I've got the baby,' came Imogen's impatient reply.

He heard heavy footsteps in the hall and the front door was yanked open.

'Oh God,' Maxwell cried. 'It's you.' He waved Matthew into the hall and shut the door. 'Well? What is it now?'

'Do you know if the Scotts knew a woman called Sarah Kempe?' Matthew asked without preamble.

Maxwell frowned. 'Sarah Kempe? Well, yes, of course they did. She was the nurse Victoria hired.'

Matthew stared at him in astonishment. 'How did Mrs Scott come to hire her? Through an agency?'

'No, nothing like that. Frye put Victoria onto her. Said he worked with her at the hospital and could recommend her. But Victoria got rid of her earlier this week.'

'Mrs Scott fired her? Why was that?'

'Victoria didn't say,' Maxwell shook his head. 'But I got the impression it was something to do with Frye. You need to ask him about the nurse. He'll tell you what you want to know.' He cast an irritated look up the stairs as Imogen shouted for him. 'For God's sake,' he muttered, and pushed Matthew aside to open the front door. 'I've got things to do,' he said as he all but pushed Matthew out.

Chapter Forty-One

Denham put his head around the office doorway. 'I just had a call from downstairs, sir. Dr Frye turned up at his house twenty minutes ago. Uniform's brought him in and I've told them to put him in the interview room.'

'Has he said anything?' Matthew asked, screwing the cap back onto his fountain pen.

'I don't think so. By all accounts, he was in a bit of a state when they picked him up. Looks like he's been dragged through a hedge backwards, apparently.'

'He's been roughed up?' Matthew asked.

Denham shook his head. 'Hungover, Copley reckons. Said he stinks of booze and his clothes are none too clean.'

'But he is sober?'

'Just about.'

'Just about will do,' Matthew said, rising and gesturing for Denham to lead the way.

Frye looked up as Matthew and Denham entered the interview room.

'I need a smoke,' he said as they took a seat on the opposite side of the table.

Matthew fished his packet of cigarettes and matches out of his pocket and put them in front of Frye.

Frye helped himself, leaning back in the chair as he took his first drag of the cigarette. His eyes closed, and as he blew out the smoke, a heavy sigh escaped his lips. 'God, I needed that,' he said.

'Rough night, Dr Frye?' Matthew asked.

Frye rested his weary eyes on him. 'You could say that. I had rather too much to drink. Christmas, you know? Time of celebration and all that. So I'd be very grateful if you could get all this nonsense over with, inspector. I'd like to take a bath and go to bed.'

'Nonsense, Dr Frye? The murder of two people?'

Frye's jaw tightened at the rebuke. 'A poor choice of words on my part, inspector. Of course, it's terrible what's happened, but it's nothing to do with me. I really can't help you.'

'When did you last see the Scotts?' Matthew said, lighting a cigarette.

Frye sighed heavily. 'I saw Mrs Scott on Monday. I hadn't seen Mr Scott for several days before that.'

'And your relationship with them was friendly?'

'Our relationship was professional. Mrs Scott was my patient.'

'And your relationship with Mr Scott?'

He shrugged. 'Cordial.'

'I see.' Matthew took a drag of his cigarette, keeping his eyes on Frye as he fidgeted in his chair. 'You've been away, Dr Frye?'

'Yes. I went away for Christmas.'

'No one seemed to know that. Not Dr Woodrow or the hospital.'

'I'm under no obligation to inform them of my movements, inspector.'

'But you were expected at the hospital. You were down for a shift today.'

Frye tapped his cigarette against the ashtray. 'Yes, of course. Forgive me. I'd forgotten. The going-away was a spur-of-the-moment decision.'

'Where did you go?'

'Just away.'

'Away where?'

'What does it matter where?' Frye attempted a laugh. 'I wasn't here. That's all you need to know.'

'All right,' Matthew said, willing to let Frye think he was having his way for the moment. 'Tell me where you were on Christmas Eve night.'

'I was in the King George public house on the high street,' Frye said.

'From what time?'

'From around seven-thirty, I think it was, until a little before closing time.'

'Were you there alone?'

'Yes.'

'All evening?'

Frye licked his dry lips. 'No, I got talking to a group of people.'

'And who were they?'

'Just people, inspector. I didn't know them.'

'And yet you left with them?'

'I may have left the pub at the same time, but I wasn't with them.'

'We have witnesses who say you left with them,' Matthew insisted.

'Witnesses?' Frye shook his head in bewilderment. 'Good heavens. Is it a crime now to make new acquaintances?'

'Where did you go when you left the pub?' Matthew continued.

'I don't remember.'

'Could you have gone to Brampton Drive with your new friends, pretending to be carol singers?'

Frye swallowed nervously. 'No. Definitely not. We didn't go anywhere near there. That's really not my kind of thing, you know. I mean, carol singing.' He attempted a laugh at the absurdity of the suggestion.

'How can you be so definite you didn't go there if you don't remember where you went?' Matthew wondered.

'No, I, er… I do know we didn't go there,' Frye blustered. 'Not at all.'

'That's very odd, Dr Frye. Because we have a witness who says he saw a man matching your description quite near the Scotts' house that night.'

'Well, he's wrong. It wasn't me.'

'This man near the Scotts' house was with a woman. Any idea who that woman might be?'

A shaking hand lifted the cigarette to Frye's lips. 'No. No idea at all. How can I have? I wasn't there. Now, is that all?'

Matthew shook his head. 'I'm afraid that's not all. Far from it. You see, if you don't tell me where you've been or with whom, Dr Frye, I won't be able to eliminate you from our enquiries.'

'Eliminate me!' Frye stared at him. 'As what?'

'As a suspect,' Matthew said.

'But that's absurd. I haven't murdered anyone.'

'And yet you won't tell us where you were or who you were with?' Matthew pointed out. 'What have you got to hide, Dr Frye?'

Frye put his head in his hand and squeezed his eyes shut. 'Look,' he said after a moment. 'I will tell you and then we can stop this nonsense. I was with a woman. So now you know and I'm going to leave.' He made to rise, but Matthew put out his hand.

'Not just yet, Dr Frye. Please remain seated.'

Frye sank back in the chair.

'I need to know the name and address of this woman,' Matthew said, and glanced at Denham who was waiting with pen poised above his notebook.

'I don't know her name,' Frye shrugged. 'And I don't know her address, either.'

'You don't know her name?' Matthew asked.

'I was rather tight, inspector, and, well, it wasn't as if I was planning on seeing her again.' He looked from Matthew to Denham and laughed. 'For heaven's sake, we're all men of the world here, aren't we?' When neither of them replied, his jaw tightened. 'I met her in the pub and we went back to her flat. I didn't leave until a few hours ago. You understand? Now that isn't a crime, inspector, unless there's been a law passed against fornication over the last few days.'

'I still need her name, Dr Frye,' Matthew said.

'For God's sake, why?'

'To confirm your whereabouts.'

'I've told you where I was and with whom. Now, I'm not going to be ungentlemanly and tell you the lady's name and address so you can embarrass her with your Puritan ideas. And if you're not going to let me go, then I want to see a solicitor. I'm not saying another word without one.'

Chapter Forty-Two

SATURDAY, 27TH DECEMBER

Lund was at his desk when Matthew entered their office the next morning.

'Hello,' Matthew said. 'How was your Christmas?'

'It was good, ta,' Lund said. 'I hear you've had an eventful couple of days. A double murder?' He shook his head with a smile. 'Why does it always happen to you, eh?'

'I wish I knew,' Matthew replied grimly.

'Denham's filled me in on the case. Says you've got a fella in the cells for it. A doctor. Has he coughed to it?'

Matthew shook his head. 'Said he had nothing to do with it.'

Lund raised a rueful eyebrow. 'Don't they all? Has he got an alibi?'

'He says he was with a woman from Christmas Eve to yesterday, but he won't give us her name.'

'Why not, if she can confirm his whereabouts?'

'Says it's ungentlemanly, but I doubt that's the real reason. There must be something about her he doesn't want us to know, although I can't think what that could be.'

Matthew sighed. 'He insisted on a solicitor before I could get anywhere with him. I left him to stew in the cells.'

'And you fancy him for the murders?'

'I'm not sure. Frye doesn't strike me as someone who would get his own hands dirty, but he was almost certainly at the house around the time of the murders.'

'So, what are you thinking?'

'It's just an idea, but he was friendly with Sarah Kempe, who is associated with Baddowes. His fingerprint is on the safe and money's missing.'

'You're thinking the three of them might be in it together?'

'Maybe. Frye has a motive for wanting Scott dead. I found a private investigator's report on Frye in Benjamin Scott's safe. He turned up some rather unsavoury things and Frye would have been keen to keep them quiet. Sarah Kempe would have been in it for the money along with Baddowes, but…' Matthew trailed off, shaking his head.

'But what?' Lund pressed.

'The murders feel like an accident. A spur-of-the-moment thing. Not a planned conspiracy between three people.'

'Maybe the murders weren't planned. Maybe it was just money they were after, and this report you found, but it all went wrong.'

'But Baddowes only took money from the safe. He didn't take the private investigator's report.'

'An oversight? Or he didn't know it was in there? Or maybe Frye just wanted Benjamin Scott shut up?'

'I suppose you could be right,' Matthew nodded.

'It does happen occasionally.' Lund called, 'Barnes! Where's that tea?'

Barnes came in carrying two cups and saucers. 'Rudd says he's bringing someone up to see you, sir,' he said, putting one cup on Matthew's desk. 'Says he has information about the Scotts.'

'Who is it?' Matthew asked, taking a sip of the tea.

'Their solicitor, apparently.'

As he said this, Rudd came to the door. A tall man, aged about forty-five, wearing a black three-piece suit and carrying a bowler hat in one hand and a briefcase in the other, was a few steps behind.

'This is Mr Deakins, sir,' Rudd said. 'Mr Deakins, this is Inspector Stannard. He's in charge of the case.'

Matthew rose and gestured for Deakins to take a seat. 'I understand you have information about the Scotts?'

Deakins put his bowler on the desk. 'I'm not sure if I'm wasting your time, inspector. I may be making something out of nothing. I am breaking client confidentiality by doing this, but...' He set his briefcase on his lap and opened it. Taking out a folder, he passed it across the desk to Matthew. 'If you look at that, I'll explain.'

Matthew took the papers out of the folder and studied the topmost page. 'A contract?'

'A setting up of a business, yes,' Deakins said. 'You see, as the Scotts' solicitor, I handle all of their affairs, personal and business. Mrs Scott engaged me to write up that contract for her earlier this month. I thought it rather odd at the time, but of course, the client's business is their own. It wasn't for me to comment. You'll see,' he leant forward and pointed, 'it's a contract between Mrs Scott and Dr Nigel Frye.'

'She was planning to set him up in a private practice?'

'That's right. For a fifty per cent share of the profits.'

Matthew turned to the last page of the document. He saw the signatures of Mrs Victoria Scott, Dr Nigel Frye and Miss Sarah Kempe! It was dated the 20th of December.

'Sarah Kempe,' he said, pointing Deakins to her signature.

'Yes. She witnessed the signatures.'

'But she has no part in the proposed business?'

'None, according to that contract. The contract was odd in itself,' Deakins went on. 'Mrs Scott had never been involved in any kind of business to my knowledge. But, and this is why I'm here, inspector, Mr Scott came to my office and told me it was all off. That I was to do no more work on it.'

'Why did he do that?' Matthew asked.

'He didn't say. But he was angry about the whole thing. I don't suppose it is relevant, but my wife insisted I come here and tell you about it after she read of the murders in the newspaper.'

'Your wife was quite right, Mr Deakins. Do you know Dr Frye?'

'No, I've never met him. And I certainly don't want to suggest he's done anything wrong. It was a perfectly legitimate business venture. But in view of what's happened...' Deakins shrugged. 'Am I wasting your time with this, inspector?'

'Not at all,' Matthew assured him.

––––––––

Matthew passed the contract to Maxwell. 'Did you know about this?'

Maxwell scanned the first page. 'A contract between Victoria and Frye? No. It's the first I've heard of it. But it doesn't surprise me. Victoria was soppy about Frye. Ben and I both thought so. And we knew he was up to something with her.'

'What do you mean, up to something?' Matthew asked, taking the contract back and putting it in his pocket.

'We thought he was after her money, her giving him a loan that he would never have to pay back, that sort of thing.

It's no secret Frye's hard up. But I had no idea he was wangling a practice out of her.'

'Mr Scott never mentioned this contract to you?'

'Not a word. But then,' Maxwell said bitterly, 'Ben always did keep things close to his chest. But I don't understand. If Victoria and Frye were going into business together, why was he suddenly *persona non grata* with her?'

'*Persona non grata*?'

Maxwell smirked. 'It means Frye wasn't welcome anymore, inspector.'

'I know what it means,' Matthew snapped as Imogen entered the room. He got to his feet.

'You have news, inspector?' she asked.

'He's asking about Frye,' Maxwell said.

'Dr Frye?' She frowned at Matthew. 'Why? What has he done?'

Maxwell answered for him. 'Your mother was planning to set him up with a private practice. And you know how she was going to do that? With your money, darling.'

'My money?'

'What do you mean with your wife's money, Mr Carr?' Matthew asked.

'Imogen gets an allowance from Victoria. Victoria said she was thinking of stopping it, and...' Maxwell laughed and shook his head. 'It all makes sense now. She said she might have another use for it, but she wouldn't tell me or Ben what she meant. Now we know, don't we? She was going to give it to that quack.'

'Mother was going to stop my allowance?' Imogen said dejectedly. She raised her hand to her head, pushing a curl back into place. As she did so, the cuff of her blouse fell back, and Matthew saw bruises on her wrist.

She saw him looking and hastily buttoned the cuff,

casting a worried glance at Maxwell. Her eyes appealed to Matthew to say nothing.

'Is that all?' Maxwell suddenly asked, watching the pair of them with suspicion.

'That's all for the moment.' Matthew nodded a farewell to Imogen and left the sitting room. As he turned the latch on the front door, Imogen whispered, 'Inspector!'

He whirled around to face her. 'You don't need to put up with him,' Matthew burst out. 'If he's hurting you—'

Imogen put her fingers on his mouth to silence him. 'It was my fault,' she said with a shake of her head. 'I got on his nerves.'

'Imogen! What are you doing?' Maxwell yelled from the sitting room.

'Do you have any suspects, inspector?' she asked, ignoring him. 'Do you know who killed my parents?'

'I have suspects, yes.'

'Dr Frye?'

'I really can't say. I'm sorry.'

'But you will tell me, won't you? As soon as you know who killed them?'

'I'll keep you informed,' he promised.

'Imogen!' Maxwell yelled again.

'You better go,' Imogen said wearily and Matthew opened the door.

'If ever you need me,' he said as he stepped down onto the front step, 'just call the station.'

She smiled as she shut the door.

Chapter Forty-Three

'Look who's come to see us,' Lund said with a warning glance as Matthew entered their office, and gestured at Walsh sitting in the visitor chair.

Walsh got to his feet. 'It's good to see you again, Stannard.'

'Were we expecting you?' Matthew asked.

'No. But there's been a development in my case and I could do with some help.'

'Again?' Matthew brushed past him to his desk. 'I'm sorry, but I've got a double murder to solve, and this time, I can't spare anyone to work on your case.' He called for Denham.

'Yes, sir?' Denham said, putting his head around the doorframe.

'I want Frye's house searched. See to it.'

'Will do, sir. By the way, Mr Palmer's arrived to represent Dr Frye.'

'Fine. Get on that search.'

'Got more evidence?' Lund asked.

'Perhaps,' Matthew said, not wanting to talk about his case in front of Walsh.

'It sounds like you might have your case wrapped up quite soon,' Walsh said. 'I have to say, from what I've heard, this doctor you've got in a cell sounds guilty to me.'

'What do you mean, from what you've heard?' Matthew demanded. 'Who's been talking to you about my case?'

Walsh gave a hesitant laugh. 'We're all coppers, aren't we, Stannard?'

'I said—'

'Why don't you get yourself a cup of tea, Walsh?' Lund cut Matthew off. He rose and held the door open, gesturing Walsh out. When Walsh reluctantly went, he closed the door and turned to Matthew with a smirk. 'You don't like him, do you?'

Matthew said nothing.

'He's as good as you at the job,' Lund went on, 'according to Rudd. Is that why you can't stand him? You're worried he's going to steal your limelight?'

'Give it a rest, Lund,' Matthew said.

'Oh, we are grumpy today, aren't we?' Lund chuckled, going back to his desk. 'But just so you know. Old Mouldy knows he's here.'

'So?'

'So, he told you to be nice, didn't he? If Walsh goes complaining to him that you gave him the brush-off—'

'He's not that petty, surely?'

'We don't know what Walsh is like, do we? Except that he knows how to ingratiate himself.' He gestured at the partition window. 'I mean, look at that. He's got Rudd eating out of his hand.'

Matthew followed Lund's gaze and saw Rudd hand Walsh a cup of tea and proffer him the biscuit tin. 'Rudd's just being polite.'

'Doesn't look that way to me. You see that look on Rudd's face? That's the look he normally gives you, and that, sunshine, is hero worship. How do you like playing second fiddle?'

'Have you come in just to wind me up, Lund?' Matthew asked irritably.

Lund grinned. 'What else do I come here for?' But then he held up his hands, and his expression became serious. 'Just remember to be agreeable when it comes to Walsh if you don't want to get it in the neck from Old Mouldy.'

'I'll bear it in mind,' Matthew muttered, watching Lund as he flicked through the pages of a case file. 'What have you got there?'

'This? Walsh's case file on his baby snatches. He gave it to me to have a look through. He reckons he's identified his snatcher.' Lund held up a photograph. 'Susan Madden.'

Matthew rose and crossed the office, taking the photograph from Lund.

Lund went on. 'Walsh wants to show that to a few of the local stations. See if they recognise her. She doesn't ring any bells with me.' He looked up at Matthew. 'What's up with you?'

'What name did you say?'

'Susan Madden. Why?'

'That's not Susan Madden,' Matthew declared. 'That's Sarah Kempe!'

Chapter Forty-Four

Matthew set the contract on the table in front of Frye. 'Do you recognise that document, doctor?' he asked and lit a cigarette.

Frye swallowed nervously and glanced at his solicitor, Joseph Palmer, sitting beside him. Palmer's eyes squinted at the document as he read.

'Yes,' Frye said. 'It's a contract Mrs Scott had written up.'

'She was planning to set you up in a private practice?'

'It was an idea she had, yes.'

'It was more than an idea.' Matthew turned to the last page of the document. 'It's been signed. By Mrs Scott and you.'

Frye nodded. 'That's correct. Mrs Scott was very keen to make it happen.'

'She was?'

'Absolutely. She did it all, that is, she had that written up without telling me anything about it. It was a surprise for me.'

'If she was so eager, why did Mr Scott inform his wife's solicitor that this contract wouldn't go ahead?'

Frye tugged at his collar. 'Well, it had seemed a good idea, but then it fell through.'

'Why was that?'

'It just did.'

'There must have been a reason.'

'We couldn't agree on the terms, as it turned out,' Frye said with a shrug.

'That must have been disappointing.'

'A little, yes, but these things happen, inspector.'

'So, who decided the practice wasn't going to go ahead?'

'It was a mutual decision.'

'Really?'

'Yes, really.'

'And amicably made? You remained friendly with Mrs Scott?'

'Of course.'

'And with Mr Scott?'

Frye's expression faltered. 'Well, it had nothing to do with Benjamin. I don't even know if he knew about it.'

'Oh, he knew. It was Mr Scott who instructed the solicitor, Mr Deakins, to tear the contract up and do no further work on it. According to him, Mr Scott was furious about it all.'

'Probably because Victoria had done it without his knowledge. Ben's very possessive, you know.'

'Was very possessive,' Matthew corrected.

'Yes, of course. Was.'

'But,' Matthew went on, 'that doesn't quite make sense. I think your relations with Mr Scott weren't quite as cordial as you make out. Mr Carr told me you were suddenly no longer welcome at the Scotts' house. Neither of the Scotts wanted you there.'

'I didn't hear a question, inspector,' Palmer said.

'My question, Mr Palmer,' Matthew said, 'is that if the parting of the ways was on friendly terms, why would the

Scotts be so angry and so unaccommodating towards your client? Dr Frye?'

Frye's mouth pursed, but he didn't answer.

'We've searched your house,' Matthew went on, nodding at Denham, who put an envelope on the table. 'We found this letter from Mrs Scott.' He picked up the letter and read aloud. '"All those old women you charmed into giving you their money. Well, that's not going to happen this time. You won't get a penny more from me!" That doesn't read as amicable to me.'

'Victoria was being melodramatic in that letter,' Frye waved his hand dismissively. 'She'd been told a lot of nonsense about me.'

'By a private enquiry agent,' Matthew nodded. 'I've read the report he submitted to Mr Scott. This agent dug up quite a lot about you, didn't he?'

'I really have no idea what he dredged up against me but I can guarantee that it will all be untrue. Men of that sort are gutter rats. They're in the business of muck-raking. They make it all up. You can't believe a word they say. In fact, I'm thinking of suing that fellow for defamation of character.'

'So, there's no truth that you had extramarital affairs? Or about the money you charmed out of your patients?'

'Infidelity isn't a criminal offence, inspector,' Palmer said. 'And in regard to these money matters, do you have any proof of them? Beyond the allegations in this private enquiry agent's report, I mean?'

'I have heard similar stories from other parties,' Matthew said. 'And the BMC held an enquiry into the allegations.'

'And they cleared me of any wrongdoing,' Frye said. 'They found nothing. It was all just jealousy. People stirring.'

'Some might say there's no smoke without fire,' Matthew suggested.

'Are you referring to gossip, inspector?' Palmer asked.

'Whatever you've heard, or what this private enquiry agent claims to have uncovered, it isn't evidence against my client of murder. So, please move on.'

'All right, Mr Palmer,' Matthew said. 'I'll move on. I'll move on to Sarah Kempe.'

There was a flicker of apprehension behind Frye's eyes. 'What about her?' he asked warily.

'You're very well acquainted with Miss Kempe, aren't you?'

'I wouldn't say well acquainted. She works at the hospital.'

'Where you've been seen in private conversation with her often. She witnessed this contract. You installed her as Mrs Scott's private nurse, even though Mrs Scott wasn't in particular need of looking after.'

'Victoria was a hypochondriac,' Frye protested. 'She wanted looking after, so I offered to find her a private nurse. She wanted one, and Sarah needed the money.'

'Did you know Sarah Kempe had criminal associations?'

Frye looked away. 'No, I didn't.'

Matthew sensed that was a lie. 'She hasn't been to work since last Monday,' he went on. 'And she cleared out of the room where she lived. Do you know where she's gone?'

'I have no idea.'

'The woman you were with on Christmas Eve. It wouldn't have been her, would it?'

Frye barked a laugh. 'Are you serious? You think I was with Sarah? For God's sake, have you seen her?' he cried. 'Sarah has the face of a back end of a bus, and you think I would—' He broke off, shaking his head at Matthew. 'I'm really not that desperate for female company, inspector.'

'Then who were you with on Christmas Eve?'

Frye glanced at Palmer, who gave him a nod. He sighed and said, 'If you insist on knowing, her name was Venetia,

and she lived in Kensington, near the Albert Hall. I don't
know the exact address, but her flat was on the second floor
of whatever building it was. You find her, inspector, and
she'll tell you I had nothing to do with the Scotts being killed.
You've got the wrong man.'

Chapter Forty-Five

Venetia was easy to find. Within a few hours, Denham discovered a Lady Venetia Hickson-Cross lived at Flat 2a, Albert Hall Mansions, Kensington and he and Matthew made their way there.

The woman who answered their knock was dressed in a green silk kimono tied loosely around her waist and, as far as Matthew could tell, nothing else. She looked at him and Denham through half-open eyes.

'Lady Venetia Hickson-Cross?' Denham asked.

'Yes,' she said, leaning her head against the door.

'Police.' He showed her his warrant card. 'Can we come in?'

'Police? Oh, what fun!'

She let the door swing open and walked away down the hall, her mules making slapping noises against the soles of her feet. Denham and Matthew followed her into a large sitting room.

Matthew's nostrils wrinkled. The flat smelt as if it hadn't been cleaned for months and it looked a mess. A large sofa draped with wrinkled clothing and blankets occupied the middle of the room, its upholstery heavily stained. Dirty plates and cups littered the floor. On the table were newspapers and magazines, dog-eared and marked with coffee rings.

Venetia sank down onto the sofa, leaning back and lifting her legs onto the seat. An arm went over her head to hang down behind her while the other dangled over the side of the sofa, her fingertips touching the floor. She closed her eyes.

'Can you sit up so we can talk, please?' Matthew asked.

'I'm listening, Mr Policeman,' she said, her mouth curving in a smile.

Matthew shared an exasperated look with Denham. 'Can you confirm you were with a Dr Nigel Frye from the evening of Christmas Eve until yesterday afternoon?'

'Who?' she asked, frowning.

'Dr Nigel Frye.' Matthew eyed the empty wine and champagne bottles littered on and around the table. 'Miss Hickson-Cross, are you drunk?'

She giggled. 'I think I may be.'

With a noise of vexation, Denham grabbed her arm and jerked her upright. 'You need to pay attention,' he said sternly.

'All right, Denham,' Matthew murmured and jerked his head for him to back away as Venetia rubbed her arm where the sergeant's fingers had dug in. 'Miss Hickson-Cross. Can you confirm Dr Frye was with you on Christmas Eve night?'

'He was a doctor? I didn't know that.' She threw herself back on the sofa, casting a sulky glance at Denham.

'He was here, then?'

'Oh, yes, he was here. I picked him up in a pub.'

'And he left when?'

'I don't know. He was gone when I woke up, thank God.'

'When you left the pub in Craynebrook, where did you go?'

'We walked for a while.'

'Where?'

'Just around.' She grinned, showing perfect teeth. 'We thought we'd sing some carols to the locals, but they didn't want to know, the spoilsports.'

'Did you walk to Brampton Drive?'

'Don't ask me where we went. I don't know.'

'It's important you try to remember. I need to know if Dr Frye left you at any time and went into a house.'

'Left me?' she cried. 'I couldn't get him off me. Clung like a barnacle. Really, old men are so pathetic.' She ran her hand through her curls, the kimono sleeve falling down to her elbow, and closed her eyes.

Matthew saw the marks on the inside of her forearm and understood. Venetia Hickson-Cross wasn't just drunk. He studied the detritus on the table and lifted a magazine, uncovering a syringe and a smear of white powder.

'What is this, Miss Hickson-Cross?' Matthew asked, pointing at the powder.

She opened a bleary eye. 'Oh,' she said, smiling like a naughty schoolgirl. 'You're not supposed to see that, Mr Policeman. It's just a little something to make me feel good.'

'Has this been prescribed by your doctor?' Matthew asked.

'What?'

'You do realise these kinds of drugs can only be prescribed by a doctor, Miss Hickson-Cross?'

'Oh, you're not going to be tiresome, are you? What is it with men from the lower classes? You're all so puritanical. Your doctor objected to my little indulgence, too. Absolutely refused to try it. Can you believe he said he couldn't risk his reputation? Do you have any idea how boring you all are?'

'I'm going to get rid of it, sir,' Denham said, reaching for the syringe.

'You leave that alone,' Venetia cried and grabbed his hand.

Denham shook her off, but she leapt off the sofa with surprising speed and gave him a vicious shove. Denham fell and cried out in pain as his back slammed into the wooden coffee table.

Matthew grabbed Venetia's arms as she continued to push against Denham. 'Enough,' he yelled at her and pinned her arms to her side.

'Get off me,' she said, and stamped on his foot.

He hissed in pain. 'That's done it. Miss Hickson-Cross, you're under arrest. Denham,' he said to the sergeant who was clambering to his feet, 'take her to the car.'

'With pleasure, sir,' Denham said and took hold of her.

'You can't do this,' Venetia yelled as Denham pushed her towards the door. 'Don't you know who my father is?'

———

The CID main office was empty when Matthew and Denham got back to Craynebrook, but Walsh was in the inspectors' office, and it was clear from the grim expression on his face that he had been waiting for Matthew's return.

Matthew turned to Denham. 'We'll leave Frye in his cell until the morning. We'll review everything then, and if we don't have any reason to hold him, we'll let him go. You can get off home now.'

Denham thanked him, bid him good night and left, casting a curious glance back at Walsh.

Walsh came out into the main office as Matthew moved to the tea urn. 'When were you going to tell me?' he demanded.

'I'm assuming you mean about Susan Madden?' Matthew said as he stirred sugar into his tea.

'About Susan Madden being Sarah Kempe? Yes. When were you going to tell me?'

'When I had a moment,' Matthew said, taking a mouthful of tepid tea. 'I have been rather busy.'

'You think I don't know what you're up to, Stannard?'

'And what am I up to, Walsh?' he sighed.

'Murder trumps baby snatching, doesn't it? You get your girl for murder, and no one's going to care about my cases. You get all the glory and I get nothing.'

'You think that's what I'm up to, do you?'

'Well, it's a chance to get your name in the 'papers.' Walsh sketched a banner headline with his hands. 'DI Stannard Does It Again.'

Matthew banged his mug down on the filing cabinet. 'You know what you are, Walsh?'

'What?'

'You're a—'

'Hello hello,' a voice said, cutting Matthew off.

Both men turned towards the door where Lund was standing, hands in his trouser pockets, rocking on the balls of his feet.

'What's going on here then?' he asked.

'I thought you'd gone home,' Matthew said.

'I'll be off soon,' Lund said. 'I wanted to find out how you got on with your mysterious woman.'

'She confirmed Frye's alibi, as did the hall porter. But it wasn't a complete loss. She was doped up to the eyeballs and shoved Denham over, so I arrested her for assault and dropped her off at the local nick.'

Lund shook his head in amused disbelief. 'Only you would go to confirm an alibi and end up arresting a dopehead.' He looked over at Walsh. 'And what are you still doing here, Walsh?'

'DI Walsh thinks I'm withholding information from him to make myself look good,' Matthew said.

'And are you?' Lund asked.

'Of course I'm not.'

'Of course you're not. So, why don't you tell Walsh what you know about this Kempe woman now you've got the time and we can all go home?' Lund raised his eyebrows at him meaningfully.

Matthew took the hint. Pulling out a chair and sitting down, he gestured peremptorily for Walsh to do the same. 'First, tell me what you have on Susan Madden.'

Lund hitched himself up on the corner of a desk, took out a paper bag of sweets and sucked one noisily while Walsh told them both everything he had found out.

'I agree,' Matthew said when Walsh had finished. 'Sarah Kempe sounds like a good suspect for your snatches.'

Walsh raised an eyebrow in surprise. 'You agree? Well, then. We're looking for the same woman. I'll come in on your case and make sure you're on the right track to catch her.'

'I don't need you looking over my shoulder, Walsh,' Matthew said. 'I know what I'm doing.'

'Oh, really? You could have brought Sarah Kempe in weeks ago, but didn't. Was that you knowing what you're doing, Stannard?'

'That was for a different enquiry, and I didn't have enough to charge her.'

'You let her slip through your fingers, and two people are dead because of it. I wonder what the press would make of that?'

'What's that supposed to mean?'

'If they found out—' Walsh began, but Lund cut him off.

'All right, Walsh,' he said, sliding off the desk. 'That's enough.'

'I want in on your murder case, Stannard.' Walsh got to his feet and pointed a finger at Matthew. 'When Sarah Kempe turns up, I am going to be there.'

'Stannard,' Lund growled warningly, staring as Matthew's fists clenched.

Matthew knew Lund thought he was going to lose his temper and punch the Essex detective. He was tempted, he had to admit, but he wouldn't give Walsh the satisfaction of seeing he had got to him.

'You can be there,' he said, shrugging as if it didn't matter to him, 'if I find her.'

'*When* you find her, Stannard.' Lund turned to Walsh, his eyes narrowing. 'He always does.'

Chapter Forty-Six

SUNDAY, 28TH DECEMBER

Maggie Piper nibbled at her bottom lip as she studied the front page of the newspaper and read the article for the third time that morning.

Mr Stone, the hotel manager, came bustling up to the reception desk. 'Good morning, Miss Piper. Rather chilly today.'

'Yes, Mr Stone, it is,' she agreed absently.

Stone flipped through the post on the reception desk, then dropped the envelopes back into the wicker basket with an impatient sigh. 'Has the lavatory on the first floor been fixed yet?' he asked.

'Not yet. The plumber is coming tomorrow.'

He tutted. 'Well, let's hope there aren't any complaints in the meantime. Having to wait three days for it to be fixed...'

'It is Christmas, Mr Stone.'

'Christmas is over, Miss Piper,' he said grumpily. 'Is there anything else I should know?'

'No,' she said, drawing the word out.

'You don't sound sure, Miss Piper.'

'I'm not sure,' she admitted. 'I may be imagining it.'

'Imagining what?'

She held the newspaper in front of his face. 'This.'

'Yes,' he said, taking the newspaper from her and scanning the front page. 'I read about those murders this morning. Such a dreadful thing. But you mustn't worry your head about it, Miss Piper. This sort of thing doesn't happen very often. You are perfectly safe.'

'That's just it. I'm not sure I am.'

'What on earth do you mean?'

'Look at the picture,' she said, rising and moving to his side. 'That's the man the police are looking for.'

'Quite the rogue, isn't he? Although my wife thought he was rather attractive. Do you think so?' He angled the newspaper to get her opinion of Nicholas Baddowes.

'Mr Stone, you don't understand.' She lowered her voice and looked around the empty reception. 'I think he's here.'

Stone stared at her. 'Here?'

'In room eleven.' She snatched up the register. 'There's two of them. They booked in as Mr and Mrs Harrison, but I'm sure Mr Harrison was this man in the 'paper. And look.' Miss Piper took the newspaper from him and pointed to a paragraph. 'They say he may be with a woman aged forty-one, who is around five foot four with brown hair. Well, that describes Mrs Harrison to a tee.'

'Are you sure, Miss Piper?' Mr Stone asked sternly.

'You take a look at them,' she said. 'Go up to their room and get a good look and then tell me I'm wrong.'

'I suppose I could,' he said, staring doubtfully at the stairs to the first floor.

'It's your duty, Mr Stone,' Miss Piper reminded him.

'Of course,' he said after just another second's hesitation. 'I'll be no more than five minutes.'

Stone made his way up the stairs and along the corridor to room eleven. He took a deep breath and rapped on the door.

There was a sick feeling in his stomach as he waited for the door to open. His breath caught in his throat when it did.

'Yes?' Mr Harrison said.

'I'm sorry to bother you, sir,' Stone said, 'but I wanted to let you know that there may still be a problem with the lavatory today. The plumber isn't able to come until the morning.'

'Right,' Mr Harrison said. 'That all?'

'Yes, yes, that's all. I shan't disturb you any longer.'

Mr Harrison closed the door in his face, and Stone hurried back to the reception.

'Well?' Miss Piper asked eagerly.

'Let me see that picture again,' he said, clicking his fingers at her newspaper. She gave it to him, and he studied the mugshot of Nicholas Baddowes.

'Is it him, Mr Stone?' Miss Piper demanded impatiently.

Stone laid the newspaper back down. 'It's him,' he nodded and jabbed a finger at the telephone on the desk. 'We need to call the police.'

Chapter Forty-Seven

Mullinger was in CID when Matthew arrived. 'You arrested a lady yesterday, Stannard!' he roared at him.

'I made an arrest, yes, sir,' Matthew said. 'I wouldn't say she was a lady exactly.'

'Don't be obtuse, Stannard. You know perfectly well what I mean. Lady, as in The Honourable, Venetia Hickson-Cross.'

'Who was in possession of a restricted drug, sir, and who assaulted one of my officers. It was my duty to arrest her.'

'She had the barest trace of heroin, I understand,' Mullinger said. 'And as for the assault, you exaggerate. Surely Sergeant Denham's man enough to fend off a woman? What kind of officers do we have here, for heaven's sake?'

'Nevertheless, sir—' Matthew began, seeing Denham out of the corner of his eye turn red with shame at the superintendent's words.

'No, not nevertheless.' Mullinger wagged a finger in his face. 'I've instructed the Kensington officers they are to release her without charge. You do know who her father is?'

'No, sir, I don't.'

'Judge Hickson-Cross, Stannard,' Mullinger roared. 'Good God, the last thing I need is him calling me and demanding to know what I'm doing allowing my officers to arrest his daughter.'

Matthew sighed. 'Whatever you say, sir. Now, if you don't mind.' He moved to step around Mullinger, but the superintendent moved to block his path.

'I'm not finished, Stannard,' he said. 'I want an update on this murder case. This doctor you have in custody.'

'Dr Frye's alibi has been confirmed and I'm confident he wasn't present for the actual killings.'

'But?'

'But it's still possible he was involved. He is associated with one of my other suspects.'

'They were in it together, you mean?'

'It's possible.'

'But you have nothing on this doctor at present?'

'No, sir. I can't hold him with what I've got, and I will be releasing him this morning.'

'I see. I daresay you know what you're doing but it's regrettable we can't close this case yet.' Mullinger glanced around, as if suddenly aware he was standing in the middle of CID with all the other officers watching. 'Well, keep me informed,' he ordered and strode out of the office.

'Rudd,' Matthew said. 'Go down to the cells and release Dr Frye, will you? Tell him not to leave Craynebrook.'

'Will do, sir.' Rudd hurried out.

Matthew went into his office. 'Morning,' he said to Lund and Walsh as he hung up his hat and coat.

'Morning,' Lund returned. 'You were right to arrest her, you know? Despite what Old Mouldy says.'

Matthew sat down at his desk and lit a cigarette. 'I knew she'd get off. It doesn't matter.'

'Giving up that easily? That doesn't sound like you.'

'I've got too much else to worry about,' Matthew said, but he knew Lund was right. He should have defended his decision to arrest Venetia, but he didn't have the energy for another confrontation. Through the partition window, he saw Barnes pick up his ringing telephone. His face became animated. Then he set the receiver down and hurried over to Matthew.

'Sir,' he said excitedly. 'I've got a lead on Baddowes. A Mr Stone, manager at a hotel in St Albans, is on the blower and he thinks Baddowes may be staying there.'

Matthew jumped up from his desk and hurried over to Barnes' desk. He snatched up the telephone. 'Mr Stone? This is DI Stannard… You believe Nicholas Baddowes is staying at your hotel?… This is very important. You're not to approach him… Yes, he might be. We'll be there as soon as we can.' He hung up the receiver.

'Well?' Lund asked.

Matthew nodded. 'The manager's sure it's him.'

'What about Kempe?' Walsh asked.

'There is a woman with him,' Matthew said.

'And a baby?' Walsh asked.

'He didn't say.' Matthew pointed at Denham. 'Get on to the local constabulary. Tell them to send two Uniforms to the hotel to keep a watch on the place. They're only to approach if Baddowes attempts to leave. Otherwise, they're to wait for us. Barnes, you're with me.'

'I'm coming too,' Walsh declared.

'Fine,' Matthew said. 'But you stay out of the way until we've got Baddowes.'

'Don't worry, Stannard,' Walsh said. 'I won't cramp your style.'

———

The police car drew up at the side of the hotel, and Matthew was glad to see that the two uniformed constables he'd asked the local station to provide had had the sense to stay out of sight. Barnes and Walsh headed for the hotel entrance while Matthew introduced himself to the constables and asked if they'd seen anything. Their reply was in the negative. If Baddowes was in the hotel, they hadn't seen him come out.

'Good,' Matthew said. 'I want you in there with us. Baddowes has a history of violence. If he's in there, I'm expecting him to put up a fight. All right?'

The constables nodded and followed Matthew into the hotel. Barnes stood by the reception desk. Walsh was leaning over it, showing a photograph to Miss Piper.

'Was it this woman?' Matthew heard him ask.

'I'm not sure,' Miss Piper said. 'I didn't really notice her all that much.'

'But it could be her?' Walsh insisted.

'It could be,' she said.

Matthew addressed himself to the manager. 'Which room, Mr Stone?'

'Room eleven,' Mr Stone replied. 'You won't be breaking down any doors, will you? I can't have our other guests disturbed. It won't do our reputation any good if it gets out we have criminals in the hotel.'

'We'll make as little fuss as possible,' Matthew assured him, thinking what happened next was out of his hands. 'Do you have the key to their room?'

Mr Stone handed him a key with a heavy wooden tag hanging from it. 'Up the stairs and along the corridor to the left.'

Walsh sprinted off, taking the stairs two at a time. Cursing under his breath, Matthew followed, Barnes and the constables at his heels. Matthew caught up with Walsh halfway along the corridor. He grabbed the inspector's arm and yanked him to a stop.

'Wait,' he said.

'I can't afford to wait,' Walsh said, tugging his arm free. 'If she's got that kid in there—'

'You barging in like a bull in a china shop could put it in danger. Have you thought of that?'

Walsh heaved a breath, and his body sagged. 'You're right,' he agreed, and with his arm flung wide, gestured for Matthew to lead the way.

Matthew continued down the corridor, his eyes marking off the door numbers until he came to number eleven. 'Ready?' he asked Barnes and the constables in a whisper. They nodded, and Matthew knocked on the door.

Nothing happened. Matthew put his ear to the door. There wasn't even the sound of movement to tell him someone was inside. With his heart banging in his chest, he fitted the key into the lock and turned it. The tumbler slid aside noisily; there was no time to lose. Matthew threw the door open and rushed inside.

There was only one person in the room, and that was Sarah. She was huddled at the head of the bed, her legs drawn up, arms wrapped around her knees. Her face was a blotchy mess, and she stared warily at the men who had burst into the room.

'Where's Baddowes?' Matthew asked.

'Gone,' Sarah whimpered and gestured at the open window.

Matthew hurried over to it and put his head out. There was a drop of around fifteen feet, but even so, Baddowes must have jumped for there was no fire escape. He turned to the constables. 'Get looking for him. And tell your station to put out an alert.'

The constables hurried out.

'I don't see it,' Walsh cried, looking frantically around the room. He clambered onto the bed and grabbed hold of Sarah's arm. She cried out as he yelled, 'Where's the baby?'

'Walsh!' Matthew pulled him off the mattress. 'For God's sake, leave her alone. You can see the state she's in!'

Walsh threw him off and turned back to Sarah. 'Did Baddowes take it?' he demanded.

Sarah sobbed and buried her head in her hands.

Matthew looked around the room. The third drawer down in a chest of drawers against the wall was open about an inch and he crossed to it. As he bent and put his hands on the knobs to pull it open, Sarah shrieked, 'NO!' and threw herself off the bed, falling at his feet, her hands scrambling at his legs. 'Don't,' she begged. 'Don't.'

Barnes pulled her away, holding her arms to her sides to stop her struggling.

Matthew tugged the drawer open and his breath caught in his throat.

'I thought it was getting better,' Sarah cried. 'It's not my fault.'

'Barnes,' Matthew said stonily, 'get her out of here.'

Barnes propelled Sarah out of the room. Walsh was staring at the chest of drawers in horror.

'Walsh,' Matthew said. 'Come here.'

'I don't want to see it,' Walsh said, turning away.

'I said come here.'

Walsh stepped over to Matthew and looked down into the drawer. 'What the—?' He stared at Matthew in incomprehension.

Matthew nodded and looked back down at the drawer and at the death-stiffened body of a tiny puppy.

Chapter Forty-Eight

The three detectives made their way to the local station and made themselves comfortable in the CID while Sarah was booked in and put in a cell.

'I want to question her first,' Walsh declared, taking a mouthful of coffee.

'No,' Matthew said flatly.

'I need to find out what she's done with the baby.'

'She hasn't done anything with it. Face it, Walsh, you got the wrong woman.'

'But everything about her fits,' Walsh insisted. 'Her history. The complaints against her at the maternity hospital. The dates of the snatches. It has to be her.'

'Could Baddowes have taken it?' Barnes asked.

'Jumping out of that window with a baby in his arms?' Matthew shook his head. 'I doubt it. And I don't think he's the type of man who will take care of a baby.'

'Not even as some sort of hostage?'

'God, I hope not,' Matthew said.

'Why did he run?' Barnes wondered.

'Maybe he guessed the manager recognised him and knew he'd call us,' Matthew shrugged. 'Maybe he saw the

Uniforms. I don't know. It doesn't really matter why. He's gone. That's all we need to know.'

'It's not your fault, sir.'

'Isn't it? I should have made it clear a Uniform was to be posted at the back of the hotel as well as the front.' He shook his head at his stupidity. 'The alert for him has gone out?'

Barnes nodded. 'I've checked, sir. And I've been on to the Yard too.'

'Good.' Matthew finished his cigarette and stubbed it out in the ashtray. 'Let's interview Kempe. Not you,' he said, as Walsh got to his feet.

'I've got to question her,' he said.

'And I want her to talk, Walsh. After the way you treated her in the hotel room, I'm not sure she will if you're in there with me. Don't worry. I know what questions to ask her.'

A cup of tea was sitting untouched on the table before Sarah when Matthew and Barnes entered the room.

Matthew pulled out a chair and sat down. Without saying a word, he offered her a cigarette. She stared at the packet for a long moment, then took out a stick. He lit it for her and watched as she took the smoke down.

'Are you feeling better, Miss Kempe?' he asked.

She gave the smallest of nods, keeping her eyes down.

'I need to ask you some questions,' Matthew went on, nodding for Barnes to get his notebook and pencil ready. 'You know you can have a solicitor with you during questioning?'

Sarah shook her head and sniffed, then took another drag of the cigarette. 'What's the point?'

Matthew was glad. 'Let's talk about Nicholas Baddowes. Where is he?'

'I don't know.'

'Any idea where he might have gone?'

'Back to his wife?' she suggested.

'So, he's left you?'

Sarah gave him a hard stare. 'Yes, he's left me. I suppose he was always going to. It was just a matter of time.'

'He stayed with you while you were delivering the goods. While you were giving him empty houses to burgle. That was you, wasn't it?'

She nodded. 'I told him when a patient's house would be empty. I thought it would be safer for him that way.'

'And safer for the people whose houses he burgled?'

'That too,' she acknowledged with a nod. She smiled ruefully. 'Nick boxed when he was younger. He always loved to fight.'

'I need you to confirm the dates of the burglaries you know he committed,' Matthew said, nodding at Barnes.

Barnes consulted his notebook and read out the names and addresses of the victims and the dates of when the burglaries had been reported.

'Those were all Nick,' Sarah nodded.

'Thank you. That's very helpful,' Matthew said, and Barnes turned back to the current page in his notebook. 'Why did Nick run?'

'He saw his picture in the 'paper. He reckoned the manager recognised him and would call you. So, he said he should leave. Said we would have a better chance if we separated.'

'So, you know about the Scotts?'

'Yes, I know about them.'

'Did Nick kill them?' She wasn't surprised by the question, Matthew saw.

'I don't know,' she said after a long pause.

'But he went there to the house?'

She nodded. 'I told him about the safe Mr Scott had in

his study. I had no idea what was in there, but if you have a safe, you must have something worth locking up in it. I'd seen where the old man kept the key. I told Nick about it, told him the Scotts would be at Midnight Mass on Christmas Eve and he could break into the house then without any trouble.'

'Were you together that night?'

'For most of it.'

'What time did he leave you to break into the house?'

'Around eleven-thirty.'

'And he came back when?'

'Around two.'

'Did he tell you what had happened?'

She shook her head. 'Nick just showed me the money he'd got. It was over fifteen pounds.'

'What kind of mood was he in?'

'Excited. Worked up. I just thought he was happy to have got so much.'

'And then you saw the newspaper and now you're not so sure?'

'I don't know. I don't want to talk about Nick anymore.'

'Then let's talk about you,' Matthew said. 'Tell me about the Scotts. How did you come to be working for Mrs Scott?'

'Dr Frye asked me if I would be interested in a private nursing job. He knew I was hard up for money.'

'So, you and Dr Frye were close?'

'Not close. It was just business. Dr Frye wanted Mrs Scott to think well of him, so he put me there to butter her up.'

'And you did?'

She shrugged. 'It was no hardship to me, and besides, she didn't need much encouragement where he was concerned.'

'And you were doing a good job of looking after her?'

'I'm an excellent nurse, inspector. Not that she was all that ill. She liked to play the invalid, but there wasn't anything really wrong with her. Mrs Scott enjoyed the attention.'

'And it was all going well. So, why were you fired?'

'Mr Scott confronted his wife last Monday and threw me out of the room, but I listened at the door. He said he'd hired a private enquiry agent to look into Dr Frye and that she would be shocked by what he'd found out. Mrs Scott had been planning to set him up in a private practice, but Mr Scott wasn't having that. She was furious with Dr Frye, and got rid of me because of him.'

'Was Dr Frye upset about his plans coming to nothing?'

'I imagine he was. I didn't see him again.'

'Did Frye know Baddowes?'

She frowned at the question. 'Of course not. He never met Nick.'

'Are you sure about that?'

'I'm sure they never met. Why are you asking that?'

'Is it possible,' Matthew went on, 'Frye paid Baddowes to kill the Scotts?'

It was obvious from her expression the idea had never occurred to Sarah. 'That's ridiculous. Frye wouldn't have the guts to do that. Or the money.'

Matthew had to concede that last statement was true. If Frye had fallen out of favour with Victoria Scott before he'd got his hands on her money, then he wouldn't have had any to pay Baddowes for the murders. And Matthew was pretty sure Baddowes wouldn't have killed the Scotts without being paid upfront.

'Would Nick—?' he began, but Sarah cut him off.

'I told you before. I'm not talking about Nick anymore,' she said in a tone that brooked no argument.

Matthew stifled a sigh of irritation, then thought of Walsh, probably pacing outside in the corridor. 'Then tell me about the puppy.'

Sarah's face softened, grew sorrowful. 'It had been abandoned. It couldn't have been more than a few hours old and it was so weak. If I'd left it, it would have died. So, I took it home. I thought I could make it better. I tried, but...' She shrugged helplessly. 'Nothing I did seemed to make any difference. Nick said I should have just left it where I found it. He wanted to throw it out, but I wouldn't let him. I'd let him do anything else but not that. Never that. It was only a poor little baby.'

'You had a baby once, didn't you, Miss Kempe?'

Her eyes hardened, the pupils contracting to a pinprick. 'How do you know about that?'

'An officer has spoken to your parents. You used to be Susan Madden, didn't you?'

Sarah said nothing.

'Your mother said you gave your baby away,' Matthew continued. 'You must have missed it very much. So much that you couldn't bear it, that you had to have a baby, even if it wasn't yours.'

She gave him a bitter smile. 'I know what you're talking about. I took that child home because her mother couldn't be bothered to collect her on time. I couldn't just leave her at the nursery. She would have been on her own.'

'You're talking about the nursery where you worked. But what about when you were working at St Catherine's Maternity Hospital? Mrs Freeman found you in her house with her baby.'

'She overreacted,' Sarah said impatiently. 'She'd left the front door open. Anyone could have gone in.'

'You went in,' Matthew pointed out.

'Just to make sure the baby was all right. I wouldn't have hurt it.'

'Were you going to take it?'

'Of course not. Why would I do that?'

'To replace the baby you lost?' Matthew suggested. He held out his hand and Barnes put a sheet of paper into it. 'Your parents live in Colchester, don't they? And you were there on November the fifth?'

'Yes. That's when I found the puppy.'

'November the fifth is when a baby was taken from a hospital. And you were also in Colchester in August when a baby was taken from a Ladies lavatory in a department store.'

'You're mad,' she said. 'Those were nothing to do with me. I would never take another woman's child. I would never, never, never do that. You have to believe me. '

'Well?' Walsh demanded as Matthew and Barnes exited the interview room. 'What did she say?'

'She denies taking the kids,' Matthew said. 'Said she would never do that to another woman.'

'And you left it at that?' There was scorn in Walsh's voice.

'The snatches are your case, Walsh,' Matthew said. 'As you keep reminding me. Now I've asked her the questions I wanted to.' He gestured at the door. 'Feel free to ask her yours.'

'You're damn right I will.' Walsh threw open the door and went in, slamming it behind him.

Matthew jerked his head at Barnes. 'I want you in there with him. Make sure he doesn't do anything he shouldn't.'

Barnes looked uneasily at the door. 'I don't think Inspector Walsh will pay any attention to me, sir.'

'Make him, Barnes,' Matthew said. 'If he steps out of line, I want to know about it. Understand?'

'Yes, sir,' Barnes nodded, and went reluctantly into the room.

Matthew returned to CID and asked if there had been any news on Baddowes. There hadn't and, his head thumping, he fell down into a chair and took two aspirin with the cup of tea a detective constable gave him. He had half an hour to himself before Walsh strode in and snatched up a telephone from one of the desks. Barnes followed a few moments later and headed towards Matthew.

'Well?' Matthew asked.

Barnes sat down beside him. 'He was all right, sir. I thought he was going to get a bit heavy at one point, but he calmed down.'

'Miss Kempe still denies the snatches?'

'Oh yes. And she reckons she has an alibi for the Bonfire Night snatch. You remember, that's when she said she found the puppy. She said it was on its own because its mother had been tormented by boys with fireworks and run off. She'd gone to the police station to demand the local bobbies do something about the kids, and she was there for about an hour from 9 p.m. onwards waiting to make a complaint. That's when the baby was snatched from the hospital.'

Matthew glanced across the room at Walsh. 'What's he doing?'

'Calling the station to see if she really did make a complaint,' Barnes said ruefully. 'He's not happy.'

'So I see,' Matthew said. 'What have you done with her?'

'She's back in the cell. I've given her a cup of tea. She's all right. Will we be taking her back to Craynebrook, sir?'

'I don't think there's any need. I'm pretty sure she's given us everything she knows. We'll charge her with being involved in the burglaries.'

'But not the murders?'

Matthew shook his head. 'I don't think she had anything to do with them.'

'You think Baddowes had something going on with Dr Frye and left her out of it?'

'Maybe.' Matthew watched Walsh hang up the receiver and make his way towards them.

Walsh halted and put his hands on his hips. 'Has he told you what Kempe said?' he asked, jerking his chin at Barnes.

'He's told me,' Matthew said. 'Did Kempe make a complaint about these boys?'

Walsh nodded. 'It's in the report book. Date and time. She was there.'

'So, she's not the snatcher.'

'Apparently not.' He glared at Matthew as if expecting him to gloat.

But Matthew rose and turned to Barnes. 'Let's charge Kempe with being an accomplice to the burglaries and get back to Craynebrook.'

Chapter Forty-Nine

Matthew climbed out of the car and walked up the steps to the station's lobby. As usual, Sergeant Turkel hailed him as soon as he stepped inside.

'A lady and gentleman to see you, sir,' Turkel said, nodding towards a couple sitting on the bench beneath the notice board. 'They said they would only talk to you. A Mr and Mrs Prince.'

Matthew told Barnes to head up to CID and fill the others in on what had happened. He waited for Walsh to follow Barnes before heading over to the Princes.

'I'm Inspector Stannard,' he said. 'You wanted to see me?'

They got to their feet. 'You're in charge of the Scott murders?' Prince asked.

'I am. You have information about them?'

Prince looked doubtfully at his wife, who tutted and addressed herself to Matthew.

'Yes, we do,' Mrs Prince said defiantly. 'My husband thinks it could be important.'

'Then please come in here,' Matthew said, opening the door to the private waiting room and gesturing them inside.

He bid them take a seat at the table and sat down opposite. Taking out his notebook, he told Prince to begin.

'I don't want to get him into trouble,' Prince began uneasily.

'Get who into trouble?'

'Maxwell Carr.'

Matthew's eyebrows rose. 'The Scotts' son-in-law?'

'I'll have to tell you from the beginning,' Prince said. 'A few months ago, Ben invited me to his office to discuss a business proposition. It turned out he wanted to sell the printing works and he asked if I was interested in buying it. I'm in the trade, too, you see, and I'd made several offers over the years to buy his business, but Ben always turned me down. So, to say I was surprised would be an understatement.'

'Get on with it, Harold,' his wife prompted irritably.

'Yes, of course, dear. Anyway, I told him I was interested, and we started negotiations. I thought the price he wanted was a little too steep, so I wanted to look into his books and make sure it was worth what he said it was. That took time, and Ben was getting impatient, but I'm nothing if not thorough, especially when it comes to business.'

'It's not a bad thing to be, Mr Prince,' Matthew said, wishing, like Mrs Prince, that he would get to the meat of the matter.

'The odd thing about it all,' Prince went on, 'was that Ben said no one was to know we were discussing the sale of the business. He wouldn't even allow me to tell my wife.'

'Why did Mr Scott want to keep it a secret?'

'I think it was to keep it from his son-in-law. Ever since I've known Maxwell, he's been talking about how he would inherit the business one day, and here was Ben, planning to sell it out from under him. I suppose Ben was worried that if Max knew he would put a spanner in the works.'

'So, Mr Carr definitely didn't know about this deal?'

Prince's body sagged. 'He didn't, not until Christmas Eve. We were close to signing the contract. The business would have been mine come the end of the month, and I wanted to celebrate. I thought that at this late stage there was no need to keep it quiet anymore. I was at a bar with some of my friends and let them in on what Ben and I were up to.' He sighed. 'I didn't realise Max was there. He heard me talking about the sale and he was very angry about it.'

Mrs Prince nudged him with her elbow. 'Tell him what he said, Harold.'

'I didn't want to get into an argument with Max, so I told him he would have to take the matter up with Ben. Max said he would and stormed out. I assumed he was heading straight for their house to have it out with Ben.'

'And then the Scotts are killed the same night, inspector,' Mrs Prince said, raising her eyebrows meaningfully at Matthew. 'Do you think that's a coincidence?'

———

Imogen answered Matthew's knock. She had an apron tied around her waist, her hair had come unpinned, and her brown curls hung around her tired eyes. She looked at Matthew and Barnes warily.

'Yes?' she asked in a quiet voice.

'We're sorry to disturb you at this hour, Mrs Carr,' Matthew said, 'but we'd like to speak to your husband.'

'We're having dinner,' she said, waving a hand at the dining-room door. 'Must you see him now?'

'It is important. Can we come in?'

Imogen hesitated, then nodded and said, 'I suppose so.' She led them to the dining room and opened the door.

Over her shoulder, Matthew saw Maxwell seated at the

head of the table. In his hand was a glass filled with what looked like a double whisky.

'Max,' Imogen said. 'The police are here.'

Maxwell slid a lazy glance over to the door. There was a languidness to it that led Matthew to think the whisky wasn't the first drink he'd had that day. 'What do you want?' he drawled.

'I'd like to talk to you about Harold Prince, Mr Carr,' Matthew said, watching Maxwell carefully for his reaction.

Maxwell took a mouthful of his drink. Then he rose, pushing his chair away with the back of his legs. 'Let's go into the sitting room. We might as well be comfortable.'

'Max?' Imogen asked as he passed her by.

'It's nothing,' Maxwell said. 'You tidy up and see to the baby.' He led Matthew and Barnes to the sitting room. 'Drink?' he offered, topping up his whisky from the sideboard decanter.

'No, thank you,' Matthew said.

'On duty, eh?' Maxwell turned with a grin and fell down into his armchair. He put his feet up on the fender.

'Harold Prince, Mr Carr,' Matthew said, taking a seat.

'Yes, Prince. I wondered when that old fool would go squawking to you.'

'Your father-in-law was planning to sell him the business?'

Maxwell swirled the amber liquid around the glass. 'So I discovered. I had no idea Ben was about to sell me down the river.'

'You found out about the sale on Christmas Eve.'

'Heard Harold telling his pals about it. He was boasting, full of himself, and there's me, hearing about him owning my business and me not knowing a thing about it. It was rather a blow, I can tell you.'

'And what did you do then?'

'I fetched Imogen from her parents, as I think I've already told you.'

'What did you say to your father-in-law about what you'd heard?'

'I really can't remember.'

'I suggest you try, Mr Carr.'

'Oh, you suggest, do you? Well, I better had then. Don't want you thinking I killed them? Because that is what you're thinking, isn't it? Yes, I can see the cogs turning in that tiny brain of yours. Well, let me see.' Maxwell sighed and rested his head on the back of the armchair. 'I think I may have said something like, "What do you think you're doing, Ben? Selling the business without telling me?" Yes, it was definitely something like that.'

'And what did Mr Scott say?'

'He said something along the lines of he could do what he liked with the business. Reminded me it wasn't mine. That I was just there on his sufferance because of Imogen.' He snorted a disdainful laugh. 'As if he'd done me a favour by lumbering me with her, not the other way around.'

Matthew bristled. 'You shouldn't talk about your wife like that.'

Maxwell's lips twisted in amusement. 'Do you know, I think that's the second time you've ticked me off for the way I talk about Imogen. Now, why is that? Has she taken your fancy, inspector? Is that it? Like the look of her, do you? Well, be my guest. Have her if you like.' He laughed again and waved his glass in the air. 'I know. I'll be like that Mayor of Casterbridge fellow who sold his wife for a few shillings at a country fair. I'll tell you what, inspector. Give me five quid for Imogen and she's all yours.'

Matthew started out of the chair, his right hand already clenching into a fist, ready to punch Maxwell on the jaw. But a hand grabbed his arm and pulled him back. Matthew turned and stared into the alarmed face of Barnes.

'Sir!' Barnes said and shook his head

'What's going on?'

All three men turned. Imogen stood in the doorway, the baby in her arms.

Matthew shook off Barnes' restraining hand and tugged his suit jacket straight. 'It's nothing, Mrs Carr,' he said, his cheeks colouring with shame at what he had been about to do. He wouldn't have minded hitting Maxwell, but he would have minded very much losing control in front of Barnes. He could already imagine what Barnes would say to the others later.

'Is Max in trouble?' Imogen asked.

'Perhaps you can confirm something for me, Mrs Carr?' Matthew said. 'After you left your parents' house on Christmas Eve, what did you do?'

'We came back here.'

'Did you go out again?'

'No, we didn't,' Maxwell said sharply.

'Can you confirm you both stayed in, Mrs Carr?' Matthew asked.

'Yes,' she said, looking from her husband back to Matthew. 'We came home and had an early night. That's right, isn't it, Max?'

'Yes, that's right, my darling,' Maxwell said. 'You see, inspector? I was here. I couldn't have done it. So if you're quite finished asking questions, I'd say it was time you left.'

Chapter Fifty

Lund was examining his tie as he shuffled into CID. He'd been in the canteen, grabbing a bite before heading off home, and he'd got jam on his tie. He'd tried wiping it off, but all he'd done was rub the jam in deeper.

'I thought you'd gone ages ago,' he said, seeing Barnes at his desk.

Barnes shook his head. 'The inspector had us over at the Carrs to question the husband about Mr Scott selling the business.'

'Yeah, I heard about that. So, what did he have to say?'

'Said he'd had words with his father-in-law, then took his wife home. His wife confirmed they were in all night.'

'So, another lead gone nowhere. That explains why the long face.'

'That's not why,' Barnes muttered.

'What was that?' Lund asked, bending over the desk and cupping his ear.

'Nothing,' Barnes said after a moment's hesitation.

'Come on. Out with it, son. What's up?'

Barnes heaved a deep breath. 'You wouldn't believe it, but I had to stop the inspector from punching Mr Carr.'

'You had to stop Stannard—? What did Carr do, for heaven's sake?'

'I don't think I should say, guv.'

'You're going to say, Barnes, if I have to shake it out of you. What was it all about?'

'Mr Carr was mouthing off about his wife. The inspector told him off for talking about her that way, and Mr Carr said that as the inspector liked his wife so much, he'd sell her to him for five quid. That was when the inspector went to punch him. I had to grab hold of him and pull him back.'

'Blimey,' Lund said, his face clouding. 'And he stopped, did he? Stannard, I mean?'

'Oh yeah. He stopped. Mrs Carr walked in then with the baby, so that sort of calmed everything down. We left right after that.'

'Where's Stannard now?'

'Said he was going home. Told me to interview the neighbours first thing in the morning.' Barnes gestured at the papers he had been working on. 'I thought I better write up my notes, so he's got them in the morning, otherwise I'll be in the doghouse, the mood he's in lately.'

'Was he all right when you left him?'

'You thought I had a long face, you should have seen his.' Barnes frowned unhappily. 'And the thing is, I think Mr Carr was right. I think the inspector is sweet on his wife.'

Lund shook his head. 'Married women aren't Stannard's style. He's too straight for that. And besides, you know what he's like with women. Treats them like princesses.'

'If you say so, guv.' Barnes screwed the cap onto his fountain pen. 'There. That's me done.'

'Is that your report?' Lund nodded at the paper. 'Give it to me. I'll put it on his desk.'

Barnes handed it over and pulled on his coat. 'Night, guv.'

'Yeah. Night.'

Lund walked towards his office, reading Barnes' report. The detective constable's reports were never wordy, so it was a quick read, and Lund saw Barnes had had the sense to leave out the details of the punch Stannard nearly threw. He pushed open his office door and started.

'Bloody hell,' he said, putting a hand to his heart. 'You made me jump.'

Walsh was sitting in the visitor's chair by Matthew's desk. 'I was just going through a few things,' he said. 'What was that I heard? Stannard nearly got into a fight?'

'That was Barnes blowing things out of proportion,' Lund said, cursing himself for not realising Walsh had been in the office. 'I'm sure it was nothing.'

'It didn't sound like nothing.'

'It's none of your business, Walsh. You mind your own. Right?'

Walsh smiled. 'Are you off?' he asked as Lund reached for the coat that hung over the back of his chair.

'It's late,' Lund said, pulling it on. 'Isn't it about time you called it a night?'

'I will soon. I just have a little more reading to do.'

'I'll see you then, if you're still here tomorrow.'

'Oh, I've got a feeling I'll be here for a few more days.'

'Lucky us,' Lund muttered.

Walsh watched Lund walk out, then turned his gaze to the report that Lund had put on Matthew's blotter. He took another glance out at the main office, made sure he was alone, and picked it up.

Chapter Fifty-One

MONDAY, 29TH DECEMBER

Barnes turned the corner onto Leyborne Avenue, already feeling the cold numbing his toes, and peered along the pavement, feeling sure he recognised the man standing beneath the streetlamp. With a start, he realised it was Walsh. He quickened his pace towards him.

'Sir?' he said as he drew near.

'Morning, Barnes,' Walsh said with a broad smile. 'I heard you were interviewing neighbours this morning and thought I'd give you a hand. That's all right, isn't it?'

Barnes hesitated, wondering why an Essex County Police inspector was offering to do what was essentially a house-to-house enquiry and the work of a junior detective. And more importantly, he wondered what would Matthew would say if he knew.

'Of course, sir,' he said, training obliging him to be polite. 'But there's really no need. It's just a few houses. I can manage.'

'It's no bother. I like to keep my hand in,' Walsh shrugged. 'So, who's first?'

Barnes pointed to the house next door to the Carrs. 'No. 19. Mr and Mrs Gough.'

'Let's go then.'

'Yes, sir,' Barnes said, and led the way. He banged the knocker of No. 19 and it was opened a few moments later by a woman in her mid-fifties.

'Yes?' she asked.

Walsh nudged Barnes aside. 'Police, madam. Sorry to disturb you, but we'd like to ask you a few questions.'

She seemed quite pleased and invited them in at once. 'What's this about?'

'Your next-door neighbours,' Walsh said before Barnes could speak. 'Mr and Mrs Carr.'

'It's about her parents, I suppose? That was awful, their being killed like that. But I don't know what I can tell you. I barely knew Mr and Mrs Scott.'

'But you know the Carrs?'

'Oh yes. I know them.'

'You get along?'

Mrs Gough raised an eyebrow. 'So so.'

Walsh nodded understandingly. 'Not the best of neighbours?'

'Well, I wouldn't mind if they weren't so noisy,' Mrs Gough said with exasperation. 'But there's always shouting or some to-do going on.'

'What are they shouting about?'

'I couldn't say. It's not as if I'm listening, although you can't help but hear. They have lots of arguments, you know. He has his hands full with her. She's a bit funny in the head, so everyone says. She went off earlier this year and he told us she was on holiday up in Scotland.' Her nostrils pinched, and she shook her head. 'We didn't believe that. We'd heard the shouting earlier in the day; we knew they'd had a row. So, we assumed she'd left him. We thought she'd gone for good, but she came back just last week with a baby, would you believe? All very peculiar, if you ask me.'

Walsh's face became serious. 'Why peculiar?'

'Because no one knew she was expecting. And if you ask me, she doesn't know what she's doing with the poor little thing. She came out into the garden while I was in ours, and I could hear it crying, so I asked if she wanted any help. But she just glared at me and hurried back into the house without a word. Charming, don't you think?'

'Cries a lot, does it?' Walsh asked. 'The baby?'

Mrs Gough rolled her eyes. 'All the time. It must have been going for an hour the other night.'

'What other night was that?'

'On Christmas Eve. It was crying for a good hour.'

'You didn't think of knocking?' Barnes said, conscious he was supposed to be the one asking the questions. 'See if she needed any help?'

'And get the door slammed in my face?' Mrs Gough cried indignantly.

'You could have spoken with Mr Carr,' he suggested.

'He wasn't there to have a word with, young man.'

'Mr Carr wasn't in the house?' Barnes started and glanced at Walsh, who was looking thoughtful. 'But he was home Christmas Eve. He told us so.'

'Well, he was for a few minutes,' she said. 'The pair of them came back just before eight. I know because I heard the front door slam. But then I was pulling the curtains upstairs in the bedroom and I saw him go off again in the car about ten minutes later. He didn't come back until the early hours. And I know that because his car engine woke me up. Cars are such noisy things, don't you think?'

'Let me just make sure I understand, Mrs Gough,' Barnes said excitedly. 'You're saying Mr Carr went out a few minutes after 8 p.m. on Christmas Eve and didn't return until the early hours of Christmas morning?'

'Well,' she said, raising her eyebrows at him, 'if you want to be particular about it, yes. That's what I'm saying.'

———

Matthew banged the knocker and rubbed the spot on his skull where it was aching. *Damn these headaches*, he thought as the door opened and Peggy Keeling peered out at him.

'Good morning, Mrs Keeling,' Matthew said. 'I'm sorry to disturb you, but I'd like to ask you a few more questions.'

'That's all right. Come in, love. Oh, you look frozen,' Peggy said as she took his hat and coat from him. 'Go into the front room. My husband's in there with a pot of tea.'

Matthew did as she said, saying hello to Mr Keeling, who was reading a newspaper by the fire. Peggy poured him a cup of tea and gave him two biscuits to go with it. He would have liked to take some aspirin with them but thought that wouldn't look right in front of her.

'There now,' she said. 'What is it you want to ask me?'

'About Maxwell Carr. I understand he came to fetch his wife from the Scotts on Christmas Eve?'

'That's right. Around seven-thirty.'

'I appreciate you were in the kitchen,' Matthew went on, 'but did you hear or see anything while he was there?'

'I was in the kitchen, yes, but the door was open, and I could hear everything. Mr Carr was fuming. He was having a right go at Mr Scott.'

'A right go?'

'Shouting at him,' she explained.

'Just shouting?'

'Did he hit him, you mean?' Peggy shook her head. 'I don't think so. I didn't hear anything like that.'

'Can you tell me exactly what you heard?'

'I heard Mr Carr shout that Mr Scott was selling the business and that he hadn't been told about it. Mr Carr said he wouldn't allow Mr Scott to do it, and Mr Scott said he couldn't stop him, that it wasn't anything to do with him.' She shrugged. 'That's all, really. The row didn't last long. And then Mr and Mrs Carr left with the baby.'

It all tallied so far with what Maxwell had told him, Matthew thought, except for the extent of his anger at the sale. But he supposed he'd be angry too if his father-in-law had been planning to do something so underhand.

'Was anything said between Mr and Mrs Scott after the Carrs had gone?' he asked.

'Not really. A few minutes later, the doorbell rang again, and it was Mrs Scott's dress turning up. She went up to try it on. Mr Scott stayed downstairs. Then she came down a few minutes later to show me just as I was getting ready to leave.' She looked up into his face. 'But that's not what you wanted to hear, is it, love? I can tell from your face.'

'I just wanted to know what happened, Mrs Keeling,' Matthew assured her, though she was right. He had wanted to hear that Maxwell had hit Benjamin or threatened him. He rose and smiled down at her. 'Thank you. You've been a great help.'

———

Rudd unwound his scarf, eyes scanning the paperwork on his desk as Barnes burst into the office.

'Where's the inspector?' Barnes demanded.

'He's not in yet,' Rudd said. 'What's up?'

'I've just questioned the Carr's next-door neighbour. You'll never guess what! She told me Maxwell Carr went out Christmas Eve and was out for hours.'

'So?'

'So, Sam,' Barnes said, 'he told the inspector he stayed in all night with his wife. And—' He broke off as Walsh strode in and, without a word, headed straight for the inspectors' office.

Rudd saw the irritated expression on Barnes' face and stepped closer. 'What's he still doing here? Shouldn't he have gone back to Colchester?'

'He was waiting on the street when I got there,' Barnes said in an undertone. 'Insisted on coming with me to question the neighbours.'

'Why'd he do that?'

Barnes shook his head, then caught Walsh looking at him from the doorway. 'Anyway,' he said in a louder voice, 'I've got to ask the inspector whether to bring Carr in or not.'

'Bring him in,' Walsh said before Rudd could reply. 'Don't wait for permission. Do it.'

'I'm not sure I should do that, sir,' Barnes said hesitantly. 'The inspector usually likes to make those kind of decisions.'

'You're a detective, Barnes,' Walsh said. 'You're supposed to think for yourself. It's called using your initiative.'

'Even so, sir—'

'You wanted to bring Sarah Kempe in, didn't you?' Walsh cut him off. 'And Stannard said no. Now, if you'd used your initiative then and brought her in anyway, the Scotts might not be dead. Do you want Carr to get away the same way Baddowes has?'

Barnes coloured. 'No, sir.'

Walsh jerked his head at the door. 'Then bring him in. But if you want some advice, Barnes, don't let his wife come with him.' He grinned. 'We don't want Stannard getting distracted, do we?'

Barnes glanced at Rudd and Rudd could see the unease in

his expression. 'Well, if you think I should,' he said doubtfully.

Rudd wanted to tell Barnes he shouldn't listen to Walsh, that the Essex detective wasn't in charge here, that he owed it to the inspector to check with him first, but before he could say any of this, Barnes had nodded at Walsh and hurried out of CID.

Rudd turned back to Walsh. There was an oddly triumphant expression on the inspector's face.

'Wouldn't say no to a cup of tea, young Rudd,' Walsh said, his lips twitching in a smile. 'Three sugars.' He returned to his seat at Lund's desk and flicked through a file.

Rudd carried a mug of tea into the office and set it down on the blotter. 'Is that your case file, sir?' he asked, knowing it wasn't.

Walsh looked up, his eyes narrowing. 'No. It's the Imogen Carr missing person case file.' His eyes dared Rudd to comment.

'I thought that case was closed, sir,' Rudd ventured.

'That's right. Imogen Carr came back. With a baby.'

'Yes, sir. She had it while she was away.'

'Away where? Did anyone bother to ask?'

'Well, I didn't work on the case, so I don't know for sure. But from what I heard, Mrs Carr didn't want to say where she'd been. And besides, she was back. It didn't matter.'

'That's what you think, is it?'

'As I said, sir, I didn't work on it.'

'Quite right. You did say that. So maybe you should get back to your own cases, Rudd, and leave me to mine.'

The rebuke stung. Rudd muttered, 'Yes, sir,' and returned to his desk, wondering how he could have been so mistaken in thinking Walsh an inspector to look up to.

Chapter Fifty-Two

'Sir,' Barnes cried excitedly as Matthew walked into CID. 'I've got Maxwell Carr in an interview room.'

Matthew stared at him. 'You've what?'

His expression made the young detective grow pale. 'He wasn't at home the night of the murders like he said he was,' Barnes explained. 'I spoke to two neighbours who confirmed he left home shortly after 8 p.m. and didn't return until after midnight.' The detective constable swallowed uneasily. 'He was lying about being at home. I thought you'd want to question him again.'

'I do, but when I'm ready for him. I should put you on report for this. What the hell were you thinking?'

'I'm sorry, sir,' Barnes said, hanging his head.

'For God's sake,' Matthew muttered and closed his eyes as a shaft of pain shot through his skull. 'Has he asked for a solicitor?'

'No, sir.'

'That's something, I suppose. But don't you ever do something like that again without checking with me first, do you hear?'

Barnes nodded. 'Yes, sir. Never again.'

'This is outrageous,' Maxwell declared as Matthew and Barnes entered the interview room and sat down at the table. 'Whatever you wanted to ask me, you could have done it at my house. Instead of which I have him,' he jerked his chin at Barnes, 'bundling me into a police car for all the neighbours to see. God knows what they'll be saying.'

'Funny you should mention the neighbours, Mr Carr,' Matthew said. 'It's them we want to talk to you about. Do you remember what you told us about your whereabouts on Christmas Eve?'

'Yes. I told you I was at home with my wife.'

'All evening?'

'All evening.'

'And yet,' Matthew consulted the notes Barnes had made during his questioning, 'we have two of your neighbours stating that you went out just after 8 p.m. and didn't return until after midnight.' He met Maxwell's gaze and held it, waiting for him to explain.

Maxwell swallowed nervously. 'They're wrong. I was at home.'

'Your car wasn't on the drive during those hours.'

'Of course it was. My neighbours are idiots. They don't know what they're talking about.'

'Both witnesses were very certain. Your car wasn't there, and neither were you. So, where were you?'

'Do I need to remind you, inspector,' Maxwell said, stabbing the tabletop with his forefinger, 'my wife confirmed I was at home?'

'I always doubt a wife's testimony, Mr Carr,' Matthew said, undeterred. 'Wives often back up their husband's statements, even when they're lying. And I saw the look that passed between you and Mrs Carr when I asked for a confirmation.'

'I bet you did,' Maxwell said, and he grinned. 'That's what this is about, isn't it? Get me in here, blacken my reputation, and Imogen's going to be a mess, isn't she? Is that the plan, inspector? You give her a shoulder to cry on?'

Matthew's face hardened. 'I suggest you worry about yourself, Mr Carr, and not concern yourself with me.'

The smile faded from Maxwell's face. 'I was at home,' he said through gritted teeth.

'You're sticking to that, are you?'

'Yes, I am.' Maxwell took a silver case and lighter from his pocket, took out a cigarette and lit it.

'I spoke to the Scotts' cook again this morning,' Matthew continued. 'Contrary to what you told me, you had very strong words with Mr Scott about the sale of the business.'

'Not contrary at all. I told you I spoke to Ben about it.'

'Yes, you did and you made it sound like it had been a calm and reasonable conversation. But according to Mrs Keeling, you were extremely angry with your father-in-law and told Mr Scott you wouldn't let him sell the business. Which I think, Mr Carr, is a very good motive for murder.'

'That's what you think, is it?' Maxwell sneered. 'In that case, inspector, I want a solicitor.'

———

Lund walked into CID, saw Rudd deep in conversation with Bissett, and frowned as he spied Walsh sitting in his office at his desk. 'Bloody cheek,' he muttered to himself before heading for Rudd. 'What's going on?' he asked Rudd as Bissett waved a sheaf of fingerprints and excused himself.

'The inspector's in Interview Room 3 questioning Maxwell Carr,' Rudd said.

'The son-in-law? Why?'

'He wasn't at home Christmas Eve like he said he was. And he's got a motive. Mr Scott was planning to sell the business. Mr Carr didn't know anything about it and wasn't happy when he found out.'

'So, the murderer might not be Baddowes after all? And I thought he was a sure bet. So what's the face for, Rudd?'

'It's Inspector Walsh,' Rudd said, keeping his voice low. 'He turned up to question the neighbours with Barnes and then told Barnes to bring Mr Carr in. Barnes wasn't sure he should. He wanted to check with the inspector. But Walsh pushed him. Told him to do it.'

'Did he now?' Lund strode into his office and glared at Walsh. 'I'll have my chair back, if you don't mind.'

Walsh picked up the case file he'd been reading, rose and headed for Matthew's desk.

'Oi.' Lund shook his head. 'That chair,' he said, pointing to the visitor's chair, 'or the spare desk out there.' He pointed out of the window at the vacant desk in the main office.

Walsh raised an amused eyebrow at him and sat down in the visitor's chair.

'I heard you told Barnes to bring Carr in,' Lund said.

'That's right.'

'Without Stannard knowing about it.'

'I told Barnes to use his initiative. It's encouraged at my station, but it doesn't seem to be the case here.'

'Taking flaming liberties seems to be the order of the day where you're from,' Lund retorted, searching through his In tray.

'Looking for this?' Walsh asked, lifting up the case file to show Lund the front cover.

'Is that—'

'The Imogen Carr missing person case file? Yes, it is.'

'What are you doing with it?'

'Just having a look.'

'Well, you can give it back. I want to file it. The case is closed.'

'Closed?' Walsh raised an eyebrow.

'That's right. The lady came back.'

'Yes, she did. She came back with a baby that no one knew she was having.'

Lund sank into his chair and narrowed his eyes at Walsh. 'I know what you're getting at.'

'So I don't have to state the bloody obvious. Not to you, at least.' Walsh cast a meaningful glance at Matthew's desk.

Lund followed his gaze to Matthew's empty chair. He had to admit Stannard had been acting strangely of late, and he didn't think it was just because he resented having Walsh around.

'All right,' he said with a heavy sigh. 'Tell me what you've got.'

Chapter Fifty-Three

Matthew told Barnes to put Maxwell back in the cell while they waited for his solicitor and returned to CID.

'How did it go, sir?' Rudd asked as Matthew passed.

Matthew grunted in response and carried on walking. When he saw Walsh was in his office with Lund, he contemplated walking out again, but Lund called to him with an urgent, 'Stannard!'

'What?' Matthew said.

'Come in here and close the door,' Lund said. 'Sit down.'

'What is this, Lund?'

'Just do it. Please.'

Matthew sat down at his desk. 'Well?' he said.

'Walsh has a theory,' Lund began. 'I think it's worth listening to.'

'Another theory?' Matthew said, raising an eyebrow. 'So, who does he think his snatcher is now?'

There was a momentary silence, then Walsh said, 'Imogen Carr.'

Matthew stared at him for a moment, then a laugh burst from his lips. 'You're not serious?'

'Just listen to him, Stannard,' Lund said.

'I don't need to listen. That theory's about as ridiculous as one of our dinner ladies being the snatcher.'

'Actually, it isn't,' Lund said. He held up his hands as Walsh opened his mouth to speak. 'I'll do this, Walsh,' he said, and opened the cover of the missing person case file. 'Imogen Carr had a miscarriage back in 1920. She was in St Catherine's Maternity Hospital. Margaret Burns was there at the same time. In fact, she was in the next bed.'

'So?' Matthew snapped. 'Susan Madden alias Sarah Kempe was also there in 1920. That turned out to be just a coincidence, didn't it?'

'Just hear me out, Stannard, please. Benjamin Scott reported his daughter as missing two days after Margaret Burn's baby was put on the church steps dead, but,' he held up a finger, 'she actually left that very day.'

'That doesn't mean anything, Lund,' Matthew protested.

'Maybe not,' Lund conceded. 'But when you realise that she had also run away for all but one of the other snatches, you have to consider it's more than just coincidence, Stannard.'

'Coincidences do happen.'

'That's a lot of coincidences,' Walsh muttered, and shook his head at Lund. 'I knew he'd be like this.'

'You made a lot of coincidences convince you Sarah Kempe was your snatcher,' Matthew reminded him angrily. 'You thought she was a perfect fit. And Lund just said, Imogen Carr was away for all but one of the snatches. Not all of them. So how do you explain that?'

'I can't. Maybe she stole that one on a day trip and took it home.'

'And her husband didn't notice she suddenly had a baby on her?' Matthew shook his head in disbelief at the idea.

Walsh made a noise of impatience. 'I don't have all the

answers, Stannard, but I do know one thing. I'm going to question Imogen Carr about the snatches.'

Matthew shook his head. 'No, you're not.'

'I'm not asking for your permission, Stannard.'

'Imogen Carr is a fragile woman who's just had her parents murdered, her husband's under suspicion of doing them in, and you want to bully her with questions about her baby? I'm not having it, Walsh.' There was a knock on the door. 'Come in,' Matthew yelled.

Barnes put his head around the door. 'Just to let you know that Mr Carr's solicitor has arrived, sir. It's Mr Palmer again. He says he wants at least half an hour with his client.'

'He can have it. When they're ready, get Carr back in the interview room and come and get me. I'll be in the canteen.' Matthew pushed himself out of his chair and headed for the door. 'I've heard enough. It's about time you went back to Colchester, Walsh,' he said as he left.

———

Matthew bit into the mince pie, not noticing the taste, not even noticing the crumbs that tumbled down his tie to collect in his lap.

He went over what Lund and Walsh had said. He hated to admit it, but if he'd come up with all those coincidences, he would have his suspicions too. But he just couldn't see Imogen stealing a baby. And not just one baby, but several over the course of ten years!

Matthew put the half-eaten mince pie back on the plate, remembering he didn't like them. He pushed the plate away and pulled his coffee towards him. Digging the aspirin bottle out of his trouser pocket, he tipped two pills into his palm and threw them down his throat, washing them down with the coffee. God, he was sick of these damn headaches!

'You're not looking quite the thing, love.'

Matthew looked up to see Mrs Parker peering at him worriedly. 'I'm fine,' he said with a smile, wanting her to leave him alone. She glanced at the aspirin bottle on the table, and he snatched it away, stuffing it back in his pocket. 'It's just a headache.'

'You want to take it easy, dearie. I've seen it before. Young men running themselves into the ground in this place. Working all hours, never having a moment for themselves or their families. You want to watch it or you'll go the same way. Before you know it, you'll be sitting up in your CID, fat, bald and drinking yourself to sleep at your desk.'

'What a lovely picture you conjure up,' he said with a rueful smile.

But she didn't smile back. She nodded seriously at him. 'Get yourself a life out of this place, love, before it's too late.' She pointed at the plate. 'You not eating that?'

Matthew shook his head and she took it away as Rudd came into the canteen. He looked around, saw Matthew and hurried over.

'I'm sorry to disturb you, sir,' Rudd said, 'but I thought you ought to know.'

'Know what, Rudd?' Matthew asked with a sigh, wishing everyone would leave him alone.

Rudd swallowed uneasily. 'I think DI Walsh has gone to question Mrs Carr.'

Chapter Fifty-Four

'Is it about my husband?' Imogen asked as she followed Walsh into her sitting room.

Walsh glanced around the room. 'Are you on your own, Mrs Carr?'

'Yes,' she said, closing the door. 'Apart from my son.'

'Oh, that's right. You have a son now.'

'About my husband?' she pressed.

'He's being interviewed.'

'Interviewed about what? What has he done? Why won't anyone tell me?'

'I'm not here to talk about your husband, Mrs Carr. I'm here to talk about you.'

Imogen stiffened. 'What about me?'

'You've been away this year, haven't you? You were away for quite some time.'

'Yes, I went away. Oh, look, if this is about all the trouble with Jane saying I was missing and Max being suspected—'

He cut her off. 'Where did you go?'

Imogen stared at him. 'That's none of your business.'

'Did you go to Colchester, Mrs Carr?'

She gasped and put a hand to her throat. 'How do you know that?'

Walsh's heart beat faster. 'Where did you stay in Colchester?'

'With a friend.'

'I need to know their name and address.' He took out his notebook and pen, then looked at Imogen expectantly.

'I'm not telling you,' she said. 'They don't want to be bothered by police.'

'I won't bother them, Mrs Carr. I'll just have a few questions for them.'

'I said no.'

'Why the secrecy about where you were and who you stayed with? Do you have something to hide, Mrs Carr?'

'Of course I don't,' she said, walking to the window. She pulled the net curtain back. 'Where's my husband? Is he coming home soon?'

'When did you have your baby, Mrs Carr?' Walsh asked.

Imogen whirled on him. 'Why are you asking about my baby?'

'When was he born?'

'The third of November.'

'You're sure about that?'

'I should know when I gave birth to him.'

'It wouldn't have been the fifth of November?'

She frowned at him and shook her head. 'The third. I told you.'

'Did you give birth at home or in a hospital?'

Imogen's breath was coming fast. 'Where's Inspector Stannard? Why isn't he here?'

'Stannard's not coming,' Walsh said. 'I'm here, and I want answers, Mrs Carr. Where did you have the baby?'

'No. I'm not talking to you.'

'I want to see the birth certificate.'

'I don't have one. I haven't registered the birth yet. I haven't got around to it.'

'You're supposed to register a birth within forty-two days. You'll get fined for leaving it so long.' Walsh looked around the room and saw a glass feeding bottle on a side table. He pointed at it. 'You're not feeding the baby yourself?'

Imogen's cheeks blazed. 'How dare you! No gentleman would ever ask a lady that.'

'I'm a policeman, Mrs Carr, not a gentleman.'

'I want you to leave.'

'Not before I've seen the baby.'

'You're not seeing him,' she said, edging towards the door and looking nervously down the hall towards the kitchen.

'Is that where he is?' Walsh said, going up close to Imogen and leaning close to peer over her shoulder. He'd expected her to move away, but she didn't.

'Get out of my house,' she said.

Walsh tried to step around her, but Imogen moved to block him, then put her hands against his chest and shoved him back. Astonished, he took a step towards her, and she stopped him with a slap across the face. Walsh felt a stinging on his cheek, put a finger to it, and the tip came away red. With a sudden burst of anger, he grabbed her wrists and wrenched them to her sides.

'Let go of me!' Imogen screeched.

'Just calm down,' Walsh yelled back, startled that what he'd intended to be a simple questioning had become a physical struggle with a hysterical woman.

'Get off me! Somebody help!'

Imogen screamed, a split second before someone banged on the front door and yelled, 'Open up!'

Startled, Walsh relinquished his hold on Imogen and she fell back against the bannisters. The banging became insistent and he reached out to turn the latch on the front door.

As soon as it shot home, the door flew open and Matthew burst in.

Matthew went to Imogen. 'Are you all right?' he asked.

'Don't let him hurt me,' Imogen whimpered, clutching at Matthew. 'Please.'

Matthew turned to Rudd who was standing open-mouthed on the doorstep. 'Get him out of here, Rudd,' he ordered.

'Yes, sir,' Rudd said, and took a firm hold of Walsh's elbow.

Walsh yanked his arm away. 'Get your hands off me, constable,' he growled. With a last look at Imogen, he strode out of the house, heading for the police car parked at the kerb.

Rudd hurried after him.

'I'm so sorry,' Matthew said. 'If I'd known he would do this…'

Imogen's bottom lip curled inwards, her teeth biting down into the soft flesh to whiten it. He saw the faded bruises on her wrists as she tightened her grip on his arms.

'You won't let him hurt me again, will you? Promise me.'

'I promise. Come on. Let's get you sat down.' He helped her into the sitting room and settled her on the sofa. Pouring a brandy, he pressed the glass into her hand and told her to drink.

She took a sip, then asked, 'Where's Max?'

'He's at the station. He's all right.'

'When is he coming home?'

'I can't say.'

'That horrible man said he was being questioned. About what?'

Matthew hesitated before answering. 'About the murder of your parents.'

Her eyes widened. 'You think Max killed them?'

'He had a motive.'

'My father selling the business, you mean? Yes. Max was very upset about that.'

Matthew sat down beside her. 'You said your husband was with you all night on Christmas Eve. It's very important that you tell me the truth. Was he really here?'

Imogen stared at him, holding his gaze. Then she heaved a deep breath and shook her head. 'I'm sorry I lied to you, but it was what Max wanted me to say. 'She sighed. 'Max did go out. He left me alone all night.'

———

Matthew climbed into the back of the car next to Walsh without a word, slamming the door shut. Rudd, sitting in the front, told the driver to return to the station, and the car lurched off. Matthew didn't trust himself to speak or even look at Walsh just yet, so he stared out of the window until the car came to a stop.

He took the stairs up to CID two at a time, Walsh and Rudd thundering up behind him. Matthew strode into his office, where Lund looked up at him in astonishment at his sudden entrance, and waited for Walsh to join him. Matthew slammed the door shut as the Essex detective stepped inside.

'You seem to need reminding, Walsh,' Matthew began, 'that you're a guest here. You have no jurisdiction whatso-ever. Which means you don't question people, especially without one of my officers present.'

'Your men are busy. You're busy,' Walsh returned defi-antly. 'And it was a good opportunity to talk to her while you had her husband in here.'

'You mean it was a chance to go behind my back.'

'You gave me no choice. I had to do it that way.'

'Is that your way?' Matthew yelled. 'Threatening? Bullying a woman?'

'When it gets results, yes,' Walsh shouted back.

Lund jumped up and moved to stand between them. 'All right,' he said, putting his hands out to keep them apart. 'Let's just all calm down. Stannard, sit down. You, Walsh, there.' He pointed to the visitor's chair and waited until both men had taken a seat. Looking through the partition window, he saw that all the junior detectives were watching, so he pulled down the blinds. 'You two are turning this into a bloody circus,' he scolded. 'I gather Walsh has talked to Mrs Carr?'

'He didn't just talk to her,' Matthew said. 'He assaulted her.'

'I did no such thing,' Walsh scoffed. 'And even if I did, it was justified. She's my snatcher, and I can prove it.'

'How?' Lund asked.

'When she went away this last time, she went to Colchester, which means she was there for both of the recent snatches. I had it from her own lips.' He grinned at Lund triumphantly. 'And there's more. She's not feeding that baby herself. She's using a bottle.'

'So what?' Matthew said.

Walsh laughed scornfully and shook his head at Lund. 'Is he really this stupid?'

'She could be using a bottle because she can't feed it herself,' Lund explained to Matthew.

'Do you get it now, Stannard?' Walsh held his cupped hands to his chest. 'She doesn't have any milk in her tits because she hasn't been pregnant.'

'That doesn't prove anything,' Matthew said, disgusted by Walsh's crudeness. 'I expect there are plenty of women who give their babies a bottle.'

'She doesn't have a birth certificate either,' Walsh went on. 'Nothing to prove the kid's hers.'

'Stannard,' Lund said. 'You've got to admit it looks suspicious.'

Matthew glared at him, then turned to Walsh. 'You know what I think? I think you're so desperate to solve your case that you're grasping at straws.'

'Some bloody straw, Stannard! There is no one else the snatcher can be.'

'That's what you want to think,' Matthew shot back. 'But I've read our case file from 1920, and I'm telling you, things were missed back then.'

'What things?' Walsh spat.

'Leads not followed up on. People not questioned when they should have been. Vaughn did a sloppy job of his investigation, and so are you with yours.'

'What people?' Lund asked as Walsh's face turned purple.

Matthew shook his head. 'I'm not doing his job for him. Walsh can find out for himself, but I don't expect he'll bother.' He pointed a finger at Walsh's chest. 'You don't go near Imogen again.'

'You can't stop me,' Walsh said stonily.

'Can't I?' Matthew countered. 'This is the Met, Walsh. You're off your patch. And if you step out of line again, I'll take it to Mullinger, and he will listen to me.'

'Sure about that, are you?' Walsh shook his head. 'I don't think so. Because I reckon your superintendent is very keen on me being here.' He leaned in towards Matthew, so their faces were mere inches apart. 'You talk to your superintendent, Stannard, and I'll talk to my chief constable. And we'll see who gets listened to.'

There was a knock on the office door.

'Come in,' Matthew barked, not taking his eyes off Walsh.

'Sorry, sir,' Barnes said, looking uneasily at the two men, 'but Mr Palmer says they're ready.'

Chapter Fifty-Five

Maxwell was smoking when Matthew and Barnes re-entered the interview room. Joseph Palmer was sitting alongside him, and he gave Matthew a rueful grimace as Matthew sat down opposite, one that said they'd met too often over this Christmas period.

'Have you advised your client that it's in his best interest to cooperate?' Matthew asked.

Maxwell made a noise of irritation, and Palmer gave Matthew a disapproving shake of his head. 'As you're well aware, inspector, my client is within his rights not to answer any of your questions if he doesn't want to.'

'I would have thought he would be eager to help me find the killer of his in-laws.'

'Well, of course I am,' Maxwell muttered, tapping his cigarette against the ashtray.

'Good. Then, tell me where you were between 8 p.m. and midnight on Christmas Eve.'

'I have told you. At home with my wife.'

'And yet your wife has just told me that she lied. That you were out all night.'

Maxwell's eyes widened. 'You've spoken to Imogen?'

'Yes, I have. I now have three independent statements saying you were out the night your in-laws were killed.'

Maxwell glanced at Palmer, who gave him a tight nod. He sighed. 'All right. I did go out again after dropping Imogen at home. I was out with another woman.'

'I need her name and address,' Matthew said.

'Linda Pearson,' Maxwell said, and gave her address, watching as Barnes noted it down in his notebook. 'You will be discreet, I hope?'

'This woman will confirm you were with her at that time?'

'Yes. We went out for a drive.'

'For four hours?'

'Well, I wasn't driving all the time,' Maxwell said with a grin.

Matthew wanted to wipe the smile off his face, especially when he saw Barnes also grinning. He glared at his fellow detective, who ducked his head down in contrition. 'We'll speak to Mrs Pearson,' Matthew said.

'I trust you will be allowing Mr Carr to return home in the meantime?' Palmer said as Matthew rose. 'As he is cooperating and his alibi will no doubt be confirmed?'

Matthew wanted to say no, that for all he cared, Carr could spend the night in a police cell, but he thought of Imogen alone in her house with the baby. She needed her husband home.

'Mr Carr can go while we confirm his alibi,' Matthew agreed. 'But I advise him not to leave Craynebrook. It's likely we'll need to speak again.'

———

Mr Pearson answered Barnes' knock.

'Yes?' he demanded, his face hardening as Barnes

produced his warrant card and asked to see his wife. Pearson shouted for her to come to the door.

Linda came down the passage towards them, and Matthew recognised her as the secretary from the printing works. He had been tempted not to spare her blushes and ask her about Maxwell regardless of whether her husband was present, but he realised as she looked at him with wide, wary eyes that he would not put her in that position, adulteress or not.

'We'd like to talk to you in private, Mrs Pearson,' he said before Barnes could speak.

'Why in private?' Pearson wanted to know.

'It's a confidential matter concerning your wife's murdered employer, sir,' Matthew said. 'I realise it's cold, Mrs Pearson, but perhaps you could step outside?'

'It's all right, love,' Linda said, taking down a coat from the hall stand and pulling it on as her husband protested. 'I won't be a minute.' She stepped out onto the path and pulled the front door to.

Matthew led her down the garden path until they were at the gate. 'Wait in the car, Barnes,' he ordered, and waited until the young detective had left them alone.

'I really don't know anything about the murder, inspector,' Linda began, pulling her coat tighter.

'It's not about the murder, Mrs Pearson,' Matthew said. 'We've been talking to Mr Carr about his whereabouts on the evening of Christmas Eve. He's told us he was with you that night. Can you confirm that?'

Her throat tightened. She licked her dry lips and cast a look back at the house. 'I don't know why he's told you that.'

'You weren't together?'

'Of course we weren't. The printing works shut down on the Monday, and even if they were still open, I don't work in the evening. So, either way, I wouldn't have been at the office on Christmas Eve night.'

Matthew too glanced back at her house and saw Pearson peering through the net curtains. 'I don't mean at the office, Mrs Pearson. Mr Carr said he picked you up in his car sometime after 8 p.m. that night and took you for a drive,' adding a little maliciously, 'among other things.'

Linda's cheeks blazed red. Her eyes flashed. 'Well, he's lying. How dare he say that! I've a good mind to tell my husband. He wouldn't stand for Mr Carr insulting me that way.'

'Mrs Pearson,' Matthew said patiently, 'please understand. I'm not here to comment on your private life or expose you. What you get up to is your business. I'm trying to solve a double murder and that's all I care about. So, I'll ask you again. Were you with Mr Carr on the evening of Christmas Eve?'

Linda opened her mouth to reply, but shut it at the sound of footsteps on the garden path. Pearson was thundering towards them.

'I'm not having this,' he declared. 'You talking to her out here. What's it all about?'

'It's just about the murders, Bill,' Linda said, and Matthew heard fear in her voice.

'She just works for them,' Pearson said to Matthew. 'Or she did. Bloody nice Christmas present that was, the old man getting murdered. You realise she's probably out of a job now?'

Matthew didn't bother to reply. He turned back to Linda. 'Is that everything you have to say, Mrs Pearson?'

Linda hesitated for the briefest of moments, then nodded. 'Yes, that's all.'

'Then I'll leave you in peace,' Matthew said. He watched husband and wife return to the house, then opened the rear car door and climbed in. 'She denies it,' he told Barnes as he got in beside him.

'So, that's that,' Barnes said. 'Carr doesn't have an alibi. Back round to his, sir, and arrest him? Sir?' he pressed when Matthew didn't reply. 'Round to the Carrs?'

Matthew shook his head. 'Not yet.'

'But he doesn't have an alibi. You can get him now, sir. Like you wanted.'

Matthew rounded on Barnes. 'What do you mean, like I wanted?'

Barnes was taken aback by his vehemence. 'I just meant…' he swallowed uneasily. 'Nothing, sir. I didn't mean anything.'

'Back to the station,' Matthew said, his jaw tightening, for he knew exactly what Barnes had meant.

———

Matthew had sent Barnes home. All the others in CID were gone too. Even Walsh had vacated, and Matthew was especially glad of that. He didn't think he could face another encounter with the Essex County detective.

He made himself a tea and carried it back to his office, where he fell into his chair and, as there was no one to see, put his feet up on the desk. Matthew lit a cigarette and blew the smoke up towards the ceiling, grateful for the peace and quiet.

Sighing, he glanced across at Lund's desk. His eyes narrowed as he saw Walsh's case file lying on the blotter. Matthew considered for a long moment, then rose and wandered over to Lund's desk and picked up the file. He took it back to his desk and flicked through the pages. It was a very thick file, the result of cases that went back a decade.

He took out his notebook to take notes but gave up after twenty minutes. There was simply too much information to take down. He would have liked to keep the case file, but knew Walsh would look for it. An idea occurred to him. Checking the clock on his wall, he lifted the telephone receiver.

When the line connected, Matthew took the cigarette from between his lips and said into the mouthpiece, 'Dickie? I know it's getting late, but I need a favour.'

———

'Are you going to tell me why I'm photographing a police file, Matthew?' Dickie asked as he took one page of Walsh's case file away from beneath the camera and replaced it with another that Matthew handed him.

'There's a lot of information,' Matthew shrugged. 'Too much to note down.'

'And you can't take the file home with you because…?'

Matthew didn't answer.

'This is a Colchester file,' Dickie said as he took another picture. 'It wouldn't belong to this DI Walsh I've heard about, would it? And you wouldn't be doing this without him knowing, would you?'

'Just make the copies, please,' Matthew said.

'I'm doing it. So, you're going to solve his baby-snatching case for him,' Dickie went on with a smile. 'Show him how it's done.'

'I'm going to show him he's chasing after the wrong woman.'

'Oh yes? And who's that? Who's this Walsh chasing?'

'Imogen Carr.'

Dickie frowned. 'Isn't that the daughter of—'

'The Scotts, yes.'

'Blimey. And how has he come to the conclusion that his snatcher is her?'

'By putting a lot of coincidences together and working them up into what he thinks is a valid case.'

'But you think he's wrong?'

'I know he's wrong. Imogen isn't a baby snatcher.'

'Imogen?' Dickie raised an eyebrow at Matthew, making his cheeks flush red. 'And you know she's innocent how?'

'Because she's not that kind of woman.'

'How do you know what kind of woman she is? You could have only met her a few days ago.'

'I just know, Dickie. And she's had enough to put up with without Walsh hounding her. Her parents treated her like a child, and her husband…' Matthew shook his head. 'He's a damned adulterer and might even be a murderer to boot.'

'You think her husband killed the Scotts?' Dickie was astonished.

'He had a motive. Scott was selling the business and Carr didn't know anything about it. And he wasn't at home during the hours they were killed. He claims he was with his mistress.'

'So, you've charged him with the murders?'

Matthew shook his head. 'Not yet. His mistress has denied they were together, but I think she's lying.'

'So, he does have an alibi?'

'I think he was with her on Christmas Eve,' Matthew said testily. 'But maybe he wasn't with her as long as he says he was. I just need to get her to tell me when they were together. If he left her before midnight, he could still have had time to kill the Scotts.'

Dickie sighed. 'It sounds like you want him to be guilty. You want to charge him with the murders.'

Matthew dropped his cigarette butt and crushed it beneath his shoe. 'I wish I could charge him for infidelity.'

'Infidelity isn't a crime, Matthew.'

'It should be. Why get married if you don't mean to stick to your vows?'

'It's not that simple. You've never been married, so you don't know.'

'I know that if Imogen was my wife, I wouldn't cheat on her,' Matthew burst out, then wished he hadn't. He didn't like the way Dickie was looking at him. He nodded at the camera. 'You're getting all the details, aren't you? I need to be able to read them.'

'They'll come out clear,' Dickie assured him.

Chapter Fifty-Six

TUESDAY, 30TH DECEMBER

Matthew tossed away the magazine as the door opened and Dr Woodrow entered the surgery waiting room.

'Inspector!' the doctor cried in surprise. 'What are you doing here?'

Matthew got to his feet, tugging his suit jacket down. 'Your secretary was kind enough to let me wait for you. I was hoping you could fit me in?'

'An appointment, you mean? Well, of course. Come in.' Woodrow waved Matthew through to his office. 'Take a seat, inspector, and tell me what the problem is.'

'It's the usual problem, Dr Woodrow. Nothing serious.'

'The headaches, you mean?'

Matthew nodded. 'I was hoping you'd be able to give me a stronger painkiller. The aspirin isn't doing much.'

'Well, a stronger painkiller would be laudanum or an opioid. But I wouldn't recommend them.'

'If they'll stop the headaches—'

'Oh yes, they'll do that,' Woodrow cut in, 'but that's not all they'll do. They dull the senses, and I imagine that isn't useful for a policeman. And I'm not in favour of these drugs at all. I rarely prescribe them because I fear they may become addictive.'

Matthew sighed. 'I don't want that. So, there's nothing you can give me?'

Woodrow shook his head. 'The aspirin will have to do. But if you'll forgive me, inspector, it is my firm belief that what you need is not drugs but rest. You look extremely tired.'

'I'm investigating a double murder, Dr Woodrow.'

'And before that, you were working on a slaughter over in Foxhall Green. Before that, the murder of a farmer. Before that, attacks on women. And before that, the murders at the Empire Club.' Woodrow shook his head. 'That would be too much for any man, let alone a man who was brutally attacked in the middle of it all.'

'I'm fine.'

'You're exhausted,' Woodrow said. 'You need a rest.'

Matthew opened his mouth to protest, an instinctive reaction, but then closed it again. What was he protesting against? he asked himself. Woodrow's common sense?'

'So, if I rest, the headaches will stop?' he asked.

'There's a good chance,' Woodrow nodded. 'I've read your medical notes. The blow you received was severe, but there is no lasting damage. There doesn't appear to be any physical reason for your headaches. It's my opinion that they are stress-related. Remove the stress and the headaches will cease. But,' he made a gesture of helplessness, 'if you insist on working yourself into the ground, I will prescribe you opiates. If that is what you want. I will have to inform your superior, however.'

'No,' Matthew said. 'I'll stick to the aspirin.' He rose and headed for the door. 'I appreciate you seeing me without an appointment.'

'Not at all, inspector,' Dr Woodrow said thoughtfully as Matthew left.

———

Linda Pearson was waiting for him when he got to the station.

He opened the door to the private waiting room and saw Linda sitting at the table, a cigarette between her fingers, half smoked already. She didn't smile or say anything as Matthew closed the door and pulled out the other chair.

'I wasn't expecting to see you, Mrs Pearson,' he said.

A shaking hand lifted the cigarette to her lips. 'I don't want to get in any trouble,' she said, blowing out the smoke. 'Promise me I won't.'

'Why would you get in trouble?'

'Because I lied to you yesterday. I'm sorry. I didn't know what else to do.'

Matthew wasn't surprised. 'Tell me the truth now.'

Linda took another drag. 'Max did come round to my house and he did take me out in the car on Christmas Eve.'

'What time was this?'

'About quarter past eight.'

'Until?'

'Half twelve.'

'Where did you go?'

'The lane at the back of the golf course. It's dark there.' She coloured. 'I know what you think of me, but you don't know what it's like at home. You don't know what I have to put up with.'

Matthew wasn't interested in her marriage problems. All he could think was that Maxwell now had his alibi. 'He never left you during that time?' he asked to be sure.

She shook her head. 'Is it all right now I've told you the truth? I won't get into trouble for what I said yesterday?'

'No, you won't get into trouble,' Matthew said wearily.

'And you won't tell my husband about me and Max?'

'I have no reason to tell your husband anything, Mrs Pearson.'

'So, I can go?'

Matthew got to his feet and opened the door. 'Yes. You can go.'

———

'Barnes,' Matthew called as he walked into CID. 'Maxwell Carr's alibi has been corroborated. Linda Pearson has just told me they were together Christmas Eve until after midnight. He's off the hook.'

'So, we're another suspect down,' Barnes said dejectedly. 'They're falling like flies. All except Baddowes and he's looking more likely than ever.'

'Why's that?' Matthew asked, seeing Lund come out into the main office. He didn't see Walsh, and he wondered where he was. Perhaps he'd gone back to Colchester, as Matthew had said he should.

'A call came in half an hour ago,' Barnes went on. 'There was a burglary over in Croydon last night and it's got Nick Baddowes' MO all over it. Glass broken in the back door, only money and booze taken. And he duffed up the bloke who lived there. The doctors at the hospital reckon he might not make it.'

'There's your killer, Stannard,' Lund said. 'If Frye and the son-in-law are off your suspect list, then it's got to be Baddowes.'

Matthew took the report Barnes handed him of the burglary. 'It certainly looks like it,' he agreed. 'Have you informed the Yard?'

'Yes, sir,' Barnes said. 'They're on high alert for Baddowes. He won't be at liberty much longer.'

'Let's hope not.'

The telephone on Matthew's desk rang, and Lund went back in to answer it. 'I'll send him up,' Matthew heard him say.

Lund returned to the doorway. 'Mullinger wants to see you,' he said to Matthew. 'You can tell him the good news. Baddowes is your killer.'

———

'Take a seat, Stannard.' Mullinger said. 'I want an update on the Scotts' murders.'

Matthew settled himself in the chair. 'I'm fairly confident the killer was Nicholas Baddowes, the burglar,' he said. 'I've just been told about a burglary committed in Croydon last night. It bears the hallmarks of Baddowes and he beat up the homeowner so badly he's in hospital and not expected to recover. If he does die, at the very least, it will warrant a manslaughter charge.'

'So, the Scotts were a burglary gone wrong,' Mullinger said, satisfied with that conclusion. 'And every effort is being made to find this Baddowes, I trust?'

'Every effort, sir.'

'Good. That's good for you.'

Matthew frowned, wondering what that last remark meant. He found out a moment later.

'I've had a telephone call from Dr Woodrow,' Mullinger continued. 'Apparently, you had an appointment with him this morning.'

'I popped in there, sir,' Matthew said, cursing Woodrow for contacting Mullinger. Whatever happened to patient confidentiality?

'He believes you're overworked. That you're in need of a rest. He's recommended your going on sick leave.'

'Dr Woodrow shouldn't have bothered you, sir. I only went there to ask for some stronger pills for my headache.'

Mullinger grunted and looked Matthew up and down. 'Nevertheless, there is no doubting you've had quite a year since coming here. I don't want to be accused of running my men into the ground, so as this Scott case is all cleared up bar the capture of Baddowes, I think it would be wise to accept Woodrow's recommendation. Lund can take over the Scott case. He seems to have pulled himself together.'

The way Mullinger was looking at him, Matthew suspected the superintendent was expecting him to voice a protest. But, strangely, he didn't feel like making one. He was sick and tired of the case. It would be a relief to give it to someone else.

'Lund can take over,' Matthew agreed. 'But I don't need to go off sick. I've got four days' leave owing. I'll take those if you don't mind.'

Mullinger's eyebrows rose in surprise. 'Four days' leave, then. Very well. Effective immediately.'

———

'What did Old Mouldy want?' Lund asked as Matthew entered their office.

'An update on the case. I told him about Baddowes.'

'So, all you've got to do is find him, and it's another case you've cracked.'

'All *you've* got to do is find him,' Matthew corrected, taking his hat and coat down from the stand.

Lund frowned up at him. 'You what?'

'I'm on leave, effective immediately,' Matthew explained. 'You're taking over the Scott case.'

'Old Mouldy's taken you off it?' Lund cried.

'No. *I've* taken me off.' Matthew shook his head and shrugged. 'I need a break, Lund. And with the whole Met out looking for Baddowes, there's nothing more to do.'

'Nah,' Lund shook his head. 'This doesn't sound like you, Stannard. Since when do you walk away from a case?'

'There has to be a first time for everything.' Matthew smiled at him. 'It's fine, Lund.' He strode out into the main office.

'Well, when are you back?' Lund shouted after him.

'In four days,' Matthew said when he reached the door. 'And I'll expect you to have Baddowes in custody.'

Chapter Fifty-Seven

Matthew went straight home after leaving the station, surprising Bella and Hobbs out of a sound sleep. He set down a saucer of milk and one of sardines for them, made himself a cup of tea and carried it to his bedroom.

Taking off his jacket and pulling on a jumper, Matthew kicked off his shoes and plumped up the pillows. He took his notebook and pencil from his jacket pocket, tossed them onto the eiderdown, and sat down on the bed with the copies of Walsh's case file and the Alice Burns papers on his lap. A few minutes later, Bella and Hobbs came in and settled around his ankles.

Beside him, he laid out all the snatch reports since 1920. Matthew drew a table with four columns in his notebook: the name of the baby, the date it was stolen and the date it was found, where it was taken from, and the person who found it and what they did for a living. After fifteen minutes, he'd filled in almost every section of the table, and he was astonished. Every child discovered at a church had been found by the church's cleaner!

It had all started with Alice Burns. Matthew remembered what he had said to Rudd about missing statements and

Rudd's reply that DI Vaughn hadn't thought the people Margaret Burns had mentioned were worth following up on. Curious whether Walsh had asked her about them, he rifled through the copies for detective's report. Reading it, he had to concede Walsh was an excellent note-taker; his report was almost word for word what had passed between him and Margaret, but he saw, not without some satisfaction, that Walsh hadn't asked the vital questions.

Disentangling his legs from the cats, Matthew padded out into the hall and picked up the telephone. The line had barely connected when Margaret Burns picked up. Matthew introduced himself and explained why he was calling.

'But I've already spoken with DI Walsh,' Margaret protested.

'I just need to ask you a couple of questions he didn't. It won't take long. In the days after your baby was taken, DI Vaughn wrote in his report that you complained the police hadn't spoken to certain people – your friend, the milkman and the cleaner. Did you mean *your* cleaner? Someone you employed?'

'I didn't have a cleaner. I suppose I must have meant the cleaner at the hospital. She was always poking her nose into the cot when she came around the ward.'

'Do you remember her name?'

'I'm not sure I ever knew it. You'd have to ask the hospital.'

'But can you describe her to me?'

'Oh, it was such a long time ago.' There was a pause at the end of the line, and Matthew waited anxiously. 'She was in her late thirties, I suppose. A little plump. Dark hair. I really can't remember more than that.'

'That's fine,' he assured her. 'I have just one more question. You also mentioned a friend to DI Vaughn. Who would that have been?'

'That would have been Imogen.'

Matthew's stomach lurched. 'Imogen?' he repeated dully.

'Imogen Carr. We met at St Catherine's and became friends. Briefly, anyway, because I must have scared her off. She didn't even come to see me when my baby was found. I never saw her again.'

Matthew thanked her and hung up the telephone, wondering if perhaps Walsh was right about Imogen after all. Yes, he'd found an important clue in the cleaner, but could it really be only a coincidence that Imogen had known Margaret Burns and had left Craynebrook the very day the dead baby turned up?

He returned to his bedroom, and Bella meowed lazily at him. As he stroked her head, his eyes fell on the copies spread over his bed and Walsh's report of his interview with Miss Richardson, the senior nurse at the maternity hospital. Miss Richardson had remembered Margaret Burns. Maybe she would remember Imogen and the cleaner too. Matthew went back into the hall and asked the operator to connect him.

'I don't know what more I can tell you, inspector,' Miss Richardson said when Matthew explained why he was calling. 'I answered all DI Walsh's questions.'

'DI Walsh asked you about Susan Madden,' Matthew said. 'I want to ask you about two other people you may have come into contact with when you worked at the hospital. Firstly, a Mrs Imogen Carr. She was there the same time as Margaret Burns. Do you remember her?'

'Imogen Carr? No, I don't recall that name. You have to appreciate, inspector,' she said with a sigh, 'there were a lot of women under my care. I don't remember them all. I only remember Mrs Burns because of what happened to her baby.'

'Yes, I understand,' Matthew said. 'What about a cleaner on the ward? Mrs Burns said the police ought to talk to a cleaner about her baby, and you mentioned to DI

Walsh that some of the staff left after Madden had a tantrum and lashed out. Were any of those who left on the cleaning staff?'

'Did I say some? I exaggerated if I did. In fact, there was only one woman who left and yes, she was one of the cleaners. I'm sorry. I didn't mean to mislead Inspector Walsh.'

'The cleaner who left—'

'Oh, she didn't leave as such,' she cut him off. 'Just didn't come back. She wasn't actually a member of the hospital staff, you see. The hospital got all its cleaners from an agency.'

'An agency. I don't suppose you remember the agency's name?'

'Baxter's Domestic Agency,' Miss Richardson replied promptly. 'Funny, isn't it? I have trouble remembering the patients, but I can recollect all the names of the people who worked at the hospital and even the firms.'

'So, you can give me the cleaner's name?' Matthew asked, and held his breath for the answer.

'Oh yes. Her name was Angela Newbury.'

Matthew let out his breath. Angela Newbury. The same woman who discovered Alice Burns on the church step.

'Thank you, Miss Richardson. That's all I needed to know.'

He hung up the telephone and grabbed his telephone directory, flipping the pages until he reached the Bs. He ran his finger down the columns, hoping Baxter's Domestic Agency was still in operation.

'Yes,' he cried when he found their listing and picked up the telephone, hoping someone there would have been working at the agency in 1920 and could tell him about Angela Newbury.

His luck held. The manageress at Baxter's Domestic Help Agency proudly told Matthew they kept all their records, even back to 1899 when they first opened, and she retrieved Angela Newbury's personnel file while he stayed on the line.

'Mrs Newbury was on our books from the 1st of March until the 23rd of November 1920.'

'Is there an address for her?' he asked.

'There is, but it won't do you any good. According to the notes in her file, she left because she and her husband were moving away.' He heard the shuffling of papers and then the voice came back. 'But I've just found this in her file. A letter asking if we would provide a character reference for her. She intended to apply to another domestic agency in the area she had moved to and she gave us an address to send it to. It was a Post Office box number in Brentwood. Is that any help?'

Brentwood! There had been a snatch there too.

'Yes, very helpful. Thank you.' Matthew put the receiver back in its cradle.

There was nothing else for it. He would have to contact all the domestic agencies in Brentwood until he found Angela Newbury. The only problem was he didn't have any telephone directories for Brentwood. Matthew got back on the telephone and asked the operator to connect him with a police station in Brentwood. When she asked which one, he replied, a little impatiently, that any would do.

When the line connected, Matthew asked the detective constable he was put through to provide him with the names, addresses and telephone numbers of every domestic agency in the area, hoping the young man wouldn't question a Metropolitan Police detective asking an Essex constabulary for assistance. To his relief, the DC called back forty-five minutes later with a list.

It was a long list. Brentwood had eleven domestic agencies, and Matthew needed to call them all. Not relishing what his telephone bill would look like at the end of the month, he picked up the receiver and began.

His first question to the manager or manageress who took his call was whether the agency had been in operation in 1922 when the Brentwood snatch occurred. If they had only opened after 1922, he didn't bother taking the conversation any further. He eliminated seven from the list in this way. Of the four that were left, only one had had an Angela Newbury on its books.

Angela had started working for Somerville Domestic Agency in January 1922 and left in August. The 8th of August, to be precise, the very day Jessica Shaw had been left on a Brentwood church's doorstep. Only she hadn't been found by Angela Newbury. The cleaner who found the baby was called Vera Rees.

'What about a Vera Rees?' Matthew asked the manager, referring to the table he had made of the snatches.

There was the sound of paper being sorted and then the manager's voice came down the line. 'No, inspector. We didn't have anyone of that name on our books.'

Matthew's excitement faded. 'Then can you tell me who Mrs Newbury cleaned for?'

'Yes, we have worksheets and duty rosters for all our staff. Is there any particular client you're interested in?'

'Did Mrs Newbury clean at All Saints' Church?' He waited, holding his breath, as the manager checked his paperwork.

'Inspector?' the voice said.

'I'm here,' Matthew replied.

'All Saints was one of Mrs Newbury's, yes.'

Matthew hung up the telephone. It was a leap, he knew, but he believed it couldn't be a coincidence Angela Newbury had moved to Brentwood and had not only worked at the church where Jessica Shaw was found but had left the agency on the very same day. There was only one conclusion to be made: Angela Newbury and Vera Rees were one and the same woman.

Chapter Fifty-Eight

Lund couldn't quite work out what was going on. It wasn't like Stannard to walk away in the middle of a case, even if it was all but over. And since when had Stannard been happy to go on leave? He had to be practically forced to take a day off, and yet, according to what Mullinger had told him, he hadn't put up even the faintest protest.

Movement outside his office caught Lund's eye. Walsh was talking to Rudd. Had Walsh done or said something to Mullinger to get Stannard out of his way? Lund wondered. Had Mullinger told him everything?

Walsh made his way towards Lund's office and sat down without waiting for an invitation. 'Rudd says Stannard's on leave. You're in charge of the murder case and that you know this Baddowes did it. So, are you charging Sarah Kempe with being an accomplice to murder?'

Lund shook his head. 'Stannard seemed convinced she was clueless about the murders.'

'Ah, well,' Walsh raised an eyebrow, 'if Stannard said so.'

'Give it a rest, Walsh,' Lund said wearily.

'I'm just saying you've got to take Stannard's opinions with a pinch of salt. After all, he flitted around with his suspect list, didn't he? First, he thought it was the doctor. Then Sarah Kempe and Baddowes. Then the son-in-law, only to discover it was Baddowes after all.'

'That's how it works, Walsh. You have a suspect list, and you work through it, eliminating as you go. You should know that.'

'I do know that,' Walsh retorted. 'It's just he accused me of grasping at straws. If you ask me, he's been doing that ever since this investigation started.'

'I'm not asking you,' Lund said. 'And you ought to watch your mouth. Stannard's the best detective I've ever worked with, present company included. His reputation is well-deserved and bloody hard-earned. The man never stops, and he doesn't do it because he's hoping to get promoted, like some I could mention.'

Walsh's lips twisted in irritation. He opened his mouth to reply when Lund's telephone rang.

Lund snatched up the receiver. 'Lund,' he barked into the mouthpiece. 'I can hear him. All right. I'm coming down.' He hung up and rose from his chair.

'What's that about?' Walsh asked.

'Maxwell Carr is downstairs, effing and blinding at Turkel,' Lund said. 'Insists on seeing someone in authority. Which means me, apparently.'

He hurried down the stairs to the lobby, Walsh following at his heels. Maxwell's voice could be heard even before he got to the bottom.

'At last!' Maxwell cried as Lund entered the lobby. 'DI Lund, isn't it?'

Lund shoved his hands deep in his trouser pockets and nodded. 'What seems to be the problem, Mr Carr?'

'This is the problem,' Maxwell said, pointing to his swollen left eye. 'You know who did this? Bill Pearson, that's who.'

'Got into a fight with him, did you?'

'I didn't have a chance to get into a fight, as you call it. I answered my front door, and before I could blink, Bill Pearson had punched me in the face.'

'And why did he do that?' Lund asked innocently.

'Because your Inspector Stannard told him about me and his wife, that's why,' Maxwell roared.

'Mr Pearson being married to Mrs Linda Pearson,' Lund nodded in mock understanding. 'Who I believe you were enjoying a bit of How's-Your-Father with while your in-laws were being murdered.'

Maxwell glared at him. 'Inspector Stannard promised discretion. Instead of which he informs Pearson about my private affairs.'

'I'm sure Inspector Stannard did nothing of the sort, Mr Carr,' Lund said. 'Perhaps Mr Pearson found out from his wife?'

'I want to make a complaint about Stannard,' Maxwell said. 'The trouble he's caused me is indefensible. Not only this,' he pointed once more to his damaged eye, 'but it's set my wife off. I've had to deal with her screaming at me because of what Pearson did.'

'Well, if you will stray, Mr Carr, you have to expect your wife not to be too pleased about it,' Lund said with a grin. 'You sure it was Mr Pearson who gave you that shiner and not your missus?'

'It was Pearson,' Maxwell insisted through gritted teeth.

'Do you want to press charges against Mr Pearson, sir?' Lund suggested. 'Of course, I can't guarantee the press won't get to hear of it. And it will certainly get out if you lodge a complaint against Inspector Stannard. The 'papers love writing about him, especially when an accusation is completely unfounded. That's happened before, you know. The newspapers had to publish a grovelling apology to him, and the person who accused him had to suffer being called a liar in the press. You see, Mr Carr, Inspector Stannard has an exemplary reputation and record,' Lund glanced meaningfully at Walsh. 'I daresay the press would reckon it's a case of sour grapes on your part. You being found out getting your leg over, I mean.'

Maxwell had turned purple with rage, and Lund was satisfied he was going to give it up.

'You said your wife was screaming at you,' Walsh said, and Lund could have throttled him for sticking his nose in.

'Yes, she was. I'm sure the whole street heard her,' Maxwell said.

'What about the baby?'

'Well, he was screaming too,' he replied as if it was obvious. 'He started as soon as she did.'

'The baby's all right, though?' Lund asked in concern.

'What?' Maxwell said impatiently. 'I suppose so. That's Imogen's department. I don't get involved.'

'He's your son, isn't he?' Lund asked angrily.

'Is he, though?' Walsh cut in, shoving Lund to one side to stand before Maxwell. 'Can you be sure the baby's yours?'

Maxwell stared at him in incomprehension. 'Are you accusing my wife of sleeping with other men?'

'Walsh!' Lund said warningly.

But Walsh ignored him. 'You had no idea your wife was pregnant when she left, did you?'

'No, she didn't tell me.'

'So, how can you be sure she actually was pregnant? After all, you've been trying to have a child for years and no luck. And then all of a sudden—'

'What are you saying?' Maxwell asked, his bluster fading.

'She's not breastfeeding, is she?' Walsh asked. 'And you must have seen her naked. Has she got the body of a woman who's given birth recently? Answer me that.'

'That's enough, Walsh,' Lund said, grabbing hold of Walsh's arm and yanking him away. 'You're crossing a line, and you know it.' He turned to Maxwell, who was staring open-mouthed at Walsh. 'Are you pressing charges against Pearson or not?'

Maxwell shook his head dumbly.

'Or making a complaint against Inspector Stannard?'

'No,' Maxwell said. 'I just want it noted.'

'It's noted. Now, I suggest you get home to your wife. And try being kind to her for a change.' He steered Maxwell out of the station doors and watched him walk away. 'Turkel,' he called to the desk sergeant. 'I want you to send a Uniform to Mrs Pearson's house straight away. If Mr Pearson has found out about her affair, then he might have walloped her too. Get someone round there to make sure she's all right.'

'Will do, sir,' Turkel said, and hurried away to find a constable.

Lund turned on Walsh. 'I've just about had enough of you. What do you think you were doing, telling him stuff like that?'

'Trying to provoke a reaction, Lund,' Walsh said.

'You'll be lucky if that's all you've provoked. If he goes home and thumps his wife because of what you've said, it'll be on your conscience.'

'I can live with that,' Walsh assured him.

Lund's top lip curled in a sneer. 'I don't doubt it.'

Chapter Fifty-Nine

Matthew's head was throbbing by the time he hung up the telephone several hours later.

As he had done for Brentwood, he did for Chelmsford. Sitting on his hall floor, he had contacted a local police station, asked for them to provide a list of their area's domestic agencies and then settled down to ring around them all.

Chelmsford had seventeen domestic agencies, with twelve of them open in 1924. None had employed an Angela Newbury or a Vera Rees, but the manageress of Johnson Domestics confirmed they had had a cleaner who was similar in appearance to the Angela Newbury description Matthew gave her, only her name had been Mary Spicer. She had gone onto their books in January 1923 and left without giving notice on the 9th of July 1924, two days after Luke McGill had been returned and found by Mary Spicer!

There was no doubt in Matthew's mind now that he had found the snatcher. His first instinct was to call the station and tell Walsh what he'd found out, but he hesitated. Why should he give Walsh all the benefit of his hard work? Would Walsh even pay any attention?

Rubbing his reddened ear where the receiver had been clamped for so long, Matthew clambered to his feet, intending to make himself something to eat. But his doorbell rang, and wondering who could be calling on him, he turned the latch and opened it.

'Don't send me away, please,' Imogen begged.

'Mrs Carr?' he blurted out in astonishment. 'What are you doing here?'

Imogen reached out a gloved hand to him, and he stared stupidly at a dark stain on the pale leather as she grabbed the fingers of his left hand. 'I don't have anywhere else to go.' She glanced down at the suitcase and carrycot on the floor beside her. 'We couldn't stay at home. Not now.'

Matthew stared at the sleeping baby in the basket. 'But how did you know where I live?' he asked.

'You dropped this when you were last at the house,' she said, taking a brown envelope from her handbag and giving it to him.

It was his gas bill. He'd stuffed it into his coat pocket the morning it arrived and forgotten all about it.

'I'm sorry,' Imogen said. 'I know I'm the last person you want to see, but there's no one else I can turn to.'

As she spoke, she lifted her chin, and Matthew saw bruises on her throat. 'How did you get those?' he demanded.

'Oh,' she said, putting her hand to her throat to hide them. 'Max. He was angry. You know it's not the first time he's hurt me.'

Matthew remembered the bruises on her wrists. 'If you want to press charges against him—'

'Oh no, I couldn't bear to go through all that. I just can't stay with him any longer. You see, I know about the woman he's been seeing. I can see from your face you know about her too.'

'I'm sorry,' he said, feeling awkward. 'Look, you'd better

come in.' She picked up the carrycot and entered. 'Go into the sitting room,' Matthew said, reaching down to pick up her suitcase before following.

Imogen put the carrycot by the side of the sofa and took off her hat and coat, stuffing her gloves in the pockets. Matthew set the suitcase down by the basket and took her hat and coat as Bella and Hobbs trotted into the room and stared at Imogen. Bella arched her back and hissed.

'Bella!' Matthew chided, and she backed away, ears flattened against her head. He turned to Imogen, who was scowling at the cats. 'I'm sorry. She's not normally like that. Can I get you anything? Tea, coffee? I'm sorry, but I don't have any sherry.' What else did women drink? he wondered.

Imogen shook her head. 'I don't need anything.' She sank onto the sofa and bent to fuss with the blankets covering the baby.

'Have you actually left your husband?' Matthew asked, needing clarification.

'I suppose I have. At least, I don't mean to go back. Not this time.'

'Where are you going to stay?'

She looked up at him with her big blue eyes that, to his horror, were brimming with tears. 'I wondered...' She broke off and sniffed. 'I hoped you would let me stay here.'

'Here?' he cried.

'Just for a few days. Until I can find somewhere. I know I'm a dreadful nuisance, but you're the only person who's ever shown me any kindness.' She reached out and slid her fingers around his hand once more. 'I'm begging you, Matthew. Please let me stay.'

Matthew knew he should say no, remind her she was a married woman, and that it wasn't right for her to spend the night in his flat because people would talk. But he also knew he couldn't throw her and the baby out or send her back to Maxwell.

'Of course you can stay,' he said.

'Thank you.' Imogen let go of his hand and patted the sofa cushion. 'I shall be fine here.'

'You'll sleep in the bedroom,' Matthew said. 'I'll sleep on the sofa.'

'Well, if you're sure. Have you eaten, Matthew? Let me cook you dinner as a thank you for putting up with me.'

'You don't have to do that.'

'I'd like to. Please.' She was already heading out of the sitting room, and he heard her say, 'Is this the kitchen?' and then the sound of her opening cupboard doors.

He took another look at the sleeping baby and followed after her. Imogen had found a steak in his refrigerator, no doubt put there by Pat while he was out, and two potatoes from the cupboard. She turned to him with a smile. 'Steak and sauté potatoes. How does that sound?'

'It sounds good,' he said.

'I think even I can manage that. Don't you watch me, though. I really will do it all wrong if you do.'

'I'll just get my things,' he said, and went into his bedroom and took his pyjamas out from beneath the pillow. He folded down the blankets, grateful Pat had also changed the sheets. He took one of the pillows from the bed and a blanket from the shelf in the wardrobe and carried them into the sitting room, placing them out of sight behind the sofa. Bella perched on the arm and peered down at the baby in the basket.

'Don't let it do that!'

Matthew turned to see Imogen hurrying towards him. She swatted angrily at Bella, who scurried away. 'Bella was only looking,' he protested.

'It might have scratched him,' Imogen insisted. 'I can't

have your cats anywhere near my baby, Matthew. Keep them away, please.'

'I will. They'll stay with me out here tonight. And tomorrow, I'll find you a hotel to stay in.'

Her face fell. 'You want to get rid of me so soon?'

'I think it would be for the best, Mrs Carr.'

She moved a little closer. 'Won't you call me Imogen, Matthew? I thought we were friends. We are friends, aren't we?'

'Of course we are,' he said, and smiled a little shyly. 'Imogen.'

Chapter Sixty

NEW YEAR'S EVE

The whistling of the kettle woke Matthew.

Opening bleary eyes, he sat up, wincing at the crick in his neck and rubbed it as he tried to work out why he was in his sitting room and not in his bedroom, and then remembered. Matthew glanced at the carriage clock on the mantelpiece and panicked when he saw it was a quarter to eleven before remembering he was on leave and didn't have to go into work.

Throwing back the blanket, Matthew reached for his dressing gown. He pulled it on, ran his hand through his hair to flatten it and went into the kitchen.

Imogen was frying bacon. She smiled at Matthew and said, 'Good morning, sleepyhead.'

'Morning,' he said, a little embarrassed to face her in his pyjamas. 'Did you sleep all right?'

'Oh, like a log. You?'

'Fine,' Matthew lied. In fact, it didn't feel like he'd slept at all. 'I'll be going out soon.'

'To work, yes, I know.'

Matthew didn't correct her. Technically, he supposed, he was working. He had planned to spend the day repeating his calls of yesterday, this time in Witham, but Imogen being there had put paid to that idea; he couldn't make police enquiries with a civilian in his flat. And if he was honest with himself, Matthew didn't want to be alone with Imogen all day. It would be too awkward. What on earth would they talk about?

The baby cried. Imogen cracked an egg into a teacup as if she hadn't heard him.

'Your baby's crying, Imogen,' Matthew said. 'Shouldn't you go to him?'

She shook her head. 'It won't make any difference. He'll still cry. I can't do anything with him.'

Matthew glanced uneasily out of the door. 'Well, it's no good my seeing to him. I don't have a clue what to do.'

She turned to him and smiled. 'You'll make an excellent father, Matthew. Your breakfast's almost ready. Go and sit down.'

He did as he was told, the baby's crying making him uneasy. Imogen came in a moment later with a plate of eggs and bacon and a cup of coffee. She set them down in front of him, bid him eat and took a seat herself.

'Is it all right?' she asked.

'It's fine,' he said, thinking the bacon was a little too crispy for his liking and the egg too runny. 'Imogen, I need to ask you something.'

Her expression became wary. 'What?'

'Where did you go when you went away in May?'

She groaned. 'Oh, why does everyone keep asking that?'

'It's important,' Matthew said. 'Please tell me.'

'If you must know, I stayed with an old friend.'

'Your family said you didn't have any friends.'

Imogen smiled. 'My family didn't know everything about me.'

'And this friend lives in Colchester?'

'I suppose that other detective told you that? Yes, she lives in Colchester. Happy now?'

'What's her name?'

'Why do you want to know?' she snapped, her eyes blazing. 'So you can check up on me?'

That was exactly why he wanted to know, but Matthew didn't say so. 'Has she always lived in Colchester?'

'She's been there for a while, yes. Now, I'm not talking about her anymore, Matthew. A lady must be allowed to have some secrets.' The baby's cries grew louder. 'Oh, for heaven's sake,' Imogen muttered and hurried out to see to him.

The noise from the bedroom lessened after a minute or two. Matthew wolfed down the breakfast she'd cooked for him and headed for the bathroom.

Washed and dressed, Matthew shut Bella and Hobbs in the box room with their litter tray and enough food and water for the day, and said goodbye to Imogen, tentatively suggesting as he went out the door that she could spend her day finding a hotel for herself and the baby.

———

'Well, well, look who it is,' DS Powell said as Matthew walked into Hackney CID. 'Matthew Stannard, as I live and breathe.' He held out his hand.

Matthew took it, feeling oddly pleased to see his old colleague again. 'It's good to see you, Powell. How are you?'

'Oh, so-so.' He peered at Matthew and frowned. 'You all right?'

'Fine,' Matthew said, wondering how bad he must look for Powell to ask. 'Busy.'

'We heard. A double murder. We've been told to look out for your suspect. Baddowes, is it?'

'That's right. But I'm not here for that. To be honest, I'm after a favour.'

Powell's eyebrows rose in surprise. 'You? Asking a favour? Never thought I'd hear that.'

Please don't be difficult, Matthew mentally begged. 'If it's a problem—' he offered, and gestured that he could leave.

'Nah. Don't be like that,' Powell said. 'What do you want?'

'Just to use the telephone for a while. I've got a lot of enquiries to make.'

'And you can't make them at your station because…?'

'Because I'm supposed to be on leave,' he admitted. 'But there's a case I'm looking into, and I don't want my guvnor knowing until I've cleared it up. So if you can let me have a desk and a telephone, I can get on with it. I won't get in your way, I promise.'

Powell looked him up and down with curiosity, then nodded. 'I'll have to clear it with the inspector, but I don't see why not. Get yourself a cuppa. Sit yourself down. I'll be back in five minutes.'

———

Fifteen minutes passed before Powell returned to CID, but he came with good news. He said he'd cleared Matthew working there, but that he would have to start after lunch because he wanted a good catch-up first. Matthew would have preferred to plough on with his enquiries, but felt obliged to agree, saying he just needed to make a telephone call. While Powell pulled on his coat, Matthew telephoned a police station in Witham and asked for a list of all the domestic agencies in the area.

To his surprise, Matthew enjoyed his lunch with Powell. They'd never got on all that well before, but it was good to talk over old times with someone who knew him before he became something of a police celebrity and it was gone two o'clock by the time they returned to the station. Matthew was pleased to see that a message had been left for him on the desk he had been given. It was a list of twelve domestic agencies in Witham. He settled in to call them all.

Only one out of the twelve agencies hadn't been in business in 1927. It took him another two hours to eliminate five more, and thirty minutes more to come across Grace Martins, the woman who had discovered Michael Perrin.

Everything was falling into place. The only thing that troubled Matthew was why Witham broke up the Colchester snatches. Had Angela Newbury, aka Grace Martins, moved to Colchester and snatched a baby in 1926 before moving to Witham and snatching another in '27, only to return to Colchester for another snatch in 1928? Matthew figured the only way he'd get an answer to that question was to ask her if he caught her.

Thanking Powell for all his help, Matthew left the station, catching the bus to take him back to Halesden. The bus was full of people who all seemed determined to begin their New Year celebrations early, and his head was thumping when he put his key into his front door lock around eight o'clock.

Matthew saw Imogen's hat and coat still on his hall stand when he opened the door. 'I'm back,' he called, rather pleased she was still in the flat. Matthew made his way to the sitting room, smiling at the novelty of having had someone to call out to when he came home. But the smile vanished as his eyes fell upon Imogen, and he saw she wasn't alone.

'Hello, Pat,' he said as nonchalantly as he could. 'I wasn't expecting you.'

'Obviously,' Pat said, glancing at Imogen beside her on the sofa. 'But here I am.'

'We've been chatting,' Imogen said. 'You never told me you had a sister, Matthew.'

He saw Pat bristle at Imogen's use of his Christian name, and it annoyed him. What was it to Pat if Imogen called him Matthew? Or was it that he hadn't mentioned her to Imogen that riled?

'What are you doing here?' he asked.

'I never needed a reason before, Mattie,' Pat said indignantly. 'I came to say Happy New Year and to see if you would come round to the pub tonight. But I suppose you're busy.' She slid another glance at Imogen, her mouth tightening in irritation.

Matthew didn't answer. He hadn't even thought about celebrating the New Year. There was an awkward silence until Imogen spoke.

'Well,' she said brightly. 'You'll have to excuse me, Patricia. Now Matthew's home, I must get his dinner. He won't be going out tonight. He's had a long day. Will you be staying?'

'No,' Pat said sharply. 'I'll talk to my brother and then I'll be off.'

'That's probably best. Well, it's been lovely to meet you.' Imogen rose and headed for the kitchen, squeezing Matthew's arm as she passed by him.

The gesture didn't go unnoticed by Pat. 'Well, she's made herself very much at home here, I must say.'

'You should have told me you were coming over,' Matthew said.

'So you could get her out of the way?'

'So I could have been here when you called,' Matthew said, but knowing she was right. He would never have let Pat know about Imogen if he could have helped it.

'I tried calling you yesterday,' Pat said, 'but the line was always busy. I even called your station this morning, but they told me you were on leave. I thought you were working on those murders we read about it in the 'paper.'

'I was, but Lund's taken over.'

'Why?'

'Because I wanted some time off, Pat,' he cried. 'The case is practically solved. We know who did it. It's just a matter of catching him, and Lund can do that.'

'Since when do you take days off?' Pat jerked her head at the door. 'Since her, is it?'

Matthew sighed wearily. He really didn't want this conversation. 'Pat—' he began.

She cut him off. 'How long has it been going on? Well, long enough for her to have a baby, I suppose. I heard it crying in the bedroom.'

'You don't understand.'

'I suppose she's why you couldn't make Christmas. You weren't working at all.'

'I was working, Pat.'

'What I don't understand is why she's been kept a secret. Is it because you thought Mum would make a fuss? Or is it that you're ashamed of us?'

'Will you shut up?' Matthew burst out, his head pounding. 'I was working at Christmas. That's the truth. I haven't told you about Imogen because there's nothing to tell.'

'Nothing to tell?' Pat shot back. 'You're living in sin with a married woman. I never thought you'd stoop so low.'

'She's not living here. She's only been here since yesterday.'

'What about the baby?'

'It's not mine. For God's sake, I only met her a week ago.'

'Then what is she doing here if you're not involved with her?'

'I'm not having an affair, Pat. She's a case.'

'A what?'

'The murder case I was working on. It was her parents who were killed. She turned up on my doorstep last night begging to stay because she had nowhere else to go. I couldn't turn her out, not with a baby. She had my room. I slept on that.' He jabbed a finger at the sofa. 'And I've been out all day.'

'Then why is she still here? Nowhere else to go?' Pat scoffed. 'You fell for that? She's got a home, hasn't she?'

'She's doesn't want to go home because she's scared of her husband. You saw the bruises on her neck?'

'I saw them,' Pat said. 'In fact, she pointed them out to me, very keen to tell me how her husband tried to strangle her. But I don't believe a word of it.'

'What do you mean?'

'I mean, if you ask me, she put them there herself. Those bruises are only on one side of her neck, aren't they? If he put his hand around her throat, there'd be a thumb mark on the other side too.'

'That's ridiculous,' he cried. 'Why would she do them to herself?'

'To get your sympathy. Oh, you're a fool, Mattie. Can't you see she's using you? Just like that other little madam all those years ago.'

'Oh, don't bring that up, Pat, please.'

'Well, someone's got to make you see sense.'

'Make me see sense?' he yelled incredulously. 'I'm not a kid anymore, Pat. I'm sick and tired of you telling me what to do all the time.'

'I don't tell you—' Pat began, and Matthew heard her voice crack with emotion, but he couldn't stop himself now, even though he had roused the baby and it was wailing in the bedroom.

'And just turning up like this,' he went on, cutting her off, 'letting yourself in. I've had enough of that too.'

'I came to see you,' Pat said, and her tears fell.

Matthew was unmoved. 'If you want to see me in future, you call me first and find out if it's all right to come round. And stop letting yourself in when I'm not here. In fact, you can give me my key back.' He held out his hand.

Pat clambered to her feet, her face a mess of blotches and tears, and fumbled in her handbag. She pushed the key into his outstretched hand and stumbled past him, out into the hall. The front door slammed.

Matthew thrust the key into his pocket and yelled, 'Imogen!'

She came into the sitting room. 'What is it?' she asked.

'Your son's crying. Can't you hear him?' He opened the cupboard and took out a bottle of whisky, pouring himself a double measure. He downed half of it.

'I know,' she sighed. 'But he'll stop eventually. Oh, has your sister gone? I heard shouting. Did you quarrel, Matthew? I hope it wasn't because of me. I was perfectly polite to her even though I could tell she didn't like me. Does she really run a public house? It sounds perfectly dreadful. You don't go there often, do you? I don't think I could be seen in a place like that.'

'Why would you go there?'

'To meet your mother,' she said with a smile. 'Maybe you could bring her here instead? That would be nicer.'

She chattered on as she laid the table, and all the while her son cried in the bedroom. The noise aggravated the ache in Matthew's head, and he wished she'd go to him.

Imogen set the knives and forks down and moved to Matthew to thread her arm through his. 'Dinner won't be long. I'll try to do better than last night. Sit down and talk to me. Tell me about your day.'

Matthew didn't want to talk. He desperately wanted to be on his own. 'I need to feed my cats,' he said, pulling out of her grasp and heading for the box room.

'Don't let them out, Matthew,' she called after him.

Matthew opened the box room door, and Bella rose from the bed he'd made her and Hobbs with a spare blanket, stretched lazily and came blinking towards him. She meowed as he picked her up and gave her a cuddle.

'Hungry?' She meowed in response. 'You've got to stay here,' he said, and put her back down. 'I'll be back,' he promised when she cried a protest as he closed the door.

He went into the kitchen and forked tuna onto two plates, tucking a saucer under his arm and putting the milk bottle into his trouser pocket. Going back to the box room, he set the tuna on the floor and poured the milk into a saucer. The cats ate and drank greedily, Hobbs making little noises of contentment. Matthew watched them with pleasure for a few minutes, then rose with a sigh and closed the door once more.

Imogen had their dinner on the table. 'There,' she said, cocking her head to one side and listening. 'He's stopped crying at last. Now we can have our dinner in peace.'

Chapter Sixty-One

The whisky had worked its magic, and the pain in his head had lessened a little, but Matthew found it easier to listen while Imogen talked and he tried to cut up his food.

Imogen saw him struggling with the lamb chop. 'I'm not very good at cooking,' she admitted. 'Of course, I never had to cook when we had a maid. Jane was quite good, and I could leave it all to her. I would like to cook more, though. I've often thought I would like to cook the Christmas lunch, but Mother would never let me. She said I'd ruin it, and she was probably right. It would be nice to try, though.'

'Well, now you'll be able to,' Matthew said, only after he'd spoken realising how insensitive his words were.

But Imogen didn't seem to notice. 'Yes, I suppose I can. I tried to make Mother understand that I wanted to have Christmas at home this year, just me, Max and the baby, but she wouldn't hear of it. She just stood there in that ugly green dress of hers and said, "Don't be silly, Imogen. You're spending Christmas with us." It didn't matter what I said.'

'At least it would only have been one day.'

'Oh no,' she said. 'Mother and Father were talking about coming to us on Boxing Day. They normally visit friends

328

then, but because of the baby, they decided they would spend it with us. You should have heard Max when I told him on the way home. He was all for telling them they could forget it. Well,' she smiled shyly, 'he didn't put it quite like that. His language was rather blue, in fact. But you know what I mean.'

Matthew smiled. Yes, he knew what she meant, though he was pleased she was too much of a lady to repeat her husband's words.

'So,' she said, pushing her shrivelled peas around her plate, 'you thought Max killed my parents?'

'For a little while,' he admitted, surprised by her matter-of-fact way of asking.

'But his mistress gave him an alibi, I know.' She sighed sadly. 'It's funny, but when I came back, I really hoped Max would love me again. I thought once we had a child everything would be all right, but it hasn't worked out that way.' With a tut of annoyance, she set her knife and fork together on the plate, and looked up at Matthew. 'What made you believe that woman when she said Max was with her the night my parents were killed?'

'I'm sorry?' Matthew said, frowning. His mind had wandered as she spoke, remembering what Dr Woodrow had said about the woman who had stolen a child to save her marriage.

'Well,' Imogen shrugged, 'surely, a woman like that, someone who has no sense of decency, who deceives her husband with another woman's husband, shouldn't be believed? After all, she's proved she's an accomplished liar.'

'You think she was lying?' Matthew asked. 'That your husband wasn't with her?'

'He could have told her to tell you they were together, couldn't he? To give him an alibi.'

'Why would she agree to do that?'

'Oh, Matthew, I would have thought that was obvious. She has a brute of a husband and wants to swap him for Max.'

'Another brute of a husband,' Matthew reminded her.

'What?' She frowned at him, then her eyes widened and she nodded. 'Oh, yes. I see what you mean. Yes, Max can be a brute.' Imogen fingered her neck gingerly.

'Imogen,' Matthew said, 'are you saying you think your husband did kill your parents?'

'He was very angry with my father,' Imogen said thoughtfully. 'After all, it was a cruel thing Father did. Maybe you shouldn't have let him go before you were truly sure he was innocent, that's all I'm saying. Maybe you ought to question him again.'

'I'm not working on the case anymore,' Matthew said, thinking maybe he should call Lund and suggest he double-check Maxwell's alibi. 'I'm on leave for a few days.'

Imogen beamed at him. 'Then you can stay at home with me tomorrow. We can have a lovely New Year's Day together.'

'I can't. I'm sorry. I have to go out again.'

'Then I'll come with you. I won't be a nuisance, I promise.'

'You might not be, but your baby would. You haven't brought a pram and we can't take him around in the carrycot.' He didn't bother to say that he couldn't take her to Colchester with him.

Her face fell. 'I'd forgotten about him. Couldn't I leave him with someone? One of your neighbours? Or your sister, even?'

'I don't think so,' Matthew said, stabbing a raw potato, wondering how Imogen could suggest his sister to babysit after the row they'd had, and especially as she knew how Pat disliked her.

'Oh, it's not fair,' Imogen burst out. 'He stops me from doing everything. Mother was right. I must get a nanny for him.'

Matthew was about to remind her she had wanted a baby when there was a thud followed by a scratching and a loud cry from the box room. Bella and Hobbs were getting restless. 'I'm going to let the cats out,' he said.

'No,' Imogen said sharply. 'I don't want them out here.'

'They've been locked up all day,' Matthew protested.

'They'll interfere with the baby.'

'He's in the bedroom, Imogen. I am letting them out.' He rose from the table and headed for the box room.

'You make such a fuss of those cats,' she said crossly and gathered up the plates. 'You don't care about my feelings at all.'

She strode out of the room, and Matthew heard her clattering in the kitchen. Bella scratched at the door again, and he opened it. She scampered out, meowing at him for taking so long. Hobbs waddled out after her.

Matthew went into the kitchen. Imogen was filling the sink with hot water to wash up, but when she saw him with Hobbs at his heels, she threw the dishcloth into the sink and declared she was having an early night. She brushed past Matthew without another word, and he heard the bedroom door slam. He stared aghast at the state his kitchen was in. Imogen had used every pot, pan and utensil he owned and she'd walked away from it all. With a loud sigh, Matthew rolled up his sleeves and got to work.

After an hour, his head pounding, his body aching, and knowing he would be spending another uncomfortable night on the sofa, Matthew decided he needed a hot bath and went into the bathroom to run the water. As he opened the door, a noxious odour hit him. He stepped inside and found the cause of the smell. Imogen had thrown the baby's soiled nappies in the bath.

Matthew's temper boiled over. He stormed out and banged on his bedroom door. 'Imogen,' he yelled. 'You've left dirty nappies in the bath.'

She didn't answer. Angry, annoyed, Matthew raised his hand to bang on the door again, but then let it fall. What was the point? He knew she wouldn't come out.

Fuming, he returned to the bathroom and opened the fanlight to air the room. Staring down at the mess in the bath, he groaned and turned on the taps. Falling to his knees, he set about washing the nappies.

'Happy bloody New Year,' he muttered as fireworks exploded outside his window.

Chapter Sixty-Two

THURSDAY, 1ST JANUARY 1931

Matthew woke early. He washed and dressed and ate a breakfast of tea and toast.

Imogen didn't come out of the bedroom, even though he knew she was awake because he heard her talking to the baby. He felt a little guilty about what had happened the previous night, even though he wasn't at all sure he'd done anything wrong.

Concerned she had spent all her money on buying food for him, Matthew put a pound note in Imogen's purse, burying it between a scribbled reminder to book a hair appointment and a receipt for a box of chocolate liqueurs. He hoped she wouldn't mind his going into her handbag, but he didn't want an argument about the money, and he wasn't sure she would find it if he left it elsewhere.

As he went to close the handbag, Matthew spotted a small black address book. Knowing he had no right to look inside, he nevertheless opened the book and flicked through the pages. There were very few entries: a couple of hairdressers, a dressmaker, other shops whose names he recognised from

Craynebrook High Street. There was an entry for a dentist in Craynebrook and under S, Scotts Printing Works and the Sherwood Close Surgery. Turning to the back of the small book, Matthew saw scrawled in pencil the name 'Canning' and an address and telephone number in Colchester. Hearing movement in the bedroom, he hurriedly copied the details into his notebook and replaced the address book in Imogen's handbag.

Shutting the cats back in the box room, Matthew tidied his pillow and blanket away and made sure the nappies he had washed the night before were hanging over the side of the bath where Imogen could see them, fervently hoping he wouldn't come home to the same scene that evening.

He scribbled a note to Imogen telling her he would be back late and not to wait for dinner for him. He added at the bottom, 'Happy New Year'. Then he put on his hat and coat and left the flat to make his way to Colchester.

———

Lund took a deep breath before he opened the door to Interview Room 1.

'Back again, Mr Carr,' he said, taking a seat at the table. 'Just can't stay away, can you?'

'Can we forgo the smart-alec comments, inspector?' Maxwell said. 'I'm here to report my wife missing.'

Lund was taken aback. 'I beg your pardon?'

'My wife is missing,' Maxwell said, enunciating each word to make sure Lund understood. 'And bearing in mind what happened last time she took off, I thought it best I come here and report it. I don't want to be accused of murdering her again.'

'Are you serious?' Lund asked, hoping this was a joke on Carr's part. But the look Maxwell returned to him made him realise he was very serious. 'How long has she been gone?'

'I don't know. She wasn't home on Tuesday when I got back after coming here. I just thought she'd gone out for a few hours to calm down. I didn't want to be at home, so I stayed at the golf club that night. Then I stayed on because they had a New Year's party. I didn't get home until early this morning, and I went straight to bed. It was only when I got up that I realised Imogen wasn't there.'

'She's taken the baby with her?'

'Yes. And a suitcase of clothes. There's no note. I've no idea where she's gone.'

The door opened, and Walsh came in. 'I heard Mr Carr was here,' he said in explanation to Lund.

'He's here to report his wife missing,' Lund told him, and their eyes met in understanding. 'The baby too.'

'For Christ's sake!' Walsh thumped his fist against the door. 'We should have picked her up when we had the chance.'

'We had nothing on her.'

'We had enough to bring her in.'

'Excuse me,' Maxwell said, 'but would you two mind telling me what you're talking about?'

Lund sighed. 'Inspector Walsh here believes that while she was away, your wife stole the baby she came home with.'

Maxwell stared at Walsh. 'You think Imogen abducted the baby?'

'I think she's abducted eight babies,' Walsh said, 'over the last ten years. And I also think she abducted a baby here in Craynebrook back in 1920 and left it dead on the church's front porch.'

'You're mad!' Maxwell cried. 'Imogen isn't capable of that.'

'Your wife is a neurotic, a hysteric. She's capable of

anything. And now,' he glared at Lund, 'we've lost her and the baby. If that kid ends up dead—'

'Don't you point your finger at me, Walsh,' Lund growled. 'Just because she's gone off again, it doesn't mean you're right.'

'Are you all stupid in the Met? How much more proof do you need?'

'For God's sake,' Maxwell cried. 'What is the matter with you? My wife's missing, the baby with her, and you stand there, arguing about stolen babies and telling me you think she killed one. You need to find her.'

'That's what we're going to do, Mr Carr,' Lund assured him.

'And you're wrong about the baby,' Maxwell said to Walsh. 'He's mine. I'll swear to it.'

Walsh yanked the door open and turned back to Maxwell with a contemptuous glare. 'Then you're as much a fool as you look,' he said.

Chapter Sixty-Three

Matthew held up his warrant card when the door opened and said, 'I'm sorry to disturb you, madam, but would you be Mrs Canning?'

The woman looked at him worriedly. 'Yes, I'm Mrs Canning. Is something wrong?'

'Not at all,' Matthew said, returning his warrant card to his pocket. 'I'd just like to ask you a few questions, if I may?'

'I suppose you'd better come in.' Mrs Canning opened the door, and he stepped inside, going into the front room as she directed.

The location and Mrs Canning herself surprised Matthew. Neither was what he had been expecting. The house was a narrow tenement on an unremarkable street, and Mrs Canning was at least twenty years older than Imogen and of a decidedly lower class. Not the type of woman he would have expected to be her friend.

'What do you want to ask me about?' Mrs Canning said, inviting him to take a seat.

'Mrs Imogen Carr.'

'Imogen? Has something happened to her? Is the baby all right?'

'They're both fine,' Matthew assured her. 'I understand Mrs Carr stayed with you recently?'

'That's right. She was here for a good few months.'

'This may sound like an odd question, Mrs Canning, but was she expecting when she stayed with you?'

Mrs Canning smiled. 'Well, of course she was. That's why she came to me. Imogen couldn't bear to be at home with all the hell her family give her, and she knew I'd look after her.'

Matthew breathed a sigh of relief. Imogen had been pregnant and the baby was hers. 'You've known Mrs Carr a while?' he asked.

'Going on ten years now. She always comes to us when things get too much at home.'

'You must be very close.'

Mrs Canning made a face. 'I wouldn't say that.'

Matthew frowned. 'But you sound almost like a second mother to her.'

'I'm nothing of the sort, dearie.' She laughed. 'If I'm anything, I suppose I'm her landlady.'

'You mean she pays you to stay here?'

'Not as such. Imogen's not what you would call a tenant. More of a paying guest. She gives us enough to cover her bed and board and a little bit extra to make it worth our while. The money's always handy. I'm not going to turn it down.'

'So, you're not friends?'

'We're friendly enough. But I only hear from her when she needs me. She just turns up when she wants somewhere to stay. And this last time, she really needed me. I delivered her baby,' Mrs Canning said, smiling. 'Lovely little thing, it was.'

'You delivered it?'

'Well, I am a midwife, dearie,' she said. 'I used to work in

Craynebrook at the maternity hospital. That's how we know each other.' She edged forward in her chair and frowned at him. 'You did say the baby is all right? I'm only asking because I had to show Imogen how to do everything. It worried me, if I'm honest, when she left, that she'd look after him all right.'

'She's managing,' Matthew said.

'That's good. But why are you here asking questions about her?'

'It's an enquiry I'm working on. Mrs Carr's parents were killed recently.'

'Oh, my Lord,' she cried, putting a hand to her mouth. 'Both of them dead? What was it? A car accident?'

'No accident. I'm afraid they were murdered.'

Mrs Canning stared at him. 'Murdered? And Imogen—'

'Is quite well,' Matthew assured her. 'She's coping better than anyone would have expected.'

Her eyes narrowed as she nodded, 'I bet she is.'

***

Dickie stepped out of the lift, crossed the hall and knocked on Matthew's front door.

He'd been having a lunchtime drink in the King George when Rudd came in. They'd got chatting, and when Dickie asked how the murder investigation was going, Rudd said it was all but over and that Lund was now in charge because Matthew had gone on leave. Astonished by this news, Dickie had grabbed the tin of gingerbread Emma had baked for Matthew as a thank-you for Bitsy and which he had planned to drop off at the police station and headed out of the pub to make his way to Halesden.

His knock wasn't answered. Dickie knocked again, and this time, he heard movement inside the flat: a door slamming and footsteps coming towards the door. It opened a moment later.

'Yes?' Imogen demanded.

Dickie stared at her in astonishment. 'Is Matthew home?' he asked at last.

'No, he's not. Who are you?'

'I'm Dickie. I'm a friend of Matthew's.'

'Well, he's not here.' Imogen moved to close the door.

Dickie put his hand out to stop her. 'When will he be back?'

'I don't know exactly. Later tonight.'

'And you'll be here, then, will you?'

'Of course I will.'

'Right. Well, could you give him this?' He held out the tin.

She took it with a frown. 'What is it?'

'Gingerbread from Emma. She baked it for him.'

'And who's Emma?' Imogen demanded.

'She's my wife,' Dickie said tersely, annoyed by her tone.

Her eyes narrowed. 'Why is your wife baking gingerbread for Matthew?'

'It's a thank you for the kitten he gave us.'

'Oh, cats again?' she groaned. 'They're all he cares about.' A loud wail rent the air. 'And now look what you've done. I'd only just got him to sleep.'

Dickie opened his mouth to apologise when Imogen slammed the door in his face.

Chapter Sixty-Four

'It's not often we get detectives from the Met here,' Colin Fowler said, inviting Matthew to take a seat. 'What station did you say you're from?'

'Craynebrook,' Matthew said.

Fowler's brow creased. 'We have an officer in Crayne-brook at the moment.'

'I know. DI Walsh. He's the reason I'm here. I've been looking into Walsh's snatch cases and I know who he should be looking for.'

'So does Walsh.' Fowler consulted a paper on his desk. 'A Mrs Imogen Carr.'

Matthew shook his head. 'She's not the snatcher.'

'That's the name Walsh gave me when we spoke yesterday.'

'He's wrong. Imogen Carr didn't take those children.'

'Then who did?'

'A woman called Angela Newbury. Let me explain.'

Matthew told Fowler everything he'd found out. How every time a baby was found, it was a cleaner who discovered it. How Angela Newbury had moved on from Craynebrook to

Brentwood to Chelmsford and to Witham, changing her name each time.

'And I'm certain we'll find her using an alias here in Colchester for each of the snatches,' he finished, handing Fowler his notebook turned to the page where he'd made his table.

Fowler studied it, shaking his head in astonishment. He looked up at Matthew. 'How long have you been working on this?'

'For the past two days,' he said.

'Two days?' Fowler cried incredulously. 'Walsh has been working on this for a year. And DI Morris three years before that. How could they both miss this?'

'I honestly don't know,' Matthew replied. 'It seemed an obvious line of enquiry to me. I can't speak for DI Morris or Walsh.'

'So,' Fowler went on, still fuming, 'you're saying this woman is working at a domestic agency here in Colchester?'

'Or was. She may have moved on by now. That was her usual MO before these latest snatches. But she's stayed in Colchester for a while now, so she must feel comfortable, maybe even safe. If we're lucky, she's still here. We just need to find her.'

'By contacting domestic agencies?' Fowler asked.

'It's how I've found her so far. But Colchester's a big place. I can't cover all of it on my own. And I'm very aware time may be running out for the baby. That's really why I'm here. I need help. I don't mean to be rude, Fowler, but I need to speak to your superior.'

'Chief Superintendent Goodridge is away for the New Year,' Fowler said, adding grimly, 'I'm in charge.' He shook his head. 'The thing is, Stannard, this is Walsh's case. And you're the Met.'

'Please don't talk to me about jurisdiction,' Matthew said

impatiently. 'This isn't the time to do things by the book. And as for Walsh. He's been chasing the wrong woman and refuses to consider any other suspect. Listen, I'm not interested in taking the credit or showing anyone up. I just want to find the baby and put this woman away. Help me do that.'

Fowler considered him for a long moment. Then he handed Matthew's notebook back and said, 'What do you need from me?'

Chapter Sixty-Five

Walsh banged his hand down on Lund's desk. 'You're wasting time. We have to alert the Yard.'

'The Yard won't be interested,' Lund insisted. 'Imogen Carr's been gone less than twenty-four hours, and she has a history of running off and coming back. All they're going to do is tell us to wait and see.'

'We need more men out looking for her.'

'And where do you suggest we start looking?' Lund yelled back. 'She's got quite a head start on us, Walsh.'

'And whose fault is that?' Walsh shot back. 'Your precious Stannard.'

'Don't start that again.' Lund caught movement outside the office and grimaced. 'Who let you in?' he yelled.

Dickie put his head around the office doorframe. 'Turkel let me up. Is this a bad time?'

'It's always a bleeding bad time for you to turn up, Waite,' Lund muttered. 'Stannard's not here, so you can bugger off.'

'I know he's not. Can I have a word, Lund? In private,' Dickie said, glancing at Walsh.

Lund jerked his thumb at Walsh, gesturing him to the

door. With a noise of irritation, Walsh went out and Dickie closed the door behind him.

'Well, speak,' Lund said as Dickie pulled a chair up to his desk.

'I heard Matthew's on leave.'

'That's right. I'm in charge of the Scott case now, and there's nothing new to tell you.'

Dickie waved his hand dismissively. 'I'm not here for the 'paper. Is Matthew all right?'

Lund sank back in his chair and sighed. 'Apparently, the doc recommended to Mullinger that Stannard have some time off. Something about chronic headaches. I don't know exactly. Why don't you ask him yourself? He's your pal, isn't he?'

'I went to his flat. He wasn't there.'

Lund tutted loudly. 'He should be there. He's supposed to be resting.'

Dickie glanced through the partition window at the pacing Walsh. 'I heard you mention Imogen Carr just now. She's the daughter of the murdered Scotts, yes? She's gone missing again?'

'Cor blimey, you don't miss a thing, do you? Yes, Waite, the lady's taken off again and we're looking for her.'

'Because Walsh thinks she's his baby snatcher?'

'Yes, he does. She's taken the baby with her wherever she's gone. To be honest, I'm worried he's right. Stannard thought Walsh was after the wrong woman, but I'm not so sure. If he's wrong and Imogen Carr is the snatcher, then that baby might be in danger.'

Dickie made a face and heaved a deep sigh. 'You're not going to like this, Lund, but I think I know where she is.'

Matthew climbed out of the police car and scanned the front doors down the street, his eyes searching for No. 113.

Fowler had given him every assistance he could have asked for, and between him and the detectives in the Colchester CID, they had discovered that a Mrs Alison Groom had gone on the books of Hollaways Domestic Agency on the 3rd of November and had been contracted to clean at the Princess Alexandra Hospital. The description the manager of the agency gave of Alison Groom matched Angela Newbury and, more importantly, she was still on Hollaways books and they had her address on file: 113 Claremont Terrace.

Fowler came up to Matthew. 'I've had a constable watching the house from a discreet distance for the past half hour. He says that a man came out ten minutes ago and headed down the street. We'll assume that's Mr Groom. He also said he saw a woman look out of the window.'

'No sign of the baby, though?' Matthew asked.

'No,' Fowler confirmed. He turned as a police van pulled up behind the car. The rear doors opened, and six uniformed policemen spilled out. He held up his hands as they gathered around and addressed them in a low voice. 'Right, men. The suspect is Alison Groom. We believe she has a baby in there. I want two men around the back of the house in case she makes a run for it. You two.' He pointed at two constables and they hurried away around the back of the tenements. 'The rest of you are going in the front. But go carefully. We don't want to risk her harming the baby if it's in there. We're just waiting for—'

Another car pulled up, and Fowler broke off. A man and a woman in a nurse's uniform got out.

'Dr Mitchell?' Fowler asked. 'My officer explained why you're here?'

'Yes,' Mitchell said. 'You think there might be a sick child in need of urgent attention.'

'That's correct. Please wait here until you're called for.' He turned back to Matthew. 'You stay here, too. I realise by rights you should make the arrest, but—'

Matthew waved him quiet. 'This is your patch. I know. It's fine.'

He watched as Fowler and the Uniforms hurried along the pavement towards No. 113. 'Please let me be right,' he muttered to himself as Fowler raised his arm and banged on the front door.

The door opened after only a few moments, and a middle-aged woman stood in the doorway. She gave a cry of alarm at the sight of the uniforms and tried to close the door, but Fowler already had one foot over the threshold and the policemen all disappeared inside the house. There were shouts and screams from inside, and neighbours rushed out of their houses to see what was going on.

Then two policemen came out with the woman bucking and kicking between them, and Matthew breathed a sigh of relief. Fowler appeared in the doorway. 'Stannard,' he called and waved for Matthew to come over. 'Bring the doctor.'

'Please come with me,' Matthew said to Mitchell and the nurse, and they all three hurried over to the house. 'Well?' he asked Fowler.

'In here,' Fowler said. 'You're needed, doctor.'

He led them down the hall and into a dingy kitchen. On the table against the near wall was a wooden crate. Matthew peered inside and saw a baby lying in filthy blankets. A strong faecal smell hit his nostrils, just like the dirty nappies in his bath the night before.

'Excuse me,' the doctor said, nudging Matthew out of the way. He already had a stethoscope around his neck, and he put the plugs in his ears and applied the chest-piece to the baby's tiny body. 'It's barely breathing,' he said to the nurse before turning to Fowler. 'We need to get it to the hospital immediately.'

Fowler shouted to one of the constables. 'Take the doctor and nurse to the hospital. Put the bells on. Don't waste any time.'

The nurse gently took the baby out of the crate and she and the doctor and the constable hurried out of the house.

Matthew felt Fowler's eyes upon him and turned to face him. Fowler didn't say anything for a long moment, then thrust out his hand. Surprised, Matthew stared at it, then took it.

'Congratulations,' Fowler said. 'You were right.'

'I'm just glad the baby's still alive,' Matthew said. 'Will you let me know how it gets on?'

'You're going?' Fowler said in surprise. 'But we've got a result. The best result. We've got the snatcher and the baby. This calls for a drink.'

Matthew shook his head. 'I wish I could, but I've got to get home. There's something I've got to do.'

'You don't look too pleased about it,' Fowler said with a grim smile. 'Whatever it is.'

'No,' Matthew admitted. 'I'm not looking forward to it.'

Chapter Sixty-Six

The bus pulled up at the stop outside his block of flats, and Matthew dropped off the back, so weary he didn't hear the conductor's cheery 'Good night' and barely noticed the porter's greeting as he walked through the lobby.

He stepped out of the lift on the third floor and fitted his key into his lock. When he opened the door, he heard voices and realised Imogen wasn't alone.

'Matthew!' Imogen cried when he entered the sitting room. 'Tell them to leave me alone.'

Three men turned to face him: Dickie, Lund and Walsh. Dickie and Lund both looked concerned. Walsh looked triumphant.

'What's going on?' Matthew asked, taking off his coat and hat and throwing them over the back of a dining chair.

'You tell us, Stannard,' Lund replied, and jerked his head at Imogen.

'They want to take my baby away from me, Matthew,' Imogen said. 'Don't let them.'

'It's not your baby, though, is it, Mrs Carr?' Walsh said. 'You stole him from the Princess Alexandra Hospital in Colchester on Bonfire Night.'

'I didn't. I didn't.'

'There's no point in lying.'

'She's not lying,' Matthew cut in wearily. His head was pounding again, and the lamplight was hurting his eyes.

'What did you say?' Walsh demanded.

'I said she didn't steal it. The baby's hers.'

'For God's sake, Stannard. How long are you going to cling to that fantasy?'

'It's not a fantasy, Walsh. I've spoken with the woman who delivered it. And the real snatcher's been caught. You should call your station. Speak to Colin Fowler. He'll tell you.'

'What are you talking about, Stannard?' Lund asked, a frown scoring his forehead.

'I found the snatcher,' Matthew explained. 'Her name is Angela Newbury. She's a cleaner. The same cleaner who found every baby that turned up. I went up to Colchester, to your station, Walsh, and asked Inspector Fowler for his help in catching her. She was arrested at around five o'clock this afternoon, and the baby was in her house. The case is over.'

'I don't believe you,' Walsh said, but the colour had drained from his face and his expression had changed from anger to consternation.

'Call Fowler,' Matthew said.

Walsh stared at him, then, his jaw hardening, jabbed a finger at Imogen. 'So what is she doing here if you're not trying to cover something up?'

'I suggest you go and call your station, Walsh,' Lund said. 'And get your arse back to Colchester before I kick it all the way there.'

Walsh turned on Lund, his face turning purple. 'You haven't heard the last of this,' he promised, and stormed out of the room. The front door banged, and he was gone.

'You were supposed to be on leave, sunshine,' Lund said,

a smile playing upon his lips. 'Not swanning around solving Walsh's case for him.'

Matthew smiled wanly and gave a shrug that suggested he couldn't help himself.

'Oh, Matthew,' Imogen sobbed and ran to him, throwing her arms around his neck. 'I knew you wouldn't let them take me.'

Matthew saw the look that passed between Lund and Dickie but was too tired to be embarrassed by Imogen's display of affection. Too tired and too upset about what he had to do. He disentangled Imogen's arms from around his neck and gently pushed her away, holding her at arm's length.

'Matthew?' she frowned. 'What's wrong?'

'Imogen Carr,' he said, 'I'm arresting you for the murder of Benjamin and Victoria Scott. You do not have to say anything—'

'No!' she screamed and tore herself out of his grip. 'You can't do this to me!'

'What the bloody hell, Stannard?' Lund cried, and instinctively grabbed hold of Imogen, pinning her arms to her sides.

'She killed them, Lund,' Matthew said with a shake of his head. 'I only worked it out today.'

'*She* killed them?' Lund repeated stupidly. 'Her own parents? For God's sake, why?'

Imogen stopped struggling and her legs gave way beneath her. She crumpled to the floor at Lund's feet but he held on to her arms. 'I had to do it,' she sobbed. 'They were never going to leave me alone.'

Matthew pulled out a chair from under his dining table and fell down on it with an exhausted sigh. He wished he was alone, that none of them were there. He rested his head on his hand and closed his eyes as Imogen went on.

'I hated them,' she said, tears streaming down her cheeks. 'Always telling me what to do, deciding everything for me. I went round there when Max had gone out. He wouldn't tell me where he was going, but he looked so guilty, I knew he was going to that woman. I wanted to know who she was. Father pretended he didn't know, but he was lying. And then Mother said it was my fault Max had a mistress because I hadn't been a proper wife to him, that I'd been a disappointment all my life. She kept on and on, and I couldn't stand it anymore, so I snatched up the knife and I stuck it in her, and she shut up at last. Father couldn't believe it. He just stood there, staring, and I thought I'd get him too. He tried to stop me. Grabbed my wrists.'

Matthew's eyes opened at these words. How could he have been such a fool? 'It was your father who put the bruises there, not your husband. And the ones on your neck. Maxwell didn't do those either, did he?'

An ugly smile appeared on Imogen's face. 'Max has never laid a finger on me. You should have listened to your sister, Matthew.'

'You deliberately tried to make me suspect him again,' he said, incredulous. 'How could you do that? If I'd listened to you, your husband could have ended up being hanged.'

'He doesn't love me,' she declared, 'so why shouldn't he hang? Why has it always got to be me who suffers?'

Matthew stared at her in horror, then glanced over at Lund and with a groan, jerked his head at the door. He wanted Imogen out of his flat.

'Waite,' Lund said to Dickie. 'Let the lads know to come up. I brought Uniform with me,' he explained to Matthew as Dickie moved to the window and waved, 'just in case we had to take the baby away and she made a fuss.'

'They've seen me,' Dickie said. 'They're coming.'

None of them spoke again until the uniformed policemen arrived and Lund told them to take Imogen and the baby to the station. Imogen didn't say another word as she was taken out. Matthew heard the front door shut and breathed a heavy sigh of relief.

'Blimey,' Lund said, shaking his head. 'I'd never have thought it. To look at her, you wouldn't think she'd say boo to a goose, and she did all that? Mind you,' he said, raising his eyebrows at Dickie, 'if you ask me, the way they all treated her over the years, they deserved it. You ought to put something about what a bloody awful family they were in your article when you write it up, Waite.'

'I will. I won't leave anything out,' Dickie promised.

Lund turned back to Matthew. 'How did you work out she killed them?'

'Imogen told me she saw her mother in the green dress she was killed in,' Matthew said, suddenly feeling more tired than he'd ever felt in his life. 'Her mother didn't get the dress until after she and Maxwell left, so the only way she could have seen it was if she'd gone back there after 8 p.m. And she had a receipt in her purse for the chocolate liqueurs that were on the kitchen table. They weren't there when the cook left at eight, so they had to have been put there afterwards. I expect Imogen took the box round as a present and forgot about them.

'And then there was the neighbour Barnes spoke to, who said she heard the baby crying for ages. It's just an idea, but I reckon he was crying because there was no one home to see to him. And now I think about it, you might want to have Wallace test the gloves in her coat pockets. One of them is stained. It might be blood. If she was wearing them when she stabbed her parents, it would explain why her prints weren't on the knife, and why the others were smudged.'

'So, what has Baddowes got to do with the murders?' Lund asked.

Matthew shook his head. 'I don't know. Maybe nothing at all. We know he was there, because he left a partial print on the safe, but maybe the Scotts were already dead by the time he got there. He may just be guilty of burglary.'

Lund shook his head in disbelief. 'Well, I had better get down to the station and get her charged.' He turned to Dickie. 'Not a word about her being here ends up in your rag, Waite. Not a word. You understand?'

Dickie nodded. 'I understand.'

Lund left, and Matthew closed his eyes once more. He heard the sound of glass clinking and, a few moments later, Dickie was beside him, saying, 'Here.' He looked up and saw his friend holding out a tumbler of whisky. He took it and swallowed a mouthful.

Dickie pulled out a chair and sat down. 'It's been one hell of a Christmas you've had, Matthew.'

'It's been one hell of a year,' Matthew returned.

'That's an understatement. I'm sorry it hasn't worked out for you.'

Matthew frowned. 'That what hasn't worked out?'

'Imogen,' he shrugged. 'I was talking to young Rudd earlier. The gossip around your station is that you were sweet on her.'

'There's gossip about me?'

'What do you expect?' Dickie said scornfully. 'Well? Were you sweet on her?'

'For a while, perhaps,' Matthew admitted, then smiled ruefully. 'But she wasn't quite what I thought she was.'

Dickie nodded. 'You can say that again. And just think. If she had got away with the murders and got her husband hanged for them, and you settled down with her, imagine the life you would have had with her. Upset her and you might have been next on her death list. If you want my opinion, Matthew, you've had a lucky escape.'

Matthew took another mouthful of the whisky and nodded. 'I reckon I have.'

Chapter Sixty-Seven

Matthew slept well that night, better than he had for months. Back in his own bed, which had the faintest trace of perfume on the sheets, he had sunk into the pillow, pulled the blankets up to his chin and felt Bella and Hobbs settle around his ankles. He fell asleep at once and did not dream. He woke late the next morning.

It was around eleven that his telephone rang. When he answered it, he was surprised to hear Miss Halliwell's voice, apologising for intruding on the last day of his leave, but requesting that he come to the station at his earliest convenience because Mr Mullinger wanted to see him.

When Matthew entered Mullinger's office an hour later, the superintendent rose to greet him.

'Ah, Stannard,' he said. 'Thank you for coming in. Take a seat.'

The cordiality confused him, as did Lund's presence. Lund occupied one of the visitors' chairs, and he gave Matthew an encouraging smile as he sat in the other. *Not a telling-off then*, Matthew thought, this reinforced by the arrival of Miss Halliwell with an extra cup and saucer. She poured Matthew a coffee from the pot on the desk, then left, giving him a parting smile.

'Imogen Carr,' Mullinger began without preamble, 'has made a full confession and been charged. The baby has been given into the care of its father. So, that's the Scott murders cleared up.'

Matthew expected Mullinger to ask why Imogen had been at his flat, but to his surprise, the superintendent seemed to have said all he was going to about her. Matthew glanced at Lund, who frowned and gave a barely perceptible shake of his head, which he took to mean that he shouldn't say a word.

Mullinger cleared his throat and reached for his coffee cup to take a sip. 'And there's news about the burglar,' he continued, setting the cup back in the saucer. 'Baddowes was picked up last night breaking into a house in Wimbledon. Once he knew we had a partial fingerprint from the safe at the Scotts' house he admitted to all the burglaries here in Crayne-brook. Not knowing the Carr woman had confessed, they also questioned him about the Scotts' murders. He denied killing them, but admitted to seeing their bodies when he burgled their house. They've charged him for their burglaries as well as our own, and he will be heading back to prison, I'm pleased to say.'

'Where he belongs,' Lund added happily.

'Quite,' Mullinger agreed. 'And lastly, I've had several telephone calls from Colchester this morning.'

Here it comes, Matthew thought. *They've complained about me interfering in their investigation.*

'They have tried to question the Newbury woman, but she refuses to say a word. Fortunately, her husband proved more forthcoming. He admitted his wife stole all the babies Inspector Walsh was investigating, including our case here in 1920. However, he denies his wife murdered Alice Burns. According to him, the baby died in its sleep. I've spoken with

Dr Wallace, who you may remember performed the post-mortem on the poor child, and he said that as he found no signs of harm on the body, it's possible the death was natural.'

'Apparently,' Lund said, 'Angela Newbury had a kid that died a few days after birth, and she was never the same again. Her husband played no part in the actual snatches. In fact, he claims he tried to stop her doing them, but she just kept on. He just went along with them to keep her happy.'

'Yes,' Mullinger growled, casting a disapproving glance at Lund for interrupting, 'but his wife had no notion of how to care for the children, and so when he felt they were in danger, he insisted his wife return them. They stuck to their pattern of putting them in the care of the church, believing that was the best way to ensure they would be taken care of. He said he was about to return the baby snatched from the hospital in November. Whether that is true, we'll never know. Inspector Fowler wanted you to know that although the baby is not in the best of health, the doctors are hopeful it will survive. The parents have been informed.'

'It was good of him to let me know,' Matthew said.

'He sends his thanks for your help.' Mullinger smiled. 'As does Chief Constable Dancey. He too, telephoned this morn-ing.' There was a note of pleasure in his voice, and out of the corner of his eye, Matthew saw Lund's lips twitch in amuse-ment. 'He sends his congratulations and commends you for your insight into the case. He was very impressed with how quickly you were able to solve it. I told him that's quite usual for you.'

'Of course,' Lund said as Matthew squirmed with embar-rassment at the superintendent's compliment, 'Stannard shouldn't have been helping at all, sir.'

'No, indeed,' Mullinger agreed. 'You were supposed to be resting, Stannard.'

Matthew opened his mouth to make some kind of protest, but Mullinger pressed on.

'In view of this, I've decided you shouldn't return to work until Monday the twelfth. I advise you to spend those days doing very little, Stannard.'

'He will, sir,' Lund said, giving Matthew a stern look. 'I'll make sure of it.'

'Very good. Well, that's all. I just wanted to let you know what had been happening.' Mullinger nodded to Matthew. 'You can go, Stannard.'

'He's as pleased as punch,' Lund said when they stood in Miss Halliwell's office a minute later. 'Getting a call from a chief constable to congratulate him on one of his men has made his year.'

Matthew turned Lund away so Miss Halliwell couldn't hear his next words. 'You didn't tell him about Imogen being at my flat.'

'He doesn't need to know about that,' Lund said. 'We got a result. That's all Old Mouldy's interested in.'

'And if he asks how we got the result?' Matthew pressed.

'Then I'll make something up. But he won't ask so don't worry.'

Matthew breathed a sigh of relief. 'Thanks, Lund.'

'I owed you one, remember? Now, you do what Old Mouldy says and go home and rest. I don't want to have to deal with you being useless when you come back.'

'I will take it easy,' Matthew promised with a smile.

'Good. Oh, before I forget.' Lund dug into his trouser pocket and drew out a small envelope. He held it out to Matthew.

'What's this?' Matthew asked, taking it.

'It's a note from my girls,' Lund said. 'They wanted to thank you for the kitten. Now, bugger off and rest. I'll see you when you come back.'

Chapter Sixty-Eight

Matthew pushed open the door of the Fiddler's Retreat, knowing he wouldn't be able to rest until he'd put things right with Pat.

The pub was busy when he walked in, full of people enjoying a lunchtime pint. Fred was serving behind the bar. He glanced up and did a double take when he saw Matthew. His face, which had been smiling a moment before, hardened.

'What are you doing here?' he growled.

'I've come to see Pat,' Matthew said.

'What? So, you can upset her again?'

'No, Fred. To apologise.'

Fred grunted. 'So you bloody should.'

He glanced at the beer pump in front of him, and Matthew guessed he was trying to work out whether he should offer him a drink like he usually did. Fred had every right to be angry with him, and Matthew didn't want anything from him that his brother-in-law wasn't willing to give, so before Fred could reach a decision, he said, 'Is it all right if I go up?'

'I don't know if she'll want to see you, but you can go up.' He lifted the flap in the bar counter to allow Matthew through. 'But so help me God, Matt, if you upset her again, you'll have me to answer to.'

Matthew nodded and climbed the stairs to the family's private area. The noise of the pub faded as he climbed, and instead his ears caught the faint sound of music. It was coming from the wireless in the sitting room. The door was open, and he saw Pat sitting on the settee, a magazine open on her lap. But she wasn't reading it. She had her chin in her hand, and she was staring out of the window. He couldn't remember ever seeing her so still.

'Pat?' he said softly from the doorway.

She didn't jump or start. Pat turned her head slowly towards him as if she were waking from a dream. Her eyes were tired and a little red. She stared at him and didn't say a word.

He entered, a little unnerved by this subdued reaction. 'If you want me to go, I'll go.'

She blinked at him, drew in a breath, but still didn't speak.

'I'm sorry, Pat,' he said. 'I'm sorry for everything I said. I didn't mean it, and you certainly didn't deserve it.'

A long moment passed, and he wondered what he would do if she continued to stay silent. Go? Stay? He had no idea what it would mean if she refused to talk to him.

But then she said, 'You hurt me, Mattie.' Her voice sounded as if she had a sore throat, the consequence, he knew, of too much crying.

'I know I did. I'm sorry. Tell me how to make it up to you.'

Pat looked away and wiped her nose with a soggy handkerchief. 'Does she know you're here?' she asked.

'She's gone and she's not coming back. Not ever.'

'Left you, has she?'

'No. She was taken into custody.' He'd said it that way deliberately to intrigue her and keep her talking.

She frowned. 'What do you mean?'

'It turned out she was the one who killed her parents.'

Pat's eyes closed, and she shook her head. 'You know how to pick 'em, don't you?'

'It really wasn't what you think. There was nothing between her and me. Nothing at all.'

'There was something,' Pat insisted. 'It was her that made you speak to me like that.'

'I don't think it was.' Matthew sat down on the settee, keeping a little away from her in case she didn't want him close. 'It was something else. Do you remember Mr Burland?'

Pat frowned. 'That mad old man who lived down our road? Of course I do. He scared the whatsit out of you.'

'You remember the way I was then? Well, it's been like that for a while,' Matthew said, feeling ashamed to admit it but knowing he had to be honest with Pat to make her forgive him. 'Only it was Gadd this time.'

'But he's dead.'

'I don't know how to explain it.' Matthew sighed. 'It's been a bad year, Pat. It's been murder after murder, and then Gadd. I know it's no excuse, but everything just...' He shrugged, at a loss how to explain the way he had been feeling.

'It all got on top of you,' she finished for him, and he was so very glad she understood. 'I knew you weren't right all this time, but you wouldn't have it, would you?'

In answer, he reached out his hand, laying it on the cushion beside her, palm upwards. In his palm was the key to his flat. Pat looked at it for a long moment, then took it.

'Forgiven?' he asked.

There was a shuffling at the doorway. Matthew turned to see his mother, looking a little bleary-eyed, standing there.

'Hello, Mattie,' she said in a voice that told him she'd been dozing. 'I didn't know you were coming round.'

'I didn't know I was either. But I've got some leave, and I thought it was high time I came by and saw you all.'

'Oh, that's lovely. So, you're stopping for tea?' Amanda asked hopefully.

Matthew looked at his sister. 'Only if Pat doesn't mind.'

Pat gave him a feeble smile and squeezed his hand. 'He's stopping, Mum.'

Read every gripping Stannard story

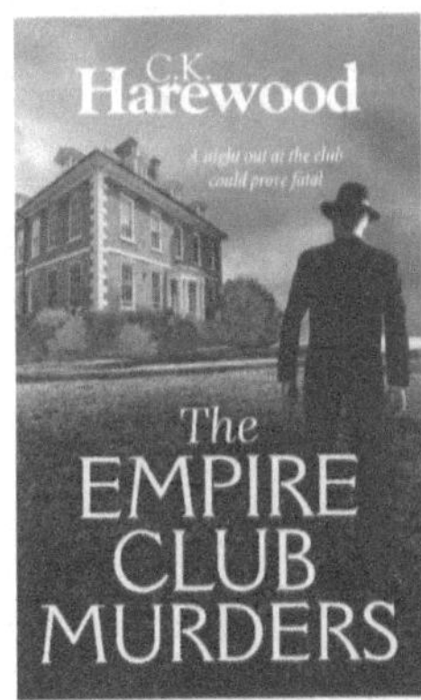

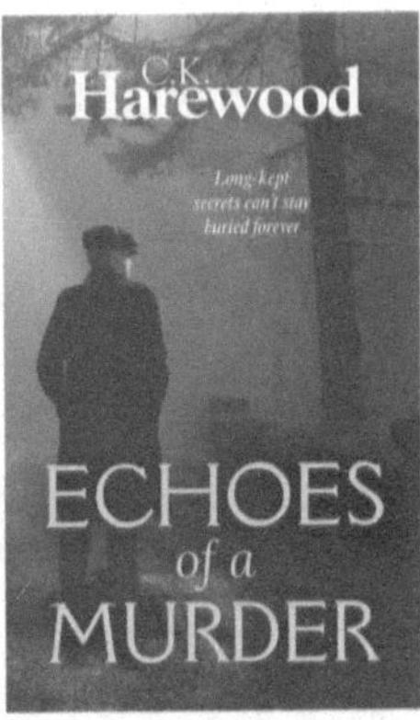

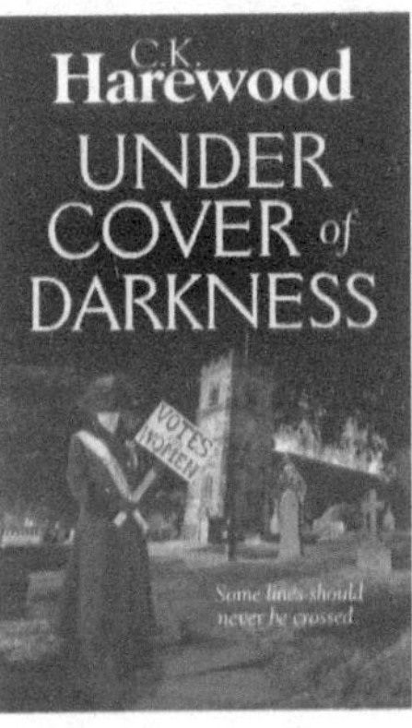

Visit
www.ckharewood.com